Sacramentum

Virtutis

Fortuna

Comes !

D. Berkeley.

Sacramentum

D J G Berkeley

Sacramentum

Published: 15th May 2012

ISBN 978-1-4716-9589-6

For Lib

And with thanks to my Elite Proof Reading Team

The Transmaritanus

2749 AUC (years since Rome's founding)

Prologue

Titus Labienus Aquilinus planned to die well: his Gladius outstretched, his head held high, no trace of fear behind his dark brown eyes: the Roman way. His training had taught him that. It had had little time to teach him much else, but it was enough: devotion to Rome; self belief; death; the rest he would be able to pick up as he went along.

His sword point twitched slightly in the bright noon-day sun and he was acutely aware of a bead of sweat dribbling inexorably towards the tip of his nose from his short cropped hair—he had once liked it long as had the girls back in Rome. The army took much from you but it gave much back too: gone was his freedom, but in return lay glory for him and for his family, and, the gods knew, the latter needed as much as it could get.

He stood firm, ignoring the sweat that itched insistently at the end of his nose. He stared at the chief, straight into his eyes. He would not let him see his fear. The man stood five paces in front of Titus—his body naked apart from a cloth tied about his waist. The eagle feathers, tied in a loose crown around his long haired head, rippled in the stiff breeze— at odds with the dark sunglasses that made his expression impenetrable. He opened his mouth betraying a row of rotting teeth, and spoke in a language Titus could not understand.

The savage's companions glared. The bead of sweat reached the end of Titus' nose, and hung there tenaciously, but he thrust the desire to scratch it from his mind. He stared at the sonifex hanging from the native's hip, clearly looted from one of Titus' dead comrades. Titus wondered whether the savage could really use the weapon; some of the native inhabitants of Transmaritanus had learnt, but most in their rebellion, had taken what lay easily to hand: their fists, farming tools, and knives. Titus looked at the knives held outstretched towards him by the chief's bodyguard, and considered his options.

His heart urged him to reach for his own sonifex, slung over his shoulder by its canvas strap. He was fast; he was very fast; perhaps he could kill one of the men, if the gods were with him? He shoved the thought from his mind: it would be far better to die with the ceremonial gladius in his hands. For he was Titus Labienus Aquilinus, the 62nd descendant of the great Titus Labienus, the Destroyer of Tyrants and the Protector of Rome; the last faint star of a dying noble family. It had always been his destiny to die well.

He thought of the men in the wooden hut behind him, their skin hanging from them in translucent sheets. He had killed the torturers; rushing upon them unseen as they were consumed in their foul work; slaying them with his gladius; spilling their blood over the polished flagstones, and listening as it spluttered over the hot irons in the brazier. He had taken the life of the condemned too, soothing their unconscious brows as he opened their veins, it had been the only merciful thing to do. But he had spared the slave child that lurked in the corner of the darkened room: there was no point in slaying a defenseless animal.

He smiled defiantly at the chief who stood before him. His parched mouth cracked and as he opened it he tasted his own sharp, metallic blood. The confidence in his voice surprised him: 'Virtutis fortuna comes.' It was old Latin and, as such, sounded magical. The motto of his family were the most befitting final words Titus could think of.

The chief's mouth hardened, as one of his guards lunged forwards, his blade aimed at Titus' face. He leapt away, aware of the knives now held

2

just inches from his back. The chief laughed and slowly lifted off his sunglasses to enjoy the spectacle. Then another laugh rang out over the courtyard, young and high pitched. It was the slave child he had spared earlier. The signum, the silver tattoo on his face that marked him out, as it did all slaves, was half obscured with the dried blood of the torturers Titus had slain. Beside the slave boy stood, hand in hand, a native girl of the same age who was watching the scene blankly. The mockery of a slave animal meant nothing to Titus, but the chief's laughter he could not permit.

With a great effort he kept his expression neutral, giving no impression of his intentions. Then he lunged forwards, a single fluid movement, and thrust his gladius into the chief's belly, and up into his chest. The man stood there for a second, transfixed, as Titus felt his warm blood trickle down onto the ivory hilt: the hilt that had once belonged to his great ancestor. The chief's eyes widened and locked with Titus'. His mouth opened and from it there issued a thin, broken sound. It sounded to Titus no different to the sound any dying man might make, but it was clearly a command to end Titus' life. He gripped the sword's hilt tightly as the bodyguards drew back to strike.

'Get down!'

Titus looked up in amazement as five of his comrades suddenly appeared on the gantry above him, sonifi pointed down at his captors. He sprung to his left, throwing himself down onto the harsh scrub grass behind the nearest guard, as his comrades opened fire.

Suddenly the air was full of blood, chips of flagstone, and the sounds of men dying. The natives that surrounded him were torn apart by the rounds at close range and the two that escaped the initial burst were cut down as they fled for the gateway out of the fortress. Titus looked up at his comrade's grim faces: they were going to kill everyone in the courtyard. He could not blame them. The battle today had been costly and they had seen many of their companions killed. He looked back at the native girl, the only person alive in the courtyard apart from Titus himself. Her eyes were wide with fear as the sonifi tore the ground up in front of her. The slave boy animal still held her hand.

Then something happened that surprised Titus: the slave stepped in front of the girl. The rounds took him in the chest, launching him backwards into her so that the pair rolled across the courtyard, eventually coming to rest in a ragged heap as the sonifi fell silent. They were still clinging to each other.

The slave boy's gaze had never left Titus' face, not until the bullets had taken his life from him, but it was not that which unnerved Titus. It was that that he had never seen an animal give its life for a person before.

The day passed in a blur.

His Centurion approached him. It was evening now and he drew his cloak in tight against the chill.

'Aquilinus.'

'Yes,' Titus replied abruptly, his mind still on the strange scene in the courtyard earlier that day. The Centurion did not know him well enough to use his first name.

He pressed something cold into Titus' hand, wrapping his fingers tightly closed over it and grunted; it was the nearest Titus would get to a thank you for his services that day.

Opening his hand Titus looked down with disbelief at the small golden circlet, The Golden Crown of Valour. He thought of how his father's eyes would light up with pride when he saw it. He smiled for the first time in months.

Back then he had felt certain that, through battle, he could one day restore his family's honour, slowly desecrated by sixty two generations of decadence, madness, and treason. How the mad, old Sybil, sitting in her dark cave at Cumae, would have mocked.

15 Years Later
2764 AUC

Luguvalium

I

It was the second day after the Kalends of August, and Titus was restless: his warband had spent two days in the same ditch, overlooking the same field. The makeshift village, hastily built by the rebellious slaves, lay some two hundred yards downhill. They were baking bread; the smell drifted up to where Marcus, Titus' second in command, crouched in a puddle of foul water. It had rained constantly for over a day now, and everything was soaked through.

Everyone spent the time before an attack preparing in their own way. Titus had practised his routine in countless sorties of this kind. In his ten years as a mercenary he had never been seriously wounded: he had his skill to thank for that. It made him wonder why the slaves rebelled at all, if all they had to look forward to was his stern justice.

Titus started his routine with a tiny shard of mirror, embedded in a camouflage case. He swung the case open and was confronted with his heavily painted face. His hair was still cut short as a throwback to his army days: dark brown, with increasingly large areas of grey now. He quickly touched up his camouflage (long marks of brown, khaki and black paste, drawn around his features like war-paint) and began laying out his equipment. First the helmet: gone were the goose feathers showing the rank (he did not need anything that would give away their position)... Titus looked around and saw that his team were also gathering their equipment ready for the attack. Titus had shed blood with his five companions more times than he could remember; they were all veterans of the infamous Transmaritanus campaigns, and respected his command without question.

Next, Titus prepared his weapon: he still carried the short stabbing sword, the gladius; ceremonial really, but once upon a time it would have been used for the infamous quick thrust to the groin. Lastly he unwrapped the oilskins he carried, and, from inside, brought out his real weapon. The other men did the same. He checked the barrel was clear and free of water—the oilskins had done their job. Water could expand in the barrel and cause an explosion; he had seen many legionaries disfigured for life for that mistake. He unclipped a magazine from under his jacket and loaded the sonifex. No need for armour piercing rounds: slaves had no armour and they had no machines, no-one had taught them the engineer's art, for such a thing would be both impossible and illegal.

Titus crept forwards to the edge of the drystone wall, separating his elite band from the slave encampment. He reached into his webbing and brought out the battered golden circlet, his Crown of Valour. He twisted it between his fingers, thinking back to when he had come so close to death back in Transmaritanus; it was fifteen years ago to the day. 'Virtutis fortuna comes,' came to his mind. He shook his head—this was not a battle. Above his head the clouds hung low and dark as he raised his fingers and, with a flick of his wrist, let the killing begin.

As Titus burst out from cover, he sped around to the western side of the encampment keeping low. The camp was far from alert, and Titus knew that the coarse foliage he had tied into his khaki uniform would keep him concealed until he was in position. Kneeling down in his new position at the edge of a bracken thicket, he could follow the outlines of his men as they took up positions around the camp. He was disappointed that they hadn't been spotted yet; he hadn't experienced a real battle for five tedious years. This was going to be far too easy. He started to pick his targets: there was a young slave pacing to and fro outside the main building; presumably he was meant to guard the chief, but he was armed only with a wooden staff.

A young girl, carrying a battered metal saucepan, was jogging away from the encampment towards the stream. Her tatty, blond hair bounced happily as she ran. Titus mused that, maybe in different circumstances, he could have had a daughter her age by now. As she approached the stream, she was pulled into the nearby rushes, and Titus didn't see her again. He looked down for a moment and closed his eyes: Antonius had had no choice but to silence her, but still Titus couldn't help thinking of another girl, on another battlefield, a long time ago.

Shaking the thoughts from his head, he concentrated on the attack. It would be the usual routine for rounding up and punishing rogue slaves. He told himself the mantra again, as if it made him feel any better. Would he feel bad about sending animals to an abattoir? If not, what was so wrong with what he was about to do? It had been drilled into him since school. He could remember the posters on the classroom wall as clearly as if had been yesterday: a slave with a pig's head, *'Servus Animalis!'* Slaves Are Animals.

He would go in first taking down any resistance: that meant killing the men. The women and children, however, would be spared and returned to the servitude they deserved.

A young man left one of the larger huts and crossed the main patch of earth at the centre of the makeshift village. Titus brought his sonifex to his shoulder, took aim using the lighted sights, and fired. The man looked down, as if in wonder, at the inch wide hole in the centre of his chest. Falling forwards, he displayed to the world the teacup sized exit wound wrought by the geometrically unstable shape of a Roman anti-personnel round. The women and children started to scream, as Titus' five companions burst from cover and charged into the dirt square.

Marcus shot indiscriminately from the square's centre. Antonius, Gnaeus, Quintus, and Tiberius wandered into the huts, occasional bursts of gunfire emanating from within. Titus ran at full pace towards the main hut. The young slave with the staff now blocked the door; he looked to be in his early twenties, with short, dark hair and his eyes were wide and his face pale. He brandished the poleaxe desperately at Titus as he approached.

Raising his sonifex to his shoulder, Titus shot the slave in the head, as he closed to ten paces. The young slave's head exploded like a ripe fruit and the staff dropped from his nerveless fingers, falling silently onto the dull earth. Titus stepped over the carcass and ducked inside, into the chief's hut. Sitting, wrapped in an animal fur, was an old slave. He was writing; an expression of calm concentration on his face.

He levelled the barrel of his sonifex at the old slave who, with broad deliberate strokes, finished his work before slowly laying the pen down across the page and pushing it over to Titus. Then he reached over to a large pile of paper at the other end of the desk, and, with effort, heaved it across, so that it sat by the piece he had just finished writing on. He stared into Titus' bemused eyes and smiled. Titus thought back to all of the slaves he had killed over the years, a creeping sickness cramping his stomach. He couldn't face where his thoughts were taking him: he roared with anger and pulled the trigger.

Outside the sonifi fell silent and the women and children were led out. In neat little lines they stood, with Titus' men keeping them penned. A few of the older men had been spared in the initial encounter and they lay face down, manacled by Marcus. Titus stepped out into the dirt square and stood over them. All eyes turned to him.

'This is the price of rebellion,' he stated. 'Loyalty to Rome is every man's duty, be he citizen or slave. Now see the price of treachery.' At this, he kicked the dead slave chief into the dirt square; his body rolled over once, coating his furs in thick mud. One of the older women, who must have been his wife, began to sob. Titus stared at the woman's grieving face. It unnerved him.

Suddenly he was back, once again, in that land where he had proved himself ten years ago. He could smell death and hear the wailing of slaves. The hissing of the Jupiter Machine, as it passed overhead and off into the far distance, filled his heart with dread: he could never accept that it brought a fair death, even to traitors. He could still taste their burning flesh whenever he thought of it. And their screams: he had learnt to live with them.

In front of him was a line of slave women and children; their men were dead: it was the Roman way. Now they would be taken back to Rome for processing. One of the young girls looked up into his face. Tears streaked though the dust on her cheeks; he knew that one day she would have been be beautiful. Her small blue eyes bore into his, and he felt a chill strike his body, the like of which he had never felt before or since. A general clapped him on the shoulder.

'Titus.' It was Marcus hissing in his ear and shaking him back to the present. 'Titus. For Jupiter's sake! Kill them.' He regained his perspective. He had a job to do. He rested the butt of the sonifex into his shoulder; it nuzzled him lovingly as he pulled the trigger. The crack of the rifle comforted him, washing away the difficult memories with its empty, consistent noise. The men's bodies jerked on the ground, as he fired into them at almost point blank range. Marcus walked along the line, shooting each in the head just to be sure, as the keening from the women became a chorus. Antonius was already eyeing them up, picking his company for the night. Titus was in no such mood. He fumbled in his pocket and took out his battered gold crown again. The glory of Rome. He grimaced.

He looked at his men standing around him their weapons pointed at the women and children, the blood from their husbands and fathers flowing past his feet. He remembered a young girl, with dust on her cheeks and a sonifex at her head; he would never be rid of her. He nearly wept.

II

To claim the full bounty from the Governor, Titus and his band would need to bring the female slaves and their children to his seat of power safely, but northern Britannia was a lawless backwater, and amongst the barely explored fells there were others who might value their cargo. To this end, Titus sent Marcus and Antonius off to look for anyone hiding out in the hills nearby. The slaves seemed less on edge once Antonius had left. Gnaeus and Tiberius began to erect a wire perimeter that would encircle their camp tonight; it gave little protection, but perhaps it would deter a casual brigand. It wasn't casual brigands Titus was worried about though—there were Reivers in these hills.

Meanwhile Quintus using his skills as a medicus, went amongst the women and children treating their wounds. One young boy had broken his arm when his mother had dropped him in panic. Quintus bound it gently and patted the boy on the head: the Governor would want the escaped slaves returned in the best possible condition.

Titus wandered alone overseeing the preparations. He felt a little sick every time he saw the large hut where the old chief had sat. He did not want to be drawn to it, but he soon found himself outside its low battered door once again. It was of typical hasty design. There was the smouldering remains of a fire at the centre of the earthen floor. Around the edges were some cooking utensils, and what appeared to be ornaments: wooden sculptures—a hunter with a dog, and a flat piece of wood with holes bored out of it; coloured bits of wood, white and black, sat in the holes. The skill of the work impressed Titus, and he wondered where this slave had managed to steal such items. He moved on to the object which had kept disturbing his thoughts throughout the afternoon: the desk. The desk was made of a rich wood, which looked, to Titus, like mahogany. Whatever it was made of, it had obviously not been made here. It looked Roman. How the slaves had got the desk here, Titus had no idea, but why they would bother in the first place, utterly confounded him. The old chief had clearly spent much time and effort in bringing it here. There was only one possible answer: it must have meant something to him. But slaves weren't meant to have feelings, not real feelings, at least not like Roman's did.

Titus thought about the old slave lying dead on the ground. They had forced the women to bury the bodies in a mass grave, but Titus remembered the old slave man, sitting and smiling, as he was at the moment he fired. Why had he not run?

Titus ran his hands absentmindedly over the wood, taking in the texture. Part of him longed to look at the papers on the desk, but he was scared of what he would find, and what it might mean. His eyes, however, were drawn inexorably towards the solitary piece of thinner paper in the desk's centre, alongside the thick pile. This was the one that Titus had seen the slave writing; the one the slave had offered him.

The piece of parchment had two words on it:
GAIUS STRABO

There was no other writing. Why would a man waste his last seconds writing the name of the Governor of northern Britannia Titus wondered? He turned his attention to the larger pile of paper pushed towards him. Why did the slave want to show it to him? He tried to stop thinking of the man and, instead, began flicking through the ten sheets of paper. Titus saw lists of numbers and dates, transaction codes and account numbers. Slaves were not allowed to use the omniajunctus, the system that connected scires all over the world, nor would their limited intellect permit

12

them to do so. This could not be a slave's account. How had it come into his possession; why did he want Titus to have it? The whole thing thoroughly confused him. The one thing Titus could see though, was that whoever owned these accounts was richer than any man he knew; probably richer than the Consuls of Rome! He laughed to himself. Looking down the list he noted that there were no names of payees, just account numbers; without access to the omniajunctus the numbers were completely meaningless. He stuffed the paper into his webbing and left the tent.

The camp was nearly ready now: a good thing, with the night drawing in. Titus knew that, despite ten years of so called peace, much of the world could still be classified as enemy territory. Once upon a time a legionary would have carried a stake and a shovel; a whole legion could therefore easily build a palisade. Titus was stunned by how fit those men must have been; there was no way he could have marched for twenty five miles a day with that additional load on his back. Now they carried a state of the art solution to the problem: a thick wire made from a titanium magnesium alloy. At a push of a button, spikes would protrude, providing a razor wire that could be safely rolled up and carried in a pack. A specially formulated glue allowed this to be cemented onto objects around the camp, creating a quickly erectable defensive cordon.

As night finally enveloped them, Titus was sitting out by a roaring fire that would be visible for miles. He knew that such a level of arrogance would most likely scare disorganised bandits away, but, just in case, he had a fully loaded sonifex in his lap with the safety catch off. Tiberius brought out his battered old ego-arca, and turned it on, bashing it against a rock as its ancient circuits failed to start up in good time. Eventually the tinny speaker hissed out some popular songs from Rome that Titus cared nothing for, but the other men knew most of the choruses, and joined in. After regaling them for a half hour or so, Tiberius turned off his ego-arca, and, with his deep voice, started the tune of an old soldier's song. Titus felt the beginnings of a smile try to creep onto his face, and the group sang together lustily, as the fire crackled in the gentle breeze. He closed his eyes. Ten years didn't seem like such a long time after all.

Tiberius was the best type of bard that a group of soldiers could ever have. He had become quite famous for it on their campaign all those years ago. The whole camp would turn out to listen, even the women, although they stayed mainly to look at him: Tiberius was incredibly handsome, and he knew it. An old girlfriend, and there had been quite a few, although Tiberius was paradoxically shy about this, and rarely spoke about them, had once described him as the very epitome of the ancient Greek's longing for physical perfection. Titus laughed to himself, remembering that Tiberius had gone as red as Mars' tunic when Titus had told him. Looking around him he saw that Quintus in particular seemed to enjoy the singing: he was always mesmerised by Tiberius' voice. The song came to an end and Tiberius nodded to show his performance for that evening was over.

Bidding them goodnight, Tiberius and Quintus retired to their tent. Antonius soon left for his tent too, via the slave pen. Marcus, thinking it probably best to give Antonius some time alone, lay down on the grass by the fire and pulled his cap down over his eyes. It looked like Titus and Gnaeus would take the first watch.

'Gnaeus, what do you think of slaves?' Titus asked, 'your family never kept any when you were young.'

'We never found we needed any,' Gnaeus replied, 'what do people need them for?'

Gnaeus was quite right, Titus thought, anything a slave did could be done by a machine, but the answer did not satisfy him. He shook his head, 'but there's more to it than that, isn't there Gnaeus? I don't need slaves, but my family always kept them because somehow, well… somehow isn't it our duty to rule them?'

Gnaeus thought for a moment before shrugging his shoulders, 'I always just felt it was wrong somehow.'

'What about killing them then?' Titus proposed.

'To be honest I try to shut it out,' Gnaeus said, 'strange how feelings change when you have a weapon in your hands.'

Titus was silent for over a minute, during which he just stared at the glowing embers of their dying fire. 'I blame the war. The things we saw, and did. It changes you,' he paused and looked across at the penned slaves. In the glow of the embers he could see mothers cuddling their children, staring back at him. He looked away quickly.

14

Gnaeus was silent: he was clearly thinking back to his past life on the battlefields of Transmaritanus. 'Get some sleep Gnaeus,' Titus said. 'I can handle the watch. I'll wake you later.'

Gnaeus nodded and lay on his back bringing his cap down over his face. A mirror image of Marcus next to him, except Marcus had become rather portly once his days in the army had finished; a subject he could become quite bad-tempered about. Gnaeus crossed his hands and began to drum his fingers on his chest. Titus could hear him mumbling quietly but couldn't quite make out the words. 'Are you praying to your God, Gnaeus?' he asked.

'Yes.'

'Is he Jupiter?'

'No, he's just God.'

Titus laughed, 'how can he look after everything by himself Gnaeus,' he teased. They had had this conversation many times before and it never ceased to amuse him how anyone could believe that there was only one God.

Gnaeus ignored him and kept praying.

'The senate wouldn't be too impressed with your heresy,' Titus said. It was a Roman's duty to worship the gods; it was a duty to your family too, if you wanted to have a job well paid enough to provide for them.

Gnaeus pulled his cap back up to roll his eyes sarcastically at Titus: as if Rome could reach them here.

'What are you asking your God, Gnaeus?' Titus continued.

'I'm praying for him to forgive us for our sins,' Gnaeus replied, pulling the cap down again.

Titus continued to stare into the fire, aware of Gnaeus still praying alongside him.

The silence was broken by Antonius noisily leaving his tent. Buttoning up his trousers he headed towards them.

'Titus!' the huge man barked. 'You sleep now. I'll keep watch.' The ground shook as he sat down heavily, stretching out his arms wide in the night breeze.

Titus lay down next to Gnaeus on the soft turf and closed his eyes. He could hear the spitting of the fire just a few feet away and the sound of

Antonius whistling tunelessly to himself. As Titus turned away to face Gnaeus again, he could see he still wasn't asleep.

'Can your God forgive sins?' Titus whispered.

'I believe that he can,' said Gnaeus earnestly.

'Then keep praying my old friend because, I think we might need him after all.'

Titus was trapped. The room was tiny, just a few feet of concrete. It was familiar: he had been here many times before in his dreams. He had barricaded himself in, and now there was only one point of entry and he could hear the enemy coming. He readied his sonifex, choosing anti-personnel rounds: they wouldn't have armour. He would sell his life dearly if need be. A grenade was tossed round the corner. He quickly flicked it back round into the corridor. No screams when it exploded. A man's head appeared at the door, painted grotesquely, with exotic feathers matted into his jet black hair. His arms held a state of the art freshly liberated sonifex. Titus fired.

The man disappeared in a cloud of gore. Over and over again, man after man came at him. His ammunition was low. Another grenade. He couldn't get to it in time. Smashed against the wall by the blast, he felt his right arm shatter. Gritting his teeth against the pain, he switched the sonifex to his left arm. He knew they must not get past the corridor. He had to protect Marcus. A shriek filled his ears. Titus heard his foes screaming in their barbarous language. He knew a few words of it, but this word sucked all hope from him.

'Gas!'

Titus awoke on the grass, cold and sweating, the fire was nearly dead now, but a few pale embers remained. He could still taste the blistering gas in his mouth. This was of course ridiculous as he knew the blistering gas did not even smell. That was why it was so deadly. He turned over and saw Gnaeus, Antonius and Marcus asleep alongside him. He looked up at the stars overhead. Antonius' watch had been typically ineffectual.

He could see the thick, milky band that made up the Road of the Gods. Only partially visible above the horizon he could see one of the Hunter's Great Dogs. It was two thousand seven hundred and sixty four years since his great city had been founded, and the war was over. It had been over for ten years. Ten years that he had spent drifting around, taking on mercenary jobs where he could. Dacia at first, rounding up escapees from the great ore mines and power factories. But Dacia was getting tame these days, and he had longed for a bigger challenge. Luguvalium, the last outpost before the Great Wall, had seemed perfect.

Technically he had never left the army, refusing to accept the sickeningly poor redundancy offer that the vast majority of the legions had been offered. For, with the whole world finally united under Roman rule, their services were no longer needed. So he still worked for Rome, albeit unpaid. But he had something that those who had accepted the Senate's redundancy deal no longer did: his pride; for he had never revoked his Sacramentum, the oath he had taken on joining the legion to serve Rome. He sighed as he remembered his dreams when he first entered the legions. This wasn't where he was meant to be: a soldier with no war, in a world of soldiers with no war. Was there any way he could have avoided this? He shook his head. The changes had been forced upon him, by a man he had once dared to call a friend. He thought back to the slave chief he had slaughtered earlier that day, and the strange papers he had given to him and shivered. But the night was not cold.

III

Ceinwyn languidly brushed her coppery hair from her green eyes and turned over, wishing that the morning would stay away just a while longer. The glow in her small room was intensifying, despite her best efforts to wish the coming day away. All around her she could hear the sounds of her room-mates getting ready for work. She would be last up again, which would mean no chance to get into the washroom until the evening; the master wouldn't like it if he thought she wasn't keeping herself at her best. She reached over to the glass by her squalid mattress. Through years of long necessity she sniffed it prior to drinking. The unmistakable smell of fresh urine filled her nostrils.

Ceinwyn hated her master with a passion only met by her hatred for most of the other slaves with whom she lived. They were of course jealous, she thought; as the daughter of a Roman lady, and a slave man, she was both taller and prettier than them. The slaves hated her for that. Unfortunately for Ceinwyn the Romans hated her even more. At first they were not sure what she was (they usually thought she was one of them) but eventually with their centuries of practice, they saw through the shape of her face, her height, and her beauty; and that look of disgust, reserved only for her kind, crossed their face. The years of practice had also given her kind a name: Half-Breed.

Today Ceinwyn would be cleaning out the master's linens for the morning; work for the master was easy, he had so many slaves there was often no work to do at all. She wasn't relishing this work though: last time she had done it the master had insisted on watching her all the time she was in his room. She felt sick whenever she thought of his stares on her body as she changed his bed and washed his clothes. She dreaded the call to his bed that so many of the slaves had had to endure over the years. The master was renowned for his unusual tastes. Yet in all of her five years in the master's house, that call had never come. Twenty three years old and beautiful beyond comparison, poor Ceinwyn, through the nature of her birth, realised that no-one, Roman or slave, would have her. She was a disgrace and an outrage to both and that would be her curse: abandoned at birth and then ignored, or worse, abused, through life. Only Cyric understood her.

Cyric was a sixteen year old slave who worked in the master's garages. He was one of the few true slaves who could almost pass himself off as a Roman if he needed to. He was unnaturally tall for a slave, and he didn't have their typical ashen skin. But this natural advantage was tempered by a thin weasely face that made him appear scheming; and wiry black, unruly hair. Although slaves were usually given only menial work, for Cyric, who had a natural ability with the workings of machinery, the master made an exception. Their master had an especial liking for ancient curri, especially racing ones, and Cyric's skill with these was too great to be wasted. The master was a poor driver himself, by all accounts, so sometimes Cyric got the opportunity to drive for him. Ceinwyn remembered one summer's day when Cyric decided that she needed cheering up. He secreted her in the boot of an ancient old off-road currus and, with himself at the wheel and the master alongside, unaware of their secret baggage, they headed off for a day trip into the mountains nearby. Ceinwyn had never been allowed out of the master's compound, except under close supervision, and even the view through the rust holes in the sides of the car fascinated her. It was her first proper view of the country she had lived in for five years. The country of her father.

As Cyric lifted her out of the car, he stared into her eyes. That was the day she realised that Cyric loved her. A few weeks later he had tried to tell her in his shy way. She remembered, with intense embarrassment, how she tried to explain that she loved him more than anything in the world, but not like that. It was surely the ultimate irony, Ceinwyn thought, that she could not return love to the only man in the world who could love her.

A little girl, barely five, tripped over Ceinwyn's slumbering head on her way to the refectory, signalling that it was, without doubt finally time to get up. She eased on a green linen shift and brushed her red hair back from her face. Everyone else had left for breakfast now, and the tiny room was dingy and lifeless. No-one had even bothered to open the shutters. Ceinwyn reached up for the wooden catch and twisted it. The wooden shutters flew apart showering Ceinwyn in dust and bright early morning light.

At the first rays of the new sun Titus also awoke. He brushed the fine layer of dew from his camouflage and sat up. From their vantage point on the mound he had a fine view of the local hills. He roused the other men around the dead fire. Luguvalium was a full day's march; it would be tempting fate to stay another night in the open with such a valuable cargo.

Marcus came up behind him and clapped him on the shoulder roughly, 'what's the plan then boss?' he asked.

Marcus had begun to call Titus 'boss' long before Titus had any rank at all. Titus had been used to being the leader all the way through his childhood: all his old friends had naturally looked to him for guidance during their old boyhood pranks. When he had joined the army, it seemed natural to him that the five men he shared a tent with, deferred to him. He had always given them the utmost respect for it though; in his heart he knew that was probably why they still followed him, now nearly twenty years from when they had first met. He trusted them all; how could he not when he had known them for so long. But he trusted Marcus the most. There was no official hierarchy in the band of men, but everyone knew that really Marcus was second in command. Now, as the sun began to peak above the hills ahead, his deputy stood before him, waiting for orders.

'Well we've got a long way to go,' Titus explained 'and we're still deep in the debated lands. I'll need you to scout ahead. You should take Antonius with you. We'll follow behind with the cargo. If you see anyone, stay hidden. Don't take any unnecessary risks. We need to get back in one piece.' Marcus nodded, and set off to scout the route, with Antonius lumbering along behind him.

At first their route snaked down from the hills by a fast flowing stream. As the gradient steepened, they were forced to descend on damp, stone slabs. The valley deepened and the steep sides blotted out the sun. Tiberius and Gnaeus drove the slaves along the path. There were fifteen women and children in all. They were not in perfect physical shape, and the rest stops were becoming increasingly annoying. Titus hissed with frustration as he checked his watch again. At this rate it would be highly unlikely that they would make it back by nightfall.

Just after midday their convoy was brought up sharp by a whistle from Marcus. Titus stopped and crouched down as Marcus approached slowly, keeping low. Together they crept forward to where Antonius lay, taking cover in some bushes overlooking the main road between Luguvalium and the chain of forts running along The Great Wall.

'Listen,' hissed Marcus.

Titus stopped breathing and opened his jaw slightly to enhance his hearing. There was an engine far away on the metalled road. Keeping his head down, he peered out from within the bracken and waited. A few minutes came and went, before, from around the corner, lumbered a battered old armoured currus. The sides were decorated with trophies, ancient body armour, useless antiquated weaponry, and bones; most of which appeared to have belonged to animals. As it drew level with them, with a great roar, the currus changed gear and lumbered on up the hill road. 'Reivers,' Marcus hissed, his eyes wide with a mixture of excitement and fear.

The Reivers were a mishmash of local men, and recruited mercenaries who plied the relatively lawless roads of northern Brittania looking for loot. They existed as a direct result of the Roman Empire's inability to control the lands north of The Great Wall. They also had a reputation for uncompromising brutality. When any man left a major town in the vicinity of The Great Wall, it would be wise for him to pay a bribe to a Reiver agent. Titus remembered his first job for Strabo, the Governor of northern Britannia and, as of two weeks ago, his boss.

A businessman had been three days overdue and Strabo, hearing that Titus' men were passing through town looking for mercenary type work, hired him to find this man and bring the documents he had been carrying safely to him. Titus got the documents and brought back the man, but Strabo had seemed to only have interest in the documents. Titus felt sick as he remembered the state of the man. Firstly he had had to cut him down from the tree the Reivers had hung him in. He was dead, but only just. He had been placed in a net and left to die of thirst above the road, and maybe it had been the thirst that had killed him. Titus hoped it was, but was fairly certain that it had in fact been the birds. Perhaps it was both, but to die of thirst with no eyes was a fate he could barely contemplate.

How many people walked past and left him there? Titus had thought. Did he cry out to them one after another begging them to help? Titus knew that most men were too afraid of the Reivers to interfere with their work.

But Titus could not afford to pay bribes, even if he had been inclined to, and he wondered how long it would be before he, too, was placed in a net, hanging from a tree. He laughed to himself. First they would have to catch him. His finger tightened on the trigger of his sonifex.

But today was the wrong day to pick a fight with the Reivers: they couldn't risk losing their precious cargo. 'Neither of you move an inch,' Titus ordered, releasing his finger from the trigger slowly.

'I reckon I can take them,' whispered Antonius proudly. 'On my own.'

'No, you fool,' Titus whispered back, 'we'll take them another day. Let them go.' The currus rolled past, and around another bend.

As the clanging receded into the distance, Antonius asked, 'are we Reivers?'

'Have you ever hung someone from a tree to die, Antonius?' Titus asked, with exasperation. Antonius paused and thought for a few moments to ponder this.

'No, not that. But we kill people for money.'

22

Titus gave him a withering look, wondering how a man as stupid as Antonius managed to actually function on a day to day basis, but then he didn't value him for his brains, Titus thought to himself. As they prepared to move on, Titus, to his surprise, found that the back of his mind was still pondering Antonius' preposterous question.

He returned to the others and explained the Reiver situation. They were all concerned at the news of a Reiver patrol acting so openly this near to the town of Luguvalium itself. 'I'd unleash the Praetorian guard!' Quintus said, 'rather than have those filthy savages on my doorstep.'

Titus nodded, aware that everyone was likely feeling the same. 'We'll report it to Strabo,' he explained, 'maybe he will act on the threat. If things get worse, we will do what we always do.'

'You mean move on again?' Quintus asked sarcastically.

'Yes, Quintus, if needs must,' he snapped. You know you wouldn't have to come with me, if you didn't want to.'

Quintus looked at Tiberius for a second. 'We're behind you,' he said, looking away quickly.

'Good, Quintus, I can always use a medic.' Titus said, awkwardly. He gestured to the worried huddle of slaves lying face down in the grass. 'Get these creatures ready to move out and keep them quiet,' he added, starting back towards the opening of the pass ahead.

They were only twenty miles away from Luguvalium now, each step bringing them closer to safety. Just before nightfall they got their first glimpse of the town, as they made the final descent down into the Caldew floodplain. Ten miles now separated them from their goal. Normally they would simply pick up curri at the main road up ahead, but this would be difficult with their slave cargo. Making their way carefully by a less used track, Titus still made good progress, but he could tell the slaves were tiring. They needed to rest: there would be no choice but to camp in the forest.

Marcus had concealed the makeshift camp well, Titus thought, as he tucked into a hunk of venison jerky, by the light of the crackling fire. They hadn't brought many provisions; not enough to feed their slave cargo at any rate. Before they had left the slave's village, they had ransacked the food stores and distributed the bread and dried meats amongst the captives. Despite this there hadn't been much to go around. The child with the broken arm was sobbing again, probably hungry, Titus thought. He opened the plastic wrapper of his jerky to bring out a second chunk. 'Quintus,' he whispered conspiratorially, 'can you give this to that child for me.'

Quintus was amused. 'You could take it yourself?'

'Yes, but, well, it just doesn't seem right really.'

'You mean with you having killed his Dad and everything,' laughed Quintus tearing a chunk of bread free from his rucksack.

'Well, if you put it bluntly,' Titus replied.

'Well I'm the doctor after all,' Quintus sighed and took the jerky, 'give me the medicine and I shall tend to my patient.'

'Very Hippocratic of you,' Titus replied.

Soon the child slept quietly and Titus took the first watch. He stared into the deep woods that surrounded them, wondering about the horrors that most likely dwelt within. When he had been a child, his family used to holiday in a small farmhouse far from Rome in northern Italy; he had fond memories of the thick forests that had surrounded his second home. During the day he had played in them, running as far in as he dared; enjoying the way the forest cut out sound and light; forcing him to navigate in different ways.

At night his mother had warned him that Caesar and his conspirators came out of their lairs and had the forest to themselves. He remembered how his father had taught him about the Great Titus Labienus, his old ancestor, who stabbed Julius Caesar in the back as he slept, dreaming of marching on Rome and setting himself up as a tyrant. He wasn't worried about mythical Caesars in the woods after that. It was only when he had grown older that he had realised the curse the Great Titus Labienus brought to his family. A man so wracked with guilt that he killed himself was never an easy stain to shift. They still had their beautiful, ancient townhouse in Rome, but inside, their family was falling down.

He sighed and looked back at the trees; the stark backdrop of foliage kept forming shapes in the darkness that his mind couldn't shake. He noticed a taller tree that, for a moment, looked like a young soldier,

24

standing in mock grandeur in front of a line of subdued trees. He turned away, trying to keep a proper watch, but he couldn't help hearing the leaves rustle, as if in the breeze of the tree man's sonifex fire. He covered his face, blotting out the images, and lay still till the memories subsided.

Titus awoke to the feel of cold steel against his face. He cursed himself for his stupidity; he had never fallen asleep on watch before. He opened his eyes slowly, already knowing what he would see. Yet he was still shocked: it was after all the first time he had stared into the eyes of a Reiver.

IV

'Get up slaver,' the bearded man grunted. He emphasised his point with a firm kick into Titus' side. The first rays of the morning light were arcing between the trees; the tiny shafts of light playing over the grimy faces of the four men who held them captive. The bearded man seemed young to be leading a Reiver band. Titus noted that their sonifi were slung into the backpacks of the four men; they had all slept as these men rifled through their camp. Either we have lost our touch, Titus thought, or these men are professionals.

The four Reivers grouped Titus and his men together at the camp's centre: this way they could guard them easily with one man. The other three went to round up the slaves from their hastily built stockade. Titus noted, as the slaves were brought out of the stockade, that three had escaped during the night. He was glad of it: Reivers had a certain reputation for their treatment of women captives. If even just some of the stories were true, the fact that some of the women were children would probably not alter their fate.

Titus was aware that the best that most men in his situation could expect was to end up hanging from a tree in a net. All he could do was hope they didn't recognise him. If they recognised him as the leader of a group of mercenaries, who owed unpaid protection money, a much worse fate could surely be created. Apparently the Reivers were extremely inventive.

The bearded man returned to face Titus. 'Slaver,' he sneered, 'you have a good haul of cargo. How you live with yourself is beyond my comprehension.' Titus didn't bother to reply, seeing as this man had likely raped more women than he could imagine, tortured innumerable honest men, and been a member of a criminal fraternity responsible for the economic stifling of most of northern Britannia. But his voice had a hint of polish, at odds with his appearance, that disturbed Titus.

The bearded Reiver seemed to read his thoughts, 'you hear tales about us, don't you,' he continued. 'I take bribes and in return I let people pass through my lands. I even protect them from scum like you.' The man stopped talking, took a step closer to Titus and kicked him hard in the groin. As Titus collapsed in a heap, the Reiver knelt down to his level, squatting on the ground. 'You think you are better than me?' the captain asked angrily.

Titus said nothing: blinking away tears of pain he realised he wasn't sure what he thought.

'We take money,' the Reiver said, rising back to his feet, 'we take your money even, but you take lives.' He gestured to the cluster of slaves, freed and standing in a group together, too afraid to run. 'You take the lives of these innocent people, and sell them to the highest bidder. So I ask you again—which of us is better?'

Titus composed himself and slowly stood up, trying to ignore the choking feeling in his stomach, and spoke: 'I once found a man hanging in a tree. He had died there, of starvation, or maybe thirst, or maybe even of despair that anyone should stop to help him.' He paused and stared into the eyes of the captain, 'a man like yourself, a Reiver, did this to him for no reason except perhaps for the fun of it. So yes, I am better than you, because at least I'm just doing my job. Unlike you, I do not enjoy it.'

The Reiver captain looked disturbed, 'I had no choice.' He looked away into the distance for some time, and Titus could see the regret etched on his face. Eventually he turned his gaze back to Titus' men, who sat together on the cold forest floor. But his expression was no longer bold. 'It is time we left here. If you value your life I would allow these slaves to go free unmolested, and I would return to Luguvalium as fast as possible.' He turned to leave and then suddenly remembered his original purpose in disrupting their camp. 'Let me see the mark before we go,' he demanded.

Titus' heart sank. He had seen a mark several times, although he had refused to buy one himself. A mark was simply a piece of holographic paper with a seal on it, most likely impossible to forge. Within the seal was a code which could be read by a scire, such as that which the Reiver captain would own. The code contained information on the owner of the seal, what his anticipated trade goods were, and what cut of them he had given to Agrippa, the Reiver agent in Luguvalium. It was this agent with an electronics dealership as a front, who would provide him with the mark. The mark would save his life in exactly this sort of situation.

Titus felt around in his webbing for something to pass to the man: a moment's distraction might allow them to overpower the small Reiver band. He didn't hold out much hope, however, because these men had their sonifi, and they were professionals, keeping back out of reach, and covering their every move.

After a moment of scrabbling, Titus' hand settled upon some of the papers he had taken from the old slave's desk. He took the top one and handed it over; he knew he had a couple of seconds at best to take advantage of the diversion. As soon as the captain saw that the paper was covered in meaningless numbers rather than a holographic Reiver mark, they would be dead. But Titus didn't expect the look of horror on the man's face, as he examined Titus' paper.

The rest of the Reivers saw the look too and, for a moment, all attention was focused on the sheet. Titus knew there wasn't going to be a second chance. He threw himself onto his feet and drew his gladius. He dived forward, throwing all his weight at the man nearest him and plunging the blade into his chest. A warm gush of fresh blood over his hands was his reward. Antonius didn't need any encouragement. Despite being unarmed, he charged headlong into two of the other Reivers, forcing them to the ground, their sonifi clattering away on the bare earth.

Titus approached the Reiver captain whose eyes were wide with fear. 'Spare my wife,' he begged.

Titus looked around in confusion, for there were no women to be seen.

'You can kill me, but don't harm her.' He looked like he was about to faint, 'I didn't know who you were,' he was trembling, 'trust me; I didn't know.'

Titus was completely taken aback. He looked behind him. His men were as confused as he was. The two men that Antonius held had the look of those who knew that all that separated them from death was suffering. 'What's going on?' Titus demanded of the Reiver captain, who had fallen to his knees in the dirt of the forest floor.

The man just knelt there looking up at Titus imploringly.

Titus offered him his hand. Taking it, the Reiver hauled himself back to his feet.

'Take my greetings back to your master,' the captain spat the last word as if forcing himself to say the phrase had cost him dearly. He tripped in the undergrowth as he and his men scattered, so eager to get away. Titus gestured to Antonius to set free the two struggling Reivers he held. Although they were winded, they also made a quick getaway; fighting with each other to be the first of the pair out of the glade.

Titus reached down and retrieved his sonifex. He was confused. By all rights he knew he should now be dead. What had scared these men so much that they had let their guard down? Why did this strutting and proud Reiver captain suddenly recoil in fear from a piece of paper? Titus paced up and down as his men dusted themselves down and retrieved their sonifi. Titus saw the crumpled up paper on the ground a few yards away—the Reiver captain had dropped it in flight. Titus stooped down low to pick it up. The sun had now risen fully, filling the forest with the soft glow of early morning light. He gently unscrumpled the paper. He was surprised when he looked at it, for he had expected it to be covered in meaningless figures. Instead there was the name of his employer in a dead slave's hand writing.

'Get these slaves rounded up. We move out in five minutes,' he shouted to his men and stared into the forest, for a moment wishing that he too, like the Reivers, could flee into the trees.

V

Gaius Strabo occupied a palace adjacent to the south gate of Luguvalium. His official role was that of Governor of northern Brittania, a role that, despite giving very little actual power, gave plenty of opportunities for mistreating the population. Rome liked to keep direct control of every one of its little provinces, so the governors were only there to prevent rebellion; they had no power to change the laws of Rome.

Titus was well aware that the further out into the provinces you went, the less the law of Rome meant; that was why he came to places like this instead of settling in his ancestral city. It was far too late to go back now, a veteran like him would not be that welcome in the Great Capital these days: it seemed that war was no longer fashionable in Senate politics.

It was strange, Titus thought, that he hadn't even seen his city for nearly ten years. He had gone back only once since the summer's day when, at the age of seventeen, he had left for the Transmaritanus and war. As the son of a noble family, he should have been expecting to fight political battles in the Senate, but he had always hated his father's dusty law and philosophy books and secretly dreaded the day he would make his first debate in the Senate House. His family's dishonour had brought him an outdoor life in the legions, which he had grown to love. But of course, like all things, the war had ended and Janus' gates had been shut firmly; most likely for evermore. Like most of the army, he had expected that some sort of ceremony would take place to mark that glorious occasion, for which they had lost so much.

And there was indeed a ceremony. Titus heard about it in a camp riddled with dysentery, waiting for marecurri that never seemed to arrive. It had been magnificent, he was told. The ancient consul of Rome, Sertorius, had presided over it, riding in triumph through the streets of Rome in an ancient chariot, harking back to the glorious days of Old Rome. The only man who served in the war itself to receive any honours in Rome was Marcus Albus, the Supreme General of the combined legions and son of Sertorius himself. A man whom Titus had once had the honour of calling a friend. All of the lesser generals, of which by this point Titus was proud to count himself amongst, received nothing. Not even a medal.

Instead, he eventually returned home to his family, to find that his mother was ill and the family poorer than ever. The walls of their townhouse were falling into disrepair and he found their once friendly neighbours cast their eyes down as he passed by. He stayed to care for his mother, finding his father distant; 'swallowed by his books,' his mother always said. She grew fainter every day and the doctors could do nothing. He never returned home after the funeral. Titus had a new family, forged in fire, and blood, and pain.

Today his new family would make itself temporarily rich. They had twelve female slaves and four children. All were in good condition. This was their best haul for the last two years. As he looked around at his friends' tired, happy faces, he was at last sure that they had made the right decision to leave Dacia and look for work in Britannia. The increased danger posed by the Reivers was more than made up for by the rewards on offer, and the life of the mercenary was based around rewards. Perhaps they could even afford to upgrade their weapons he thought, looking at his battered old sonifex as it bounced in time to his step at his hip; it had been the same one he had first used in the Transmaritanus fifteen years ago. It had never misfired in all that time though—a testament to Vulcan's forge (the huge weapon factory just outside Rome), and its fastidious approach to weapon craftsmanship.

They crossed the threshold of Strabo's compound and stepped across the cold marble floor. Outside it had begun to rain. The bustling market that thronged the southern gate was being covered hastily with polythene sheeting to try to keep the few customers there were. The weather was renowned for being bad for business in Luguvalium, and what with that and the Reivers, it was a wonder Strabo managed to thrive so well.

A beautiful girl met them at the gate and ushered them into a small waiting room complete with plush armchairs and a hookah pipe imported from Asia Minor. The girl bobbed her head of beautiful red curls and left quickly.

'We should do more jobs for this man,' Quintus said nodding in the direction in which the girl had gone. Titus was aware that the constant moving around was a struggle, especially for Quintus. Sometimes he wondered why Quintus stayed with them: he could have been a proper doctor, maybe even a famous one in Rome, instead he plied his trade as a field medic and trained killer. It was no life for him.

'We will stay here for now,' he said, 'if Strabo can get us lodgings. If he has more jobs we'll take them.' This seemed to please the men, but Titus had an uneasy feeling. For all his pleasure at the great haul of slaves, he knew there was something not quite right about this. As he saw their slaves dragged away into the courtyard, and out of sight, he felt that he would be happy if he never had to touch a slave again.

'Aquilinus, Aquilinus, come through,' a jolly voice boomed from the room next door. Titus opened the door to see a rotund man about his own age, sitting at an expensive looking, mahogany desk, similar to the one the old slave had been writing at only two days ago.

'Tell your men to smoke as much of that flavoured tobacco as they like; it's the best. Comes direct from the fields of Hakim Shariff himself. Have you ever been to Asia Minor Commander?' he asked Titus.

'Never had the pleasure sir. Britannia has very much become my home: I am somewhat reluctant to leave these days,' Titus said, trying to sound as respectful as possible. Despite being hired twice now by this man, he had never had the opportunity to meet him face to face.

Strabo rubbed his podgy fingers together, 'a good haul of slaves. My agent mentioned to me that there would probably only be half that many. I am very impressed with your abilities.'

'It seems to have become our specialty sir,' Titus replied, not sure that he should really be that proud of having this sort of skill.

Strabo played with a silver figurine on his desk and smiled awkwardly, 'did you find any stolen property at the camp?'

'What do you mean sir?' Titus asked.

Strabo played with a loose thread at the edge of his sleeve and continued. 'Well, one of the slaves you were hunting was once my slave. He stole from me the night he ran away. You know what they're like: nothing more than stupid animals. Well, this animal, well, he was a magpie. Liked pretty objects. Somehow he stole a desk just like this one!'

Titus opened his mouth to tell Strabo all about the mahogany desk and the strange writings he had found, but something in the way Strabo looked at him warned him against it, and he quickly shook his head.

'I'm not surprised you didn't find it,' Strabo said quickly, grinning inanely. 'Stupid fool probably burnt it for firewood.' He laughed, clapping Titus on the shoulder, encouraging him to join in but Titus wasn't in an especially jovial mood.

'Lets get down to business then,' Strabo said, stepping back behind his new desk. 'Would you like to do more work for me, Aquilinus?' he took out a leather wallet and brought out a tiny scire. 'I pay handsomely—here, I'll show you. Give me your team's account details.'

'We don't have an account as such,' Titus said, feeling slightly behind the times, 'we usually take cash.'

Strabo glared at Titus momentarily, and then laughed. Titus couldn't help noticing that he had begun to dribble slightly. Strabo lifted a spotless, silk handkerchief to his mouth to clean it up. 'So much hilarity.' He giggled for a few seconds before letting out a loud sigh. 'How about your own accounts then Commander Aquilinus—I'm sure you will dispense it equally amongst the men.' The way he spoke clearly suggested the opposite was more likely.

34

'I'd still prefer cash sir.'

'I don't deal in cash; account code only. Didn't my agent make that clear when you took the work?' Strabo said. Colour was rising in his cheeks and he was clearly getting annoyed. Titus didn't want to ruin his relationship with his potential new employer so soon. He handed over Marcus' account details. A few key presses and scrabblings of podgy fingers on the touch screen later, and the money had been passed to Marcus, the only member of their team with an online account. A piece of thin paper spooled out of scire. Strabo tore off the receipt and passed it over.

Titus had worked for the slave markets for years in Dacia, but he had never met a man who paid as handsomely for a slave as Gaius Strabo. This was far too much. Strabo smiled at Titus, aware of where his thoughts were going.

'Consider it advance pay, Aquilinus,' he said, smiling. Seeing Titus begin to frown with concern, he continued quickly, 'Titus, I'm not sure if you are aware of the disappearance of Decimus Petronius? He was the Chief Legate of our Praetorian guard.'

Titus nodded, 'I've heard a little of it.'

'Not been seen for several weeks,' Strabo reclined in his wicker chair—his massive bulk testing the seat to near breaking point. 'It's a nasty business. It seems that the Reivers may have got him. The Senate have appointed me in his place temporarily, until of course he is found. This is where you come in, you see Titus; most of my men are busy trying to find this man, or at least discover what happened to him. While they are performing this sacred task, handed to me from on high, I have no-one to take care of my usual business.'

Seeing that Titus wasn't convinced, he changed tack, 'sleep on it, if you're not happy then don't do the job and I'll take 25% back off what I just paid you.'

Titus realised that even taking 25% off they had made an exceptionally favourable deal. He nodded slowly and promised to return the following day.

Strabo had put them up in a row of houses that overlooked the river Caldew as it coursed down into Luguvalium from the hill country. It was on a quiet street only occasionally disturbed by the hum of curri. Titus had been given the largest of the houses: he had two bedrooms, as well as reception rooms and a cellar where he could keep fine wines and slaves, if he had had any. Titus was surprised to find a young, male slave already in the house when he arrived. It turned out that Strabo had sent him from his palace personally to prepare the place for his arrival. Titus felt that he could probably have coped by himself, with the lights being voice activated, and the house having all the modern conveniences. It even had a new toy: a fusion amplifier. Titus had worked around fusion amplifiers for years in the military; it seemed that the technology had eventually filtered down to the commercial market. The principal was simple: generate your power in as messy a way as you like, somewhere you don't much care about, Dacia for instance, then beam the power around the world using electromagnetic induction. A fusion amplifier could pick up this power and use it locally, the upshot being that almost all electrical items could now be fully portable. Titus flopped down in an armchair and dismissed the slave.

He turned on the giant screen that made up most of the side wall of his sitting room. The first thing to pop up was amusingly an advert for the very fusion amplifier he was using to watch the commercial. It depicted a happy Roman household, probably up on the Palatine hill in Rome itself. Titus wondered if that family knew how the fusion amplifiers they used to cook their fine food and straighten their hair had been first put to use. If Titus closed his eyes and opened his mind, he could still hear the otherworldly sound of the Jupiter machine preparing to destroy. He shook his head as if to rid himself of a memory he knew he would never be truly free of.

As he began to relax in his new home, his attention was drawn to his pocket and to the small piece of thin paper that Strabo had given him. Besides the large sum for the slaves there was an account number. Somewhere in the back of his mind Titus knew where he had seen this before. He found himself taking out the papers he had found at the slave camp, not entirely sure that he wanted to look at them. He didn't want his suspicions to be confirmed. Yet they were.

Every perfectly justified line of print proved him correct: these accounts he held, of the richest man he could ever hope to meet, were those of Gaius Strabo himself. It was inconceivable that a regional governor could be this rich. In fact Strabo's generosity surprised him even further now: it had always seemed to him that the richer a man was, the harder it was to get a fair payment from them. Strabo was obviously the exception. Or more likely, maybe he was just so rich he no longer cared any more.

Titus looked out of the window at the rain hammering down on the metalled street outside. The market must surely have closed in this, he thought. No matter how he looked at it, Titus knew that Strabo could not possibly have amassed such a fortune through taxes and slaves. Even counting bribes it wasn't possible. There had to be something else. The thought of wheels of intrigue spinning, with him merely running around the periphery unable to see the grand plan, frightened Titus. Yet he could imagine Quintus' look of despair as, yet again, he told him they were moving on. It wasn't fair to move his men on again just yet, especially when they were being paid so well. But no matter how hard he tried, Titus couldn't shake off the idea that the more they dealt with Gaius Strabo, the further into his world they would be thrust. He had to protect his friends from that. There was only one thing for it, Titus thought, as he began to unpack his belongings: work for Strabo; take his money; let him trust us. But don't trust him, Titus mused, don't trust him an inch.

VI

Ceinwyn was scared. Three days ago she had shared a room with five other girls; now there were only three. The worst of it was that no-one seemed to want to talk about what had happened to the other two: there was no gossip, just dead, expressionless eyes whenever she mentioned the other girls. It was as if her companions had simply forgotten their existence. She had mentioned the strange disappearances to Cyric, of course, but he was just interested in her safety, shaking her by the shoulders and telling her not to ask questions like that.

'Keep your head down and don't let them see you are worrying!'

He looked like he did that day he had tried to kiss her; the day Ceinwyn kept trying to forget. She promised him she would stay safe, and she meant the words, but in her heart Ceinwyn knew herself better than that.

Going about her daily tasks it was relatively difficult to seek out new information. A week ago however, it would have been impossible. The master had been following her even more than usual, and she had barely had a second's reprise from his beady eyes poring over her body. Then something terrifying had happened. He had touched her. Ceinwyn couldn't remember being touched by a Roman before, they tended to keep away: Marcus Albus, the Consul of Rome, had decreed Half-breeds unclean years ago. He could now be proud of a Rome cleansed of them. Ceinwyn thought of her old home in Rome; she had never known her mother, but her father, a British slave named Devin, had managed to shelter her and bring her up alone.

She still remembered that day five years ago as if it was yesterday. Devin crying as his master threw Ceinwyn onto the street; the master beating Devin as he tried to go to her. Eventually she stopped waiting outside the house. There were no others like her that she knew, so she had no-one to team up with. The soldiers moved her on until she was outside the city gates, then they left her to her own devices. She had thought that her old master had been harsh on her, but only after being sold to Gaius Strabo did she fully appreciate how unpleasant Romans could be.

His greasy fingers had closed on her wrist as she was about to make her way to bed. He had moved towards her, his piggy eyes ogling her body. She thought he was going to try to kiss her. She felt the bile rise in her throat, she mustn't be sick, she must hold it in, she must tolerate him, she knew, or she would die. But she couldn't overcome her revulsion. Her efforts were to no avail: he could see her disgust clearly in her eyes. That was the last time he had looked at her. For the two days since her rejection of him, he had pointedly looked the other way, with an air of haughty dignity whenever she had passed him. But she knew that, behind the apparent disregard, he was planning to punish her, and she shivered at the thought of her fate.

He had been spending more time downstairs as well, behind the two black metal doors with the keycode, in the basement of his compound. The slaves were not allowed to go in there; very few people were. Ceinwyn had watched the master go down, and from time to time officials arrived with large briefcases. No-one knew what happened down there. No-one even asked, apart from Ceinwyn. After several days of investigation, all she had discovered was that one slave girl swore blind that the two missing girls had both been ordered downstairs before they disappeared. Presumably they were still there. Ceinwyn knew there was only way to find out.

VII

Choking with laughter, Marcus looked like he was going to die over his breakfast. Clearly the others thought it was the funniest thing they had ever heard as well. 'Sorry, let me get this straight,' Marcus said, in between outbursts of mirth, 'you actually asked Strabo for cash?'

'Yes,' Titus replied wearily, unsure what the fuss was about, 'you know I don't trust the omniajunctus.'

'It can't go wrong! It's completely safe,' Marcus groaned, weary from having to explain this very simple principle, yet again. 'These big governors in their fancy palaces, they don't deal in cash any more. You're barely thirty for goodness sake; get with the times!'

'It's not safe Marcus. I want my money to actually exist.'

At this, Marcus launched into a tirade, most of which Titus didn't understand, apart from the bit about the omniajunctus having been around for almost fifty years and being completely safe. Titus left any of their work that required knowledge of scires, to Marcus. He didn't know much about scires, but he did know that what Marcus didn't know about them probably wasn't worth knowing. This didn't stop Marcus from going on about them a bit more than might be necessary however, thought Titus.

Today they had another job to do. Strabo's agent had woken Titus at the first signs of dawn and given him the details of the work. A simple enough job to do as a favour—not quite to his taste Titus thought, but the truth of the matter was that the six of them hadn't found an employer as good as Strabo during their whole ten years as mercenaries. The houses they had been given were amazing in comparison to what they had put up with throughout numerous other small cities and towns.

'It looks like we're staying,' Titus remarked to the group after they had finished the hearty, slave cooked breakfast of bacon, famous Luguvalium sausage and eggs. None of them could remember when they had last eaten so well.

Quintus looked the most relieved, which in turn relieved Titus. He doubted how much longer Quintus would have stayed with them, if it wasn't for Strabo's generosity. Quintus' leaving would have taken Tiberius too. Like a Legion tent group, his group was also meant to have six, the army had taught him that.

'What are our orders then, boss?' Marcus asked.

'It seems that Strabo has some business associates who have been somewhat, how shall I put it, reluctant to follow through with business transactions. We have been asked to', at this he paused, with a smile on his face, 'persuade them otherwise.' A moment of silence passed around the table and then everyone, Titus included, burst out laughing.

'You managed to sound just like him,' Gnaeus exclaimed.

Titus thought of the gross man in his immaculate toga, and understood why Strabo needed men such as him to do this sort of job. No-one in their right mind could be scared of Gaius Strabo in person.

Their first debtor lived in the merchant quarters towards the western edge of the city where the great canal wharfs brought in cargo from around the world. Strabo's instructions as to their appearance had been very exact. They were to be dressed in full regimental legionary uniforms, (none of them had worn one since their graduation day at the great Field of Mars Military Academy): interlocking burnished plates of metal with a red cape fastened at the shoulders scraping the ground beneath; it would be ridiculous on a battlefield. Strabo had guessed their sizes quite accurately, and they had taken great enjoyment in putting on the regimental uniforms again: it brought back fifteen year old memories from a time where the world was a simpler place. Back then, Titus thought, you could solve problems with a sonifex, or maybe just a well timed round of drinks. He thought about Strabo; the mahogany desk strewn with papers; his own rage as he slaughtered the old slave to silence his thoughts. A sonifex could not solve this.

Now, with red wool playing at his ankles and a horsehair plumed helmet to show his command, Titus marched along the dusty streets of the Merchants' Quarter, with his men filing along behind him. At the canal edge men were working at giant cranes using magnets to lift the metal crates from the docked marecurri. The smell of freshly gutted fish drifted down to them from the fishing currus docks further ahead. This was one of the few parts of the town that still thrived. The Reivers couldn't halt the influx of bounty that chugged slowly up the canal from the sea. Titus and his men ducked under a narrow entrance to a portacabin, and addressed the young, overly made-up receptionist. 'We are here to see Plublius Fabius,' Titus said sternly.

The rest of his men filed in behind him, entirely filling the reception room of the cabin. The receptionist played with her dyed hair, whilst pretending to look at some papers on her desk. 'Plublius Fabius is in a meeting, you'll have to come back later,' she mumbled disinterestedly and went back to reading her gossip magazine. The front cover mentioned some scandal in Rome and promised, 'full and exclusive cover interviews with our supreme leaders Marcus Albus and Decimus Catula,' the two elected Consuls of Rome.

Titus wondered how much Marcus Albus must have changed since the days that he had fought with him in the Transmaritanus. He remembered him as a proud man, five years his senior and more privileged. Titus remembered his obsession with Romanness, in fact most of their pre-battle meetings had been pure rhetoric on the subject: Marcus Albus was not fond of non-Romans.

For a brief second Titus was back on that ancient battlefield once more.

The smell of death filled his nostrils again. The line of women and children stretched away into the distance. He saw the young girl again, for some reason he couldn't see her face clearly today; just the tears on her cheeks. A general clapped him on the shoulder ready to give an order. He looked up at the handsome young face of Marcus Albus.

'This is his office right here,' Marcus interrupted his reminiscence by tapping at the brass name plate. Titus looked at the door whilst Antonius stepped over to it.

'You can't go in,' said the young receptionist, worried now.

'Antonius,' Titus ordered, 'take down the door.'

A heavy booting from Antonius would knock down most things. The flimsy portacabin door buckled easily and the six men filed through into Plubius Fabius' office. The man himself was sat behind a battered old desk; he was busy eating some kind of fish stew. The office was strewn with papers, books and fishing apparatus; it was clear that no-one had been allowed to clean it for several days.

'I would offer you a seat,' Plubius said in a brash accent that sounded as salty as the sea itself, 'but there be quite a few of you.' He took another mouthful of his stew, 'one of you is quite a strong lad I see,' he gestured towards Antonius, 'ever worked on a ship lad?'

There was no reply.

'Well how about you then lad,' Plubius said, gesturing at Tiberius, 'there's always room for a pretty boy like yourself on one of Plubius' vessels.'

'They all work for me,' Titus stated slowly.

'And you I suppose,' Plubius replied, 'work for my dear friend Gaius Strabo?'

'Your dear friend Gaius Strabo, to whom you owe a rather large sum of money?' Titus countered.

'Owe him money!' Plubius laughed. 'He owes *me* money! The way he governs these harbours has nearly ruined me.'

Titus leant on the desk, his assault sonifex slipping from his shoulder to hang menacingly from his hip.

Plubius instantly broke out into a sweat and began to fish around in his desk hastily, for some notes, 'much of my funds have been wiped out by some trouble with the omniajunctus, but let me see I always keep some hard cash handy.'

Eventually Plubius managed to dig out enough greasy sestertii notes to fulfil the orders from Strabo. Titus couldn't look the broken captain in the eye, so he turned on his heel and stormed past the receptionist who was furiously pretending to read her magazine, and back onto the street; his men following closely behind.

After an afternoon mostly spent forcing small businesses into near bankruptcy, Titus had begun to have enough. He had never relished the idea of doing this job for Strabo, and the reality of it began to hit home, as the people he was ordered to take money from became poorer and poorer. One man was clearly running his business from home: Titus had had to send Marcus round the back to stop his wife bolting with their possessions. The man had actually begged Titus on his knees not to take the money. With the Reivers crippling business, this was a bad time to be trying to earn a living in this town. Titus wished there was something he could do, but he was simply following orders. Strabo was Rome's presence in northern Britannia: he had to support Rome.

The final name on the list led them to the tallest building in Luguvalium. A glass fronted, five storey building: the local branch of a major stock trading firm. Titus had fewer qualms about this final part of his mission: no-one inside this building could be classified as poor and needy.

'Appius Scribonius does not wish to see you,' the smartly dressed concierge said, as Titus demanded an audience.

He pulled out a seal from his pocket, similar to the ones the Reivers used. 'I am here under direct orders from Gaius Strabo,' he said, 'he has given me the authority to act on his behalf. He commands that I be allowed to speak with Scribonius.'

'Gaius Strabo may be the Governor,' she replied, 'but he has no power to demand when he, or any of his minions for that matter, will see our staff. If you do not leave I will have to call security.'

Her finger rested on a rather obvious 'concealed' button beneath the desk. Titus couldn't be sure if she had pressed it or not. The receptionist was right of course: Gaius Strabo was the Governor of northern Britannia, but that position, by law, didn't entitle him to much official power. On the other hand, everyone knew that Strabo could get away with doing pretty much whatever he liked. Therefore Titus had to tread a careful tightrope: use Strabo's position, but hint rather than threaten directly. He heard the sound of a safety catch clicking off, and held out a hand to stall Antonius.

'I'm sure there will be no need for that,' said Titus, 'you have to understand that I have important information for Scribonius; you must allow me up to speak to him.' Titus was well aware of how he looked, standing in his flowing cape in the centre of that impressive marble floor. He hoped it was enough to persuade the concierge of his authority.

The concierge waited a moment, clearly weighing up the situation. Titus meanwhile was doing the same: there were eight security guards in the atrium, two of them had assault sonifi such as theirs. They would not be able to fight their way in. Even if they did, Strabo would have to deny all knowledge; as the Governor he might even have to sentence them to death, Titus thought, laughing to himself at the idea.

'You may go up,' said the concierge eventually shaking her head slightly with exasperation. His persistence had paid off. 'If he asks you to leave you must do so immediately.' Her finger remained under the button for a second, before moving to adjust the clips at the back of her tightly bunned hair. Titus understood now why Strabo had insisted he wear the uniform.

Appius Scribonius' office was on the third floor; the lift seemed to take forever to get to the top. The glass sides gave them a good view of the complex as they travelled upwards; it was far grander in its own way than Strabo's palace, all marble floor and glass walls. Titus could see why someone might want to work in a place like this, but for him he knew that the outdoors was the only workplace. He knew in his heart that he couldn't stay living in a city forever: he needed to see the sky. He looked over his shoulder to see Tiberius and Quintus engaged in some good natured banter. He hadn't seen Quintus so happy in months.

The lift doors swished open with a gentle, mechanical whirr. Titus led his team along the corridor. As his footsteps echoed along the cold, marble floor, Titus passed a procession of statues lining the walls; they were clearly tribal, originating from the ancient Britannic peoples.

Titus thought of the part his name-sake ancestor had played in the liberation of this part of the world. He had been fighting for Caesar then; the man he would one day betray and murder. He paused by a framed iron arrowhead, almost all rust now; maybe the Great Titus Labienus had used his tower shield to block an arrow just like this one. He liked to think of his ancestor in this way, as a great warrior. That way he could look up to him, and understand him. Everyone else saw a different side of the Protector of Rome and Slayer of Tyrants. To most he was a man who had averted disaster by killing his one time friend , who had gone dangerously egotistical. But whenever Titus thought of his ancestor, all he could see was a terrified coward stabbing his friend in the back whilst he slept.

Titus came to a halt outside the office of Appius Scribonius and was surprised to hear a young voice from inside when he knocked on the door. Despite the refined beauty of the building itself, Titus was still surprised by the quality of this young man's office. He looked to be no more than in his early twenties, yet he was in such a high position. It took an awkwardly long time for Titus and his team to cross the expanse of swirled, rose marble to the desk, during which time Scribonius was clearly unsure of how to act. He welcomed them as they reached the halfway point between the door and his desk, but he still had to raise his voice to be heard, even at this distance. The relics of the ancient world motif was clearly evident in this room as well: a piece of the original Great Wall stood proudly in the corner, adjacent to a huge portion of the thick curtain from the ancient temple in Jerusalem.

Titus eventually came within reach of Appius' desk and spoke. 'My name is Titus Labienus Aquilinus,' he reached in his pocket for Strabo's seal, 'we are here on the official business of Gaius Strabo the Governor of Luguvalium.' Looking at the awkward young man in front of him, he was unsure how best to proceed. This was not what he had expected.

The silence was broken eventually by the young stockbroker. 'You have come for the money,' he stuttered.

Titus nodded slowly. The young man played with some papers on the corner of his desk never quite meeting Titus' eye. 'I don't have it.'

Titus stared at him.

The young man nervously looked up at him from under his dark, thin, eyebrows. 'I told him there were no guarantees. It's not my fault,' he continued, his voice faltering as he looked at the weapons carried by Titus, and his men.

'I care nothing of this,' said Titus, dismissing the man's explanations: this was the last debtor on the list and it was getting late. 'You must pay Strabo. There is no choice.'

'I don't owe him anything. You have to understand, the Governor, he came to me to invest some, actually, quite a lot of money into. . .'

Titus cut him off. 'I'm sorry, if you can't pay yourself, you will have to draw money from your company.'

'I don't own this place,' the young man shouted, now halfway out of the chair. 'If they hear what happened they will sack me. I'll be ruined.'

Titus didn't know what to say, but with surprise he found himself looking on the young man with compassion. 'Calm down,' he said gently. The young man sat back in his fine leather office chair. 'You are an intelligent man—there must be a way out of this for you. Think for a minute.' He gestured to his men to be at ease. They dispersed and started looking at the fine collection of statues that decorated the south facing glass wall. Titus wasn't near enough to see through the glass at the correct angle from this height, but he was fairly certain that the massive window gave a view over the whole of Luguvalium, all the way over to the fells of Rheged, twenty miles distant. His thoughts were interrupted by the young man.

'There is no other way,' he whispered to himself, 'no way out. No way.' His hands opened a drawer under the desk and at the last minute, Titus realised that he was not drawing out sestertii. A handheld sonifex appeared from the bowels of the desk. The world seemed to slow down for Titus as his training took over. In one movement he dived to the right, whilst simultaneously slinging his sonifex from his back holster into his hands. The safety catch clicked off and Titus brought the weapon to bear on his would-be attacker. Then he stopped himself. The young man was not pointing the sonifex at him, but instead simply staring at it as he held it in his tight, pale, grip. Sweat was pouring down his face. He turned and looked at Titus accusingly with his piercing blue eyes. Then suddenly he brought the sonifex up, placed it into his mouth, and pulled the trigger.

The young man's head disintegrated in a burst of ragged tissue and bone fragments. His body flopped back down into the leather office chair, which was slowly propelled backwards by the force of the impact, one of its wheels squeaking repetitively; its deceased occupant spurting bright arterial blood liberally over the rose marble flooring. Titus slowly drew himself up from the ground and looked around to see his men, sonifi drawn, staring in disbelief at the scene before them. The sound of pounding boots filled the corridor behind them. Titus had seen the security presence on the way into the building—this was not going to be easy to explain.

VIII

It had cost Ceinwyn a large forfeit to buy the code to the black metal doors downstairs. The frumpy old washer-woman she had bought it off had worked at the compound since the master had had it commissioned. She was a Roman, but a poor one, forced to work for a wage that barely paid for her food and upkeep; provided by the master, of course. In reality she was little more than a slave, Ceinwyn thought, but she did have one thing Ceinwyn didn't, she was accepted anywhere she went as an actual person. Ceinwyn would be lucky to be spat at out on the street; she had heard of worse happening of course, and slaves had no recourse to the legal system. It was far safer to stay in the compound.

She would now be doing clothes washing for two days for this woman, but she was in possession of the digital code for the basement. It was the master's birth date, of course. As Ceinwyn thought about her red, raw hands from that morning's clothes wash, she couldn't help but remonstrate with herself for not just trying to guess the combination. But she knew that she would never have had the guts to stand by that door in plain sight, and work out the code. The simplicity of the numbers confused her.

Either the master was as stupid as he looked to use a code so weak, or maybe there was in fact little of interest to guard in the basement.

A shiver of fear passed through Ceinwyn as she thought of a third possibility, maybe the master wasn't too worried about people breaking into his basement as long as they never got out again. She shook the idea from her head—three of her one time companions were gone, and they had been some of her few friends in the compound; it was her duty to find them. She just had to pick her moment.

Dusk fell and Ceinwyn still had linen to fold and put away for the staff at the compound; the extra washing duties ate into the time for her officially assigned chores. She lifted up one of the piles of sheets and took out the small bag she had concealed inside it. It was time.

Opening the bag she took out the black shift she had taken from one of the master's mistresses; it was beautiful. She slipped it on; admiring herself in the mirror, she enjoyed the feel of the fabric on her skin. For a minute she allowed herself to imagine herself with a man on her arm. An image of Cyric appeared in her mind, breaking the fantasy. She turned her attention back to the dress, angry at herself. Why couldn't she make herself love him? He was the kindest man she had ever met. Her hands worked quickly at the frills of the dress, tearing them away and packing the excess material into her sack. The largest frill made a perfect headscarf to cover up her tell-tale red curls.

Once Ceinwyn felt suitably camouflaged, she headed out into the now much darkened cloister. She edged around the stone pillars that surrounded the first quadrangle. She could hear the soft murmuring of the fountain in the middle. It was a statue of Aeneas and Dido, an original from the tenth century since Rome's foundation, if she remembered right from the inauguration speech the master had made them all sit through when he had it installed. That meant it had only been made two hundred years after Jesus had been executed.

Ceinwyn wondered if the artisan who had carved the beautiful sculpture had known about Jesus; as a Roman, he certainly wouldn't have been able to speak about him. Ceinwyn, as a non-Roman, was allowed some freedom in this way: she was at least not expected to worship the Roman gods. To be honest, she thought, they probably didn't even credit her with the intelligence to hold a belief of any sort, let alone articulate it. This thought comforted her. Here she was, about to break in to the master's secret place and rescue her comrades, yet those proud, true Romans she served wouldn't even think her capable of planning such an action, yet alone pulling it off successfully. Keeping low and close to the wall she headed off further into the darkness.

Ceinwyn was brought up short by the sound of voices ahead. She pulled in close to the wall, hoping her camouflage would save her. She stretched the black frill covering her hair to veil her face: a bride in mourning. The men were dressed in white coats, and the nearest carried a large metal box. They spoke in hushed tones as they approached her hiding place.

She had seen people like them before. It was always the same: the white coats, and the business-men. Once, a few weeks ago, she had seen some very rough looking people allowed into the basement, which had surprised her, because usually it was the respectable sort: the ones who would look at her and stare at her beauty for a fraction of a second before a part of their mind would suddenly realise what she was, and would turn away. She hoped these two would turn away too. She knew well the dangers of being caught disobeying—the master enjoyed administering punishment. Ceinwyn felt sick as she remembered the last time she had seen him wield the electric baton: it was on a slave boy who had been caught stealing, if she remembered correctly. By the time the master had had his fun, the poor boy had lost control of his bowels, and ultimately his mind.

The men were only metres away now, and Ceinwyn knew there was no way she would not be spotted: the alcove she was in was only half a foot in depth and a floating electric light thirty feet away cast a faint glow that couldn't help but betray her; besides, with it still being summer, it wasn't quite dark yet. Six feet away the men stopped, turned, and started down the steps to the basement. Ceinwyn let out her breath slowly, suddenly desperately aware of the need to breathe.

Once the echoing of the men's footsteps had disappeared, Ceinwyn slowly left the scant safety of her alcove and cautiously tiptoed to the stairs herself. The huge, black metal doors were slowly closing. Taking care to move as silently as possible, she edged herself round one of the slowly moving doors and peered in. A brightly illuminated, white corridor lay ahead. There was no sign of the two men. Cursing herself for giving up so much for the code, she slipped through the gap in the slow moving doors which closed tightly behind her with a soft click; in the absolute silence of the corridor it made her jump. She began to walk down the corridor, moving quickly now, as there was no cover. She knew that the sooner she found her companions, the faster she could get out of this place.

As she reached the halfway point of the corridor, she met a thick wire running along the ceiling, which hummed gently; unsure as to its purpose she continued to the end of the corridor following it. There was a T junction. Two perfectly white corridors led away from her perfectly white corridor, at right angles. Ceinwyn felt disorientated, floating in a sea of white. Looking up she let the thick wire choose: its reddish hue the only non-white object, seemingly, in the basement. It turned to the left.

The corridor continued past several offices. At first she was careful to lean inch by inch around the window until she was certain it was unoccupied. After the third unoccupied office she decided that everyone seemed to have gone home, apart from those two men she had seen enter earlier. Yet there was no sound apart from her own footsteps, and the sound of her heart beating hard in her chest.

She still hadn't fully decided what she would do when she found her comrades. When she had first thought about getting the code, and successfully stole the beautiful nightgown, she had grand day dreams of sneaking them out under the very noses of multiple guards, armed to the teeth. She hadn't considered that the place might be empty. Feeling more and more unnerved, she began to speed up and before she had a chance to stop herself, realised she was running. Panicking now, she began to sob slightly as her breathing quickened with the exercise. She managed to bring herself to a halt at the end of the corridor. She was trembling, not sure if she would have the courage to make it back up that otherworldly, white corridor.

The room ahead looked more inviting. It was dark, with a faint glow from screens within. The wire she had been following ended at this room too, disappearing into a large box on the wall. She took a step inside: there

52

were several desks within, all dark metal; they looked very modern to Ceinwyn's eyes, which surprised her—the master tended to prefer antiques. On top of each desk was a screen upon which digits, and figures danced. Ceinwyn moved closer to take a look: a list of names and numbers scrolling down slowly. She didn't recognise any of them. She read the last name out loud; the only sound in the room apart from the quiet hum from the screen itself.

'Titus Labienus Aquilinus.' It had a nice ring to it, she thought. She felt a hand close on her shoulder.

As the security detail neared the office, Antonius crouched down, sonifex aimed plum at the door's centre. Titus saw his thumb flick from standard ammunition to the antipersonnel, short range, grenade launcher attachment. The huge man was ready to fight to the death if need be. Quintus and Tiberius scuttled across the floor, taking covering-fire positions behind the desk; Marcus and Gnaeus kept in close to protect Titus in the inevitable gunfight. He surveyed his men: to them he was the Centurion. He must not be allowed to fall.

'Stand down,' he ordered, 'I am very honoured that you would sell your lives here. You are all great warriors, but if we fight here we die. We must run.'

Antonius growled angrily at this.

Titus shouted an order to him, 'move the desk to the door! Do it fast! Barricade us in!'

The desk looked as light as a feather in Antonius' bear-like grip. He jogged as fast as he could across the rose marble, sliding the desk into place forcefully at exactly the same moment that the first security guard opened the office door. From the commotion outside, Titus supposed that the impact of the opening door against the guard must have knocked him clean off his feet. In the meantime Marcus had been planning a way out of this mess, for there were no other doors and the barricade would surely not hold for ever.

'The window,' he shouted to Titus, 'it's the only way.' The sounds of men attempting to break down the door echoed across the huge office. Antonius had piled a large amount of the antique Great Wall in front of the door now: it looked like the guards would not be gaining access for some time. From his vantage point at the base of the massive glass wall Titus surveyed the whole of Luguvalium: he had been correct—he could see the fells of Rheged in the distance, with the receding glow of the sun now set behind them. Three storeys down small curri filled the main approach to the city centre. There was a patch of grass directly beneath the building, but the fall was at least thirty feet—they could never survive that.

'Gnaeus get the hell away from that relic,' and come and help us,' Marcus snapped.

Titus turned and saw Gnaeus running the old temple curtain through his fingers.

'Your God might have hidden behind that two thousand years ago, but right now I don't care,' continued Marcus.

'He tore it in half,' Gnaeus said.

'What?'

'My God: he tore it in half two thousand years ago,' replied Gnaeus haughtily.

Titus was about to join with Marcus in exasperation at this pointless waste of time. But Gnaeus' words kept echoing in his mind. 'By the gods! You've got it Gnaeus,' Titus ran up to him excitedly, and grabbed him by the shoulders, leaving Marcus standing by the glass wall, bemused. Titus drew his ceremonial gladius from its sheath. 'I apologise to your God, Gnaeus,' he said as he drew the sword along the longest length of the thick curtain, splitting it in two. A loud thud came from the far corner of the office where the door stood: several stone chunks from The Great Wall had come dislodged from the top of the desk. The guards were using a ram. They needed to work fast. 'Marcus, what sort of rounds did you pack today?' Titus shouted whilst fishing in his webbing for the all purpose palisade glue. It was force of habit that had caused him to fill his ceremonial webbing with the modern day materials he would take on campaign; force of habit had saved his life before.

'Standard only,' replied Marcus with regret, checking the load on his sonifex—he now understood what Titus intended. 'Preparing to fire,' he said loudly. Everyone turned to watch. The silencer ensured that the sonifex fire was eerily quiet, even in the confined room. After a five second burst the huge, plate glass window was merely cracked and a foot wide grubby smudge extended across the surface. Marcus shook his head grimly. The security guards at the door had clearly heard the thudding of silenced rounds into glass, and were redoubling their efforts, with the result that Quintus, Tiberius, and Antonius were now pressed against the door too, desperately holding it shut.

'Search your webbing—we need armour piercing rounds now!' Titus shouted. After a few seconds of fiddling around, it was clear no-one had the rounds they needed. He felt ready to give up and just hand themselves over, when suddenly Antonius grunted, reached beneath his jacket into a small pocket in his shirt, and pulled a single round out, throwing it towards Titus. It landed short and rolled elliptically across the marble floor, stopping against Titus' boot. He scooped it up. The first thing that struck him was the full metal jacket encasing the round: this would do the trick. 'Marcus, take off your silencer! You'll need the extra power,' he ordered. As Marcus unscrewed the length of grey metal from the end of his sonifex, Titus was struck by this bullet's age. It was corroded, and whilst it fitted the calibre of a modern day sonifex something in the way of its design told Titus it dated from earlier. It had two initials carved into the base, R.V. Titus could see they would not affect the firing mechanism, but who had scratched them there? And why?

'You have the round?' shouted Marcus, urgently.

Titus tossed it to him.

'Preparing to fire.'

They all covered their ears. The shot was painfully loud in the confined area. The massive wall disintegrated, showering shards of glass over the rose marble. Gnaeus dragged over the two halves of ancient curtain, now glued solidly together. Antonius heaved over large stones from the remnant of the original Great Wall, using them to weight one end. Tiberius and Quintus went first, easing themselves over the lip of the shattered glass wall. Titus watched as they slid down to the ground below, dropping the last few feet as the curtain ran out. Despite his protestations, Titus insisted that Marcus went next with Antonius and Gnaeus. As

Antonius turned and dropped his body over the lip, Titus spoke to him, 'R.V?'

'Later,' came the curt reply. Suddenly the door burst open and several security guards burst into the office, covering the ground between them and Titus worryingly fast. They carried their sonifi at the hip, firing as they came. Titus leapt backwards, agile as a cat and caught the edge of the curtain as it flowed down the building's side just below the wall. Ignoring the horrific, burning pain in his hands, he slid down fast, nearly landing on Antonius, who had only just dropped from the end as Titus arrived.

Recovering quickly from the heavy landing, Titus led his men at a jog into the heart of Luguvalium. Apart from the guards standing on the lip of the disintegrated wall staring down at them, there was no sign of further security forces. Disappearing into the maze of side streets in the merchant's quarter, Titus knew they could quickly shake off any pursuers.

He whipped out his global positioning handset; Strabo's compound lay two miles to the west. He kept the handset out; on these unknown windy streets he knew that local knowledge would have been better, but this was the best he had. Dashing fast around a corner, their boots clattering on the metalled road, they twisted and turned through alleys and across grassy squares. Their military uniforms drew occasional glances from the commuters along the busy streets, but most were so caught up in getting home as fast as possible that no-one took much notice. After they had run hard for twenty minutes, Titus brought them down to a halt and breathed a sigh of relief. Strabo's compound lay just ahead with the electric lights floating over the main arch shimmering in the warm night air. They were safe for now.

IX

The plush waiting room was as well appointed as before, Titus thought to himself as his men huddled together, unsure of their reception. They had been waiting for over an hour now, Strabo was next door. Maybe he was listening to them, Titus thought; he had already ordered his men to be careful what they said. They sat in silence, reliving what they had just seen silently in their heads, the huge pile of pipe tobacco in the middle of the table was no longer a draw for them, and the water pipe remained unlit.

They sat and they waited, the sun well below the horizon now. No-one called them through. Strabo was clearly extremely displeased with them: they had failed to obtain the money from their most important target, as well as creating a degree of unwelcome attention in the process. Titus wasn't sure that Strabo could smooth things over even if he wanted to. It would be far easier to pass justice on him. That would mean execution: a mix of unpleasant chemicals. Would it hurt? It was certainly meant to. Titus remembered the pictures of crucifixion he had studied in his history lessons: at least he wouldn't have to endure that, a slave's punishment.

His thoughts were interrupted by a commotion outside. There was the sound of running feet, and shouting. He rose to his feet and peered into the gloom outside to see a figure flashing past the doorway and running in panic towards the compound's gates. Titus realised that no-one had shut them since his men had entered; maybe he had been meant to shut them himself.

As the figure ran into the distance, Titus noticed that it was the girl with red hair who had greeted them the day before. She was young, probably in her early twenties. There was something odd about her. Something other than her panicked state, and the fact that she appeared to be wearing an extremely expensive dress. He couldn't quite put his finger on it.

Three more figures ran past, two in the black uniform of Strabo's security guards and one in a white coat. Titus could see that there was no way they would catch the girl before she got to the gate; if she had any sense she would hide out in the alleys nearby. They would probably never find her out there.

The same thing had obviously dawned upon her pursuers. The white coated man came to a halt ten paces away from Titus, who stared at him through the portico as he bent over, panting for breath, clutching at his arm and cursing at the back of the girl's bobbing head, which was now receding far into the distance. The security guards stopped at the gate and closed it firmly. They did not intend to pursue the girl into the town. Titus had a feeling that Strabo would not be best pleased if he discovered their laziness.

As the men walked back to the central compound, Titus tried to listen to their animated discussion; he couldn't hear exactly what they were saying but it was clear from their gestures that they were not too impressed with whoever had left the gate open. He hoped that the identity of the persons responsible would remain a mystery: he was already in enough trouble as it was. The white coated man walked back the way he had come, obviously disappointed that he had not caught his quarry. As he drew near, Titus could see why he wanted to catch her. On his arm were two pretty curves of bloody holes. The girl clearly had a strong bite.

'Come in Aquilinus,' boomed the voice from next door, making Titus jump.

He rose and entered the small office, and was surprised to see Strabo smiling back at him.

'Aquilinus, well done. Well done. You have obtained a lot of money for me today.'

'Thank you sir,' Titus said, unnerved by his host's good spirits. 'I know that we could have done better, if only...' he continued.

'Nonsense,' Strabo interrupted, 'that little, hiccup, at Strabionus' and Lucilius', its all sorted.'

'Strabionus was a partner of the company?' exclaimed Titus. The man had looked so young.

'Yes, and a very promising young man by all accounts. Such a shame to have such a profitable life, extinguished.' Strabo lingered over the last word, drawing it out, enjoying the sound of the syllables on his tongue. 'Still,' he continued 'sometimes these things can't be helped. I had a chat with my friends at the Praetorian guard central office here: they are prepared to, how should I put it, overlook what happened this afternoon. Of course it may have helped that I now am in sole charge of the Praetorian guard until our old friend the Chief Legate turns up.' He smiled widely, obviously very happy at this turn of events and, no doubt, the extra profit it would bring him. He turned to Titus conspiratorially, 'the official story of what happened this afternoon is that, apparently, the young man couldn't cope with the stress of his high powered job and shot himself. Was that what you saw, Aquilinus?'

Titus' hopes soared, and he began to let himself believe that Strabo would not only forgive his mistake, but actually cover for him. 'Yes sir.' But the words tasted surprisingly sour in his mouth: a young man had died and here he was only interested in saving his own skin.

'There was no talk of him owing me money was there?'

'Of course not sir, nothing of the sort,' Titus said.

Strabo rubbed his hands together with glee. Titus breathed a sigh of relief. He turned to go, but Strabo stopped him with a wave of his hand. Titus' heart sank; he just wanted to go home and pretend the day had never happened. 'Good. I see we can trust one another then,' Strabo said, his voice calculating again. 'I will have more jobs for you soon—I think we can benefit each other well.' Strabo turned his attention back to the console screen beside him.

Titus thought about the young dead investor and what he had said about Strabo. Anger rose inside him as he stared down at this disgusting, bloated man tapping away at the screen in front of him. He thought about his men sitting outside: he had to do the right thing for them, they were what mattered—they were his family. He thought about Quintus, and the look he would get from him when he told him what he had done, but there was no choice. Strabo had not left him any. Quintus would understand. They would find somewhere else and start again. They always did.

'I will not extort any more money for you.' Titus declared finally.

Strabo continued typing for a few moments. Then he stopped and slowly turned to face Titus. 'What was that you said?'

'I don't want to work for you any longer.'

'But we were getting on so well!' exclaimed Strabo looking hurt and gesturing for Titus to sit back down.

He preferred to stand.

'What is this business of extortion anyway? These people owed me money, you obtained it. There's nothing wrong with that surely?'

'That's not what the young man told me,' said Titus.

Strabo's smile ended abruptly. 'He chose my investments poorly: he paid the price for losing my money. I do not have to explain to a common mercenary, such as yourself, the complexities of the way I work, but listen to this, Aquilinus. I reward good work well; better than anyone else. You already know that. Earlier today, in that office with that incompetent young man, you saw how I reward poor work.' The colour in Strabo's cheeks had now risen and he looked almost demonic in his anger. Still he had not raised his voice. Titus could see he was sweating again.

Neither man spoke. Titus was unsure whether he could leave or not; did Strabo have more to say to him? Was he being threatened? He felt he needed to put matters straight. He sat down. 'Sir, let me explain. I understand what you have told me about your rewards and your punishments.' Titus had dealt with men like Strabo before, and he knew that flattery was the way forwards. 'Your way seems very fair,' he

60

continued, 'but we, as a group, have decided it is time to move on. We may travel to Londinium and see how the work is there.'

'I can assure you there will be more work here. In fact I can guarantee it for you. You know there is always the most work where there is the most disorder. You won't find a more chaotic place than the lands around Luguvalium.' It was almost as if he was proud of it.

Titus thought of the Reivers at work in the forests around the city. What Strabo said was true: their presence certainly generated extra work, even whilst it choked the town's economy; if not checked it would soon bring Luguvalium to its knees. Titus thought about the heaped tobacco in the room next door, the expensive floating lights in every room, and the fashionable linens worn by the man in front of him. Something about this did not make sense.

'Our minds are already made up sir. I'm sorry.' Titus declared. He was about to push himself out of his seat, but was stopped by Strabo.

'I'm sorry too, Titus,' he said. You don't mind if I call you Titus do you?'

'No,' Titus said surprised, only his closest friends and family would use this name. He didn't want to count Strabo as one of those, but to refuse would have been too rude.

'Well, Titus,' Strabo said, 'I have many jobs that need doing. I was hoping you would be the right person to do these jobs for me.' His speech was cold and measured. It unnerved Titus. 'Your father is not well is he,' Strabo said suddenly, looking straight into Titus' eyes.

Titus felt the hairs on his neck stand up. 'That is true.'

'I also hear you haven't seen him for some time?'

'Not for five years.'

'Do you not feel you've let him down at all?' Strabo said softly, leaning forwards to study Titus' reaction.

He didn't reply.

Strabo paused. It was clear he was enjoying this. 'So, I have a proposition. My informants tell me your father needs regular treatments to stay alive; it seems however that your family has sunk so low that he can no longer afford even the lower tier of healthcare.'

Titus reeled at this. His father wrote to him occasionally, but he had heard nothing of this; it was typical of his father to be too proud to ask for help, Titus thought. In his heart he knew what Strabo was saying was true: all that his family had once been was now gone.

'If you work for me,' Strabo's voice echoed over his thoughts, 'he will have access to that better healthcare he needs: my men in Rome will see to that.' Strabo fiddled with the catch of a drawer beside him. 'Of course, if you wish to leave you can. I won't stop you.' For a moment he seemed to let the threat hang in the air, not even whispered. But he could not resist it, 'my men in Rome, they can of course make sure your father receives no treatment at all.'

Strabo turned away from Titus. 'I wouldn't want to do that of course,' he added, quietly. Then suddenly he fixed Titus with a piercing stare, 'you wouldn't make me have to do that? Would you?'

X

The strumming of Tiberius' lyre filled the crowded bar. He had been re-working some of Virgil's *Aeneid*, bringing it up to date. By the look of the number of women surrounding him, it seemed that this popularist approach to the classics did indeed work.

'Aeneas climbed a rock, battered by the sea.'

Titus turned to Marcus and refilled his ale mug, drunkenly slamming the pitcher down onto the oak table, nearly shattering the glass. The rich ale spilled over the edge, running in brown, treacly rivulets onto the stone flagged floor of the tavern.

'Why so glum Titus?' asked Marcus. 'It's not like the Praetorians are coming for us—you got us off that one!'

Titus didn't reply.

'Sat atop the rock he stared around, he saw the storm with all its force.'

'Come on Titus,' Marcus said clapping his friend on the shoulder and picking up the half full pitcher of fine local ale, 'have another drink.'

'Of his friends there was no sign, dear Antheas was gone.'

'I don't feel like it,' Titus said.

'Suit yourself,' said Marcus sarcastically. He took a deep drag from the pitcher itself, pausing to wipe a beer moustache from his top lip before continuing. 'It's pretty good ale this you know, an old Britannic recipe apparently.' He paused again to sample the fine brew, 'they say it's something in the water,' he added conspiratorially.

'Then suddenly behold below three stags appear on the shore.'

'Tiberius' song's not bad,' Marcus said, beginning to slur his words. His glass was empty again.

Titus refilled it, still silent.

'I always found the *Aeneid* a bit dull myself. Still, look at *that* one Titus,' Marcus said, suddenly losing the thread of the conversation and pointing at one of the more attractive of the girls surrounding their bard. 'If only I was a bard,' Marcus lamented.

'Marcus, not being able to sing is the least of your problems with women, believe me,' said Titus, pointing one of his fingers into Marcus' now ample belly. 'Too much easy living that's what it is. Well it's going to change—I have a feeling Gaius Strabo is going to have rather a lot of work for us.'

'Cheer up Titus! Come off it!' Marcus implored, changing the subject, 'look it's meant to be a celebration. Even Antonius is enjoying himself.'

Titus looked across to where the big man was sitting chuckling to himself and reading a letter. He saw Gnaeus and Quintus watching Tiberius' performance. Gnaeus seemed to be deeply interested in something a young blond girl was whispering in his ear. Quintus too had some interest from a lady, one of the barmaids, and quite attractive, Titus thought. Quintus was doing everything he could to ignore her affections; Titus could see he only had ears for the music. Besides, Quintus was married. Titus couldn't remember a time when Quintus had gone to see his wife though, in fact, he thought to himself, in the whole time he had known Quintus, he had never met her. She lived in Rome of course, probably still with her parents. Titus shrugged his shoulders—it wasn't really his business.

Tiberius' song came to an end. After much applause, and a few kisses on the cheek from his new admirers, Tiberius asked for requests. All around the bar there came shouts for drinking songs, love songs, folk songs. He smiled, and waited for the crowd to decide. Quintus walked over and spoke to Tiberius who nodded and waited for silence. Then he began to play a more modern song; it technically required more instruments and was in an odd time that made it impossible to tap your foot to. Titus hated this sort of thing and it was clear most of the rest of the bar did too. Quintus and Tiberius enjoyed the music together as Quintus tapped his hands on the bar, somehow managing to keep time with the odd music. The army of admirers slowly shifted away to other parts of the bar, and the two were soon alone with the tune.

'What's that you're reading Antonius?' Titus asked. It was rare that the big man was in a mood for talk, Titus thought, shrugging off the depression he had felt earlier, realising that he should make the most of the time in the bar.

'Letter from mother,' Antonius said in his terse way. 'She drew me some good pictures—look here,' he pointed at drawings of a house with animals outside, with a wide grin. Titus laughed at it too. Turning it over and passing it back to Antonius, he saw a letter written on the reverse.

'You've read this Antonius?'

'Sort of,' Antonius said, 'I prefer the pictures.'

'Do you want me to read it for you?'

'Yeah, don't pretend to be girl when you read it though.'

'I'll try,' Titus said, trying to keep a straight face. 'Ok, here goes: *Dearest Antonius, thank you for the money you sent us this month, it keeps us going knowing you support us. Your father is very proud of you....*' Titus continued reading the letter all the way through, with Antonius nodding occasionally. When he had finished he noticed that Marcus had refilled his beer glass. What the hell! There's nothing better I can do! He mused as he drained it. He thought of his father receiving the better treatment in hospital. It was meant to be a celebration after all.

Titus stumbled through the dark alleys back to his home. How on Earth had he managed to lose the others, he thought to himself, as he tried to focus clearly on the street signs. The area of the town he was in was particularly downtrodden, and the graffiti on the signs made it even harder for him to make out the correct direction home.

'*Strabo mutto sugit.*' Titus wondered whether the man who wrote that was still alive.

'*Bibere quod facere.*' Why write that? '*Drink what you make.*'

Images of his father ill in hospital kept flitting into his head, although he kept trying to shake them out. The bargain he had made with Strabo scared him deeply. He didn't trust the man at all, and now he had entrusted his father's care to him. He knew, with a dreadful utter certainty, that he would be drawn further into the criminal machinations of the Luguvalium Governor. He wanted no part in his murky world whatsoever, but he had no choice now; he had sold it to the Governor the moment he had first walked into his office. He worried for his men as well, Gnaeus in particular. He thought about how Gnaeus could, with a few words, somehow lighten the mood in a room. It was a skill *he* didn't have. He wasn't sure exactly how Gnaeus did it, but he was pretty certain it was to do with his innocence. Titus laughed to himself. It was ridiculous to refer to a man who had killed as many people as Gnaeus as an 'innocent'. Titus came to the conclusion that there wasn't really a word to describe what Gnaeus was, but what Titus *did* know was that people like Gnaeus should not be expected to be part of some grotesque protection racket, or even worse.

Titus shook his head as he stumbled along, trying to keep it clear to find the way forwards. He didn't want to get involved in this mess. Why hadn't he just got out as soon as he felt unsure about the situation? That was what they usually did. But he was so tired of running.

A scream up ahead caught his attention. He felt adrenaline surge through his body, miraculously clearing the alcohol from his bloodstream. There was the scream again. It was a girl, only a few hundred yards away. Titus ran up a side street towards the sound, with no idea if it was the right way or not. The scream rang out again, reverberating off the metalled road and into the cold night's sky. It was slightly to the right. Titus ran faster now, conscious of how loud his footsteps must be; perhaps they would scare away the girl's attackers, he thought to himself. Finally he found a side street to the right, and ran at full pelt down it. He ran past numerous other side streets. Which one should he take? Why didn't the girl scream again? Images of her dead body filled his mind, pushing aside all the previous worries of the evening.

He was running so fast that at first he missed the action. His peripheral vision caught sight of three figures down a narrow cul-de-sac but before he could stop himself he had overrun. Coming to a sudden stop, he doubled back and advanced slowly towards the figures, trying to control his breathing. They must not see that he was out of breath.

Ahead, two young men with short hair, wearing military combats were wrestling a girl to the ground. Moonlight, shattered into shards by the branches of an overhanging cherry tree, illuminated the scene. The girl screamed again and bit one of the men. He slapped her across the face, 'dirty whore!' he shouted, and spat on her. The other man began to tear at her dress. As Titus drew nearer he could see the dress properly—it looked surprisingly expensive. The men still hadn't noticed his silent approach.

'Good evening gentlemen,' said Titus firmly, as he reached the end of the alleyway.

The man nearest him jumped a foot into the air, letting out a startled shout. He turned swiftly and faced Titus. The man was in his early twenties, as was his companion. They were clearly new army recruits, presumably on leave from one of the few remaining manned hill stations on the Great Wall. Titus' heart sank. The Great Wall saw little action: these men would be desperate to prove themselves to each other.

'Get lost old timer,' the first man said, recovering his swagger; he was drunk but not as far gone as Titus.

The second one turned his attentions back to the girl. 'You don't want to tangle with army boys.'

The girl was screaming, begging for help.

The first man glared in the moonlight. 'Unless you want to join in of course—sloppy seconds is all you'll get mate but, you are getting on a bit for this sort of fun.'

'Let her go,' Titus said, irritated that they considered thirty to be 'getting on a bit,' 'or I can promise neither of you will fight again for a long time.'

'Is that meant to be some sort of threat?' the larger of the two men hissed, lumbering over towards Titus menacingly.

'Seems we have an old boy who thinks he knows a thing or two about fighting do we?' said the other soldier ,approaching Titus.

The larger man left the girl and edged around to Titus' side, as the girl began to get to her feet. She had a veil over her head, and face, and her dress was torn to shreds.

The first kick came from the side and caught Titus unawares. Before he knew it he was on the floor and the two men were laughing. 'I think you've had a bit too much to drink mate,' the first man jeered.

'We're going to properly fuck you up now,' the second man added. 'You ever seen a soldier before? You've never fought in your life have you! Now you know why you never mess with the Roman army!'

An explosion of pain from Titus' ribs told him another boot had struck him. The two men stood on either side kicking mercilessly into Titus, who was still too winded to defend himself. After a minute or two he lay still and they stopped. The first man drew a knife which glittered in the pale moonlight. The blade focused Titus, removing the last vestiges of his intoxication. He saw the girl whimpering on the floor. He knew they would rape her for as long as they wanted, and then most likely kill her: that way there would be no case against them. Titus thought back to his own training; he had fought beside men like these two in the Transmaritanus—men whose training had taught them to be the best for so long that they truly believed they were above all. Titus no longer had any such beliefs: any he had once had, were now mingled with his blood in the soil of those far away battlefields.

The man with the knife stooped down low. Titus knew that they would probably scar him as a punishment and then drag him away—they wouldn't risk killing him if he just lay still. But he was not in the mood to receive a scar. The second man was standing alongside him with his back towards Titus; he was staring at the half naked girl on the ground. It was the perfect moment. Swinging his body round forcefully, Titus struck his outstretched foot into the side of the second man's knee.

A hideous cracking sound was his reward, as the soldier's knee dislocated, throwing him to the ground in agony. Titus leapt to his feet as his other assailant thrust the knife at his throat. Titus lunged forwards and grabbed the soldier's wrist, twisting him the opposite way to his stroke. The man grunted as he was forcibly bent over double, with Titus holding his knife arm outstretched behind his back. A swift measured stroke to the underside of the soldier's elbow resulted in a sickening pop, as it, too dislocated. As the man opened his mouth to scream, Titus filled it with his boot, scattering his teeth across the cul-de-sac.

He roughly grabbed the man with the ruined knee and got him onto his good leg, the other helping him with his one functional arm. 'A Roman soldier does not abuse his position of power,' he said. 'You may not be Britannic, but you can't treat local people like animals.'

'This one *is* an animal,' one of the soldiers said, between tears of pain. 'Look she's just a slave.' Turning he began to hobble away, dragging his comrade with the dislocated knee as fast as he could behind him. Titus looked back at the girl on the ground. He walked over to her and held out his hand. She looked up at him, her big green eyes visible, almost glowing with a bewitching luminescence in the moonlight. Her veil had slid up above the forehead, betraying copper coloured curls. He could see that she had made the veil herself from bits of her own dress. Why on earth would she want to do that? he thought, as he reached down and helped her to her feet.

He looked at her properly for the first time and simultaneously realised two things: firstly that she was unmistakably the same girl who had been running from Strabo's compound earlier that evening; and secondly, that she was the most beautiful woman he had ever seen.

Then he realised there was indeed something different about her; something he had not seen before up close. The soldier had been wrong, for she was not a slave. That was obvious from her appearance: she was pale skinned, yes, but not wan as most slaves were; besides, she was too tall, and her features too regular. Then her veil slipped down and Titus drew breath sharply. Across her right cheek was a stylised 'S' pattern in spidery silver. She had a signum, she must be a slave. He stared at her, puzzled. She was tall, even for a Roman woman. Then it struck him: he did have a word to describe what she was. As soon as it had reached his lips he wished it hadn't: 'half-breed.' The girl's eyes narrowed and then closed. He just caught her as she fell.

XI

Titus didn't know why he took the girl home. She was so scared she kept whimpering to herself. She hadn't said anything to him. Maybe it was because he had called her a Half-breed, Titus thought. He hoped she had been too dazed to hear and comprehend, but he had seen the look on her face; she had heard. He had never met a half slave, half person before: the penalties for producing one were too great for them to exist in great numbers.

Titus thought of the cocktail of noxious chemicals used for an execution. Under Marcus Albus' Senate, a Roman who produced a Half-breed would receive that if they were caught, it was the same as the punishment for a loving union with a slave in the first place. Rape of slaves on the other hand, as exemplified by the two young men earlier, was condoned, especially amongst the young who didn't know better. But to have love for a slave and not hide it away; that would never go unpunished. Not by Marcus Albus at least. Titus thought back to how he had known Marcus Albus, as a man just five years older than himself, spouting rhetoric in the General's tent. Most people found slave-Roman interaction an embarrassment; it was something you didn't talk about openly. But that man hated slaves like no other, and he had brought the whole thing into the open.

He looked down at this girl lying in his arms; the girl for whom he had taken a beating to save. He had no idea why he had saved her, and he had no idea what to do now. A mercenary might have done this for money, but no thought of a reward had even crossed his mind. His life was straying from the path, and he did not know where it would lead. He had certainly not expected to feel compassion for a slave. Where were her parents? Presumably she was the product of a rape, as long as the man had stated this as his intention he would be free from the guilt of producing her. Her father might even be a soldier on the Great Wall. Her mother would have had much less chance; unless she had hidden her away she would have most likely been caught. Even if she had been raped she would still have been punished for her part in bringing this girl into the world.

Titus shuddered at the thought. He had never liked the idea of torture and had always managed to refuse to take part in it when offered. Crucifixion was torture. A slave's execution.

Titus was at the door of the house with the girl still groggy in his arms. He had a choice. Ever since that afternoon Strabo had owned him. He was now as much a slave as any in his compound. This girl could perhaps buy his freedom if returned to Strabo. However, if discovered hidden by him, he would most likely be killed; and, without doubt, so would his father. He had to take her to Strabo immediately. The girl opened her eyes and wiped her face clear of tears. Titus let her feet gently down to the ground, as the emotions raged inside him he couldn't bring himself to look at her properly.

'You saved my life,' came her lilting voice as she smiled, her face lighting up with a keen intelligence as she studied him. 'Why?'

Titus' world crashed down around him with that one word. The thoughts that had made him kill the old slave crowded his mind once more. He was going to be sick. He had known the truth for so long, ever since he had seen that slave boy give his life for another all those years ago. An animal would never have done that, and an animal would certainly not question whether it merited being saved from death.

He was guilty of mass murder.

He looked down at the girl he had saved: his first chance to make something right. His hands were shaking.

Titus reached for the pass-card from his pocket, and swiping it deliberately, unlocked his door; he would disobey Strabo to save a life. But he knew in his heart that one life could never atone for the death of hundreds. It would take his whole life to pay off that debt.

'You are like me,' the Roman said. The look of embarrassment on his face made it clear he wished he had thought more before opening his mouth. Ceinwyn frowned at him, then laughed. She understood his confusion. This was fascinating: she had never spoken properly to a Roman before. She studied him; he was in his early thirties, she thought, with greying brown hair. Despite her many reasons to hate him, she surprised herself. There was something simple and trustworthy about him; as if for him the world was black and white. Maybe he was a good Roman? If such a thing could even exist. She couldn't believe she was actually in this man's house, didn't he know that he would be in serious trouble for harbouring a Half-Breed?

'We are *all* like you—every one of us. Let me show you. Do you have any Slaves?' she asked.

The Roman blushed again. 'Just the one,' he said and clapped his hands, the universal summoning gesture. Ceinwyn had to stop herself from reacting to it, but managed to stay in her seat. A young man ran up the stairs from the cellar. The blood drained from his face as he saw Ceinwyn.

'Don't be scared,' she said tenderly, patting the boy on the arm, 'tell him about yourself.'

The boy trembled in front of his master, building up courage. Eventually he opened his mouth. 'My name is Brice, sir, and I hate you and all your kind.' Ceinwyn could see that he was not sure whether such a frank outburst would be tolerated, but he had many years to build up that hate.

The Roman was stunned. Ceinwyn looked into his eyes and felt she could almost see the collapse of the world he thought he lived in, but there was something else too, something falling into place as if a long confirmed worry, that had been nagging at him for years, had been finally swept away.

'Don't be scared boy,' the Roman spoke, dragging a chair out from the kitchen table at which they sat, 'sit down here.' Then he just stared, first at Ceinwyn, then at the boy.

Ceinwyn broke the silence, 'once upon a time Romans subjugated people they conquered to work their land for them, to use them as slaves. Over time you forgot that we had once been people too, from all the corners of the globe. You set laws that stopped us breeding with your kind and you segregated your cities. We became a race ourselves, completely subservient to yours.' She paused, 'or so you thought!'

'How do you know so much about our history?' asked the Roman. He clearly didn't buy her explanation.

'Devin told me,' she said, purposefully adding nothing else. She liked the air of mystery she was casting. She looked into the Roman's eyes and smiled. She rather enjoyed having his undivided attention. He just stared into her eyes, waiting for her to continue. Eventually she relented. 'He's the wisest man in the world, and he's my father.' The Roman laughed again; she liked his face when it laughed—laughter brought it to life.

'My father thinks he is pretty wise too, but he has brought my family into ruin. What makes yours any different?'

'My father is a historian. He keeps the history for all the Slaves in Rome, and it seems,' she said, pointing at the Roman, 'for you lot as well, since you don't bother remembering the past for yourself.'

The Roman seemed to accept this explanation. He began to speak again, firstly to the boy. 'Well. It seems an introduction is in order. I never introduced myself, and for that I can only apologise. You can see why I did it can you not?'

The boy nodded.

'What is your name?' The Roman asked, looking at her.

Ceinwyn spoke her name quietly, not sure if the Roman could pronounce it.

'I am Titus Labienus Aquilinus,' said the Roman.

She was puzzled by the three names—which should she use? Then she remembered back to the scire room in her master's compound; was that the name she had read? If it was, what did that mean?

The Roman obviously sensed her confusion and explained, 'people who have just met me would call me Aquilinus, my friends would call me Titus.'

'Good to meet you Aquilinus,' Ceinwyn said, surprised at the look of regret that passed quickly across the Roman's face.

The boy nodded as well, in agreement.

'Why do you work here Brice?' the Roman asked.

Brice laughed emptily, 'did you think I had a choice?' He smiled bitterly and continued, 'I was payment for a debt. The master was owed money by a family who owned my family; it was only a small amount, but they paid with me instead. I am not permitted to see them.'

'Who is not allowing you to see them?' asked the Roman.

'My master of course.' Brice replied angrily.

The Roman gestured around the room. 'Do you see your master anywhere in this room.'

The boy didn't reply but just stared dumbly at the Roman.

'Go!' he said, smiling, 'I'm not going to tell him you've left, and after what I've heard tonight I'm never going to have a Slave again.'

As the boy ran out of the house excitedly, Ceinwyn was pleased that her words could have such an effect on the man, but was sad as well because she had wanted to stay with this exciting new Roman she had met. She began to get up to follow Brice.

'No, no,' said the Roman, sensing her concern. 'You can stay as long as you want.'

'What makes you think I want to stay near a Roman now that I am free?' Ceinwyn said, more boldly than she had meant to, staring into the Roman's handsome face.

He looked hurt. There was a moment of awkward silence, and then both of them tried to speak at the same time. Another silence, then she said:

'Perhaps I will stay one night, till I can find somewhere safer. I can sleep in the cellar; Brice had a bed there didn't he?'

He laughed again. 'You don't think Strabo would give me a house with no spare room do you! Come upstairs I'll show you.' He moved to help her upstairs, but she immediately began to cry. 'What's wrong?' he asked, putting his hands on her shoulders, trying to comfort her.

'You work for him!' She screamed and tried to escape his grip. She wormed her way free, and began to run for the door, but at the last minute realised she needed the pass-card to open the door now that Brice had shut it firmly on his way out. She darted across the room to the table where the card lay, but tripped on the carpet and slid to her knees sobbing in despair, and pain.

Then she heard the Roman speak over the pounding of blood in her head: 'I hate that man, I loath him with every fibre in my body, and I will resist him in any way I can.' He walked up to Ceinwyn and took her by the hand, helping her to her feet. He stared into her deep green eyes. 'If looking after you and protecting you from him is all I can do to resist him, I promise you I will die, if necessary, doing just that.' He reached towards her, wiping her tears from her face.

Images of Cyric doing the same flooded back to her, but where that had been embarrassing, this time she felt something she had never felt before. When Cyric had done this, he had tried to kiss her. She shuddered at the thought. Did she want this Roman to kiss her? He just stood there holding her hand, seemingly unsure of what to say next. For a moment she was touched by his shyness, but then she remembered who he was and scorned the soft, emotional part of her brain. This man was the enemy.

She pulled her hand from his and, numb from the gamut of emotions she had already run that day, climbed the stairs to the spare room. As she lay in the soft spare bed, another new experience for her, she knew for the first time in her life that she was safe. But still she could not sleep. Her enemy wanted to protect her, he had said he would die for her—she didn't know what to think.

Titus lay in bed; he should have been asleep. He would need to make some plans in the morning—he had just put his life, and those of his men in mortal danger. He didn't think many of them would understand, apart from Marcus. Maybe Marcus would understand. As he thought back over the evening, he couldn't help but kick himself with embarrassment. He had called her a Half-Breed: he had accused her of being stupid, thicker even than that brute Antonius. He laughed to himself—he had always had a way with women. That's how Tiberius would have put it at least.

He turned over and tried to sleep. Images and words kept creeping in and preventing it. 'People who have just met me would call me Aquilinus.' It had been the right thing to say—no-one would call him Titus unless they were his closest friend or family; not even lovers always used each other's first names. But Titus couldn't help thinking of the strangely beautiful girl with the odd lilting accent, sleeping only a few feet from him, separated only by a wall; perhaps one day she could call him 'Titus'.

It would never happen of course, he knew that. She should hate him. He was a Roman. Before he'd even opened his stupid mouth she must have hated him; knowing what he did now he found it impossible to think that any Slave didn't hate the Romans. Images of him rounding up Slaves like cattle kept intruding on his thoughts. He pushed them away; he couldn't deal with them now. As he drifted off to sleep, he tried to keep away the dreadful thoughts of his past actions, seen in the new light of day, with an image: a girl dressed in a torn, black dress that could only have been stolen, for a reason as yet unknown, her copper hair piled on her pillow, her deep green eyes shut; a girl who felt safe for the first time in her life. The only good thing he had ever done.

The line of Slaves snaked into the distance along the beach. Titus held a fully loaded sonifex in case they should try to break free and run. They must be flown back to Rome safely for processing. The volacurrus touched down effortlessly beside him, its plasma engines glowing purple against the dusky sky. He would need to file the Slaves on board. The girl was looking at him again. He couldn't meet her piercing green eyes right now, instead he focused on her tear-streaked cheeks. It was no wonder she was crying: her father was dead. Her mother cradled her in her arms. She showed only hate on her face, no tears. The volacurrus doors opened and Marcus Albus in full military regalia descended the platform, his red woollen cloak billowing in the wind eddying across the beach. He clapped his hand on Titus' shoulder. 'Good work my old friend.'

'I didn't capture them all myself Albus.'

Marcus Albus laughed at his joke, 'you may proceed.'

Titus gestured for the Slaves to start moving forwards and a slow shuffle of movement began.

'No, my friend,' Marcus Albus held out his hand to stop the Slaves. 'I want to see you prove your commitment to Rome.'

'I'm entirely committed to Rome, sir,' Titus replied, showing him his badge of rank, 'they even made me a general for it.'

He laughed with Marcus Albus, enjoying the feeling of being young and alive; they both remembered it had been the same Marcus Albus, the Consul's son and Supreme General who had bestowed the honour on Titus in the first place.

'Oh, I'm sure you are.' Marcus Albus' voice was polished from years of command, and an upbringing amongst the nobility. Titus was very lucky to have such a man as a friend. It was exactly this sort of friend that could help his family from their present predicament. 'But prove it anyway: kill these animals for me. We already have enough cattle in Rome.' He spat on the ground in the direction of the Slaves.

Titus let off the safety catch of the sonifex. It was clear the Slaves had understood what Marcus Albus had said because they huddled together in fear. Titus brought his sonifex to bear, clicking the selector from single shot to fully automatic. He brought it to his hip: there would be no need to aim at this range.

'Do it now Titus,' he heard Marcus Albus speak forcefully. He had never called him by his first name before: he must truly count him as a friend after all.

Titus looked for one last time into the tear streaked face of the young child. She stared right back at him. He pulled the trigger.

'Titus! Titus!' he was woken by a girl's voice. 'Are you going to come and eat this breakfast or not?' There was a pause. 'Sorry, I got your name wrong didn't I.' She sounded embarrassed.

'No Ceinwyn, Titus is good,' he replied, his heart soaring in spite of the knowledge that she had used his first name only as a mistake—she didn't know what it meant to him.

Bleary eyed, he trod downstairs to see the most wonderful platter of food ever assembled in his house. A big plate of fried eggs sat alongside a pile of circular Luguvalium sausage. In the kitchen Ceinwyn stood, holding a frying pan, from which was emanating the delicious smell of thick, smoked bacon. She squeezed some maple syrup over the rashers and kept frying.

78

'Erm,' he said, unsure what he had done to deserve this. 'You still remember that I'm the enemy right? A Roman.' He laughed.

'Maybe it's poisoned.' She stared darkly into his eyes before grinning.

Titus nodded and picked up two plates, taking them across to the table, and seating them opposite each other. Ceinwyn brought the smoking bacon across to the table and started to share the food out between them.

'When your whole life changes in a single moment... what can you do to adapt?' he asked.

Ceinwyn shook her head. 'I've had a whole life knowing what would happen every day, until now.'

'So we are in this together.'

She smiled. 'Until I find someone who can help me better than you can.'

'What do you need?'

Her expression darkened, 'I need someone to kill your boss.'

Titus saw her pale cheeks colour with anger, as she thought back over Strabo's injustices towards her and her friends. Her signum darkened too—a deep silver blemish on her face. It was strangely beautiful. His eyes filled with admiration for her. 'I think I know someone who might be able to help you with that.'

She raised an eyebrow, 'thought you might.'

'But it won't make up for everything he has done wrong in the past.'

'But its a start,' replied Ceinwyn.

XII

The sound of a firm knock on the front door disrupted breakfast rudely. Titus cursed—he had managed, this morning, to exchange more words with a girl than he had done in the last five years put together. Quickly he hid Ceinwyn upstairs, before jogging over to the sitting room and pulling the front door open quickly, nearly toppling Marcus, who had been leaning against it.

'Messenger came from Strabo this morning,' Marcus said irritably.

Titus felt his stomach lurch. Marcus fished around in his pocket and drew out the orders. As Titus ran his eyes over it, he felt his heart sink even lower. Marcus read his expression, 'I'm bored of collecting more slaves for that man as well, but what can we do? We do need the money after all.'

Titus nodded and beckoned for Marcus to come in.

As he clattered around in the kitchen trying to make Marcus a drink, Titus' mind was working frantically. He looked at the plump figure sitting at his table, reading the morning newspaper that he had brought round. Titus had always relied on his own ability to work his way through difficult situations; he even admitted to himself that he did have a knack for that sort of thing. But that alone would not be enough now: he needed intelligence; intelligence to match Strabo's; and he would be the first to admit that he knew cleverer men than himself.

'Why are there two places set here?' Marcus asked.

'Erm,' Titus thought quickly, why had he not cleared the other place away before opening the door? 'In case you came for breakfast?' he said slowly.

Marcus looked at him as if he had gone mad, but seemed to buy the ridiculous explanation. Or at least if he didn't, he wasn't suspicious enough to question further.

'Marcus do you trust me?' Titus said passing him a cup of tea.

'To the ends of the Earth.'

Titus knew it was true: the pair had history.

'You saved my life, if you remember,' Marcus continued.

Titus cut him off: he hated it when Marcus mentioned this. It was old history, and it didn't seem healthy to him for Marcus to dwell on it as much as he did. 'I don't want you to mention that ever again. It doesn't count any more.' He took a deep breath. 'I haven't been entirely honest with you Marcus.' It was a good start—it was the truth.

'Anything to do with why you were in such an awful mood last night?' Marcus asked, sipping from the steaming mug.

Titus nodded. 'You know that Strabo is not the sort of man you would want to get on the wrong side of?'

Marcus nodded, sipping cautiously from the hot brew.

'I think I've got us on the wrong side of him.'

Marcus stopped in mid sip and looked straight at him. Titus saw a brief flicker of concern across his face, quickly replaced by intense thought. He took a big mouthful of tea, swallowed it, and put the cup down on its saucer thoughtfully. He did not speak, sensing that Titus needed to. And so Titus began to explain about his bargain with Strabo and his father.

'So we're stuck here.' Marcus said.

'I am,' Titus agreed, he looked at Marcus earnestly, 'but you're not. You could all leave.'

'If we did, you would never be able to do his work; it would be as good as us killing your father.'

'Possibly,' replied Titus, 'but none of you belong to me after all.'

'You know that isn't true, after what you did for me.'

'No, Marcus,' Titus shouted with frustration. 'Enough.' He threw his hands in the air and began to stalk around the room.

Marcus looked down at the newspaper in front of him, but it was clear he wasn't reading it.

'Sorry, I shouldn't have shouted,' Titus said, returning to his seat. 'It's just that I knew we should have left here days ago; I just wish I'd listened to my instinct.'

'Perhaps,' Marcus replied, looking back up. 'But we're not leaving you behind.'

'How can you speak for the others?' Titus asked.

'I won't ask them,' he replied and turned his attention back to the newspaper.

'You mean we should keep this a secret?'

'How do you think Quintus is going to take this!' Marcus said, looking back up. He folded the paper and placed it in front of him on the table.

Titus nodded.

'What we really need to do is figure out how to get out of this mess though,' Marcus said. 'We can't just keep doing missions for Strabo: everything we do for him is a show of weakness, and our reluctance to oppose him.'

'Agreed,' Titus said, 'so you think we should refuse to do this?' he asked, gesturing at the latest orders from Strabo. Could he perhaps get round the problem without mentioning Ceinwyn? He hoped he could—Marcus finding out about her would complicate things even more.

'We can't refuse to work for him,' Marcus' shaking head, dashed Titus' hopes, 'but we can delay. I suggest we say we need time to prepare. We can buy days, possibly even weeks that way.'

Marcus was clearly warming to command, Titus thought; a far cry from the shy young man he had fought beside in the Transmaritanus.

'What we really need is a weapon,' Marcus continued, 'something we can use against him. Strabo is completely reliant on his position granted by Rome. Now, he is effectively blackmailing you, so you need something to blackmail him with.'

Titus had already begun to walk over to the desk below the main wall screen. Reaching into a drawer, he brought out the accounts he had kept hidden since the raid on the camp. 'Like these you mean?' he said, sliding them across to Marcus on the other side of the table.

Marcus' eyes lit up as he looked over the list of figures. 'This is insane,' he said, 'where did you get these?'

'They were given to me by a Slave,' Titus replied.

Marcus looked incredulous. 'When?' he asked.

'It was the old man who led that group of Slaves we killed; he left them out for me in his hut.'

'Right,' said Marcus, looking increasingly confused. 'Well, these look like fairly important documents.'

'Maybe that's why we were sent to round up the Slaves in the first place,' Titus said, unsure if he was just being paranoid now.

'You think Strabo knows these are missing then?' Marcus asked, gesturing at the papers with worry in his eyes.

'He questioned me about the contents of the chief's hut,' said Titus, realisation dawning.

Marcus pored over the documents for a few seconds before looking up, 'what I don't understand, Titus, is who wrote these papers? A Slave gave them to you, fair enough. But you know as well as I do that a Slave could not be an accountant: they're just animals.' He laughed, 'for heaven's sake Titus, a Slave couldn't do this! The chief must have stolen them, but why would he do that?'

'To pass them onto someone who might have the power to use them against their creator?' Titus replied, bracing himself for the inevitable. More secrets would have to be revealed.

'Marcus, there's more I haven't told you. I...' but he never got to finish his sentence. As if on cue, a beautiful girl descended the stairs to tell another Roman that the majority of his life was built on lies.

'I think Ceinwyn here can explain better than I,' he said, gesturing her to a seat at the table with them.

Marcus listened intently as the young girl explained who she was. He listened as she told him about her treatment at the hands of Strabo. He listened as she tore his world down around him. As he looked across at Titus, they shared in that moment. From now on everything would change. Marcus gazed out of the window, for the first time setting eyes on a world that made sense. He had spent his life in pursuit of other's deaths, at first for honour, family, and Rome; lately for money, and Titus, his old friend. Now he had a new master to fight for, and she was nothing if not beautiful.

Marcus looked at the beautiful girl with the strange voice, and, upon the new life she instilled in him, vowed that Strabo would pay for everything he had done to her. He took strength from the tiny seed this bewitching girl had planted, and as he looked at her, she caught his gaze and seeing the wonder in his eyes, she smiled at him, and he felt the seed burst into life.

Marcus had spent most of his life with little confidence in anything, let alone himself. He would have died in dishonour had it not been for Titus, and the shame still burned deep inside him. But now together. Himself and her. They would crush Strabo. And then remake the world. He laughed at himself.

He had to tell her how he felt first.

After Ceinwyn had finished speaking, Titus sat still, waiting patiently for Marcus to speak. Eventually, he began to tell Titus what he should do, 'get her some clothes,' he said, gesturing at the black dress she had clearly slept in.

'And please let me go with her.' His heart wished, but his cowardly lips would not speak.

XIII

The afternoon sun sank low in the sky, as Titus stared out of the kitchen window; summer was nearly gone. On the table in front of him were the plans drawn up between himself, Marcus and Ceinwyn earlier that morning. He placed his finger on the 'white corridor,' and traced a path following the 'red ceiling cable.' It had been difficult to get the details from Ceinwyn who was understandably still quite traumatised by her experience in Strabo's compound. From her information Marcus and himself had decided that exploring the east part of the complex seemed most useful: the best chance of getting information to augment the papers they already had.

Titus sighed as he thought about Ceinwyn again; he wished it could have been he who had taken her to the market. He trusted Marcus implicitly of course, and knew that he understood the importance of them both keeping a low profile, but despite his best efforts, he couldn't quite convince himself that this time spent poring over the plans couldn't have been put to better use. He laughed at himself—he hated shopping, did as little of it as possible. But somehow this was different.

He angrily turned his attention back to the plans. Marcus had been adamant that Titus would hate the market, and that he was doing him a favour by taking Ceinwyn there himself. He was probably right, Titus thought, remembering with acute embarrassment how he had called Ceinwyn a 'Half-Breed' to her face. His fingers drifted over the page of hastily sketched map and landed on 'place where I bit white coated man on wrist.' He liked the thin writing: despite its spideryness it was still better than his.

The place that Ceinwyn had indicated was on the opposite side of the facility to the scire room. Whoever had found Ceinwyn there, and dragged her away, wasn't trying to take her out of the facility. If they had, they would surely have used the white corridor Ceinwyn used to get in to the complex. Instead, strangely her captor had chosen to drag her further into the facility.

He examined the map further. It did not proceed past the biting annotation: Ceinwyn had obviously had the presence of mind to retrace her steps even whilst being pursued. She had avoided running further into the facility towards where she was being taken. Titus' hand kept being drawn to the patch of bare white paper to the west of the facility. What was there? Why did they want to take Ceinwyn to it?

They planned to break in tonight if possible: with the now unfeasible Slave catching mission looming ahead, they had no time to spare. Titus walked over to the sofa in the corner of his sitting room. Piled high, in a teetering mountain, was his war gear. It had been kept in the spare room, but, to make space for his guest, it now cluttered up his front room. Titus didn't mind particularly though; he had never been especially tidy, just as long as he knew where everything was. Digging through the mountain of gear, he found what he was looking for—a Dacian head-scarf. As he ran the rough fur through his fingers, he thought of the legionaries who had invented them over a thousand years ago. The Dacians could of course cope with the harsh climate of their native country, but Roman invaders in winter needed protection. The holes for the eyes and the slit for the mouth looked sinister in the light of dusk, but would provide camouflage and, importantly, protect their identities. Titus put it to one side ready for the evening's action and turned back to the pile.

86

Ceinwyn's laughter from the changing room carried all the way across the department store floor to where Marcus was eyeing up some waterproof gear. Rain was an inevitability of life in Luguvalium. Although he hoped that the slave catching mission could be prevented by their work tonight, he was, if ever, a pragmatist. He fished through the racks to find a waterproof jacket and trousers his size, as usual the trousers and sleeves were too long, if they were to fit him elsewhere. With summer ending he would need new waterproofs. Snow was rare these days even in the north, it just rained instead.

Marcus had finally found a waterproof jacket that fitted, when Ceinwyn came up behind him. 'Look at this,' she whispered suddenly, causing him to nearly drop the jacket with shock.

He turned to see her dressed in a toga with a light blue sash. The sight took his breath away. 'You look...' he stammered.

'Like a Roman,' Ceinwyn exclaimed proudly.

She looked like a Roman woman heading to the temple on her wedding day. He wanted to tear the toga off and kiss her; taste her. 'It's OK.' Marcus replied, nodding, cursing his inability to find the right words yet again. 'Are you sure you don't want something a little bit more inconspicuous?'

She smiled at him, but made no move to take the toga back.

'I like it though,' he carried on, not sure of what else to talk about.

Her smile broadened. He smiled back, wishing she could read his mind.

He wanted to say: 'Up until this morning my world was confusing and often sad, now it is more confusing, but the sadness has lifted. Why? You might well ask—because now I know you, I also know about the subjugation of an entire people. But as well as that sad knowledge, you brought *you*. Your face, your hair, your laugh. Your body. I have never been so excited by anyone in my whole life. And I would die for you.'

But Ceinwyn could not read minds. And Marcus' shy tongue would not allow him the words he needed to tell her.

He looked up from his frustrating thoughts to see Ceinwyn's excited face at the other side of the shop, as she held up some cotton trousers with animal prints on. He smiled back, and looked down at his chosen waterproof again. It was red. 'Idiot,' he exclaimed quietly to himself and put it back on the rack. 'Better wet than dead,' he muttered, continuing his search, but limiting it now to waterproofs of a khaki hue.

A milky white hand brushed over his and grasped hold of one of the jackets. 'Try this one,' said Ceinwyn.

'I'm not sure it'll fit,' replied Marcus. He felt his face begin to burn and cursed himself for his weakness.

'Try it anyway.' She passed him the jacket—it was already camouflaged. Marcus turned it over in his hands.

'Its a hunting jacket.' He explained.

'That's what you do isn't it,' Ceinwyn said, looking straight into Marcus' eyes, 'you hunt people.'

She stared at him. 'I am sorry for everything I've done Ceinwyn, I want you to know that.'

'Rome isn't sorry.' Ceinwyn said angrily.

'Rome would never agree it was even wrong.' Marcus replied.

'Will you hunt for *me*, Marcus?' Ceinwyn said, coming to the point. She saw the flicker on Marcus' face as he realised she had used his first name. She had hoped for it.

Marcus looked over her shoulder; on the other side of the road a toddler was jumping up and down, pointing excitedly at a young girl standing in the Slave shop window. As Marcus watched, the mother dragged the small child in mid-tantrum, yet still pointing, away. 'Mummy! Please can we have it?'

'What do you need me to do?' he asked quietly, not sure he could trust his voice.

'I need you to save someone for me.'

XIV

'Quiet,' Marcus hissed at Titus, 'they'll hear us.' They were crouched behind the quadrangle wall yards away from the entrance to Strabo's cellar. The patrolling pair of security guards whistled tunelessly as they passed a couple of feet away from Titus' head. The security so far had been stronger than Ceinwyn's description had suggested. Her escape must have led to a doubling of the guard. The darkness was absolute, and apart from a strange hunting jacket that Marcus had insisted on wearing, they were both clad head to toe in black. Only their voices, if heard, could jeopardise the mission.

'Explain to me again how we are going to save this boy, what's his name, again?'

'Cyric.'

'Yes that's the one,' Titus continued, 'so we are going to break in to the compound, steal information, and then smuggle out another Slave?' He looked quizzically at Marcus. 'Did you perhaps not notice the guards?'

'We snuck past them a second ago,' Marcus retorted.

'Yes, Marcus. You and I just managed it; do you fancy trying to sneak past again with a non-camouflaged Slave boy?' Titus gestured over to where they had concealed the boy amongst some bushes in the lower quadrangle. 'He isn't exactly inconspicuous is he.'

It was true, Marcus thought, that the boy didn't appear to have natural aptitude for stealth. At well over six foot tall he looked like an awkward beanpole.

'We have to do it,' Marcus said, louder now, 'for her sake.'

'I suppose you're the expert on Ceinwyn now, aren't you,' said Titus, turning away from him.

'It's not like that, it's just...'

Titus cut him off: 'shush, they're coming round again.' They waited, huddled together as the guards made another circuit.

'Now,' Titus whispered. The two men moved silently across the tightly cropped grass, and effortlessly rolled over the low wall, keeping close to the ground. Titus quickly checked down both sides of the cloister. The guards were still at the other end of the quadrangle. Titus could make out the glow of a lighter as they lit each other's cigarettes.

Marcus was the first to speak again, 'if they catch us we're dead.'

'No, my friend,' Titus whispered with a grin, his angry words forgotten, 'if they catch us, *they're dead*.' He shifted his coat slightly; the sharpened gladius blade glimmered in the far off floating light.

'That old thing again!' Marcus laughed

'This, *old thing*, has saved my life many times Marcus. And yours, if you remember.'

'I thought you said you didn't want to mention that again.' Marcus replied, sullenly.

'Old habits die hard,' Titus said, and fell silent—lost in the past.

Both men stared into the darkness together in silence, 'how long do those guards have to take to smoke their cigarettes?' Titus wondered to himself.

The crisp sound of footfalls on gravel focused him once more. The guards were moving. Titus crept silently across the cloister path and began to descend the steps; the concrete echoed with his footsteps despite his best efforts. The guards, twenty yards away, and on the other side of the quadrangle didn't look up; their torch beams swung gently before them as they strode along the cloister, completely oblivious to the two intruders.

90

Titus reached the huge, black door to the basement. He reached for the code panel. The guards must be half way round the quad by now he thought. That gave them around thirty seconds; they could not help but be spotted if they were not inside by then. He quickly punched in the code to the door; Ceinwyn had been right, the pompous fool was so proud that he hadn't changed the code from his birth date, despite having a previous break in. The door swung open and Titus and Marcus stepped inside. A red rubber button on the wall led to a junction box above the door controlling the lock. Titus pushed it. Ten seconds to go; he counted them down as the doors began to close.

Peering through the ever diminishing gap between the two doors, he caught a glimpse of torchlight playing on the basement steps, but it was quickly cut off as the doors clicked shut. In the near silence of the underground corridor the noise seemed to echo forever. Both men stood together, ears at the metal door, waiting to see if the guards had heard it too. Neither heard any call from the men outside. Most likely the guards had not noticed; they didn't seem particularly competent. But Titus couldn't shake the thought that the door was awfully thick and heavily soundproofed.

In the bright lights of the white corridor their camouflage felt conspicuous; Marcus wore his new jacket picked out by Ceinwyn earlier that day; Titus wore a long military great coat. Their features were completely concealed beneath Dacian head-scarves. Titus scanned the sides of the corridor looking for hidden cameras. He saw none, but kept the scarf on none-the-less. For all his earlier bravado, Titus knew that if Strabo found out that they had been here, they would most certainly suffer.

At the end of the corridor Titus followed the red cable, as Ceinwyn had done a week earlier. It led to the left, down to the eastern edge of the complex. The place seemed completely deserted. As they arrived at the first corner, Titus reached into his webbing and brought out an oculus—a small piece of plastic about the size and shape of a table tennis ball. He placed it on the floor and rolled it gently around the corner. On a small handheld scire he could see the sensor's view of the corridor ahead. It was clear. The three offices were dark, and the doors were shut. Everyone had gone home. Titus and Marcus, confident that the coast was now clear, stepped around the corner, and calmly continued down the corridor to the gloomy room which lay at its termination.

Within, lay a series of scire banks with large screens blinking in the semi-darkness. Titus was amazed by the scale of the facility. He couldn't place exactly where beneath the compound he was, after the disorientating effect of the white corridors. However, he was fairly certain that they were outside the compound's boundary, far away from Cyric, left trembling in a bush yards away from the security patrols. He wondered how long he could stay hidden—would his nerve hold?

'You need to work fast,' he whispered to Marcus, who was staring in wonder at the red cable which was inserted into a grey metal box, halfway up the wall nearest the door.

'Have you seen this thing?' Marcus asked.

'Is it going to get us anything to blackmail Strabo with?' replied Titus tersely.

'No, but,' Marcus replied thoughtfully, 'it doesn't quite make sense.'

'Go, on.'

Marcus began: 'You remember the war.'

'Yes, we all remember the war,' Titus said, exasperated.

'Well, yes; if you remember towards the end of it they put me in charge of part of the communications grid, dealing with data transfers between the Transmaritanus and Rome,' said Marcus.

'You were always pretty good with scires,' said Titus irritably, checking around the corner back into the white corridor. There was still no sign of any security presence.

'Yes, I'm all right with them,' replied Marcus before continuing, 'but that's not the point; this type of cable, I've only ever seen once before.'

'And where was that?'

'At the interface between the omniajunctus hub for our operations in the Transmaritanus, and the omniajunctus itself.'

'So you're saying it's pretty rare then—could be worth a bit maybe?' replied Titus, enjoying winding up his friend.

'I'm saying,' Marcus replied evenly, 'that this cable can carry a *lot* of information.'

Titus looked at his friend and saw the colour had drained from his face. He was genuinely worried.

'Titus, you need to take this seriously and listen to me now. There is a lot more going on here than either of us realise,' Marcus said, 'I don't know what Strabo's doing; I don't even know if I have the means to find out with this cheap crap,' he gestured at the small scire he held in his hands. 'All I know is that whatever he is doing is on a huge scale, hugely complicated, and almost certainly hugely illegal.' He paused for a second and looked at Titus, 'I don't want to try blackmailing a man whose business needs that,' he gestured at the red cable.

Titus looked intently at his old friend, 'we're here now Marcus. We must find out what's going on, or else all of this has been a waste of time.'

'We could just save Cyric and leave,' Marcus said, gesturing at his scire. 'I don't think I can hide the trace when I hack into his omniajunctus with this thing. It's not safe.'

Titus walked over and put his hand on Marcus' shoulder. 'You want to impress Ceinwyn don't you?'

Marcus nodded sheepishly.

'Let's return with two things tonight then,' continued Titus, 'an old friend of hers plucked from the jaws of death, and the means with which to take down her hated old master. I think she deserves that.' He thought it best not to mention Ceinwyn's request of him.

'Right,' said Marcus, taking a deep breath, 'in which case you better grab hold of this cable.' His scire's screen glowed faintly in the dimly lit room as he booted it up. 'It will just take a second to gather the data,' he said, now utterly absorbed in his work, 'plug it in over there.'

Titus sat down with his back to the warm metal of some unnameable piece of scire machinery. His right hand held the end of the cable Marcus had proffered him; there wasn't much space under the desk, and he was having trouble finding the right socket. The sounds coming from Marcus a couple of feet away, suggested he was already totally exasperated with Titus' inability with all things electronic. That was why he had a team, Titus thought to himself. He was about to comment on this to Marcus, but was interrupted by the unmistakable sound of footfall somewhere down the entry corridor.

'Go for cover,' he hissed at Marcus, as he wriggled further beneath the desk. Out of the corner of his eye, he caught sight of Marcus diving behind the desk opposite. The boots were nearer now. Titus listened to them intently; he could tell that there was more than one man, but beyond that he could only guess at the numbers. He wriggled backwards as far as he could, dislodging wires in the process. He heard a soft plinking sound and the machine above him turned off as he accidentally unplugged its power connection. He stopped in his tracks; he was as hidden as he was going to get without making his hiding place obvious. Marcus looked worryingly conspicuous on the other side of the room. He gestured at the machine he cradled in both hands, mouthing words that Titus couldn't make out. But it was clear that the connection was working and, despite the interruption, Marcus was trying to complete their mission.

Titus held his breath and waited. He could hear the man behind him—the back of the desk gave him complete protection from this angle.

'They're in here somewhere! Keep looking!' The rough voice rasped over the top of the desk, down to Titus' ears. He turned his head and realised that he could see the tip of the man's boot beneath the base of the desk. As the man continued to prowl around the room, Titus spotted the other man standing directly behind Marcus, who lay completely still. Titus recognised the man as one of the guards from the quadrangle earlier. Clearly the basement doors had not closed as quietly as he had hoped.

At least that probably restricted the number of men to two, Titus thought. Fighting was the last thing he wanted to do because it would leave certain evidence of their presence. Even if their Dacian head scarves successfully protected their identity, they would never be able to break in so easily again.

The man nearest Titus had circled around the room now and was walking down the aisle between Marcus' and Titus' hiding places. Titus knew this was the moment of truth. The two men were muttering to themselves, complaining of hunger. If they could stay hidden just a few moments longer, Titus was sure the men would give up, assume they had heard nothing after all, and return to their endless patrol loop, and cheap cigarettes.

The man drew level with Titus. He could see him from the waist down. He was only half a foot away, so close that Titus knew he could kill him with his gladius before the man had a chance to react. It was risky. Maybe the men would just give up and leave? His grip tightened on the gladius' wooden handle. Instinct caused him to begin drawing it from its sheath. The man shifted, the black metal of his fully automatic assault sonifex popping momentarily into view from around his hip. Titus froze. The man reached into his pocket and pulled out a packet of cigarettes. He drew one out and began fumbling again for his lighter.

'The boss won't be impressed with you smoking in here,' the other man called from across the room.

The first man cursed and threw the cigarette on the floor.

The second man was clearly in charge, 'pick that up! You can't leave litter in here. The boss would have you killed for less,' he growled from across the room.

'Fuck you.' The tone was investigational.

'Do you want me to come over there and make you?'

The man turned, facing away from Titus now, and slowly bent down. Marcus kept stock still, but there was no way of avoiding the guard's field of vision. The guard froze, half bent at the waist, staring right into Marcus' eyes. Their cover was blown.

XV

Ceinwyn poked the fire in the grate, turning over the green logs, enjoying the popping from the fresh wood. The heating in the slave quarters at the compound had been meagre, she had often found herself wearing all her clothes during the long winter nights. She removed her gown, sitting on the floor wearing only the light cotton clothes she had had bought for her by Marcus earlier that day. The fire was a luxury really: it wasn't cold enough for her to need it yet. But the most novel thing, and that which she was enjoying the most, was simply being alone. In her five years under Strabo's roof there had not been a moment unspied upon.

The first seventeen years of her life had been happy mostly; she had few friends as no-one, neither slave nor Roman, wanted to associate with her due to the affliction of her birth; but she had had her father, and his books. Strangely, she had felt privileged during most of her childhood, for she had received something no other woman ever received, an education. Roman women were barely educated, and no Slave was at all. Her father, having no other children to dote on, had tried to teach her everything he knew. She had taken in as much as she could, mainly history and politics. Her smile faded as she remembered how she had been taken from him.

She looked up at the shelves in the sitting room. Titus hadn't fully unpacked, leaving the room only sparsely decorated. However, alongside the equipment he had lying about in disorderly piles, there was a single decoration, a picture sitting on the mantelpiece. In the picture were two figures. Ceinwyn got to her feet lightly, and gently stepped over to it. The picture was old; Ceinwyn could see how the edges had been torn and how it was held together only by the frame which clasped it. In the centre were two characters in camouflage gear, jubilantly embracing, beneath them was an annotation, 'Rowena Valley'.

Ceinwyn marvelled at the sight of the younger Titus. He looked to be in his early twenties she thought, his hair was dark brown with none of the grey which flecked it now. The shorter figure was clearly Marcus.
Ceinwyn laughed as she realised he hadn't changed at all. As she stared at the picture, she imagined Titus here in the room with her and smiled. She would enjoy being alone for now.

Before the security guard had a chance to make a sound, Titus made a split second decision. Rushing from his cover in one movement, he found himself on the back of the half bent-forward guard. The man was hopelessly off balance and still shocked from the surprise of seeing Marcus crouched beneath the opposing scire bank. Titus' weight bore the man face down onto the ground. He quickly got his right arm around the man's neck; he couldn't see the other guard, but he knew he had seconds, if that, before he must reach them.

The guard beneath him struggled, one arm trapped beneath his body, but with the other he grappled with Titus, trying to pull his arm from around his neck. Titus was far too strong for him. The man's struggling increased frantically as Titus twisted his neck like a vice. Then came a sharp crack, and the struggling abruptly ceased.

Titus rolled over quickly. The second guard was charging at full pelt along the aisle straight towards him—he had no time to avoid him. He launched himself forward, diving at the man's knees, tackling him to the ground. The two men wrestled on the floor. Titus managed to get his hand to the pommel of his gladius, but the guard had his hand in a firm grip and Titus could not draw the weapon. Meanwhile, with their free hands the men fought to grab each other's throats. Rolling around the floor they brought scires crashing down around them. This guard was stronger than Titus and with every second Titus knew his grip on the man's arm was weakening. The guard was beginning to exert real force on Titus' throat; he felt the blood pounding in his head as the veins draining through his throat were crushed by the powerful grip.

He could not release the grip on his sword for fear of it being turned on him, so with the other hand he struck repeatedly, as hard as he could, at the guard's arm, desperately trying to weaken his choking grip. His vision was dimming now and he knew he was seconds from losing consciousness. All he could see was the grim face of the guard glowering at him as he tightened his lethal grip on Titus' neck. It would be the last thing he ever saw.

Then suddenly the grip loosened, the man's eyes glazed over and he fell forwards against Titus' shoulder. Titus coughed and rubbed his throat, his vision slowly returning. The figure of Marcus appeared behind the man, a large screen in his arms. He reached over and helped Titus to his feet. 'Thanks,' Titus grunted through his painful throat.

'What shall we do now?' Marcus asked, looking down at the two guards on the floor.

'You're not going to like this Marcus,' Titus said, bending down over the figure of the unconscious guard.

'But he doesn't know who we are,' said Marcus pointing to his Dacian head-scarf.

Titus shook his head, 'they must think this was another inside job; they mustn't suspect anyone else knows about this place. They must think we are Slaves; this man can tell them we were professionals. If he does that we will never get into this place again.'

'It doesn't seem fair.'

'It's not,' said Titus, reaching for the unconscious guard's neck, 'but we have no choice.' He snapped the unconscious man's neck—a single sharp motion. Looking up at Marcus' appalled face, he spoke, 'Strabo set this in motion; we have no choice, but to see it through.' He walked over to his old friend, 'have you got everything you need from the system?'

Marcus nodded and showed Titus the display he held.

Titus peered intently and noticed names along with numbers. 'What does this mean?' he asked.

'It's the same as the papers you found in the slave camp—its Strabo's accounts. But this is the full version, which is stored on his secure server. We have the names of the accounts as well as their numbers and the amounts they have paid and received.'

Titus clapped Marcus on the shoulder, 'there will be something we can use in this.'

'I'll analyse it for you when we get back.'

Titus nodded, pleased he had someone in his team who understood scires. 'I wish we could have told Quintus about this too.'

'I don't trust him,' replied Marcus.

'You never have, I understand, he isn't easy to talk to. But he is a good man. That's one thing I'm sure of.'

Marcus began to walk back down the white corridor towards the exit of the basement, followed by Titus, then he stopped and turned around. 'If you trust Quintus so much, why haven't you told him about Ceinwyn?' He asked.

Titus thought for a long time before replying. 'Because Marcus, I don't know what he'd do.'

'And you still say you trust him?'

'What else can I do? He is my friend.'

From the tone of his answer it was clear that the conversation was over. The two men walked on and were soon at the T junction. The basement doors were off to the right, only thirty yards away. Ahead lay the corridor heading towards the west wing; Ceinwyn's map showed little beyond this point.

'I say we have a look,' Titus suggested, keen to find out as much as possible about his enemy.

Marcus looked afraid, but nodded and the pair set off. As the corridor continued, there were more offices on both sides of the passage. All were dark inside however and the doors were firmly locked. The whole place seemed deserted at night. As the pair proceeded deeper into the facility, Titus began to feel uneasy. It was the same feeling that Ceinwyn had had the first time she had explored the basement; it was too quiet. Titus was becoming increasingly aware of his breathing, and his beating heart, for they were the only sounds, apart a distant, tortured, screeching sound—like metal grating on metal. Looking across at Marcus he could tell he was feeling the same.

'Do you want to go back?' Titus asked.

'Maybe we should just have a look around the corner.' Marcus replied, from his expression, clearly surprised by his own bravado. The screeching noise was getting louder; its source didn't sound far away. Titus reached into his pocket for the oculus. It wasn't there. Thinking back, he realised he had never picked it up after the last time he had used it. How had he managed to forget to collect it? he thought, cursing his stupidity.

'Marcus, go and check it out. I'll cover us,' Titus whispered over the humming sound.

Marcus crept over to the wall and peered around the corner. After a few seconds he turned to Titus, 'I'd come and see this if I were you.'

Titus joined him at the corner; looking around it he saw rows of metal trolleys against the wall. They were all covered with blue sheeting. The sound was louder than ever. There were several corridors leading off from this area, and Titus couldn't tell which one was the source of the unsettling sound. Every part of his body was telling him to leave now; Marcus clearly felt the same as he was already backing away down the corridor. However, Titus had to know what was under the sheet. He walked up to the nearest trolley and lifted the corner.

As Titus lifted the corner of the sheet, the screeching sound down the corridor abruptly stopped. He froze, his hand still on the sheeting. He looked down at the surgical implements that had been concealed beneath, some of them still fresh with blood. In shock he staggered back around the corner, just as a voice sounded from a distant room.

'This one's finished.' The voice was male and it sounded educated, yet brutal. It chilled Titus to the bone.

'Let's get out of here,' whispered Marcus, gesturing back down the corridor.

He nodded, still staring at the trolley and its harrowing contents. He turned to see Marcus already half-way down the corridor. Titus began to run after him, but was brought up short by the sight of him turning in his tracks, and running back towards him. 'This way!' Marcus called as he ran back past Titus, and kicked frantically at a low lying ventilation duct. Within seconds he had the duct cover free. 'Get in, now!' he hissed at Titus, who obeyed immediately.

Once within the duct Marcus carefully replaced the duct cover.

'What's going on?' Titus asked.

'Quiet,' Marcus whispered, 'they'll hear us.'

Titus listened intently. He could hear footsteps in the distance. As the sound grew closer, he realised they were coming from the direction Marcus had run in.

They waited, huddled together in the ventilation duct watching as the pair of guards' feet passed at eye level. A few moments after the feet had passed, the guards came to a halt. They began to talk to a third man; clearly the educated one Titus had heard earlier. He strained hard, but he couldn't make out all of the conversation from the duct. The educated man's voice carried better than the others. He heard him repeatedly mentioning a 'procedure,' but he received no further clues as to what this was. He was interrupted from his thoughts by Marcus tapping his leg and pointing further down the duct. Titus agreed that they needed to move from here.

The thin metal ventilation duct was just wide enough for a man to crawl down; Marcus, despite his extra bulk, was just able to manage, albeit at a slow pace. This Titus thought, was actually a good thing as it kept the amount of noise made by the crawling to a minimum. He was completely disorientated now, and had no idea where they would come out—he hoped it was onto the main corridor, but for all he knew they could be travelling further into the west wing. He pulled out his GPS to check his location, but received no link to the satellites this far underground.

After ten minutes of crawling, which seemed like an hour to the two men, they came out of the vent into a cramped utility room. There was a rusty boiler against the left hand wall, its warmth palpable from the other side of the room. Next to the vent they had crawled out of, there stood a ladder fixed to the wall, extending vertically approximately twenty feet. A hatch at the top clearly led to the surface above, but into what part of Strabo's compound it opened, they could only guess. Both men looked around for a safer option. The room was so noisy they could barely hear each other.

'What's that noise!' Titus shouted

'Sounds like water,' Marcus shouted, pointing at a hatch in the floor with a wheel handle.

Titus nodded and gestured to Marcus to open it. He placed his hands on the rusty wheel and slowly twisted the lock open. The sound was even louder now. Both men peered down into the darkness below the hatch. Titus flicked a tiny torch out of his jacket and shone it down into the abyss beneath.

Far below, a torrent of water cascaded down the side of a concrete weir before disappearing beyond the penetration of their torch light.

'The Aqueduct,' Titus shouted. 'It runs underground from the hills before coming back up into Lugavalium.' Both men looked at the rusty ladder leading down towards the water; they presumed there must be some sort of ledge at the bottom, but then what? Marcus shivered at the thought of falling into that torrent; dragged under; lungs bursting, before being torn to pieces by the various filters and additive pumps that lay ahead. He shook his head and pointed upwards at the ladder leading back up into Strabo's compound.

Titus was the first to start the climb. With trepidation he lifted the hatch a crack, but, peering out, he was pleasantly surprised to find himself staring out over the main quadrangle through which they had crept at the start of their evening's work.

He hauled himself out onto the neatly trimmed grass of the quad, and scanned all around carefully for any signs of guards—there were none. He had not expected to see any as he was almost certain that the two guards they had killed in the east wing scire bank were the two who had been patrolling this area earlier. He gestured for Marcus to follow him up into the pitch black night. Once the two men were out of the duct, they gently let the hatch close. Despite their care it snapped shut with a loud clang that sounded even louder in the deserted courtyard. It seemed impossible to open again from the outside.

'Don't forget Cyric,' Marcus hissed at Titus, as they began to move over the closely cropped grass past a statue of Dido and Aeneas.

'How could I,' Titus replied sarcastically.

Leaving Marcus by the statue, Titus headed back towards the bush where they had left Cyric. He whistled quietly to attract his attention, but there was no movement from inside the bush. Titus tried again, looking all around for signs of life. He wished his mouth was able to make owl sounds for use as signals: this whistling could easily attract unwanted attention. There was still no movement from the bush.

A long groan emanated from the other side of the quadrangle. He froze and turned slowly, trying to catch sight of whatever had made the sound. Attached to the other side of the quadrangle Titus could make out the shape of a crude, metal cage bolted down to the concrete ground, clearly no more than a metre and a half in any dimension. The source of the moan was squatting on the floor, a dishevelled figure Titus could barely make out. Keeping low he jogged across the deserted quadrangle towards the figure.

A hand clamped down hard on his shoulder as he entered the colonnade, bringing him up sharply. He swung round, throwing the hand off, whilst his hands went straight to the throat of his assailant. 'It takes four pounds of pressure to break a man's neck,' his training muttered to him at the back of his mind. To Titus it was a constant companion—a sixth sense able to operate before his conscious mind could. This time his conscious mind kicked in just in time. 'Cyric,' Titus dropped his hands away from Cyric's throat as he gasped his name.

'That's Tristan,' Cyric whispered, eyes wide with fear as he realised how close he had just come to death.

Titus did not move. 'Who is Tristan?' he asked.

'Tristan is an example.' Cyric did not elaborate.

'An example of what?' Titus asked.

'He stole from our master,' he said, spitting the word, 'you don't want to steal from the master, and you especially do not wish to be caught stealing from the master.'

Titus felt the hair's on the back of his neck rise up at Cyric's words. 'What did he do to him?' he asked.

'You don't want to know,' Cyric replied, glaring at Titus, '*I* know what they did though, because we had to watch whilst he tortured him, and all the way through the master demanded to know what sort of person he was.'

'And what did you tell him?'

'With a whip at your back there is only one thing you can say—what you know he wants you to.'

Then Tristran screamed. 'The master was merciful! the master was merciful!' It was an inhuman sound which rang out over the quadrangle, mad and slurred through tortured lips.

Cyric waited, patiently, for it to stop. 'That was my answer as well,' he replied.

Titus took Cyric by the shoulder, 'you have seen a lot here that you should not have done boy, but now, thanks to Ceinwyn, you are free.' At that he began to head for the gatehouse, and the waiting figure of Marcus in the gloom.

'Stop Roman,' Cyric said bravely. 'You have waited here long enough; you have heard his story. Now what will you do about Tristan?'

Titus stopped, and turned to face Cyric for a brief second, 'Tristan is mad. What can we do for him now?'

'Take him from this place! Save him as well!' Cyric replied, nearly shouting now in the deserted quadrangle. What had started as a test of Titus, had turned more personal than Cyric had expected it to. He turned and headed towards the huddled figure in the cage.

Titus leapt onto him and pinned him down to the ground. Covering his mouth with one hand he hissed into his ear, 'if you ever endanger me or my men again, I promise that you will die. Do you understand?'

Cyric made no sound.

'Do you understand?' he hissed again, more insistent this time.

Cyric mumbled an affirmation through Titus' fingers and tried to nod his head. Titus released him. 'Tristan is beyond saving, Cyric. Do you really think we could get him out of here silently?'

Cyric stared blankly back at Titus, refusing to accept his logic. Titus looked away, the decision to manhandle Cyric had cost him, but it was the right one; maybe Cyric would accept it in time. He gestured for Cyric to keep low as he crossed the quadrangle over to Marcus.

'Why did you leave the bush?' he asked Cyric.

104

'I saw the guards heading after you, Roman. I wasn't going to hang around on the off chance you escaped. Do you have any idea what they would have done to me if they had caught me in that bush?'

Titus was clearly not impressed with his charge's attitude. 'Not as bad as what I ought to do to you for not being back in the bush when we returned. You realise that every second I spend here increases my chance of being caught?'

'Typical!' Cyric snorted, 'threaten me, why don't you. You don't frighten me Roman! I have been treated like shit by you people my whole life.'

'We are risking our lives for you Cyric,' Titus replied quietly, 'the least you can do is show us some respect.'

Cyric shrugged his shoulders at Titus and began to walk over to the figure of Marcus crouched near the fountain. Best to leave the boy to his thoughts, Titus decided, as he followed the boy, shooting glances all around to make sure the coast was still clear.

Together, the three men crossed the final piece of ground to the gate of Strabo's compound.

When they reached the gatehouse that guarded the main entrance, Titus crept forwards to inspect it. The guard inside was fast asleep in his chair, with a biscuit crumb strewn newspaper lying across his lap. The screen in the wall behind him was blaring out the latest news; the noise would cover their exit nicely. Titus beckoned for Marcus to come over, along with the young Slave. He placed one hand on the door of the compound and looked hard at Cyric.

'Tonight boy I give you your freedom. But I ask you now—will I regret it?'

The boy looked up at the Roman veteran and sneered at him, 'you can trust me,' he spat.

Titus thought hard, looking up into the dark night's sky. He already hated the boy. But Marcus seemed to think that Ceinwyn valued him. He stared at the boy once more and pushed the door open. The hanging lights above the main gate illuminated them brilliantly, as they headed at a trot out onto the street, before they eventually receded into the distance as the trio disappeared into the gloom.

XVI

Ceinwyn threw her arms around Cyric and squeezed him as hard as she could. She could not believe that finally her and her best friend were together again, and almost free at the same time. She winced at the pain in her nails as she hugged him; during her long night-vigil of pacing the front room she had chewed her nails down to the quick. She let go and noticed that Cyric was blushing. Looking down she noticed the swelling in his trousers, and looked away quickly. But he had noticed where her gaze had fallen and his redness deepened.

She pretended she hadn't seen and quickly turned to Titus, thanking him with a kiss on the cheek. He almost ignored her, nodding curtly and making a sort of half grunt which she took as an acknowledgement of her thanks in saving her friend. He stomped past her, kicked off his boots and sat down on the sofa, pointedly looking away from her and Cyric. Marcus remained outside; he too looked glum.

'Come in Marcus, tell us how you managed to break in to Strabo's compound. It must have been really difficult,' she said, trying to raise his spirits with a bit of flattery.

He shook his head at her, 'getting late. Better go home,' he pointed down the road to the house he shared with the others.

'Come on! You have just saved my best friend. Let me at least thank you properly.'

Marcus looked back in at Cyric, framing the door behind her, 'I think you have plenty of catching up to do already.' He had emphasised the words 'catching up' and Ceinwyn felt a blush start. Surely he didn't think? She opened her mouth to correct him, but Marcus was already striding away, head down. She closed the door.

Cyric reached down and kissed her cheek.

'Good night,' came Titus' voice from across the room.

Ceinwyn looked up as Titus rose from the sofa, waved in her direction and started to climb the stairs. He stopped awkwardly, half way up the stairs, 'oh, Cyric, there is a bed for you in the basement. Ceinwyn's room's upstairs. Or,' he paused and put his hand to his brow in thought. 'Or whatever you want.' He tried not to catch her eye as he finished the climb up the stairs, but Ceinwyn could see his anguish plainly.

Cyric had already worked out how to get the screen on the wall working and had found a program in which three middle aged Roman men were messing around in racing curri. She grabbed hold of the moment, and quickly followed Titus upstairs, with Cyric barely noticing her absence. She caught up with him just as he reached the top of the staircase, with one hand on his bedroom door handle. He turned to face her. 'I thought...' he trailed off. He looked bemused, but hopeful. Ceinwyn felt her heart quicken and she smiled at the sensation. She understood.

'You think,' she paused to laugh, 'me and Cyric?' She took a couple more steps towards Titus and whispered in his ear, 'I could not love him.'

His arms moved around her back and made the lightest contact as if he was not sure what he wanted. She felt her breathing quicken; the 'enemy' was so close. This man had killed so many of her people. Surely what she wanted to do now was wrong. What would her father think? But he might even be dead for all she knew.

She kissed him on the cheek again. This time he seemed more interested.

'Thank you,' she whispered. 'You were brave for me tonight.' She brushed her mouth over his as she kissed his other cheek. She could feel

107

Titus' heart deep in his chest. She wanted to hold him. He moved his head slightly to intercept her next kiss. She moved towards him, eyes closing, ready for the moment she suddenly craved. Her mind was finally made up: this 'enemy' was what she wanted. It didn't matter anymore to her what he had done, besides he was trying to make amends. It was time to show him.

'Oi, Roman, have you got anything to eat in this hovel? I'm starving!'

The pair jumped apart in shock at the call from Cyric downstairs. Ceinwyn started playing with her hair awkwardly. They listened as Cyric stomped sullenly down the basement stairs to his room.

'I was just going to go to bed.' Titus said eventually, avoiding her gaze as he swiftly stepped into his bedroom and closed the door. She looked away too. The moment had gone, and for the briefest of seconds Ceinwyn wished Titus had left Cyric behind in the compound. But even that small, angry thought only worsened her heartache as she realised that Titus had rescued him, in spite of clearly believing her, and Cyric to be lovers. She took a step across the landing and rested her hand on the handle. Her hand tightened to open it, her heart fluttered. She let go. He had walked away; if he really wanted her, he would come to her.

Her decision cost her sleep. Laying awake, she was tormented by the thought that this strange Roman, who seemed to care so much for her, was literally on the other side of the wall by her head; if there had been a hole she could simply have reached through and stroked his face. He cared for her, and she was safe, and she was one step from his bed.

The next four weeks seemed to pass in an instant for Titus. He spent as much time as he could with Ceinwyn. They could not go out openly during the day when, instead, they had to talk under the watchful eyes of the jealous Cyric, but at night Titus would take Ceinwyn for walks. They would walk together on the banks of the river Caldew and sometimes Titus would take Ceinwyn further afield into the hills where few Romans bothered to venture, and they were at last safe and alone. For the first time in his life Titus felt close to a woman. They talked about everything, and their days were punctuated with the ever present sound of laughter, yet the almost-kiss on the stairs was never repeated, as if in some way to give in to their feelings would simultaneously shatter them.

But through all of this happiness there ran an undercurrent of sadness in Titus, for he knew that it could not last. As the summer finally drew to a close, the night walks became less and less practical, the rains fell harder than before and the chill began to draw in. The leaves on the great oaks lining their road turned golden and beautiful, before finally beginning to fall, and then, one bitterly cold afternoon, Strabo's messenger returned.

XVII

'There is no way we can make this look convincing,' Marcus said, in their makeshift hide, high above the Slave encampment. Titus was inclined to agree with his friend. There were barely twenty Slaves, and none of them seemed to be carrying weapons. They had to botch the job, but it had to look genuine, not just for Strabo, but also for the rest of the men.

'If they find out then your father dies.' Marcus said, blunt as always.

Marcus was right and Titus knew it, but it was hard to accept. 'We'll have to lie forever,' he said, 'every time he sends us out for more Slaves, we will have to do this again. We can't live like that.'

'We'll just have to take it as it comes!' Marcus laughed, 'maybe he doesn't really need more Slaves—the gods' know what he does with them! Our next mission we might be sent to kill some Reivers. Now that would be a proper mission wouldn't it?' He clapped Titus on the shoulder, trying desperately to cheer him up. It was to no avail, when Titus got into one of his black moods it was nigh on impossible to jolt him from it. He had been in an uncommonly bad mood ever since they had left Luguvalium six days ago. The cynical part of Marcus wondered if the separation from

Ceinwyn was responsible for his friend's recent terrible moods. He recognised the seed of jealousy growing inside him and once again tried, without success, to stifle its unrelenting, corrupting growth.

'There is, of course, another option,' Titus said, 'we could succeed in the mission and bring the Slaves back to Strabo...'

'Could you do that, knowing what you do now?'

Titus thought about the old man in the tent, slaughtered whilst trying to help him; he thought of a girl on a far-away shore; he thought of Ceinwyn. 'No.' He could never be responsible for the death of a Slave again.

'Me neither. We need to devise a plan. First though, I want to show you this.'

Marcus drew out a folded piece of handwritten parchment and showed it to Titus.

It was a list of names.

'The main contributors to Strabo's fortune,' said Marcus proudly.

'Graham Armstrong.' Titus turned the name over on his tongue. 'A local name.'

'Yes. Strange. I'd have imagined a man like Strabo would only deal with Romans.'

Those without citizenship were second class citizens, unable to hold any political office, local or in Rome. Their prospects in business were also, more often than not, poor.

'Hmmm.' Titus peered at the other name on the sheet.

'*Vivlter*?'

'Yes, I don't know what that is, some sort of political group maybe?' Marcus wondered. 'Never heard of it before. But just look how much money they have paid him, and regularly too.'

Titus looked at the figures, 'this is more than I was paid for the entire Transmaritanus campaign.'

'By far!' Laughed Marcus; Roman legionary pay was not as good as people imagined.

'If they are so rich though, how come we don't know about them?' wondered Titus.

'I imagine they must be in Rome, or they are extremely secretive and dangerous of course,' Marcus laughed. 'Hopefully not, but knowing your luck Titus, they will be. The strange thing is,' he added taking the parchment back, 'that the money has been sent to Strabo from Britannia; I can't determine where from but it certainly isn't Luguvalium.'

'Are there any other sources of funding?' Titus asked, gesturing at the paper.

'Yes, he uses the omniajunctus to defraud people, steal their money, break businesses etcetera. The usual things you would expect a governor to do, except on a much greater scale—probably why he needs that heavy duty omniajunctus connection.'

Titus thought about this for a second before he realised the implications, 'you mean like what had happened to most of the people Strabo ordered us to debt collect from?'

'It would seem so,' Marcus said gloomily, 'I imagine that's his way of getting back at people who have got in his way. A man in his position could easily ruin a small businessman like that.'

'But why ruin a small business in his own town?

'Your guess is as good as mine, Titus. Perhaps he doesn't plan on staying there for ever. Do you?'

The pair were distracted by rustling in the grass behind them. Marcus froze, Titus gesturing to him to stay perfectly still. The rustling was getting nearer, whatever it was was doing an extremely poor job of creeping up on them.

The undergrowth rippled and then began to thrash madly. For a second both men thought it must be a pack of Reivers and then simultaneously realised it was just Antonius. The brute of a man lumbered towards them and set himself down out of sight of the Slave camp behind his comrades. Titus gestured for him to whisper; he knew from experience that Antonius had never really grasped the basics of stealth. 'I'm looking forward to getting into action.' He spoke extremely slowly, but the volume was not greatly different from usual. He had at least tried.

'Is that all you came across here to tell us?' asked Titus.

'I was talking to the others. We were thinking—are we going to take them now?'

'You're certainly eager, my friend, but Marcus and I think next morning would be better. Need some time to draw up a plan.'

Antonius forced his huge bulk between his two friends and peered down into the Slave encampment. Titus held his breath, expecting a shout of surprise from below.

Antonius surveyed the scene for a moment and then crept back slowly. 'Don't seem many of them to me,' he said, leaving at least a second before each booming word. 'I'll kill them now. We could be home by tomorrow?'

Titus laughed, 'have you got a particular reason for wanting to be back tomorrow?' Antonius blushed; something neither Titus or Marcus had seen him do before.

'He's got a woman.' The educated voice came out of nowhere.

All three men jumped out of their skin. It was Quintus who had somehow crept up on the three of them completely silently. Titus greeted him and he came over to join them in the hide. Titus watched for any hint in Quintus' face that he might have overheard any of the earlier conversation, but there was none. It seemed so far they were safe.

Eventually, Antonius and Quintus left: apparently Gnaeus had managed to bring down a deer, and was busy spitting it in their camp half a mile back. Both Titus and Marcus longed for the food, but both knew the very existence of their group depended on the quality of their plan. The food would have to wait.

'Good venison,' remarked Gnaeus, nodding towards Tiberius, acknowledging his abilities as a chef.

'Best I could manage at short notice,' Tiberius replied, shrugging his shoulders and ripping off a chunk of smoking deer meat with his mouth

'The rest is going to be cold if they don't get back here soon,' said Quintus

'Yeah, what the hell do you reckon is taking them so long?' asked Tiberius.

'Don't know,' said Quintus irritably, 'something about planning the attack. Didn't seem that hard to me—a few huts, a few mindless Slaves. I'd have just walked in and let rip with the sonifex. It's like they are planning some sort of military operation—I mean for Jupiter's sake it's just a bunch of Slaves.'

'I'd trust him if I were you,' interrupted Gnaeus, irritated at the way the conversation was turning.

Quintus looked at him angrily, still chewing the venison. 'Is that meant to be some sort of threat?'

'No, not at all, you need to calm down Quintus. Just think how long you've known Titus; it's at least fifteen years isn't it. In all that time has he ever done anything to betray your trust?'

Quintus thought hard, still chewing. 'Never,' he admitted.

'So, it would have to take something pretty big to change the habits of fifteen years. Trust him. He trusts us, we should trust him.'

'Your God teaches you to trust I guess?' Quintus scoffed.

Tiberius and Antonius looked away, Gnaeus' faith in one God was an embarrassment to his family and, by extension, his friends as well. They tolerated it, unlike the Senate who could formally exile him from Rome if he made too much of a fuss about it. Despite their tolerance however, it was rarely talked about. Only Titus ever asked Gnaeus about his God.

'Actually it's more that he teaches me to question,' Gnaeus answered.

'Do you think I care?' Quintus said, 'leave that talk for Titus.'

Gnaeus shrugged, 'you asked,' he said calmly and continued eating.

'I wouldn't need to if you'd just do your civic duty, and worship the real gods,' Quintus said, goading him.

Gnaeus rounded on him, 'funny that, your talk of duty. When did you last see your wife, and perform your 'civic duty' with her?'

The colour drained out of Quintus' face at his words.

'I don't pry into your life,' Gnaeus continued, 'neither does Titus. If he has secrets, then I don't think they are anything that would affect us.'

Quintus quickly dropped the subject, as Gnaeus knew he would, and returned his focus to eating. The conversation around the fire was more muted now; Quintus' outburst against Titus was unusual and none of them quite knew how to react to it. There was also the uneasy feeling going through the four men's minds that Titus did seem unusually remote; maybe he was indeed keeping something from them.

114

The feast was interrupted by the sound of footfall at the far end of the camp. All four men listened intently. Was it Titus and Marcus? Or someone else? Quintus called out the watchword for the evening but there was no response.

'Antonius, come with me! Keep low!' hissed Quintus.

The big man lumbered after the more nimble Quintus. 'Store tent,' he said.

'Circle round to the left,' Quintus replied, 'if any make a break for it. Take them out.'

Antonius disappeared into the gloom.

Quintus made for the entrance to the tent. There was a dim glow inside: a lantern. The click as he took the safety catch off his sonifex made him catch his breath. He made a mental note to email the munitions company about the appalling design fault. The flickering light inside the tent moved again. Quintus leapt through the opening in the canvas, and brought the muzzle of his sonifex to bear on the intruders, his eyes squinting against the lantern's light.

'What the hell are you doing Quintus?' asked a bewildered Marcus, an open kit bag in his hands.

'I heard noises, I thought I'd... You didn't reply to the watchword.'

'I didn't hear you call it out,' replied Titus, who was standing near the electric lantern on the other side of the tent filling up some webbing. Quintus stared at him and the webbing he was holding.

'Could you lower the gun Quintus?' Titus asked slowly.

The barrel slowly lowered, but Quintus didn't leave. 'What are you doing?' he asked.

'Preparing for tomorrow,' said Marcus angrily.

Quintus stared at him for a long time. Finally he nodded. 'All right,' he pointed in the direction of the fire, 'venison is getting cold, I better head back.'

'We'll join you once we've sorted the kit out,' said Titus.

Quintus backed slowly out of the door. Marcus peered after him, watching as the huge figure of Antonius burst out of the tree line from his ambush point and, like an excited dog, bounded back to the camp. He let the tent flap fall back into place and wiped his brow of the cold sweat that had formed on it.

'That was far too close,' Titus exclaimed.

'It's done now and I don't think he suspects,' Marcus replied.

'We won't know till tomorrow.'

'Is there anything else to do?'

'Apart from eating venison, no, not really,' Titus said.

Marcus' stomach rumbled again, 'you're right, it is getting late after all.'

'If it doesn't go to plan tomorrow, at least we tried,' Titus said.

'Ceinwyn isn't going to buy that,' replied Marcus.

'I know.'

'Did you tell her where we were going?' Marcus asked.

'I told her it was a mission for Strabo, she understands, and she trusts us.' His heart wished he could have told her the truth.

'Did you explain about how we would try to spare the Slaves?'

'I didn't tell her it had anything to do with Slaves. I didn't know how to tell her. If she finds out,' Titus drew a deep breath, thinking about Ceinwyn's wrath, 'she will kill me.'

'And more importantly,' Marcus replied, with a glint in his eye, 'I'll have absolutely no chance with her.'

As he mentioned her name, Titus felt the sickness in his stomach. Marcus clearly adored her. How could he tell him how *he* felt about her? As he sat down, and began to chew on the venison, another thought crossed his mind. The nausea was even worse now—what if the plan didn't work? What if Slaves died? What if Ceinwyn found out? Whichever way things turned out Titus knew one thing: he would lose one of them soon—his oldest friend or the strange, red haired, beautiful girl.

He looked up into the sky and found what he was looking for quickly. The hunter's belt. To the right was the ancestral star, a huge red giant burning millions of light years away. Jupiter apparently lived there, and with him everyone's great ancestors. Titus Labienus, the Destroyer of Tyrants and the Protector of Rome, should be there by rights. Titus didn't believe in Jupiter, or the ancestral star, but for the first time in his life he wished that he did.

116

'Labienus, my friend,' he spoke in his head. 'I have found a woman.'
The star shimmered a deep, orangey red, but no sign came.

'I have never felt this way about anyone.'

The star stared impassively back. Titus wanted to curse it. 'Help me!' he implored. 'Make my plan work.' The star ignored him.

He looked down at his feet and tried to summon the courage to admit his feelings to the star, to himself. 'I love her.'

He looked up, expecting to see a shooting star, or some other sign. But the ancestral star remained expressionless.

'I love her.' He almost whispered out loud. But either the Great Titus Labienus had better things to do, or was long dead, his decayed bones deep inside the Earth rather than floating, ethereal, above some far away star.

Titus closed his eyes. He could trust in nothing but himself. He just hoped he was up to the task.

XVIII

Quintus cursed as the thick marsh beneath his feet slurped over the top of his boots. With every ounce of strength he managed to wrestle one free. Crouching down for extra leverage he managed to wrestle the other leg free too. 'What the fuck am I doing here?' he shouted into the bright morning sky.

He looked down at the watch on his wrist. He had seventeen minutes left. Looking up he scanned the marsh for any sign that would point him in the direction of the Slave encampment. The tree on the rise up ahead looked familiar. The slope looked treacherous however, a mixture of scree and crag. Quintus had never been the best climber. Not for the first time that morning he asked himself why Titus had volunteered him for this job.

When they had sat down earlier in the morning to discuss the plan, Quintus had expected, as usual, to act as sniper. He knew his skills lay in accuracy rather than brute strength and close-quarters combat; that was left to Antonius. However it seemed that today the others would do the shooting from afar. The idea was to scare the Slaves down the slope to the west of their camp, towards where Quintus was hiding. He would start a massacre, causing the Slaves to run back to the others, and give themselves up. Usually the men would be killed; and the women and children returned to slavery. That was the Roman way. However Strabo's orders this time had been to bring back every man, woman and child that they could. Quintus had seen the orders himself, and was incredulous. It was madness to bring a wild male Slave into captivity; they were known to be virtually untameable.

Quintus checked his load, popping the magazine out from beneath his sonifex. It was full of anti-personnel rounds—he would cause havoc amongst the Slaves. Yet he had no idea how far he still had to go to reach the position. From above, it had all looked so simple—a distance of only a mile. The route he was supposed to take had been scouted by Titus and Marcus the day before; it was completely concealed from the Slave camp and, according to Titus, would be easy. That was why they had agreed to synchronise watches and give him half an hour exactly to get into position. Half an hour should have been enough. Quintus checked his watch again—fifteen minutes to go. He quickly adjusted the load on the backpack and, with some trepidation, began the climb.

Titus watched the Slaves collect water from the nearby river, in complete clarity through his telescopic sights. To his left lay Gnaeus and Antonius, to his right Marcus and Tiberius. Each was ten paces apart from the next, completely concealed in the undergrowth. Titus felt a bead of sweat form in his hairline, and trickle down his camouflaged cheek. It wasn't even warm this morning; a fine dew lay on the grass about them. He wondered how Quintus was doing. He felt bad for sending him on the mission but he knew that he was too accurate to be allowed to shoot with them. He would easily see through the plot. Titus could imagine what Quintus was going through right now; he did not envy him—that route they had picked was hell. Even a superhuman effort would not be enough to get to the correct point in half an hour. He looked down at his watch. It was nearly time. He flicked the safety catch off his sonifex. His team followed his lead.

Quintus grunted with pain as he tore his knuckles on the exposed rock above him, the weight of his pack pulling at his aching forearms. The next move was the hardest—an overhang of rock. It had seemed simple from

119

below. He made the fatal mistake of looking back over his shoulder; although the drop was forty feet at the most it sucked at him, sapping the strength from his legs. He pulled himself in closer to the crag, a sob of fear escaping from his tightly clenched mouth. This was wrong. He knew a little about climbing, enough to know that it was essential to lean out a little, to give yourself space from the rock. Yet in his worsening panic he was just clinging onto the rock with every point of contact he could possibly make available. His knees shook against the cold stone. He had to move. He could not climb down safely, nor did he have the time to find a way round. He tried to look at his watch but his body would not allow him to loosen his grip on the crag that he so desperately clung to. He thought of the Slaves running free, of the accusing stares of his friends for letting the animals escape. He could not face them like that; he would not be a coward. Slowly, with a superhuman effort of will, he inched his body away from the rough crag. He let out his tightly held breath slowly, finding that his feet felt secure, and he had one good handhold with his right hand. He paused to recover his breath and focus his mind on the final stage of the climb.

Looking up at the overhang again he was astonished by how near the top he already was—the overhang was the crux of the whole climb. He thought back to his days in the military training school in Rome. Once when he was seventeen he had raced Titus on the climbing wall. He had been desperate to beat him, but to no avail. He was never able to beat Titus at the military academy, although he had tried to at almost every physical test. Maybe that was why he had trained further to become a medic? Titus couldn't claim that he could save lives, Quintus thought happily, although a part of him worried that maybe Titus would have been a better doctor than him, if he had gone to medical school rather than chasing girls. He brushed the thoughts from his mind. Titus was not here now—he was alone on the crag.

He took his left hand from its poor hold, and found a better one slightly higher up. Then, using all his strength, he threw his legs high up into fresh holds just beneath the overhang. Contorted, he paused briefly for breath. He needed to get one leg over the rock above, if he managed that the rest would be easy. He steeled himself for the final push. The right leg was his strongest; he pulled the foot from its hold, trying not to look at the sickening gap between him and the ground beneath. He kicked his leg upwards—the side of his foot grated on the edge of the overhang and fell back down. No hold. He had to try again. This time he reached further. His other leg began to cramp up with the effort of holding him in place. He knew this was his last chance. He kicked his leg upwards once more, this time it caught. With his last reserves of strength, he used it as a pivot to pull the rest of himself up and over the obstruction.

Crawling now, with blood oozing from his torn fingers and dust caking his lips he pulled himself over the lip of the crag. Panting, he rolled over. Every part of him cried out for rest, but he knew he had to keep going. There was no time to even look at his watch. He ran to the tree. Looking down he saw the brook running into the woods beneath. The foliage blocked his view of the camp. He had to get to the river. He ran again, his heart pounding in his chest. He tripped on the mossy ground, cursed and threw himself back onto his feet. He was sprinting now. Then he heard the dreaded sound of sonifex fire in the distance. He fell to the ground in shame. He was only a few hundred yards away, but it might as well have been a hundred miles. He hadn't made it. He had cost them the mission.

'Now!' Titus roared, as he knelt up above the bracken that gave him cover from the Slave encampment. The look of horror on the Slaves' faces filled him with pity. He opened fire. Three hundred yards away he would have expected to hit only a few Slaves, as they presented fast moving targets; today he confidently expected the body count to be zero. His companions, following his lead, opened fire at the camp: a crescent of death. As Titus had expected, the Slaves turned tail and fled west, away from the sonifex fire, down to the brook, and away down the fell side. So far no Slave had been injured.

Titus looked to his left and saw Antonius concentrating hard as he tried to pick off a straggling Slave. Despite his efforts the Slave escaped. Antonius stopped firing as the Slave disappeared into the distant woods by the brook. 'None,' he exclaimed. He threw the sonifex down in disgust.

'Don't worry,' Titus said reassuringly, 'Quintus will get them; we were only meant to drive them towards him anyway.' He hoped desperately that

121

he would be mistaken in his prediction. The men waited. Five minutes passed with no sound from the ambush point.

'What the hell is he playing at?' Gnaeus said, 'the Slaves must have reached him by now.' Another five minutes passed but still no sound.

'He hasn't made it,' said Tiberius glumly.

As Titus looked around at the disbelief on the faces of his men, he began to realise the harm he had done Quintus, 'if he hasn't, we mustn't blame him, there must be a good reason he couldn't get there.' His words didn't have quite the effect he had hoped; there was a small nod of agreement from Tiberius and Gnaeus, but Antonius face was a picture of barely controlled fury.

Half an hour later the men were still waiting for any Slaves to make their way back to the camp to give themselves up. The mission was clearly a complete failure. Titus collected up Antonius' fallen sonifex, 'we go back to camp. We'll wait for Quintus there.'

They all jumped at a ragged shout from below them.

'You'll wait right there.'

The voice came from a clump of bushes beneath their position. The branch of the nearest shrub parted as Quintus strode out. He was plastered with mud and weeds from the waist down, and his arms were criss-crossed with angry looking scratches. His sonifex was pointed straight at Titus' belly.

'Easy Quintus,' Titus said, 'what happened to you?'

'Where were you?' shouted Gnaeus accusingly, 'you let them get away.'

'You better ask him,' Quintus said, gesturing at Titus with the tip of his sonifex. He was still panting from his exertion earlier. 'Look at me. Half an hour was never enough to get into position on that path. Were you trying to kill me?'

'Put the weapon down Quintus.' Titus still held Antonius' sonifex, the barrel pointed towards the ground. His fingers moved round to the safety catch instinctively. He stopped them: a rifle full of blanks could not harm anyone.

'Not until you explain why you purposefully let those Slaves get away,' Quintus shouted.

'I don't know what you are talking about Quintus,' replied Titus, 'it was your fault the Slaves got away, not mine.' As the words left his mouth, he hated himself for saying them, heaping more blame on his blameless friend. But he had to divert attention away from himself, or the whole plan would be ruined, and with that, his father's chance of life; as well as any chance he had with Ceinwyn.

As he saw the grim faces of his men staring angrily at Quintus, he nearly lost his resolve; only the thought of Ceinwyn kept him going. He stared right into his friend's eyes as he spoke. 'This is your fault Quintus.'

In that moment he was consumed with hatred for Rome, and how it abused Slaves. He hated Strabo for trapping him, and setting the fates, that had brought this terrible moment upon them, in motion. But most of all he hated himself for not being able to find another way to save his men, his father, and his love. This was the only choice and he had made it, hard as it was, and he was not sure he would be able to face the consequences.

Quintus looked like he had been punched in the stomach. Seething with anger he turned around and began to walk away. Gnaeus tried to follow. Titus stopped him. 'No Gnaeus, you stay here. Let him think.'

Back at their makeshift camp Titus and his men cleared the camp away in silence. Gnaeus tried to add some cheer to the atmosphere by handing round some chocolates he had had imported from Italia. He took Titus' glare to be a refusal. He considered trying to talk his friend round, but by the time he had thought better of it, Titus had already stalked off to the store tent with their sonifi. Gnaeus turned instead to the remnants of last night's fire. It was important that it was cold before they left. It wasn't so much that they were concerned about the fire spreading, more the ever present threat of a Reiver band tracking them. A dead fire was less likely to arouse interest than warm embers.

Gnaeus poured a jerry can over the ashes, which hissed and spat as the cold water met the few remaining coals. He kept enough water back for their journey home—it should take them no more than two days. If only Strabo had lent them a currus, they could have been back in half a day. Despite their good work for him, they seemed oddly out of favour.

Gnaeus put the jerry can down. As he did so he noticed a small metal object on the other side of the steaming ash pit. He walked over to inspect it. The object was black and curved like a banana: it was a sonifex magazine. Gnaeus looked up to call out to the others to ask them whose it was, but the fire pit was now deserted; the others must have moved to help take down the storage tent. He looked down at the magazine again. It was closest to where Tiberius' tent had been—he must have left it there whilst clearing the tent out, and forgotten to return it to Titus. Gnaeus picked it up and walked over to the storage tent to pack it away for him. As he did so he looked into the top of the magazine at the single remaining bronze coloured cartridge within. It didn't look right.

He popped it out and examined it more closely. The end of the cartridge case was simply crimped off; there was no round in the end. It was a blank. His mind turned over the day's events: the Slaves running; their inability to hit the Slaves; Titus offering to stow their sonifi in the munitions tent after the mission. It all fitted together, but made no sense.

Gnaeus looked around again but there was still no sign of the others. He wasn't sure what to do. He thought again about what he had said last night about trusting Titus, and made up his mind. He kicked his heel backwards into the soft earth and made a small hole. Dropping the blank into the hole, he quickly buried it before stamping the earth down firmly. Turning around, he made his way to his tent in silent thought, and began to pack away his gear. He would trust Titus even though he did not as yet understand his motives.

He was interrupted from his thoughts by the sight of Titus running up to him from down the hill beneath the camp. 'Thank the gods you're safe Gnaeus!' he shouted, out of breath, 'I thought we had lost you as well.'

Gnaeus looked at him in bewilderment. 'I've been here all the time though?'

'We thought you had followed us—Marcus and I went off to find Quintus, the others followed. I didn't know you had stayed behind.'

'I was just clearing up the camp for you.'

'Quintus is gone!' Titus said.

'Gone?'

'We found some of his clothes and equipment not far from here and some blood as well. Come quickly.'

At this he began to sprint away and Gnaeus followed him.

'At least they didn't get you, Gnaeus,' Titus said.

'Who didn't get me?'

'The Reivers of course!'

The mention of the Reivers made both men fall silent as they thought about the ordeal Quintus would be facing at this very moment. Titus remembered the man suspended from the tree. The Reivers were not fond of captives they could not ransom.

Titus rounded the corner and the forest clearing, where his other men had waited together, loomed ahead, Gnaeus was close on his tail. Why had he not thought to bring the sonifi? Titus thought, cursing himself for the oversight.

Quintus' jacket lay on the soft turf in the clearing. It had been trampled on and the grass around it had several marks where a struggle had clearly taken place. To Titus' trained eye, it was clear that several men had taken him.

'We might still catch them...' Marcus started, but was cut off by Titus.

'If I had brought the sonifi, then maybe. By the time we have returned to camp and come back here, no chance. They will have a currus somewhere in the woods nearby—we do not. All we can do is hope they want a ransom, if so we have to hope we can pay it.'

'What if they don't ransom him?' Tiberius asked, seemingly on the verge of tears.

'We have to pray that they do,' Titus said.

His men just stared at him, expecting him to have a way out of this.

'That's all we can do.' He turned away and began to walk back to camp, partly because he was desperate to get away from this place, and partly so they could not see the tears he felt he was certain to shed. This was all his fault: he had shamed his friend into leaving the safety of the camp, and his friend had paid the price *he* deserved for his own cowardice. All he could think about was Quintus hanging from a tree, or worse.

He had heard other tales of what the Reivers did to those who wronged them. Some of it was most likely myth, but he doubted that all the tales were completely far fetched. If there were truly people who were animals it was not the Slaves, it was the Reivers. The tears he worried about never came, not even when he turned to see Tiberius picking up Quintus' jacket and tenderly storing it in his webbing, to return to him later. Titus tried to pull himself together, realising that he too had to have hope that Quintus was alive and well. He owed it to all his friends to get their comrade back. He owed it to himself. But he knew that Quintus only had one hope, and that hope was a man who was unlikely to do him any favours.

But Titus had started this, and he had to see it through: he had no choice but to ask Gaius Strabo for help.

XIX

'Let me get this straight,' Strabo rubbed his podgy fingers together and stared up at Titus from his plush chair, his eyes full of pure malice. 'You want me to divert the Praetorian Guard from their duties in order to find some useless mercenary who wandered off in the woods and got himself lost?'

'He was taken by the Reivers, sir,' Titus replied, refusing to rise to Strabo.

'You saw him taken by them?'

'Not exactly.'

'So what did you find 'exactly'?' Strabo asked.

'A torn jacket; some blood; his sonifex abandoned.'

'Sounds like a wolf to me,' Strabo replied, dismissing Titus' idea with a wave of his hand. 'You were near the Great Wall were you not?'

'That's true sir, but...'

Strabo dismissed Titus' words with a wave of his hand. 'It was clearly a wolf then; they often venture down from Caledonia. You can't expect me to send out the Praetorians on the off-chance the Reivers have your man. Their job is to protect the city itself, and prevent the Reivers infiltrating it. The Reivers can have the woods and the hills for all I care.'

'With all due respect sir,' Titus replied, gritting his teeth at having to show respect for the disgusting man in front of him, 'wouldn't it make more sense to take the fight directly to them? They must have camps. The Praetorians could be used to subdue them.'

Strabo laughed. 'Since when did I ask you to give me military advice? A mercenary who can't even round up a rabble of slaves! We'd need an army: the Praetorian Guard versus every vagabond in the North of Brittania?' He bowed his head in mock penitence, 'forgive me Titus if I choose to defend my capital instead.'

'Sir, it's your duty...'

Strabo laughed again, a globule of his spit landed on Titus' arm but Strabo didn't seem to notice. 'I have no duty, but to this,' he held up a beige sestertii note from the drawer in his desk. 'I am in charge of this city. I administrate it as I please, and I do not take advice from mercenary captains under my command. You are dismissed.'

The two men stared at each other over the mahogany desk. When it was clear that nothing further was to be said, Titus turned to go, knowing that it would be fruitless to argue further. Strabo would only continue to taunt him if he persevered. If he was to rescue Quintus he would have to do it himself, but how five men could take on the Reivers he had no idea. As he reached the door he turned, unable to resist a dig in return.

'Decimus Petronius would have helped me.' Strabo jumped at the mention of the missing Praetorian Guard chief legate, but he quickly managed to regain his indifferent facade.

'Decimus Petronius isn't here.' He was suddenly anxious, his fingers playing with a fine wooden sculpture on the edge of the desk.

Titus took the opportunity to continue his attack. 'When he is found, I'll make sure he finds out what you did today. Rome appoints the legate to defend its citizens.'

Strabo sneered at Titus, 'I think it is highly unlikely that Decimus Petronius will ever be found and if he is, one day, I seriously doubt he will be in a fit state to cause me any harm.'

'You seem to be very sure of that,' Titus said. He knew he should stay silent; he was treading very dangerous ground here.

'I know what the Reivers do to those who they count as enemies.'

128

Titus bristled with anger. How could Strabo talk like this when his friend was in the Reivers' clutches? Summoning up every last ounce of strength he feigned deference to Strabo, nodded, and, not trusting himself to speak to him again, he turned and left.

The walk from Strabo's compound to the street where their two barrack houses were seemed longer than usual that evening. As Titus walked past the remains of the old Roman fort that had once been the centre of the city, now merely a tourist attraction, he paused to peer into the distance across the waters of the Solway. The sun was setting over the outline of Criffel in distant Caledonia. Had the Reivers taken Quintus across the Wall?

He had heard rumours that some Reiver families were allied to Pict families, and that blood loyalty ran far deeper than any love they might have for their home country, or Rome. Every minute he wasted, Quintus could be taken further away, that was if he was even still alive.

Once upon a time, Titus would have known exactly what to do—that was the Titus Labienus Aquilinus, who had commanded a thousand men across the seas. Titus sat down on the grass by the ruined fort realising, with a wave of regret, that that man he had once been was now dead; he had not nurtured him; he had allowed him to die. Rome had abandoned him, Marcus Albus the consul had abandoned him. He was alone; him and his old group of men from the army. They were all that was left of that life he had loved. The only life he had ever really known. The only reason he bothered living at all.

But he hadn't factored in Ceinwyn. She had brought him a chink of light, fluttering high above, just out of reach. He thought of Quintus again; reaching for that chink had cost him dearly. The worst of it was that he knew in his heart that his betrayal of Quintus, earlier that day was not to save his father from Strabo's friends in Rome, nor for the Slaves in the camp—it was all for Ceinwyn.

He turned and looked down the hill; he was only half a mile from home. The half mile had a month ago been lined with boutique shops, and department stores. Now most of the boutiques were boarded up or for sale, and the department stores stood dark and half empty of stock.

'*Te occidi familia!*' scrawled in whitewash over the frontage of an electronics store. A final message to Strabo from the owner - '*You killed my family*'.

The Reivers had Luguvalium on its knees, and still Strabo would do nothing. He punched the earth in anger; everything that had gone wrong since he had come to Luguvalium was due to Strabo. The man would seemingly not be content until everything in the city, including Titus and his men, was ruined. He felt more alone than he had ever felt in his life, but then he realised that there was one other person he knew who would understood how he felt. The girl that he loved, only minutes away.

He loved her—he had to tell her. He jogged home, paused briefly for breath, and for courage and then he opened his front door and stepped inside.

A frying pan caught him hard on the side of the head, throwing him off balance. He tumbled headlong over the side of his sofa, ending up spread-eagled and dazed half on and half off it. 'You bastard!' Ceinwyn shouted, aiming a blow at his groin with the pan.

Titus recovered enough to dodge it taking the blow on his left knee instead. The pain was immense and he rolled away to avoid the next attack.

'I knew you Romans were all the same.' She raised the pan to strike again.

This time Titus caught it mid strike, leaping up from the sofa. They stood there together in the middle of the room; his hand around hers on the pan handle; the other round her back, preventing her from breaking loose.

'I hate you,' she spat, her signum shining bright as her usually pale face glowed with anger.

'What have I done?' Titus asked, wanting to loosen his grip on her hand, as he could tell it hurt her, yet unable to do so, at the risk of further blows.

'You know everything about my people, you pretend to care, you even rescue my friend.' She paused for breath, still trying to pull the pan free of Titus' grip, but to no avail. 'Then you take your men and kill my people like cattle, for money!' She started to cry.

130

Titus stared at her, unable to understand why that old history still bothered her. 'Ceinwyn, you know about that already, I have done many things I'm not proud of. But I'm different now. Put the pan down.'

'Stop pretending Titus,' Ceinwyn snapped at him through her tears, 'I know what you have been doing. I know about your last mission. Cyric told me everything. You killed my people, rounded them up and sold them to my old master.' She looked him right in the eyes, 'tell me it isn't true.' She did not gloat, even though she had caught him out—she was too upset and too disappointed in him.

It was a look Titus never wanted to see again.

'Don't even try denying it,' she said, her green eyes flashing with rage, and hurt, 'Cyric spoke to Strabo's messenger after he had given you the mission.'

Titus was stunned, he opened his mouth to protest his innocence then, with horror, the significance of Ceinwyn's words hit him. 'He talked to the messenger?'

'Yes. Cyric told me not to trust you. He was right. I was a fool to listen to you over him, to feel. . .' She trailed off. The anger had gone now; she was simply aloof. Titus noticed a small bag in the corner—it contained her few worldly possessions.

'Did the messenger see you as well?' He asked urgently.

'That makes no difference. Cyric talked to him, and I trust Cyric, I don't need to hear it first hand; you Romans are...'

Titus released the pan and grabbed her by the shoulders. 'Ceinwyn, listen to me. It's important. Did he see you?'

'No, I was upstairs. Why does it matter?' She was curious now.

Titus half expected a blow to the head from the now released frying pan, but it did not come. 'It matters because Strabo now almost certainly knows where Cyric is,' Titus explained, 'frankly that doesn't bother me that much really, apart from the fact that you happen to live in the same house as him. When they come for him, then they will find you too.'

Ceinwyn dropped the pan.

'We need to get you out of here—somewhere safe.'

'It's all right,' she said gesturing to her bag, 'I'm already leaving, actually.'

'Not on your own—I mean with me. We'll leave. Leave the country if need be. I'd go anywhere with you, if it meant you were safe.'

'But you would still kill my fellow people?' she said, staring at him with that accusing gaze again.

'Ceinwyn, Cyric was right about the mission. That was the order.'

Ceinwyn frowned with surprise at his admission of guilt; she had not expected it.

'But did you truly believe that I could carry it out, knowing what I did, feeling what I do? I love you Ceinwyn. I botched the mission on purpose, for you. I love you. Even if you never trust me enough again to let me near you, I will still love you, and, if need be, I will die for you.' He let go of her shoulders and stood waiting for her response. Her face was impossible to read. She made no movement at all for several seconds; to Titus it was an eternity. Then slowly she leaned forwards, and put her arms around his neck.

It had been over five years since Titus had kissed a woman. Tiberius, in particular, mocked him about it, usually whilst he was in the company of some seedy bar prostitute, but Titus didn't care. He knew he had more taste than Tiberius.

The kiss was all he had been expecting. He had waited for her for so long. As he felt her soft lips brush against his, his hand reached round, and undid the ribbon holding her dress at her waist. She kissed him again, pushing her body up against his. His hand slid down her back, resting just above her buttocks. As he pulled her, towards him her mouth opened, and she moaned softly with need. Her dress slipped down to the floor and she kicked it away.

She took him by the hand and rushed upstairs, giggling as she tripped halfway, bringing Titus crashing down upon her on the stairs. They kissed again, Titus' hands running up her arms and caressing her cheeks as they stared into each other eyes. He didn't feel so alone now.

He let Ceinwyn escape from underneath him and she used the freedom to run upstairs to her room. Titus followed but was surprised to find the door locked shut.

'Ceinwyn!' He called surprised. 'Let me in.'

'One minute,' she shouted back.

Titus tapped his foot impatiently. Was she having second thoughts? Maybe he was taking things too quickly? But then they had waited nearly four months since they had met. He had never known a girl for this long. The door clicked open; the room inside was almost dark. He stepped in.

Five candles burnt on the high wooden bed rail, and in the corner a small incense burner had been lit and was pouring out the smell of sandalwood. Ceinwyn sat on the bed. She was wearing the tie for a toga wrapped around her middle, and nothing else. Titus gasped and was suddenly desperate for her. She beckoned him over and took off his clothes slowly, kissing his bare chest as she eased off his shirt. She knelt down and, undoing his belt, pulled his trousers to the floor. As she looked up at him and smiled, he suddenly felt slightly sick with fear—would he be able to make her happy? It had been so long. She took him in her hands and he closed his eyes to enjoy the sensations. She bent forwards. He felt warmth engulf him, and a groan escaped his tightly clenched lips.

She stopped and looked up at him again, 'I don't know what I'm doing.' Her voice was shaky and he could see her hands were trembling. 'It's my first time.'

He took her by the hands and pulled her back to her feet. 'I've never loved anyone before, so its new for us both.' He kissed her. 'Lay down.'

She lay on her front on the bed. Titus couldn't help but stare at her beautiful bottom and the perfect curve of her hips. Did she realise how beautiful she was?

He lay down next to her and began to rub her back gently, starting at her shoulders, letting his thumbs work their way between her vertebrae. He felt her begin to relax. He reached over and let his kisses trail his fingers; kissing her neck gently; feeling the downy invisible hair that all women had; enjoying it standing on end as his breath cooled her skin. His kisses reached her hips and he felt her tense. Sensing her excitement he teased her, changing the angle so that his mouth ran down the side of one buttock and down her left leg. She groaned and moved her legs apart.

'Titus, I. . .' Her voice was husky. 'I need you.'

He put pressure on her hip, helping her roll over. Her face and chest were flushed dark pink with excitement. He looked down at her perfect firm breasts, and the beautiful nest of copper curls between her legs. He wanted her too, but he had to make it special for her.

'You are beautiful.'

She smiled and started to cry.

Reaching forwards, he kissed her face as she sobbed, trying to take her tears away. He held her tightly.

'Am I?' she managed to croak. He nodded and held her more tightly. 'I never looked right. I'm not Roman, but I'm not Slave either. My father always said I was beautiful, but he had to say that.'

'You are, and I'm going to show you.' He lay her back on the pillow, and kissed her neck. She arched it and he felt her body rise up towards him as his kisses moved downwards towards her breasts. As he reached the left one, he paused before cupping it gently in his hand, and taking the dark nipple in his mouth. She moaned again and he saw her head thrash from side to side for a couple of seconds as he drew the nipple further in and licked. His hand gently stroked the side of her breast as her breathing quickened.

'Titus please.' She was insistent now. He took his mouth away from the nipple and kissed further down, just under her belly button, next to the blue toga tie which lay loosely over her tummy. She moaned with frustration as his kisses moved further towards her. He took her legs in his hands, gently parted them, and moving her to the edge of the bed, knelt down.

'I love you.' He liked the phrase, and wondered if he would ever tire of it. She was too excited to reply. He remembered his first time, and wished he had had someone who had some idea of what they were doing to teach him then. He let the tip of his tongue linger just below her opening and braced himself. Her whole lower body arched in the air as she cried out. He waited for her to recover before letting his tongue gently fall back into place. He let it caress up and down, always stopping short of the bundle of nerves at the front of her.

'Titus,' she gasped, trying to stay still, 'that tickles.' She laughed.

Titus laughed back so hard that he had to stop for a second. He stood up and kissed her mouth again. 'Sorry,' he said.

'I didn't mean you to stop,' she said, smiling seductively again. 'More.' She laughed again, obviously enjoying ordering a Roman around for the first time in her life.

Titus nodded and knelt down again. He started to kiss her again as before, but she was more used to it now and pushed herself forwards trying to get his tongue where she needed it. Eventually, when she couldn't cope with it any more, he let her.

Her gasps were so loud now that he was sure Cyric would hear them down below in the basement. He tried to forget about him, but he couldn't help but share in his pain. If Ceinwyn had been there now with Cyric, he knew exactly how he would feel. Ceinwyn's mouth was wide open, every stroke of his tongue bringing out a fresh cry of pleasure. He could tell she was close. He used his hand to gently tickle the top of her legs, and as he did so he felt her whole body tense. Laying completely rigid with her back arched in the air, she seemed to breath in constantly for an age and then let it out in a long, satisfied moan.

Titus stood up and lay down next to her. He kissed her closed eyes and rubbed her back gently. She started to shiver, so he covered her over with the sheet. She seemed tired; maybe he should let her sleep? His whole body hoped she was just enjoying the moment. Then she opened her eyes.

'I think it's your turn.'

He smiled and started to move over her.

'No. You lay down.'

Titus was surprised, but did what she asked. She sat up and putting one leg over him sat on the top of his thighs straddling him. She reached down and undid the toga tie. He closed his eyes, expecting her to slide forwards onto him but instead he felt cool material brush over him as she wrapped the toga tie around him in a simple loop. He groaned as she slowly pulled the material from end to end, causing it to twirl around him. She changed the angle slightly so that the material coursed up and rubbed over the tip of him, and he opened his mouth, and gasped. 'Ceinwyn, please.' Then he realised what she was doing and laughed. 'Enough teasing now.'

She nodded and slid forwards onto him.

He looked up and watched her gorgeous body bounce up and down gently on him in the soft candlelight. Her eyes remained fixed on his; he felt like he could see into her soul. His hands caressed her bottom as she gently moved him closer to finishing. He felt the moment coming and pulled her forwards to him, so that she lay on top of him, her breasts pressed hard against his chest. She was moving faster now, and his hands pressed firmly into her back guiding her.

She tightened again and he felt pleasure come on her in waves, as it had done before. She clenched her teeth, but the moan was still loud enough to carry to the basement. It was too much for Titus, as her pleasure carried him over the edge as well.

As the pleasure slowly faded, he realised she was still laying on top of him. He rolled onto his side so that they lay side by side, but still locked together. He kissed her and slid out, missing the warmth. He felt a brief moment of sadness; it felt like regret, but he regretted nothing; the *parva mortum*. He took a deep breath and hugged Ceinwyn close to him. She was already half asleep. He closed his eyes, hoping they could share dreams.

Then suddenly, and with no warning, a plan slipped fully formed into Titus' mind. A genius plan; one that would save Quintus. He looked down at her sleeping figure.

'Thank you,' he whispered.

XX

'Londinium? Marcus splurted into his coffee. 'Why on Earth would you want to go there?'

'To ask for help: the Praetorian Guard here are subordinate to the guard headquarters,' Titus replied. 'If I can persuade them to help, there is nothing Strabo can do but go along with it.'

'He won't like you going above his head.'

'That's why I have to leave today, before he has a chance to stop me,' Titus said, thinking of the checkpoint at the main road into the town.

Marcus nodded in assent, sipped from his glass of water and grimaced.

'Urgh. What's wrong with your tap?' he said.

Titus sniffed the water, 'smells fine,' he remarked. He tasted it, 'hmmm. Actually that's really stale.' He rose to get a fresh glass from the kitchen tap.

'What about Cyric, and Ceinwyn?' Marcus asked.

'They need to be moved—my house is no longer safe. We need to hide them somewhere, but don't worry, I've thought of that too.' Titus walked back from the kitchen and sat down. He had a feeling that if

Marcus found out how this inspired plan had come to him, they would no longer be friends.

'I know a place, deep in the hills—a remote cave. Gnaeus told me that a Christian priest once hid there from persecution. You could hide them there.'

'Do you know where the cave is? You can't take Gnaeus with you.'

'He showed me on his maps when he told me about the priest. He planned on taking a look next summer. I reckon I could find it.'

'I don't think we should hide them together,' Titus said, 'they have fallen out.' He wished he could explain to Marcus why they had fallen out, once again cursing his cowardice. He thought of Cyric's face earlier that morning as he had walked downstairs from Ceinwyn's bed; the mixture of loathing and jealousy. The worst of it was he could imagine the same look on Marcus' face. He didn't trust Cyric around Ceinwyn any more. Some time apart would most likely help restore their friendship.

'We have to keep them together,' Marcus said, 'otherwise they will be alone until you come back. They will need someone for company.'

'You could look after them,' Titus suggested.

'I can't look after them both unless they are together. I can't be in two places at once!' Marcus said, laughing.

'Why don't you look after Cyric then,' Titus said, 'take him to this cave, and I'll take Ceinwyn to Londinium—she'll be safe with me,' he smiled at his plan, imagining himself, and Ceinwyn exploring the Britannic capital.

'Take Ceinwyn to Londinium? Are you insane? Disguising her as anything but,' he paused, 'what she is, would be nearly impossible. But Cyric could pass as your Slave. He would make you less conspicuous than if you were on your own.'

Titus smiled at his friend's obvious ulterior motive and he wished he could find an easy way to tell him what had happened between Ceinwyn and himself last night, but he was unable to find the words. He nodded assent and Marcus, clearly excited by the prospect of a week or more alone with Ceinwyn, explained that that he would lie to the others, claiming to be going to Londinium with Titus. There was no harm in telling the others of their intentions, as long as they did not mention Cyric, or Ceinwyn.

138

The last part of the plan was the bit that hurt Titus the most, even more than a week away from Ceinwyn. Once the Praetorians had rescued Quintus they would run. He had wrangled with his conscience most of the night, because it put his father at great risk from Strabo. However it kept his men safe, and would take Ceinwyn far away from her former tormentor. Perhaps if he got to Rome fast enough, he could still save his father. But the plan still felt cowardly.

'Kill your boss for me.' Her words to him, and his promise to her still echoed in his head. This plan ignored his promise, but there was no other choice, Strabo was too powerful. She would understand.

He looked down at his breakfast, neglected and almost cold. He didn't have the stomach for it anyway. He reached for his glass of water and downed it in one, grimacing at the, still bitter, taste.

As darkness fell over Luguvalium, Titus and Marcus made their move. The others thought they were heading out alone, and to a casual onlooker they appeared to do so. Only a careful observer would have realised that the two figures following a hundred yards behind, wrapped up against the bitter cold, were in fact tailing them.

Titus stopped by the two curri at the end of the road. 'These things are knackered Marcus! What were you thinking?'

'They are unobtrusive,' Marcus replied, haughtily. It was certainly true. All curri, bar a few reserved for the nobility, were ex-military specification. Most had been painted and had the tracks replaced with wheels to be more attractive and practical on the roads, and all had had the weapon emplacements removed. These two rust coated behemoths before them hadn't even been painted; they were dented and coated in filth.

'Where did you find them?' Titus asked.

'On a farm to the south of the city.'

Titus still looked uncertain.

'They were cheap,' Marcus added.

The two slaves had reached them now. Ceinwyn removed her shawl from round her head; it took all of Titus' will power to do nothing more than smile at her. Cyric's scowl was visible even beneath the Dacian head-scarf Titus had lent him. They had both agreed to the plan—Ceinwyn with tears at first, when she learnt of her enforced separation from Titus, but once she had understood the reasoning she was happy enough. Titus knew she had a great liking for Marcus; the two of them would be happy together while Titus was gone.

Cyric was still scowling. He had not taken well to the plan, particularly as he understood much of its necessary complexity was due to his foolishness in trying to turn Ceinwyn against Titus, and revealing himself to one of Strabo's messengers. But Titus wondered if, in his place, perhaps he would have done the same.

'Get in,' Titus snapped at Cyric, who stamped his way round to the passenger side, and wrenched open the battered door.

'This is a piece of shit, Roman.'

'It was cheap.' Titus replied, 'and it is the best you're going to get, unless you want to go back to Strabo.'

'If I go back to Strabo she goes back too.' He smiled at Titus mischievously.

Titus had not expected him to appreciate the tension between himself and Marcus over Ceinwyn. He paused for a second, not sure how to react, as Cyric continued.

'You wouldn't like that would you? I guess you wouldn't mind if I was taken back though, but then I don't have...'

'Shut up, get in the vehicle, and strap in,' Titus roared at the boy, who jumped into the vehicle as fast as his legs could carry him.

Marcus looked at Titus quizzically.

'He's a strange lad,' Titus said.

'Indeed,' Marcus replied.

Had he guessed? Titus could not be sure. He turned to Ceinwyn, 'Marcus will look after you now.' She nodded and walked towards him. Her hair was still partly covered by the shawl, yet a few copper strands rippled loosely in the cold night air. He wanted to kiss her again, take her to Londinium with him, spend another night with her. She reached her arms around him and hugged. He returned the hug (trying to make it seem as friendly as possible), whilst over her shoulder he smiled disarmingly at Marcus.

Ceinwyn seemed to understand the predicament she had put Titus in. After hugging him, she turned to Marcus, threw her arms round him too, and whispered in his ear. He smiled too, returning her hug far more eagerly than Titus had. Yet throughout the whole of their embrace, her eyes never left Titus'. 'I love you,' she mouthed silently over Marcus' shoulder. Marcus didn't seem to notice, excited as he was at the thought of him and Ceinwyn alone, just the two of them. The thought filled Titus with dread.

Londinium

XXI

Not for the first time that day Titus wished that Cyric had died trying to escape from Strabo's compound. The sulking adolescent was more than he could bear. Every time that Titus chided the boy for his insolence he just retorted with 'you made me come with you.' Titus would have loved to simply leave the boy at the edge of the road, but he had promised Ceinwyn he would look after him. Although Ceinwyn clearly did not love the boy, as she had proven to him rather emphatically last night, it was clear that she cared deeply for him; a care born out of a long imprisonment, with each looking out for the other. He could not harm Cyric, and in truth he felt sorry for him: there are few men who have not felt the pain of losing a woman to another man. He thought about Marcus and the pain that inevitably he would suffer. He sighed.

The road south curved its way down past the hills of Rheged, weaving a tight course between them and the long line of hills that formed the backbone of Britannia. The old currus drove as badly as it looked and Titus kept his hands firmly on the wheel for fear that it might spin off the road at any moment. Cyric mocked him again as yet another young Roman with a fast currus shot past him. He remembered the days when he had been young and he, too, had enjoyed the thrill of a fast currus. There were companies that could do pretty much anything to them for the right price. It didn't stop the drivers looking like idiots though, Titus thought laughing to himself. Cyric refused to laugh, even when Titus made an obscene gesture at the driver suggesting that the fast currus, with the extensively modified exhaust system, might be making up for an inadequacy elsewhere in his life, but Titus laughed enough for both of them.

As they continued further south the ground flattened out. Titus had spent time in many parts of Britannia, but he always felt that the high places were the best. He had no love for Londinium, a place he had only visited once, and then only briefly, and he had no love for Cyric, but necessity dictated his current actions. This would be a trip to be endured.

As they passed through other settlements, it was clear which parts of the towns were Roman and which were mainly inhabited by Slaves. There were always too many Slaves for Romans in the provinces. Many had no choice but to find corrugated iron to make shelters and live their lives on the edge of society, as best they could. Cyric glowered at Titus every time they drove near one of these shanty towns.

'How long will it be before you decide to kill us?'

'What?' Titus asked, confused

'Slaves. Like me. When will the genocide happen.'

'I don't understand.'

'Look out there,' he said, pointing at the corrugated roofs packed tightly together. 'You don't need that many of us.'

'No.' Titus agreed, but still didn't get Cyric's question.

'You don't need us anymore: you have machines to do everything we can do.'

Titus understood, but surely the Senate would never condone slaughter on that scale? But Slaves were animals in the Senate's eyes. He felt slightly sick, and not just from the uneven rocking of the broken currus.

'What was she like?' Cyric spoke again, changing the subject.

'She is the most lovely person I have ever met.' Titus replied, sidestepping the question.

'You know that's not what I asked.'

144

'You know I'm not going to tell you.'

Cyric folded his arms over his chest again and sighed loudly.

Titus tried to break the animosity, 'for what it's worth Cyric, I am sorry I hurt you.'

Cyric did not reply.

'I do love her, you know,' Titus said.

'I love her too.'

'If you truly love her Cyric, then you have to let her choose.'

'Even if she chooses some Roman bastard, who cares nothing for her?' Cyric spat on the floor of the currus. The rain started coming down hard, battering the windscreen.

'I love her,' Titus reiterated, and pulled on the small lever that started the wiping blades.

Cyric shook his head. Neither spoke for some time, but, instead, stared out at the driving rain, listening to the rhythmic squeaking of the worn blades on the blurry glass. High on the hillside above, a farmer was driving a small reconnaissance vehicle up a nearby fell side, to bring his sheep in for the coming winter.

As the currus lumbered south both men noticed how the land became more prosperous; as the North country ruled by Strabo was left behind, they drove through towns full of shops. As the weather improved, they noticed markets in some of the villages they passed by. There was production, and produce being sold. The Reivers did not venture this far from the north lands. It was a vision to Titus of what Luguvalium might have been like, before the Reivers had strangled it.

'You hate Strabo?' Titus asked, it was more of a statement than a question.

'He is a Roman, so, yes, I hate him.'

'I'm going to ruin him.'

'You should kill him,' replied the boy, '*he* has no qualms about killing.'

'He needs to be exposed for what he has done,' explained Titus, 'killing him would only lead to a worse life when someone else takes his place. Rome needs to investigate, and employ someone respectable in his place.' He did not believe his own words, so how could he expect Cyric to.

'Did Rome not appoint Strabo?'

'Even Rome can make mistakes,' Titus replied.

'I doubt Rome would make such a convenient mistake,' Cyric replied, 'Strabo seems the sort of man Rome would want in Luguvalium; a harsh ruler, greedy, someone who can extort and won't let people get in his way. Rome has no love for Luguvalium.'

'Rome must care. Why else safeguard the lands at all?'

The boy took a moment to reply while he stared at the road ahead, his sullen expression now gone; he was enjoying the discussion. Finally he spoke: 'Rome only cares for Rome. Rome wants land for money and produce and it needs governors who can get that. That is why Strabo is there.'

Titus shook his head, 'I hope that whoever comes next will be better than Strabo, I will do what I can.' He stroked his chin knowing that, sadly, he had little power to do anything about who was the next governor.

'You don't plan to be the next governor, do you?' the boy asked, the scowl back on his face.

'I can see no way that could ever happen—you would have to be a noble for a start.'

'Ceinwyn told me you are a noble,' sneered the boy.

Titus ignored the insult, 'yes I am, and I was once proud of it,' he added. 'But the years have been harsh on us; my nobility was as good as lost when I entered the army too low for my social standing. We could not afford to buy the commission.'

'So you fought your way to the top?' Cyric seemed quite interested now.

'Yes, and then all the way to the bottom again once we had won the last war.'

'They didn't need you any more.'

Titus nodded his head.

'I imagine they gave you a pension, homes, healthcare,' Cyric asked with a knowing smile.

Titus shook his head.

'And you still think genocide for my people is far fetched? They didn't need you, so they discarded you. They don't need us.'

'I still can't believe Rome would do that.'

146

'You know Strabo! And you dare say that? Did you not see what he did to us?'

'I am not like Strabo.' Titus said, 'and not every Roman is either. I hate the man. I treat Ceinwyn well and with respect. I love her, and I promise you, as I have promised her, that I will do everything in my power to oust Strabo from his position, and make him pay.'

'Your word means nothing to me Roman,' Cyric folded his arms and turned to stare defiantly out of the currus window.

Titus nodded, 'that's fair—you have no reason to trust me yet. Give me some time.' The boy huffed and stared out of the window again, but Titus could tell his words had at least had some effect.

He looked to the south. To his left the sun was now above the horizon and the dwindling rain now swirled above the rich farmland in incandescent light. He smiled to himself, wound down the window and breathed in the crisp morning air. He felt alive again, for the first time since the end of the war he was fighting for something he actually believed in.

It was late in the afternoon by the time they reached Londinium. The air was noticeably warmer than in Luguvalium, surprisingly so for winter. Apparently it had not snowed in Londinum for ten years. No one knew why but it had just got too warm. As they approached the city, they were directed down a slip-road. The screens above the road dictated that they should slow down to accept a scan.

Despite the ostensibly peaceful nature of the Roman Empire, it was still necessary to scan all vehicles entering the larger cities; there was the ever present threat of unrest and, more recently, the occasional home-made explosive device smuggled into a public place. Titus, with his new knowledge, now suspected that it was perhaps the work of Slaves. However with the public perception being that Slaves were nowhere near intelligent enough to construct the crude bombs, it was attributed to separatists from Asia Minor. It was not a war: the media made this very clear—there had been no war for ten years; a point that Marcus Albus made much of in his speeches, to a Rome finally weary from nearly two millennia of subjugation.

It was simply unrest.

Titus sensed Cyric's worry as they slowly passed the scanning gantry; a beam of light passed around the vehicle betraying the low dose of X-rays they and their luggage were receiving. Ahead was a portcullis gantry—a sheet of reinforced metal ready to fall should the scire system decide that they needed a more formal search. Titus was not unduly worried for they carried nothing contraband—his sonifi were all legal. He had purposefully not brought any explosives; as a mercenary he would probably have been able to leave them at the gates, however he did not think it likely he would ever get them back. Much of the equipment he carried would fetch a good price on the black market.

The light on the portcullis above stayed red as they approached.

'They're not going to let us in,' said Cyric, his voice rising with fear.

Titus didn't reply. He just kept driving at the open portcullis, hoping it would not shut. He wondered if maybe it could shut on the currus, but brushed the thought from his mind realising there must be safeguards to stop that from happening. He distrusted machines deeply though, and the worry remained. Why can't we just go into Asia Minor and wipe out the terrorists? he wondered to himself as the light turned green and Cyric let out a long held breath.

Leaving the portcullis far behind, he drove into the heart of the city. The streets became more crowded the further in they travelled. Titus realised how much cleaner than Luguvalium it was: there was no rubbish piled up and many of the houses were brand new. Unlike Luguvalium however, the people seemed far less approachable, staring at the ground as they walked hurriedly, trying to avoid eye contact with each other.

Titus wasn't entirely sure where the Praetorian Guard headquarters was but he knew it would be in the ancient centre of the city, rather than a new development. All Romans liked history and tradition—the Praetorian Guard more than most.

As he drove slowly under the rotting walls of the old city of Londinium, he thought back to the people of Britannia who had built them in the first place—the Britons, Ceinwyn's people. There were many of them still in Britannia, and the few who had not gained Roman citizenship tended to live in remote areas.

Once through the old walls they left behind any vestiges of normality. The city within was a museum, paved in old stone, with the great towers, built by the great General Vespasian, soaring into the sky over the Senate building. This was of course only a replica of the Senate building in Rome to remind the people of Britannia who ruled them; no Senate ever sat in it for only one Senate could exist, voted in by all Roman citizens around the globe. Titus wondered how on Earth the senate had managed to organise elections fifty years ago before the omniajunctus was invented. People would have had to travel all over the world to Rome to vote in the ballots on the Field of Mars. The vote could not be carried out in the provinces, for that was against Roman law. The omniajunctus allowed the vote to be collated centrally in Rome, but people could vote from a scire locally; a neat loophole which had greatly increased the electoral turnout, and had benefited Marcus Albus and his family immensely. Their popularity in the provinces meant that a member of his family had been consul every year since the new system was brought in.

It wasn't easy for Titus to find a place to park the currus, for it would be taken away and destroyed unless left in a designated space, and there were few of those and many curri. The city was far too busy.

'What do we do now?' asked Cyric, his sullen expression back once more.

'Too late to go to the Guard tonight. It looks like we have to find a place to stay.'

The pair only had to walk a couple of hundred yards before they came across a suitable pub.

The Consul's Head, the battered hanging sign read. Titus tutted to himself as he realised that they had got the cases backwards, so it actually read *The Head's Consul*. Out in the provinces, far from Rome, grammar could get lax. Still, once the door was open and the warmth from the open fire reached them he managed to forgive the proprietors for their illiteracy. Even Cyric seemed pleased, and Titus wondered if maybe the young man had never been in a pub. It was unlikely that he had—Strabo wasn't exactly likely to have taken him out for the evening.

The bar was perfect. Dingy, with small tables secreted into nooks and arches around the ancient walls. Looking around he noted that most of the clientele kept their heads down, nodding surreptitiously to their companions. It was the sort of pub where secret dealings were allowed to stay that way. The pair made their way to an empty table far away from the fire; no one turned to look at them as they passed. 'You ever drunk beer boy?' Titus asked Cyric, who laughed. 'You know we can't.'

Titus shook his head at his own stupidity. Slaves were almost exclusively unable to process alcohol, if they drank any they got drunk very quickly, felt hot and then vomited. If they drank too much they could even die. Their genes were different.

'But I have tried beer,' Cyric said, surprising Titus, 'a friend who worked on the markets for Strabo smuggled some in one night. I had a bit, and I felt OK. Maybe I'm one of the lucky ones.'

'Good lad,' Titus said, remembering his days in the military academy when similar incidents had occurred.

'Dead lad.' Cyric whispered pulling the torn cloak up over his face, a mark of respect to the Romans in the bar, who should not have to look upon the face of a Slave whilst revelling unless they should wish to: even Cyric understood that this was not the time to be overly conspicuous.

Titus didn't reply. He got up and went to the bar returning with two pewter mugs brimming with ale.

'This is the good stuff, brewed next door—the small breweries are always the best.' He lifted the mug to his lips, 'drink to your friend's memory?'

Cyric, his mug halfway to his mouth, slammed it back down onto the table. 'How dare you drink to his memory, Roman?' he hissed.

Silence fell suddenly over the previously lively bar. Everyone in the pub was looking at them now. Cyric realised it and took the scowl from his face, trying to look submissive to the people in the bar, whilst maintaining his defiance for Titus to see.

'If you do that again, I promise I will beat you,' Titus hissed quietly, but loud enough for the other drinkers to hear. They went back to drinking; a large group of men in the corner went back to their gambling on red and black cards. 'Everyone here expects you to obey me: we have to act as master and slave, or else we will be discovered.'

150

'Why don't you just tell them the truth?' Cyric whispered, his head bowed in apparent deference before Titus.

Titus didn't reply.

'It's because you are a coward,' Cyric tried to say it with conviction, already knowing the answer but unable to accept it.

Titus spoke the truth—Cyric already knew. 'They won't understand, look around you.' Titus gestured at the drinkers clustered around the fire, all old Romans. 'Do you truly believe that if I stand up and tell them the truth, they will do anything whatsoever about it? Their own Slaves are probably too scared of them to corroborate our tale. They don't want to believe that Slaves are more than animals, so they never will.'

'But you have standing amongst them,' Cyric continued, exasperated.

'A mercenary! To them I'm scum.'

Titus took a long drink, thinking about how he had fallen from being a general. 'How strange,' he confided in Cyric. 'You know I used to long for peace. I never thought of what it would bring.'

'You would rather be at war?'

'I would rather have a purpose. Like this, petitioning the Guard for my friend; its better than just fighting for money.'

'Easier than doing something that might make a *real* difference.'

The boy took a sip from the pewter tankard, and grimaced at the taste.

'Too strong for you?' Titus asked.

'No, just perfect thank you,' Cyric replied, downing the rest of the pint; there were tears in his eyes when he had finished, and just the hint of a flush to his face. Perhaps Cyric was one of the lucky slaves who could drink a little alcohol.

Titus laughed. 'You do have spirit you know, I admire that.'

The boy just glowered at him as Titus realised that, despite his misgivings and against his better judgement, he was actually starting to like him.

XXII

The bed was probably the least comfortable that Quintus had ever slept on. He thought back over the Transmaritanus campaign, dwelling on the nights sleeping rough, but no, nothing had been quite as bad as the hovel that the Reivers had given him. The main problem was the leash around his neck, bolted into the rear wall. The cable on this was only a couple of metres long, which prevented him from leaving the hovel to relieve himself. It would make sense, Quintus thought, for them to have left some sort of pot for him to go in. Presumably it was all part of the entertainment. They did seem to find him rather entertaining.

In the five days since his capture Quintus had come to learn a fair bit about the Reivers. At first of course he had expected to die, and so drinking in every last detail about their society, and trying to work out the location of the secret camp they were in, was far from his mind. However, after two days and nights of expecting imminent death Quintus began to relax slightly.

They didn't treat him well of course; he was beaten and booted around the camp when he wasn't tied to his leash. But they seemed genuinely keen to keep him alive, even to the extent that when a beating resulted in a large cut across his back, they actually sent the camp doctor to stitch the wound, without anaesthetic of course, but then he had at least prescribed some unpleasant tasting antibiotics afterwards. They were not what Quintus would have prescribed himself of course, but then they were out in the sticks.

Conditions seemed to have improved since the self appointed leader of this band of Reivers had returned from a sortie, and discovered that they had a high born captive. The Reivers were very family orientated, this man, it seemed, owed his high position to the fact that his family were at that moment the most powerful and, as the head of the family, he therefore lead the Reivers. Although this was the first band that Quintus had come across he gathered that there were others nearby, and that they were loosely allied. It also seemed from the behaviour of envoys from other camps, that they saw this man as a chief over their own chiefs.

It was hard for Quintus to tell much more as the Reivers tended to speak in their old Britannic language. The few months they had spent in Britannia had only been enough for Quintus to pick up a little, but that which he knew was mainly pleasantries, and these didn't come in particularly useful in the Reiver camp. He spoke Latin to the Reivers, mainly cursing them, which they clearly understood, even if they only cursed back in Britannic.

Sitting in his hovel, in the one patch that was so far free of his own excrement, Quintus decided how best to ration the one can of corned beef he still had from before his capture. While he agonised over this, he listened to the conversation going on in the camp below. Britannic sounded like a man choking to death on his own phlegm. He longed to hear Latin spoken again.

He wouldn't have to wait long.

Later that evening, Quintus awoke to the sound of commotion in the camp; there was a chill in the air and the sun had sunk down almost to the horizon. The Reivers were getting into defensive positions, picking up their weapons from where they had drunkenly dropped them the night before. A few men pulled on army jackets, clearly looted from previous victims, but most wore dirty civilian clothes augmented with trophies. These ranged from bandoliers of rounds that did not fit the gauge of the sonifi they carried, to idols of the gods looted from unlucky travellers. There was even some contraband on display—one man had a crucifix around his neck. Quintus hadn't seen many of those before, making one was illegal, wearing one was to invite banishment. Gnaeus had one, but even he wasn't foolish enough to wear it openly. Presumably this Reiver had no idea of its significance, or then again, as an outlaw, banishment was probably the least of his worries—where would he be banished to?

The men didn't seem to be expecting an attack. They stood at their posts smoking, eating and shouting; the three things that seemed to feature most heavily in a Reiver's life, when he wasn't off pillaging. In fact they seemed to have gone to their positions only to show a readiness to defend their camp, if it was truly threatened. It was a show of strength. Something which they did not bother with when visited by Reivers from another camp, which could only mean that whoever was approaching was important and foreign to them.

Quintus moved to the door of the hovel, as far as his leash would permit. To his frustration he still could not see what was going on. From the sound of things a man was being greeted, and there was the sound of a currus being parked. It sounded very different to the dejected ones owned by the Reivers. The engine was smooth and new, whoever had bought it had spent a lot of money converting it. He wished he could see it and the person it carried. He craned his neck forwards and strained to see if he could make out any of the few words he knew. He needn't have tried so hard for the guest was a Roman, and was not in the mood to speak any Britannic.

From the sound of his voice the man was well bred but it was not a voice he recognised. The Reiver who spoke with him was definitely none other than the Captain himself. He had questioned Quintus after his capture, and spoke Latin relatively well, albeit with a strong accent.

Quintus wouldn't go so far as to say that the Captain liked him, but he did seem to realise his importance as a hostage. Had it not been for him he expected the others would have put him to death by now. The looks they cast in his direction when they used the door of his hovel as a latrine, told him in no uncertain terms what they would like to do to him if their leader would allow it.

154

Despite being only a few yards away, Quintus didn't catch all of the conversation. Whenever something interesting was mentioned it seemed that a Reiver close by would have a coughing fit and prevent Quintus hearing most of it. Whether this was done on purpose or was more to do with the horrendous sanitary conditions impacting on the Reivers' health, Quintus was not sure.

'How is your master?' he heard the Reiver Captain asking.

'Well enough, I suppose. He comes to claim what is his.' It seemed from the silence that followed that the Reivers had not expected the Roman to get to the point so soon.

'We will provide the money,' the Captain replied gruffly, clearly angry that his word had been doubted.

'When?' The Roman was persistent.

'You can have it now, part paid in goods, or all in a week once we have traded the goods for sestertii.'

'And what if my master wants it all in cash, now?' The voice was menacing, but controlled.

'He cannot have it.' From the intake of breath down in the camp, Quintus could only assume that the Captain had turned his back on the Roman visitor.

'Can I remind you,' came the Roman's voice, 'that if it were not for me and my master you would have nothing.'

There was no reply from the Reiver.

'Ten percent is all we ask for. Ten percent of nothing is, of course, nothing.'

'Tell your master he can wait till next week, or he gets nothing.'
Another fit of coughing from below left Quintus seething with frustration.

'Any prisoners?' Quintus heard the Roman ask after the coughing. He was not sure how the previous argument had been settled, if indeed it had. Still, the Roman had changed the subject, his voice cheery now, but a hint of malice remained.

Quintus' heart leapt; maybe this Roman would pay his ransom. He opened his mouth to shout out, but then to his surprise he did nothing. He could have called to the man, he was only a score of yards away, but something in his head told him that being a prisoner here was safer than being free with the Roman.

It mattered little though, for here was the chance for the Reivers to ransom him. He waited for the Captain to give him away, still unsure why that thought worried him.

'No. We have no prisoners.' Quintus coughed with shock, bringing his hand to his mouth to muffle the sound lest he be heard by the Roman.

'Are you sure?'

Quintus was confused by the Roman's words—why would he be so persistent?

'No,' the reply was emphatic, 'we have no prisoners.'

'A mercenary was lost in the woods a few days ago,' the Roman was all matter of fact now, too much so. 'You wouldn't know anything about him would you?'

'There are a lot of wolves in the woods.'

Silence again. Quintus wondered if the two men were staring each other down, waiting for one to break. Still no words came.

'Take my compliments to your master,' it was the Captain bidding the Roman goodbye.

Quintus sat back, listening, as the currus drove away. From the sound of the tyres he could be certain that the road leading from the camp became metalled within a few hundred yards. They couldn't be too far from civilisation. He filed the information away, and put his head in his hands to think. Nothing that had been said between the Roman and the Reiver made any sense.

He was woken again with a rough shake of the shoulders. It was dusk the sun's last rays playing over the hovel as the wind blew the bare branches above.

'What is your name, mercenary?' It was the Reiver Captain again. He had asked Quintus' name before, but all he had received was a shake of the head, for which Quintus had received a beating, quid pro quo.

Quintus shook his head again.

'Why did you run away?'

'Run away?' Quintus said, confused and still drowsy, could they have slipped something into his water, he wondered?

156

'Run away,' the Reiver reiterated, 'do not be ashamed; I would run from your employer as well.' The man chuckled, 'look, I have brought you some ale—it's a bit stale but it's the best I can do,' he looked around furtively before adding, 'don't tell my men—I have a reputation to keep.'

'Why did you not ransom me?'

'To draw out your death of course!' The Captain tilted his head back and laughed raucously. 'We are Reivers! You've heard the stories; evil bastards who come in the night, rape the women, carry the children off and pillage the lands.' He smiled, and Quintus realised that the Captain was not being entirely serious.

'Where are you from?' asked the Captain, changing the subject.

The question was so out of the blue that Quintus found he had answered it before he could stop himself—they must have drugged him.

'Rome, eh?' The Captain played with his beard, deep in thought. 'That makes sense.'

He leant forwards so his face was nearly touching Quintus'. 'Between you and me,' he whispered, 'I think our master is too rich to be from these parts originally. Rome makes sense. Why did he send you here?'

Quintus shook his head. 'I haven't been to Rome for years.'

The Captain looked confused.

'You say you know your master is rich?' asked Quintus.

'Did you hear the amount they tried to take from me? Daylight robbery!'

'I thought that was your speciality,' replied Quintus.

The Captain frowned for a second, then suddenly his face split into a wide grin and he laughed; a huge booming sound that filled the hovel. Quintus realised he was much younger than he had thought, in fact not much older than himself, and he was sure he had seen him somewhere before.

'Night time robbery, that's more my speciality. Now what is your name?'

Quintus told him—it couldn't do much harm now. He asked the Captain his in return.

'Graham Armstrong.' The name meant nothing to Quintus. 'Leader of the strongest Reiver family, the Armstrongs' he continued, shaking his bicep in Quintus' face; obviously the sign of the family. It made sense when Quintus thought about it.

At this the Captain left the hovel, stalking off into the darkening evening. Quintus lay down to sleep, or at least he pretended to, but beneath the facade his mind was working fast with only one goal. Escape.

XXIII

Titus stood in the crisp morning air outside the gates of the Praetorian Guard's Britannia headquarters. Despite its ancient grandeur, Titus thought it was still a shadow of its counterpart in Rome. The Praetorian Guard had once been elite soldiers of Rome, designated to protect the Senate. In time though, as all things do, the situation changed. The army was away on permanent duty as the wars intensified, and the Praetorian Guard had increasingly found themselves a police force rather than a ceremonial guard. They put down unrest when needed; they even took over from the Lictors (bodyguards who had once followed senators around ready to beat away any troublemakers with their bundle of rods—the fasces). Eventually they had become a power in their own right, although one very much under the control of the Senate. But one thing had not changed, for, like the Lictors before them, they too carried fasces.

Titus could see Cyric staring in awe at the fasces held by the nearest Praetorian. The guard stood stock still, clad head to toe in black body armour; only his eyes and mouth were visible under the riot helmet. The fasces looked menacing, and indeed it was, a blow could either stun or kill, depending on the setting chosen by the bearer. There was no unrest in

Londinium at present so Titus assumed this guard would have the fasces set to its lowest setting. He could see the occasional flicker from the induction coil set in its base, as the power it gathered from the underground transmitters ebbed and flowed. Titus shivered at the thought of that power somehow being beamed around and through him; every scrap of matter that made him somehow permeated by it. Yet he could not feel that awesome force which passed through his body. He had felt it before though, when enough of it had been concentrated in one place. It had been long ago, but he remembered it as if it was yesterday: the buzzing in his ears first; then the hairs rising up all over his body; the pressure building up. That otherworldly whine of the Jupiter machine grating in his ears.

'Remember, you are my Slave,' Titus spoke to Cyric, clearing his head, as they approached the wrought iron gates gilt with the SPQR of the Roman army. The guard remained still, but spoke into the tip of the fasces, his voice suddenly rising from an intercom to Titus' right.

'State your business or leave.' The voice sounded almost mechanical.

Titus, irritated by the brusqueness replied curtly, 'I am Titus, of the noble Labienii family. I come to seek an audience with the Supreme Legate of the Guard.' There was no reply from the storm-trooper beyond the gate. The two men looked at each other.

'Maybe we should get out of here,' Cyric suggested.

'Wait, he will let us in—he has to.'

The guard didn't move. He didn't look especially concerned that the Roman and the Slave were waiting outside.

'Have you seen that stick he is holding? He doesn't *have* to do anything.' Cyric said, his eyes still fixed on the deadly staff.

'You should be more worried about the sonifex he has concealed behind his body armour,' replied Titus knowingly, and at that moment the guard shifted his weight to the other foot, betraying the outline of the sonifcx strappcd to his back to an impressed Cyric. 'Besides, as a member of the nobility, no matter how dishonoured, I have a right to an audience with the Legate.'

They waited for several minutes, but still nothing happened. 'Are you sure about these rights?' Cyric asked sarcastically.

'The Supreme Legate is not a noble; he would dearly love to be, but that is conferred by birth. He couldn't get away with treating a proper noble like this, but me, he can make me suffer for a bit.'

'You mean he takes revenge for the misfortune of his birth out on you?' said Cyric. 'It must feel good to do that.'

'Revenge is a strange thing Cyric. Do you really think you'll ever be able to right every wrong done to you?'

'One day, I promise I will,' Cyric said, anger smouldering behind his eyes.

The sun was beating down on the bustling square now, bringing warmth even in the heart of winter. All around, Romans and Slaves went about their business within the ancient centre of Londinium. It was mainly home to the larger banks and trading companies, which was reflected in the smart togas worn by the workers. Titus looked out of place in his military clothing; even some of the Slaves seemed better dressed than him in this place.

Lunchtime came and went. A man crossed the square selling snacks, but most of the businessmen seemed uninterested, rushing away to the temptation of a fat working lunch instead. Titus saw Cyric eyeing up the snack trolley and sent him off to get some dormice. As he devoured the small creatures drenched in honey, he closed his eyes and pretended he was back in Rome. He couldn't remember the last time he had tasted a dormouse; food was usually much more basic in the provinces. Cyric had clearly never tasted one before but, egged on by Titus, managed to eat a couple of the small creatures. 'Try dipping them in the garum,' Titus suggested. Garum was a sauce made out of fermented fish, which people had enjoyed for as long as history could remember.

Cyric grimaced at the thought, and looked down at the dead mouse in his hand. Titus was fairly certain the boy saw the practice of drowning small mice in honey to be yet another manifestation of the degeneracy of the Roman people, but he did seem to enjoy eating them.

The sun sank lower into the sky and the long shadow cast from the statue of General Vespasian, his pilum buried deep in the throat of a hapless Celtic chief, enveloped them. Cyric stared up at the statue which towered over them.

'I hate that man,' he said calmly.

Titus nodded. 'He is the one responsible for conquering your people all those years ago—I can understand that.'

'I hear that they honoured him in Rome for his triumphs as well.'

'You mean the Colloseum?' Titus spoke the word quietly; everyone did.

'It was built by the Senate to thank Vespasian was it not?' Cyric replied, echoing Titus' tone; it was one of awe, tinged with more than a little fear.

'It was built for him—an honour for conquering your people.'

'What goes on there?'

Titus had been expecting an angry retort from the boy, but it seemed his curiosity had got the better of him. 'Remember Tristan?' Titus asked.

Cyric nodded, thinking about what had been done to him, what he had had to watch.

'You don't want to know.'

Eventually, as the sun began to glow a deep orange on its descent to the horizon, the heavy oak doors behind the gate creaked open a crack and a wizened old Slave limped out towards them. The iron gates that for so long had barred their path, swung open automatically at his approach.

'My master welcomes you, Titus Labienus.' Titus ignored the insult, as a noble the correct formal address would be to use his first name and common name, *'Titus Aquilinus'*; to use his first name and family name, as the slave had, implied he was a commoner. To be honest though, Titus thought, with his father ill and his family bankrupt his grip on the nobility was fading. It would not be long, he thought, before they would be forced to sell the family home in Rome, and there were many rich common families who would love to get their hands on its exclusive address.

The Slave led the pair through the great hall of the Guard. Mounted on the walls was a succession of uniforms showing the evolution of the Guard. At first a simple tunic and iron helmet, from around the time of the first Punic War; then a more ceremonial red tunic with a cape, from around three hundred AD, prior to the Great Expansion. The helmet with this was iron with a great white horsehair plume. Titus chuckled under his breath; everyone knew that back then legionnaires had had goose feathers

162

in their plume. That didn't stop the historical replica industry getting it wrong, the horsehair did look impressive he admitted.

The final article on the wall was a modern day Guard's uniform—black body armour interlaced so that the joints could move easily but remain protected. Titus shivered as he looked into the empty eye slit of the helmet; it looked even more evil without anyone inside it. Beneath the suit lay the great door that lead into the Listening Chamber where the Praetorian Guard would try those who had been accused of a crime. It was rarely needed however; the Praetorian Guard were permitted to carry out sentences for most crimes without the need for a trial, only a high born Roman citizen could realistically expect to receive one. A Slave would never be permitted inside, as indeed Cyric was not, the old Slave directing him to sit on the floor by the door. Cyric flushed angrily, but a look from Titus stilled him to silence. The old man sat down beside Cyric; he too forbidden from entry by the nature of his birth.

Titus paused beneath the door. It was inscribed with the names of every Legate who had ever sat in judgement here. Britannia had been occupied for almost two millennia now, and a Legate had sat here for over half of that time. There were a lot of names on the door. The last name read Vibius Modius, the man whom Titus was about to implore for help.

Titus had only his wits with him. He would be forceful and persuasive, and that would win them over. He looked down at the dirty combat jacket he wore, wondering if maybe he ought to have hired a toga for the day. Still, it was too late to worry about that now.

'Come in.' A voice sounded from behind the door. Titus was about to open it when the motto above caught his eye,

For the glory of the gods, the protection of Rome, and the destruction of Tyrants

It might as well have been his family motto, for it was his great ancestor who was the Destroyer of Tyrants. No-one seemed to remember that any more. In Rome he would be a laughing stock, even in Londinium there would be those who knew, and looked away when they heard who he was. In Luguvalium, no-one knew, he could just be himself. He pushed the heavy door open, and walked inside.

He hadn't expected there to be so many Listeners in the Listening chamber. The Supreme Legate sat in an ancient wooden throne on a dais at the left hand side of the chamber. Flanking him were other members of the Guard's high command. They wore ceremonial guard uniforms. Titus noted the ubiquitous use of horse hair plumes, again having to conceal his amusement at these supposed great warriors' poor knowledge of military history. No one spoke as he crossed the floor and stood in front of the eagle shaped lectern. Behind him were empty stalls where his legal assistance could sit, but he hadn't brought anyone; he wasn't meant to be on trial, but he felt as if he was. The galleries above were thankfully devoid of any audience; Titus didn't feel that he would have had the courage to speak in front of so many.

It was strange he thought that once he could have spoken in front of thousands before a battle. His confidence was a different kind to that required here. He had to control himself well to prevent a stutter, as he began his plea. Nodding in acknowledgement to the Supreme Legate he began.

'Fellow Romans, I have travelled all the way from Luguvalium to ask for your assistance against the Reivers.' He paused for dramatic effect. The silence in the room was broken however by the loud snores of the book-keeper seated to the left of the Supreme Legate.

'Get on with it,' droned the Legate's assistant, thumping the floor with the base of his ceremonial fasces. His booming voice woke the book-keeper with a start.

Titus mopped his brow of the fine sweat which had formed on it, and continued. 'The Reivers have taken one of my friends; right now he may be being tortured by them, or possibly even sold as a Slave. This man is a Roman countryman, an ex-soldier of Rome and a trained war-medic. A rescue party needs to be sent out immediately...' He was again interrupted by the Legate's assistant.

'Where did this take place again, Aquilinus?'

'Luguvalium, sir,' his anger rising—they weren't even bothering to listen.

'In which case, Aquilinus, why do you bother us here? You should have spoken to the Chief Legate of the guard in Luguvalium. This seems like a simple matter that can be dealt with by a provincial legate. There is no need to waste our time here with it.' He turned to the Supreme Legate,

'I suggest we consider the case dismissed?' The Supreme Legate looked up from a book he was studying, and nodded.

Titus was furious, but with great effort he choked back his anger and continued cordially. 'With all due respect sir, I did attempt to resolve this locally before I made the long journey to Londinium. Surely you are aware that the Chief Legate of Luguvalium recently disappeared?'

The Supreme Legate let out a sigh of boredom, 'do you come all this way to inform me about the affairs of my own Guard? Of course I know about Petronius. A sad affair', he added, bowing his head with regret. 'Good old Strabo has taken his place though—a thoroughly decent man. He will see you right.'

At this the Legate's assistant waved his hand to signal Titus from the room.

He stood his ground. 'The Reivers took him.'

'What are you talking about?' It was the Legate's assistant again.

'Petronius,' Titus said, 'they say in Luguvalium that the Reivers took him.'

'The Reivers are too weak, they are broken, a spent force.' The Legate's assistant's barked out.

Titus could not believe what he was hearing, these old men sitting on the dais were entirely out of touch with reality, whilst back north, Luguvalium was strangled. He had to put them straight.

'I'm sorry, but that is simply not true,' he said, with exasperation beginning to edge into his voice. He wanted to shout at them, wake them from their stupor, but he realised that these men were used to reasoned argument, and shouting could only be counterproductive. 'The Reivers are stronger than ever. They threaten the very existence of Luguvalium!'

'A spent force!' The Legate's assistant reiterated, this time reading from a paper before him and turning to show it to the Legate himself, 'I quote from the latest report from Strabo, who reports that the Reivers are broken, scattered and bloodied.'

'And it's all lies,' Titus roared, stepping forwards, 'they hold Decimus Petronius and my friend too. Strabo cannot see beyond his own greed.'

'Be careful what you say Aquilinus,' said the Supreme Legate. His voice was kindly but firm, despite his many years. 'Remember where you are. You choose to accuse Strabo of lying to his superiors? If so, choose your words wisely and be ready to summon a legal counsel to assist you, for I assure you, a man as great as Gaius Strabo will command great respect in a hearing in this court.'

He might as well have just said that his case was utterly hopeless. The Supreme Legate would side with Strabo. Titus had no real evidence, only a vague suggestion of some mild corruption on Strabo's part, which was to be expected for that was part of his job as Governor. More importantly he had no legal council, and no friends to call as witnesses. As far as the Guard were concerned, everything Titus said could be a lie. He would receive no help whatsoever from these people.

The court too sensed that the proceedings were effectively over, and began to talk amongst themselves. The Supreme Legate reclined in his chair and closed his eyes. Titus nodded, turned sharply on his heel, and marched back out of the room. If he was going to rescue his friend, then he would have to do it by himself.

XXIV

Ceinwyn reached forwards and collected the battered mug from the edge of the cave. The rainwater pouring from the lip had filled it in seconds, and she took a big gulp before setting the mug back down. She hadn't realised it was possible for it to ever rain this much. People said it rained more in Luguvalium than in other parts of Britannia, but Luguvalium was nothing compared to the high hills that surrounded it.

She lay down upon the mossy interior of the cave and stared out into the gloom outside. Mist swirled over the barren ground before her. In the brief intervals of clemency she had gone for short walks around the cave, which was high up in the centre of a horseshoe of mountains. It was certainly remote she thought to herself. The cup was almost full again—soon there would be enough to cook with. Ceinwyn smiled to herself; she far preferred this way of collecting water than climbing down seven hundred feet to where the small tarn lay. The rainwater tasted fresher as well and the cave was perfectly positioned so that it stayed dry inside even in the harshest of weather. All around the cave walls were clothes and cookery equipment. She had everything she needed to survive. The only thing she missed was human company.

She clicked the lighter switch on the side of the stove causing it to roar into life as the gas ignited. Usually stoves were electrical, but with no induction loops nearby the power could not be transmitted to the stove. The larger an electrical item, the larger its receiving loop was, so bigger items could work further from an induction loop. A little electrical stove with its tiny receiver would have stopped working almost as soon as she left the city limits, and would have been completely useless.

Supper this evening was to be jugged rabbit. She had crept out of the cave that evening, as she had the three evenings before, to retrieve it from where Marcus had left it. She sighed to herself as she gutted the animal and placed it into the boiling water. Scattering some herbs into the water she pulled out the picture she had smuggled out with her.

'Rowena Valley,' she said to herself, taking the black and white photo out of its silver frame. She stroked Titus' face with her soft fingers. It was what she had done for the last three nights; the three nights since she had last seen her love. There was little else for her to do. She looked at the picture of Titus and his best friend—they both looked so happy. Marcus was beaming out of the photo at her; she had not seen him now for two days, although he kept bringing her food. As she thought about his leaving, and how different his expression had been from that on the photo, a tear began to course its way down her cheek. She was alone, her love was far away, and she had broken a man's heart.

The wind howled outside, louder than before. She reached out to stir the rabbit, its blood oozing out into the seasoned water, forming a claret coloured sauce. She wished she could take her words back. The blame was hers alone and that knowledge gnawed at her as she lay alone on the soft moss, flitting in and out of a troubled sleep, whilst the rabbit gently bubbled in its own congealing blood.

Outside the storm had intensified, lightning struck every few seconds, although Ceinwyn, who had been taught about the relative speeds of light and sound as a child, could count it and thought it still some distance away. The rabbit tasted delicious and she licked the small bones clean. Although she loved to eat the food Marcus brought, she still wished he would not, it only made her feel worse. She knew that somewhere out on the fell side Marcus lay sheltering from the storm. Her guilt soured the food she had been enjoying. How could she have hurt him so badly that he couldn't even bear to see her?

She cursed Marcus' stubbornness: if he hated her so much why did he insist on providing for her still—he could just return home? She knew the answer of course. Marcus only hated knowing that he could not have her. He would never abandon her. Ceinwyn thought back and realised how devoted Marcus had been to her since he had first met her. Still, she knew she had made the right choice in Titus, no matter how sorry she felt for his friend.

She thought back to three nights before with embarrassment. The start of the trip had indeed been most exciting. The furtive creeping through the darkened streets of the city; Marcus playing up the danger to excite her; then the way that they had curled up like children to stay unnoticed in the back of a supply currus, and the way she had felt so free as the currus clattered its way up the tortuous mountain roads. She had lived in Luguvalium for five years, ever since she had been sold to Strabo, yet never in that time had she been allowed to walk freely in the hills. Marcus would not tell her where they were going, but she knew it was the hills. There was something romantic about the fells that would appeal to him. It should have been a warning to her.

Once they had wriggled out from amongst the beer kegs in the currus, they fled into the dark night whilst the driver was busy supplying the inn at the top of the remote pass with fine local ale. Running hand in hand, they eventually collapsed exhausted and laughing through aching lungs with the excitement of it all. Marcus was certain they had escaped detection even though Strabo would clearly be on the look out for his escaped Slaves. It was all going so well, until they reached the Priest's Cave.

The problem, when it came down to it, was one of space, for the cave was not a large one and the pair were forced to sit close together. This in itself had not posed a problem, until Ceinwyn became aware of Marcus edging closer. It was a small thing at first: a cup would be placed in such a way that he would have no choice but to move slightly to retrieve it, or the food would need stirring, but it would be slightly out of reach. Every time he shifted closer in the cave as they sat and talked, she wriggled further away—she had hoped he wouldn't notice, but he must have done for he became more obvious.

Ceinwyn had almost wished that she did love him, but then she thought of Titus, whose strength and simple devotion was so much more appealing than this cleverer, complicated and woefully desperate man who was attempting to woo her.

He should not have tried to kiss her.

If only she hadn't explained why she had turned away, Ceinwyn thought. After her refusal he did what she expected. He tried to turn it into a joke.

'It was nothing!' he had insisted. 'A stupid mistake.' He did everything to persuade her that he had simply been overcome by the romantic surroundings. But she knew that inside his heart was splitting in two. She should not have told him about Titus when he could have easily talked his way out of his feelings. She sat glumly with her head supported on one hand, staring out into the storm outside. Marcus was out there somewhere, probably close. She hoped he would not die out of stubbornness.

XXV

The hound was close. Quintus shifted instinctively further into the gorse thicket that sheltered him from the storm above. He had picked a good night to make his escape. It was the beginning of the run up to the Midwinter feast and the Reivers had been celebrating. That meant ale, mead and even, Quintus saw to his surprise, a few vintage bottles of Roman wine had been liberally consumed by the camp. The Captain had smuggled some up to his hovel in the evening. Quintus had never been fond of ale, but the fine wine was more than able to meet his refined tastes. He was surprised the he shared it with him but he seemed to enjoy his company despite their differences. As usual the Captain had left, hurling abuse and curses at Quintus, as his men cheered him on.

The rain had started soon after the festivities, and it wasn't long before the revellers were shrouded from Quintus by sheets of water that lashed the camp. Most had wisely withdrawn inside. It was too good an opportunity for him to miss.

He had spent most of the previous day and night pretending to sleep, his hands tightly clutched beneath his stomach. Secretly though he had been twisting and shaping the key from his tin of corned beef. It had been hard to bend and it was entirely the wrong shape, hours of sharpening on a pebble he had found in the corner of the hovel had been required. At first he had feared that the guards would be able to hear the noise as he sharpened the key, forming it into the tool he needed. He needn't have worried: the guards evidently believed him to be soundly asleep, and he was able to keep the movements of his wrists small so as to avoid suspicion.

The sharpened and twisted key had worked like a charm. As the storm reached its height and the lightning sounded like it was coming down amongst the very trees above him, Quintus made his move. The handcuffs came off easily. His two personal guards were far away, sheltering, probably unconscious with drink. He began to run.

He initially followed the metalled road, hoping for some sort of sign that would point him in the correct direction. In his darkest thoughts he had felt that he would happily walk in any direction as long as it did not lead to Luguvalium—he could barely think about Titus without wanting to kill him. However, he knew he couldn't leave his comrades without first saying goodbye to Tiberius. Maybe he could even convince him to leave too. Quintus smiled at the thought of Tiberius and himself returning to Rome. He could maybe get a job in the General Hospital as a medic: he could easily train up to a post there. His skills at battlefield medicine could be turned to civilian needs. Tiberius could do anything; he could play the lyre in a band; he could even be a professional wrestler. They could make a new life for themselves, away from Titus and his lies.

But as he thought of Rome his gut had tightened at the thought of seeing his wife again, every time he thought of her he wanted to cry. Not because he missed her, although she was a pleasant enough girl, but because of his shame. He had tried so hard to make himself love her, for his family and for her. He cursed himself every day for what he was—what Rome would not permit. How could loving Tiberius be wrong? But it clearly was, for if it were not why would he be so ashamed of it that he couldn't even tell the man he loved. Could he persuade Tiberius to leave with him at a moments notice? He doubted it, and so he was stuck, for he could never abandon him. His thoughts turned to Titus. He had known him since he was fifteen; he had trusted him for almost

172

half his life. Besides everything that Titus had said was true. He had failed him. He had let the Slaves get away. As he stood there drenched in the rain cascading off the trees around him, he realised that he could not leave for Rome yet no matter how much he yearned for it. He had to make things right with Titus first. Perhaps then one day Tiberius and he would leave amicably.

In the end he did not have to make the decision, for there were no road signs pointing either towards or away from Luguvalium anywhere along the thin winding road. Instead, with no idea where he was, or where he was going, Quintus stumbled on through the night, the rain blinding him and the mettled tarmac jarring his feet with every step. Thank goodness the Reivers had left him his boots he thought as he blundered on, half blinded by the storm

When he thought he had travelled for around three miles he stopped. He had no real idea of how far he had come; in the rain every inch of this forest looked the same. However his watch said he had travelled for thirty minutes, so he could assume the distance travelled from that. He paused for a quick rest, stooping down to scoop water from a pothole in the road. The water was gritty despite the huge volume of rain. He spat it out. That was when he first heard the dogs. He had thought that the rain would wash away his scent; he had hoped he would not have been missed until the morning when bleary eyes would have taken some time to realise he was long gone. Now he had no choice but to leap for the nearest cover he could, and cower there. The gorse spines, sharp as ever despite the damp, cut into his exposed arms—why hadn't they allowed him to keep the jacket?

Deep in the thicket now Quintus knew there was no point in making a run for it. It was too late. Better to wait and hope. The barking got louder still. Then he heard a rustling in the gorse. Looking round in fear, he saw the huge muzzle of a Germanic Shepherd fighting its way into his gorse thicket. The dog growled, filling its nose with the scent of Quintus. He could hear excited shouts of men from further up the road. He had to move now.

He wriggled deeper into the undergrowth. The gorse bit into his arms and face, his fingers bled profusely from the sharp spines but he kept moving, he knew it was his only chance. A sonifex was fired repeatedly into the air only a few yards behind; they were signalling to the others.

Quintus reached the far side of the thicket, before him, through the sheets of water lashing the ground, he could see the wood continuing into the inky blackness. He could lose them in the trees. In one lightning move he tore himself out of the cover of the bush and darted away; he made no effort to move stealthily for he knew they must see him move regardless. Speed was all that mattered now. A Reiver shouted in his filthy Britannic language. Quintus could not understand it, but it was clear that the man had seen him and was giving chase. The dogs would not be far behind.

Quintus sprinted; every step was torture, his heart beating so hard he felt it must surely tear itself free from his chest. The forest blurred before him, reflexes helping him leap from side to side avoiding the trees. A depression approached. He fell as he fled down the slope, rolling down in the thick mud. Striking a tree with his back he lay dazed and sore. Shouts from the lip behind him focused his mind. The Reivers would kill him if they caught him.

He got to his feet with great effort and shook the dizziness from his head. He began to run again, slipping on the thick mud which now lay everywhere. Would the storm never end? Quintus had never experienced anything like it. The ground was becoming treacherous now—a quagmire. The men were so close behind that there was no time to find a way round. He waded into the mud which gripped his knees with its glutinous hold. He looked behind; a lantern was swinging madly in the distance, descending the hill he had just fallen down. He waded forwards and the mud crept up his legs now almost reaching his hips. No effort on his part could drag him further in; it was all he could do to wrench his body free onto some firmer ground to his left. He lay on the ground panting, terrified at the near miss he had had. He felt sick as he imagined the feeling of cold mud slipping down his throat, filling his lungs, his stomach, his nose; his life ebbing away in an eternal tomb of silt.

The dog's bark was so loud it could have been next to him. He got back to his feet, shaking the worst of the mud from his legs. He forced himself to go on, and staggering onwards into the swamp, he found to his surprise that the firm ground continued. He could make out a thin path ahead through the marshes. Looking up he could see a faint glow in the sky through the tree canopy—dawn was approaching. The sounds of the men and dogs receded further into the distance, perhaps they had not found the safe path through the mire, Quintus thought, allowing himself to hope at last that he might actually escape.

When he was certain that his pursuers were far behind, Quintus slowed to a jog, letting his breathing ease as he caught up with the oxygen debt to his aching muscles. He looked up at the sky again, feeling the cold rain on his face, letting it wash him clean. He was finally safe.

He continued his jog, still unsure where he was in the deep forest. He could wander for days in here, and still be lost. He looked around to try to catch his bearings as he jogged slowly, dreaming of somehow finding his way back to Luguvalium before daybreak, and surprising them all over breakfast. Then a tree root caught his left foot, tripping him.

As he overbalanced he flung his arms out to catch at a tree branch, but it was flimsy and snapped under his weight. He felt like he flew through the air for ever, but in truth it was for less than a second. The ground was soft and yielding. He felt the quagmire's tendrils creep up his neck, around and into his ears, and finally into his mouth; his feet churned slowly in the thick mire unable to find purchase. He screamed, an animal cry of fear as he sank deeper into the filth.

XXVI

'Bastard.' Marcus cursed Titus for the umpteenth time that night. He had found a hollow on the leeward side of a sheep track. It was barely wide enough for him, resulting in a constant trickle of water on his forehead and into his boots. Not for the first time that evening he considered returning to Luguvalium. True, Antonius and Tiberius did think he was in Londinium with Titus to get help to find Quintus, but he could make something half believable up. Any amount of lies would be better than spending another foul night in this place utterly forsaken by the gods.

It had all looked so lovely three days ago he thought, with the clouds rolling over the tops of the high fells. He couldn't have thought of a better place to begin his life with the girl he longed for. He stamped his feet in anguish as he thought back over what had happened, the things he had said. He clenched his fist and forced it into his mouth, biting down hard on his knuckles as he remembered his greatest humiliation. His tears flowed to join the rain-water that splattered his face.

At his feet were the remains of a rabbit's kitten. It had had barely any flesh on it; in fact it would have been barely worth cooking had he even had a stove. At least the young meat had been tender enough to eat raw.

He had longed for the mother rabbit he had killed with it. He imagined how Ceinwyn would have cooked it; in the short time they had been together in the cave he had discovered what a wonderful cook she was.

Neither creature had been easy to catch. When Marcus had been a young boy his father had shown him how to hunt. The family had owned a large farmhouse outside Rome and, where possible, they had enjoyed being able to live off their land. Marcus had learnt to make traps with wire and a wooden peg that would eat into a trapped rabbit's neck, cutting further the harder it struggled. He had also learnt to shoot the rabbits with the small air powered sonifex his father gave him for his tenth birthday. He had always been a good shot.

Right now he had no sonifex, he had left it in the cave and in his shame-driven hurry to leave had forgotten it. Sitting above the rabbit's burrow with a heavy rock held outstretched over the opening for four hours had nearly overcome his stubborn pride, yet he still did not retrieve the weapon that would have made his life so much easier. He would rather his arms ached and that he would go hungry.

His stomach rumbled again, reminding him that the larger of the two kills had been taken to Ceinwyn. He left them a few hundred yards from the cave. The spot had been well chosen; it allowed Marcus to watch the cave from cover first to ensure that Ceinwyn was not in the entrance or nearby, then he could rush forwards, leave the food and retreat before she had a chance to speak to him. It seemed that she kept a similar watch too; he had once heard her call his name as he ran off into the tall, dead bracken; the anguish in her voice tearing at him. Yet he chose to remain in the hole, the pain he felt turning to anger, partly against himself, for being stupid enough to be taken in by the girl, but mostly against Titus. Whenever he thought of his friend he felt a rage he could hardly control build up inside. He thought of Titus as a brother, but he could not cope with the idea of him being with the girl he loved.

As Marcus lay still dreaming of his lost love, the storm began, at last, to relent. He was soaked to the skin—with the weather the way it was he knew he would stay damp for days. He shivered in the chill morning air suddenly aware of how cold he was. Despite three layers, the easterly wind coursing over the fell-side bit deep into his skin. He reached into his pouch and plucked out his last two cereal bars. Hungrily he devoured the most battered of the two before smoothing out the packaging on the other and replacing it safely in his webbing. He would leave it by The Priest's Cave for Ceinwyn before going back to Luguvalium for the day he decided.

Even allowing for the walk in and back, there should be plenty of time to get more food and change his clothes. He could get Ceinwyn something special for supper as well he thought, as he tramped across the damp upland turf, better than that stringy rabbit from last night. As he walked his rage began to dissolve. He waited for his usual cheeriness to replace it. But it did not come. He felt nothing. He would never have Ceinwyn. He no longer had anything to prove, or anything to lose. He tried to smile to himself, but it felt wrong—more like a grimace. He thought of Titus, but his rage would not come, instead he felt something which scared him, something he had never realised he possessed: cold hatred.

As the mud's grip tightened upon Quintus, the panic eventually ran its course to be replaced by an eerie calm. He felt the mud in his mouth, filling his ears, pressing on his tightly shut eyelids. He was going to die.

He had often wondered what it would be like to die. He had been taught that if a Roman died having lived a good life he could go to Elysium. Yet he did not know if such a place existed, or if it did whether he had been good enough to warrant a place there. Whatever happened, he thought, it would be better than the cold, thick mud.

His mind wandered from topic to topic as that of the dying man does. Mainly his memories were of Rome. He had missed the metropolis so much, if Elysium was Rome he knew he would be happy eternally. He remembered his medical training; he knew how he would decompose. In the mud he wondered if the process would be different. Maybe he would be preserved? He thought of the plaster casts formed from the outlines of the dead found at Pompeii after Vesuvius erupted. They were interred on view in a museum in Rome, and he had been taken to see them as a child. Only their outlines had survived, empty chambers in the rubble that had once housed their bodies, a hole the shape of a person in the posture in which they had perished. Quintus wondered if the mud might preserve

178

him in this way. In expectation of such a fate he straightened his legs and folded his arms across his heaving chest; he would not be preserved for all eternity waving his arms around like a terrified girl. He was a Roman soldier, and he would die like one.

When the first pair of hands grabbed him he was unable to distinguish what they were. In his dream he was suddenly shaken awake by his mother, and reality took a long time to return. By the time it did he was aware that he was lying in the cool light of dawn. The ground was damp, and he was spluttering. A river of corrupted filth retched forth from his throat. He had been rescued, but by whom? He tried to look up but another wave of retching struck him.

Once he had finished he lay still on the ground gasping for breath. As the thunder in his ears subsided he became aware of the speech around him; there was no mistaking the guttural tones of Britannic. Quintus groaned at the realisation of his re-capture. Looking up he saw the barrel of a sonifex levelled at his head. He was too weak to contemplate flight, let alone attack, besides there were a dozen of them at least as well as the dogs. It was probably the dogs that had saved his life; their keen sense of smell had been his rescuer. What had their rescue saved him for though, he wondered?

He waited for the shot to be fired; he knew enough about the Reivers to be certain that they would not allow an escape to go unpunished. Their Captain may have wanted to keep him alive for now, but surely after trying to escape they could not allow him to live. The fact was irrefutable. Yet no shot came.

Despite the fact that he could not understand the language, it was clear that the Reivers were arguing amongst themselves. Eventually it became clear that those who wished to keep him alive had won, and, with a look of irritation, one of the more angry Reivers, having clearly lost the argument, stowed his weapon, and hauling Quintus to his feet began to drag him back the way they had come.

Quintus lost count of the number of times he fell during that journey. His weakened legs were barely able to carry him. Every time he fell the big Reiver who led him would kick him in the ribs before hauling him to his feet again. Quintus was starting to wish that he had simply been left in the peace and quiet of the mud, by the time they at last came across the Reivers' currus.

The first thing Quintus noticed about it was the smell—the stench of death. Row upon row of skulls hung on the side: macabre trophies of the Reivers' trade. The smell inside the vehicle was nearly as bad. The upholstery had clearly never been cleaned and was smeared in a mix of mud, oil, blood and, what appeared to be, human excrement. Quintus was propped in a corner, and the vehicle began to lumber back towards the main Reiver camp, and certain death.

XXVII

Dawn broke with a firm frost over the rooftops of Londinium that morning. Smoke from the factories oozed in tendrilous coils over the icy streets. It was the first frost—it came later each year. Titus took a deep breath, enjoying the taste of the icy air on his tongue. How much crisper would it be away from the pollution he wondered. He contented himself with the thought that he would soon be back in Luguvalium where the air was clean. He thought about his coming reunion with Ceinwyn. If only he was returning under different circumstances. His head told him not to worry; Quintus was dead, probably killed the day they lost him. The manner of his death would likely have been horrific in the extreme, but it was over now; there was nothing Titus could do. But that was his head talking.

There was a much bigger part of him that knew that Quintus was alive; it was the part that remembered every day of his life since he was sixteen till now, still in his prime, approaching his thirty second birthday. Every moment of his life from that time had had one constant: his men. Even war had come and gone, but his friends had stayed. When he thought about Quintus he could picture hundreds of times that the man had infuriated him, but he could equally think of moments where his quick

temper and constant challenging had been a source of laughter. He had
saved Titus' life before, and Titus had saved his. The two were bound
together for ever despite their differences. All his men were bound by
blood spilt together, their own and that of their enemies. Titus knew that
he would know if one of them were dead. Instead he was certain that
Quintus was alive. Somehow, he had no idea how, he had survived, but he
needed help, and at the last Titus Labienus Aquilinus, the 62nd descendant
of the great Titus Labienus, the Destroyer of Tyrants, and the Protector of
Rome, had failed him. It made Titus sick to the stomach.

He slammed the shutters closed hard, snapping some of the brittle
wood into dust which shimmered in the red winter sunlight streaming into
the dingy bed-sit. 'Get up,' he said quietly waking Cyric. 'We leave today.'
A week ago he might have snarled those words at the insolent boy, but he
had no place for anger anymore. Part of him rather liked the young Slave's
company, confrontational and questioning: he reminded him of Quintus.

They could not wait in Londinium any longer: they had already spent
the last five days waiting to see if the Guard would listen to them again. It
was now clear that they would not be granted a further audience. The pair
packed their few belongings in silence, and left the inn through the back
door, striding out along the icy street to where the battered old currus
waited by the side of the road. Londinium was slowly waking, the ground
seemed to vibrate beneath their feet with the life. It both frightened and
excited Titus. He realised that if he had followed the path of politics in
Rome and the Senate ordained for him by his birth, he would have found
Londinium quaint in comparison to Rome.

His memories of Rome were vague now; the wide open countryside
was his home, the trees his cover, and the sonifex his guide. He felt out of
place here. He even had to keep his weapons concealed. Carrying a
weapon openly was a privilege only for the Praetorian Guard. However,
judging from the wicked looking sonifi sported by most passers by it was
clear that the rule didn't seem to be strictly enforced here. It was a
different story in Rome he had heard, where civilians were banned from
carrying any sonifex, and even the Praetorians were forbidden from
carrying any weapon apart from the fasces. Marcus Albus was clearly not

taking any chances these days with the worsening political problems in Asia Minor.

The currus was right where they had left it, already too damaged to be an interesting target for vandals. The roads were packed with other currus jostling for position. Titus, unused to driving in this way, and with only a rudimentary knowledge of the route, was soon exasperated. After an hour they had moved less than ten miles and were still within the city despite the fact they had left its ancient walls behind over half an hour ago. That would have been impossible in Rome.

It was a strange paradox to Titus that the greatest city in the world should be one of its smallest. In sharp contrast to Londinium Rome had never expanded beyond the Pomerium, the sacred boundary ploughed by Romulus over two thousand years ago. The defensive walls had been strengthened, but the city had never grown beyond their defensive might. Titus had forgotten much of what lay within the walls but what he remembered was far different from Londinium. The sky was empty here. The sky above Rome was always full in his childhood memories, as he looked up now thinking of the Great City he could almost see the volacurri from all around the world, flocking to the air dock at the base of the space elevator stretching upwards into infinity. The sky was never dark, even in the deepest winter nights.

As Titus gathered speed he began to forget he was driving in a city. His driving skills, although not best suited to city driving, were excellent and he soon found he was exceeding the speed limit by a good margin. Seeing as only the most inept members of the Praetorian Guard were placed on traffic duty he had little worry about being caught. For the first time in the day his bleak mood began to lift.

'What will you do now, Roman?'

The question was barbed, Cyric knowing Titus' mood wanted a bite. He had long ago understood that his friendship with Ceinwyn prevented Titus from causing him actual physical harm, no matter how sharp his tongue became.

'I don't know.' The fact terrified him; he always had a plan.

At that moment he was cut off from his thoughts by the look of alarm on Cyric's face and he looked back at the road ahead which he had been neglecting. As if in slow motion, he turned to see a suited man carrying a black box crossing the road directly in front of him. The man seemed frozen to the spot with fear, one hand outstretched, the box in midair, falling to the ground. Titus hit the brakes; the currus began to skid as Titus wrestled it to the side of the road, over the kerb and sideways into the unyielding side of a large rubbish skip. The impact threw them forwards hard against the seat restraints.

The box hit the ground, splitting open, splattering its contents over the road in a crimson stream. The man, suddenly regaining his composure, turned and fled away from the building he had been heading to. As Titus watched in surprise, the man vaulted a fence tearing his suit on the rusty wire, and at a full sprint fled back to the city.

Titus opened the door of the car, letting Cyric out of his side as the passenger side door had buckled with the impact. He stared at the fleeing man in confusion as he disappeared around a bend in the road. Why would the man flee? He had made him drop his package, the man should be angrily demanding compensation. With the sound of the buckled metal of his currus pinging in his ears behind him, he approached the stricken box gingerly. Its contents had been spread widely over the road, a multitude of small pinkish objects. He bent down to examine one more closely. He tried to pick it up but it was freezing cold, and slipped through his fingers. It was a piece of ice. Titus moved closer to examine the box and saw that it had burst at the bottom corner but the lid was still in place. He undid the clasp and slowly lifted the lid. What he saw inside made him gasp involuntarily with complete surprise.

It was a human heart, packed with ice.

Suddenly he was aware of Cyric standing above him also staring at the strange find. They both looked up simultaneously at the marble façade of the building the man had been heading towards. The name of it, scratched in clear, deeply etched letters across the beautiful surface brought hope to Titus.

'Vivlter'

XXVIII

Gnaeus crept from sleep slowly, his head feeling several sizes too small for his brain. He knew that the drinking last night had been unwise, the contest with Antonius had been foolhardy in the extreme. He rolled over slowly, hoping to trick his brain into believing he was still flat on his back with his eyes closed. It didn't work. The bright light streaming in and reflecting off the frost on the terraced roofs on the other side of the street seared the back of his eyes and awoke the pounding in his head. Just when he thought things couldn't get any worse, a chorus of horns and whistles began in the distance. He groaned, it was Saturnalia again; it had crept up so quickly this year. Out on the streets of Luguvalium stalls would be being set up laden with the finest winter foods.

In Luguvalium that would mean sausage. But without doubt there would also be ale, fresh bread and fine winter cakes imported from Germania. None of this much appealed to Gnaeus at the moment. Saturnalia had been a magical time for him as a child, but with no Slaves around the house little would change for the week long festival. For during Saturnalia Slaves were temporarily freed.

But Gnaeus remembered the festival from his childhood, and the mixture of awe and fear he had used to feel on Saturnalia itself, the final

185

day of the festival, when the Slaves were freed from their work, and allowed to sing their otherworldly songs. It had once been his favourite time of year, but that was a lifetime ago. All that Saturnalia now meant to Gnaeus was death, pain, and the cold; they should have all been distant memories but ten years seemed like yesterday to Gnaeus, though he tried not to let the others see it. He remembered above all else, the cold.

Rising painfully, he made a cup of coffee and, relaxing in his dressing gown, switched on the opening of the festival in Rome on the wall screen. No-one was permitted to carry filming equipment into the temple of Saturn itself, but since most of the festival took place outside there was still much to see and broadcast around the world. Decimus Catula opened the proceedings as a Consul of Rome. He was a bull-necked brute of a man, but he was loud and well connected. He was a good choice to open the ceremony, speaking the sacred prayers clearly in the old Latin. Two semi naked vestal virgins posed on either side of him, trying not to look uncomfortable in the chill breeze.

The Senate were arranged in a semicircle behind him, seated in the open air but wrapped up in ceremonial robes. In the centre of them sat the real power in Rome, Marcus Albus, the second Consul; a quieter man than Catula, tall, wiry and fair. If Catula was Rome's mouthpiece everyone knew that Albus was its brain. Whilst to Gnaeus, Catula seemed like a bull, powerful but foolish, he saw Albus as a spider, sitting content at the centre of his web. The sight of the man sent shivers down his spine. He didn't seem much older than when he had known him.

Known was the wrong word really, but he had spoken briefly to the man; they all had. He had wanted to meet Titus before promoting him to a command that would make him his near equal. Titus of course had simply thought him friendly, poor foolish Titus, but Gnaeus knew the real reason Marcus Albus had sought out his friend before promoting him. He had wanted to ensure that the rumours he had heard about Titus, Titus' family to be exact, were unfounded. He did not wish to have a general alongside him who was not in his little exclusive members club.

Titus had never told Gnaeus what price he had to pay to join the club, but Gnaeus had seen the look of utter desolation in the eyes of his friend later on that day. He wondered if the prize had been enough; the short

186

term friendship of a future Consul. Days later they had all been forgotten, as soon as the volacurri arrived to take the nobility back to Rome following the success of the campaign. Rome had subdued the Transmaritanus Rebellion; the world was safe again; the terrorists were dead, and freedom would rule forever.

But Titus would stay with the men (the other generals could return to their private member's clubs in Rome—the little orgies laid on specially and the free flowing expensive wines), but Titus would stay with the men, the only General to remain behind and watch his men starve on the freezing beaches, as Rome seemingly forgot its army. Titus could believe Marcus Albus was an old friend with whom he had lost touch if that was what he wanted, but Gnaeus knew differently.

'Remember what we were doing this day ten years ago?'

Gnaeus jumped at the voice, spilling the lukewarm coffee into his dressing gown. 'Morning Tiberius,' he rasped through his dry throat.

Tiberius nodded and poured himself a cup, 'refill?'

'Yeah go on,' he replied, his voice hoarse from last night's drink.

Tiberius threw himself down onto the sofa next to Gnaeus. 'Antonius not up yet?'

Gnaeus shook his head.

'Still drunk probably.'

'He didn't seem that drunk last night!' Gnaeus said, remembering his humiliation in the drinking contest.

'You've got to be joking, he was broken. That's his trick though,' Tiberius added conspiratorially, 'he doesn't let you know he's drunk, demoralises his opponents you see. He was toying with you.'

'Oh, right,' said Gnaeus, remembering the endless shots, culminating in the endless vomiting into the canal running past the ruined Luguvalium castle. 'Are you sure he's not just in bed with that girl—you know the one he met in that bar last month?'

'What Octavia?' Tiberius laughed, 'that was last month. He has a new one now, not sure what she's called though! Anyway, I don't think he's with her now though, poor fool couldn't possibly get it up with the amount of ale inside him.'

'I see,' said Gnaeus sleepily, and turned back to the screen where Catula was about to strike the chains off the statue of Saturn and signify the opening of the holiday. The Pontifex Maxiumus reached up from the entrails of the goat he had just slaughtered and declared the portents good. There was a huge crowd watching but no-one seemed particularly interested. Temple attendance had decreased spectacularly over the last fifty years. Even the Pontifex Maximus, the Chief Priest in the state, seemed to simply be going through the motions.

'You do seem in an uncannily good mood this morning Tiberius.'

'Of course, it's Saturnalia! Who isn't happy?'

'Quintus?' Gnaeus said.

Tiberius' expression drooped.

Gnaeus immediately regretting bringing the subject up tried to change it. 'At least it's better than it was ten years ago, even for Quintus.'

'So, you do remember what we were doing then?' Tiberius said quietly.

'How could I forget, for it has been ten years to the day since I first tasted human flesh,' said Gnaeus quietly.

They both stared towards the screen, but neither were watching it.

Saturnalia

XXIX

'This will never work,' hissed Cyric from beneath his cowl.
'Stay quiet, and remember you are my Slave,' Titus replied. The bed sheet he was wearing as a makeshift toga was far from convincing he thought to himself, as they strode towards the revolving door of *VivIter*. The toga should have been rimmed with purple to show his nobility. At least it was relatively clean. It was the best they could do at short notice.

'Oi Roman, don't you remember what day it is today?'

'Do enlighten me?' Titus replied sarcastically.

'It is the first day of Saturnalia, Roman,' stated Cyric.

'Is it?' replied Titus with genuine surprise. 'Is it already? How could I have not noticed?' Looking around he realised that everyone did look surprisingly informal and the Slaves were walking around, for once with their heads held high. It was Saturnalia after all. Cyric was grinning despite his near death experience in the currus only a few minutes before. 'In which case, you can be a Slave celebrating Saturnalia, but not yourself, remember these people don't know the truth about your people.'

'How could I forget?' said Cyric angrily.

'But you can ignore some of my orders, and I can be kind to you once in a while, it is Saturnalia after all.'

Passing from the cold into the warm blast from the air conditioning, he entered *VivIter* for the first time. He was not sure what he would find within, but the opportunity to explore the organisation, contributing to the largest portion of Strabo's fortune, was too good to miss. Within these walls was his best chance of finding something to use against Strabo. Raising his head as a noble should, Titus strode with as much confidence as he could muster, towards the stunningly beautiful receptionist.

'Welcome to *VivIter*, sir,' she beamed at Titus who was sure she was being sarcastic. 'Are you here for one of the treatments?'

Titus looked around the plush waiting area; dozens of clearly unwell Romans were dotted in chairs, drips attached to their arms. Despite their obviously advanced states of disease, Titus was suddenly aware that he was by far the least well dressed of them all. He turned back to the receptionist. 'No, I am here to discuss my account.'

The receptionist nodded, digging a ledger out of the desk beneath her. 'Certainly sir, if I may just have your name?'

Titus nodded, hoping his face didn't betray the anxiety he was feeling; this was a desperate chance—the stakes becoming higher every second. He smiled disarmingly at the reception girl, 'Gaius Strabo. My name is Gaius Strabo.'

The sound of heavy footfall outside jogged Tiberius and Gnaeus from their dark thoughts. The ceremony in Rome was long finished and the big screen now showed only an educational film about the never-ending power of Rome; reminding its audience about the wonderful gifts granted upon non Roman populations by their new rulers, and the eventual gift of citizenship for all those who accepted the might of the new empire. So many people had citizenship now. Those who couldn't get it, or hadn't applied, were mostly stuck in dead end jobs, or were Slaves.

'Antonius,' Gnaeus said cheerily, as the huge man entered the house, 'good to see you at last.'

The great man groaned as he fell clumsily into the nearest chair. 'You bastard,' he said, gesturing vaguely at Gnaeus, and vomited bile onto the carpet. His face was as green as his sick.

'I thought the shots were your idea.'

Antonius waved his hand contemptuously, clearly neither could remember whose idea it had been, but both clearly agreed it had been the wrong one.

'Looking forward to Saturnalia?' Tiberius asked Antonius.

'More than ten years ago.'

'Funny, we were just talking about that,' Tiberius said.

'There are better times to remember,' said Antonius. 'Rowena Valley,' he added, looking wistfully into the distance.

'You enjoyed Rowena Valley, didn't you?' Gnaeus said.

'I have no idea how you managed to; it was the worst experience of my entire life!' Tiberius said laughing.

'Marcus hated it too,' Gnaeus said, remembering the events from long ago as if they had occurred yesterday.

'I learnt from it,' Antonius replied.

A loud explosion from the screen startled them. 'Terrorists attack Pompeii,' the newscaster exclaimed excitedly, whilst pictures of the breaking news flashed on the screen. It was clear from the images that tourists had been the main targets.

'Another bomb?' Tiberius exclaimed. 'It will be separatists from Asia Minor again,' he continued, 'it's not going to be long before the Senate has to do something about them.'

'And have to open the gates of war in Janus' temple again!' Gnaeus laughed, 'I think Marcus Albus would rather have a few tourists killed in Pompeii now and again than risk the political implications of that. They've only been closed for ten years.'

The news programme had moved on now, there were a few quick seconds left after the headline story to mention a political scandal involving Marcus Albus. Compared to the terrorist attack however, it seemed inconsequential, and little was mentioned about it.

'Doors open or closed *we* have been at war for the last ten years regardless.' Tiberius said.

'But that was our choice,' replied Gnaeus.

'As have most of the other men I knew from the army,' Tiberius continued, ignoring Gnaeus' words, 'do you know anyone who made a decent living after the army?'

'Me.'

Everyone turned to look at Antonius who spoke only rarely; usually this would be a sign that when that person *did* speak their comment would in fact be one of great pertinence. Antonius was not like other people however.

'I signed up to the army to fight, I always wanted to fight, and I still want to fight. If they call us up to Asia Minor, I would fight.'

'Perhaps,' Gnaeus replied, 'but have you never wanted to just settle down in one place?'

'What's the point,' replied Antonius as he began to pull his coat back on. 'If I stayed in the same place eventually I would kill all the men, and fuck all the women, where would the fun be in that?' As if to accentuate his point he rose from his chair, and strode out onto the cold street.

'Want to see the Saturnalia celebrations?' Gnaeus asked.

'Might as well,' replied Tiberius as the two strode out after him, their noses following the smell of ale on the cold winter breeze.

It was exceptionally cold that morning in the town centre. Gnaeus' breath condensed as he breathed and the wind gusted hard as he crossed the bridge over the canal by the old castle. Behind him stood the infirmary with its great chimney belching clouds of acrid smoke as it burnt clinical waste. Gnaeus had awoken one morning to find ash on the street by the house; it was a universally accepted fact that the hospital needed a taller chimney.

As the bitterly cold wind found its way between his clothes, it reminded him of that winter ten years ago again. It had been much colder than this one. He tried to shake the memories from his head; Antonius had been right, Tiberius had been wrong to speak of them. It was in the past, although Gnaeus knew that the things he had seen would never truly leave him. Far better to remember the great victory at Rowena Valley than that final long winter and the snow covered desolate beaches littered with their own dead. He felt sick, and tried turning his thoughts to what would be taking place within the town.

Saturnalia lasted for seven days; it had once been only three but its popularity had meant that the Senate eventually relented and made the unofficial week that everyone took off work official. Everyone looked just a little bit cheerier, even the keepers of the few remaining stalls that lined the road seemed less morose than usual. It was no surprise Gnaeus thought. With the town in the bad way it was, and most of their competitors already forced to shut up shop, the resilient few shop keepers who remained could take advantage of the Saturnalia boom. Not that people had much to spend as it was. The Reivers had taken almost everything over the last few months.

Gnaeus wondered what the Reivers would do with the things they had taken, if they did not wish to be part of the Roman community they would certainly need money to support their own. Did they celebrate Saturnalia he wondered to himself? Probably not, they had their own pagan festivals. Looking at the free people of Luguvalium milling around him he wondered how many of them actually believed in Saturn, a Roman god transplanted thousands of miles to a new land. At least the Reivers were free to celebrate what they liked, how they liked. His hand subconsciously slipped into a concealed pocket in his thick coat to finger his iron cross. Would he be safe to wear it here he wondered? As a Roman he was expected to do his 'ceremonial duty', in short he should worship the Roman gods publicly, if not privately. It was not actually illegal to hold a belief in one god, so he would not be punished formally but he had known plenty of ridicule for it. Officially under Marcus Albus' new rules he would no longer be welcome in Rome itself; if anyone in power knew of his secret belief that was.

He decided to keep the cross concealed, despite Saturnalia's proximity to his own God's holy birth day; the Praetorian Guard had eyes everywhere and, although he doubted whether anyone in Rome cared a single sestertii about the movements of one of their many forgotten soldiers he knew one day he might have to return to Rome. In the meantime he could celebrate Saturnalia in name, but in his heart the birth of his Saviour.

Arriving in the town square Gnaeus and Tiberius headed straight for the beer tent—sure enough Antonius lurked within. 'Trying to invent your own special hangover cure?' asked Tiberius clapping Antonius around his broad shoulders.

The big man laughed raucously and downed the rest of the thick ale. 'Special Saturnalia brew,' he remarked, with wonder in his voice.

'I can smell it from here,' replied Tiberius nearly overcome by the fumes.

Gnaeus turned away to look out into the square, at the centrepiece of which was a huge barbeque. The people of Luguvalium were queuing up where a member of the Praetorian Guard was handing out piles of roasted meat. Saturnalia, itself, was in seven days, and no one would be going hungry in the run up to the great festival's climax. As was customary there would be free food twenty four hours a day for the whole week, all paid for by the Governor. The long queue was full of Romans, locals, and with it being Saturnalia, Slaves as well. But Gnaeus noticed that far from seeming excited to share this free food with the others, most of the Slaves looked pale and haggard. He watched as one took the plate, ate a mouthful and promptly vomited it back up right next to a guard. The guard kicked him hard in the ribs, and the Slave crawled away retching. Some of the Slaves were eating but most looked too ill to take much interest in the food.

As he looked on, a family were examined by an agent who, having checked his papers, turned them away. As Gnaeus looked on in confusion, he realised that Tiberius was also watching. 'You know, I'm not sure that food's actually free,' Gnaeus said.

'What!' Tiberius laughed, 'impossible.'

'But the guard turned away that family.'

'No one seems to be being charged though, they just seem to want to check their papers,' said Tiberius pondering why the family might have been turned away, perhaps they had entered Britannia illegally.

A man in a grey jacket was next in line to have his papers checked. As he approached, a banner proclaiming the festival was raised into place obscuring the scene. Gnaeus tutted with frustration. The man had seemed oddly familiar. He began to talk with Tiberius again, but suddenly caught movement out of the corner of his eye. The man in grey was now running from a pursuing Praetorian. The pair disappeared into an alley, with Gnaeus still not having managed to get a good look at the man.

The shunned family were walking past now; a five year old boy clung to his mother who was trying to look as dignified as was possible in the circumstances. A twelve year old girl followed. All three looked starving. Gnaeus fished into his military coat and found some dried meat. A good legionary's ration but hardly the food a child would eat. He handed it to the girl anyway as she passed; it would be better than nothing. As he reached his hand out the girl recoiled and ran to her mother, who stopped and turned angrily on Gnaeus.

'I didn't mean to scare your daughter,' he said, 'I was offering her some food; it's not very much, or very nice, to be honest, but it's something.'

'What makes you think we want charity?' the woman asked angrily.

'The Guard, they turned you away.'

'I'm glad, it is better than the other choice.'

'To get free food?' asked Gnaeus surprised.

'Free!' the woman laughed. You have no idea what that food would have cost me. At this she grabbed the dried meat and, turning around, strode off into the crowd pursued by Gnaeus.

'Lady,' he said grabbing her shoulder, 'I am sorry to ask but what do you mean about a choice?'

'Why do you care?' the woman hissed. Gnaeus could see that behind the façade she was terribly afraid.

'Is it Strabo?' Gnaeus asked, hoping his intuition was right. The woman froze at the sound of the name.

'You are friends of the Governor?' She was shaking.

'Not exactly,' Gnaeus admitted, 'look, things are not right around here; the town is poor; the Reivers predate from all sides—yet nothing is done. He obviously doesn't care about his people. Yet he gives out free food, but not to all. I only seek to understand.'

'He gives out free food to those who are with him,' the woman spoke much calmer than before.

'And you are not?'

'My husband was once a businessman, he worked at the docks. He was ruined by Strabo, who pursued him for his debts when he knew he could not pay. There is only one honourable way out of that situation.'

Gnaeus nodded, understanding the man's predicament; for a Roman, dishonour meant taking your own life.

'He ruined your family. Why punish you more?'

'He wanted Cornelia,' she said.

The little girl, standing a footstep behind her, jumped at the sound of her name.

'She was to be payment for the debts of my husband.'

'Was your husband's life not enough,' Gnaeus asked incredulously, 'he would also have taken your daughter as a servant?'

'Servant?' the woman said slowly, then shook her head. 'No, he wanted Cornelia for his bed. But I would rather starve.'

At these words she took her daughter by the hand and led her slowly away, the little boy still clinging to the edge of his mother's coat, until the group were lost in the crowd.

As if in a dream he wandered aimlessly through the Carnival. A loud laugh cut through from the beer tent. He knew it was Antonius yet he did not go to him. The sound of a lyre being strummed as an impromptu band improvised by the Roman Dead Memorial; he knew it was Tiberius, yet he did not go to him. Instead he thought about what the woman had said. This was the man they worked for who was tormenting them: he was an animal. How could Titus keep them here fighting for this man, Gnaeus wondered? Then he thought back over all that had happened in the last months; the blank rounds, the distance that Marcus and Titus had kept from them. He trusted both of them, that was why he said nothing, had done nothing. When the time was right he knew they would let him know what was going on. But Gnaeus could see no reason why Titus would endure working for such a man as Strabo, and for the first time, the thought occurred to him that Titus and Strabo's alliance was not all it seemed. There was only one way to find out. He headed for the barbeque.

XXX

'N ame!' The praetorian shouted at Gnaeus, louder than was entirely necessary.

'Gnaeus Lartius,' he said boldly. As a mercenary working for Strabo he should expect a larger than usual portion of free food.

The Praetorian looked down the list. Gnaeus shuffled uneasily; it had seemed like a good idea in his head as he approached the Guard. But as he stood before the Guards he realised that if his suspicions were correct the outcome could be far worse than just being refused the free food.

'Lartius, Lartius,' the Praetorian spoke to himself, as his finger settled on a name on his list. 'Lartius, Gnaius Lartius,' he said, his finger having found the name and read the accompanying note attached to it. 'You should know better than to show your face here!' At that he nodded briskly, and Gnaeus instantly felt two hands grasp his shoulders. Before he was able to protest he was being hauled away.

He was quickly dragged away from the square. Staring around him in shock, Gnaeus was surprised by how few people even looked in his direction—let alone tried to help. The Praetorian who was dragging him was surprisingly strong.

'I think there has been some mistake,' Gnaeus spoke as calmly as he could as the guard started to frogmarch him down a nearby alley.

'Shut up. Keep walking.'

'I am a Roman citizen and...' Gnaeus' breath was knocked out of him as the Praetorian lent his fasces into his back, the electric shock catapulting him forwards, forcing him to trip. Gnaeus sat up slowly, surprised to find himself unable to stop hiccupping.

'It's the stick,' the Guard said, clearly proud of his knowledge of the weapon. 'That's the lowest setting.' The words were spoken as a clear threat. 'I have some questions for you,' he continued menacingly.

'Questions from whom?' Gnaeus asked, his composure returning. He brushed his jacket to remove the brick dust it had collected from the floor of the alley. Finished, he drew himself up as tall as he could, which was not very, and stared straight at the Guard. He had met people like this man before, and knew exactly how to handle them.

'From Gaius Strabo, of course. Your boss?' the Praetorian replied as if Gnaeus had forgotten who his boss was. 'He wants to know where your leader is.'

'My leader, what are you talking about?' Gnaeus replied. He had no intention whatsoever of getting Titus into trouble, and he was fairly sure he could talk his way out of this situation. The man glared at Gnaeus and moved his fasces so it was only a few inches from his testicles. His thumb worked on the small metal dial halfway up the shaft. The resonator at the bottom of the stick glowed a little brighter and Gnaeus became aware of a faint humming sound from the fasces. Perhaps he would not be able to talk his way out after all.

'I mean your leader, Titus Aquilinus,' the Guard replied. 'Where is he?'

'He is in Londinium,' Gnaeus replied, 'doing your work for you.' It didn't matter what he told the Guard now; he already knew how this had to end.

The Guard nodded, pleased at the information he was receiving. 'And the girl, the red haired one, where is she?'

Gnaeus shook his head, 'I really have no idea what you are talking about.'

The Guard nodded imperceptibly, telling Gnaeus that it had been a shot in the dark anyway. He asked the same question again, the fasces moving even closer to Gnaeus' nether regions. A shot in the dark perhaps, but this guard clearly wanted to show the well spoken, better dressed Gnaeus who was in charge. It was time to end this charade.

'What, do you mean your Mother?' Gnaeus said, pointing to the guard's own mop of red hair. 'I know where she is, waiting in my bed desperate for me to come home.'

The guard did not react immediately, his mouth just hung open as he contemplated what Gnaeus had just said to him. Then suddenly he roared with anger, drawing back the fasces like a primitive club. How typical, Gnaeus thought as his hands closed around the guard's neck, that even the most well armed men will act like fools if not trained adequately. The guard's neck snapped easily in Gnaeus' practised grip. It did not require strength, only the correct technique.

He dragged the body further down the alley and around the corner. A waste bin sat propped open with the remains of a broken chair. Gnaeus lifted the Guard's body with difficulty and heaved it into the bin, kicking the chair out of the way to allow the metal lid to slam shut. He looked both ways quickly to ensure he had not been seen before striding off nonchalantly back to the Carnival. He gave the Praetorians a wide berth, yet he wondered how much attention they were paying anyway, half of them were already so drunk as to be rendered barely conscious.

As he walked he tried to piece together the fragments in his mind. How had Titus got on the wrong side of Strabo? Surely just going AWOL would not be enough to have them all blacklisted? If they were so unwelcome why were they not just thrown out of the city? Strabo owned the houses they lived in anyway. Gnaeus had the uncomfortable feeling that he already knew the answer to his last question. He had not tried to leave the city of late, now he wasn't so sure he should try at all. Who knows what might be written by the names on the list held by the Guard on the town gate. An interrogation at Strabo's compound would likely be far more harrowing than what he had been subjected to in the alley a few moments before. The infuriating thing was that he couldn't quite work out what had they done wrong?

As he trod through the Carnival he began to look for his friends. Poking his head into the beer tent he saw that Antonius had gone, most likely to sleep off his second binge in as many days. Gnaeus suddenly remembered that he too was meant to have a hangover and his headache returned almost immediately. He looked over to the street corner where the musicians had been, but that area was now deserted. Deciding to head home alone he began to leave.

Then he saw that the man in the long, grey jacket, he had seen running from the Praetorian's earlier was walking just ahead of him. His hood was up, again frustrating Gnaeus, who was sure he knew him. 'Excuse me sir,' Gnaeus shouted, 'but do I know you from somewhere.'

The man stopped, and for a moment Gnaeus thought he would turn around so that he could see his face, but then, without warning, the man began to run. Panicking he tore down the path by the temple of Jupiter with Gnaeus in pursuit.

Then three things happened in quick succession. Firstly Gnaeus noticed something in the way the man ran—the awkwardness of it was in itself familiar. Secondly, the running man turned slightly to see if he was outrunning Gnaeus and failed to navigate a bollard as well as he otherwise might have done. Lastly as the man fell he twisted in the air, landing awkwardly on his back so that his hood fell from his face. Gnaeus recognised him instantly, and came to a sudden halt with the surprise. For in front of him, panting for breath and clutching at his injured leg, lay none other than his old friend Marcus.

XXXI

Gnaeus stared down at Marcus, lying prostrate on the cold tarmac. 'You are not in Londinium,' Gnaeus said quickly, before realising the point seemed rather obvious. He paused for a second, confused. 'Why?' he asked, offering Marcus his hand.

'Someone's got to keep looking for Quintus,' Marcus replied, still winded and gladly taking hold of the proffered arm.

'Then why not come home to your house?'

'Titus told me to keep a low profile,' he began to go red.

Gnaeus laughed, 'stop it Marcus, you know as well as I do that I am no fool.'

'But it's the truth,' Marcus began to protest.

'I know about the blanks.' Gnaeus stared into Marcus' eyes looking for a reaction.

Marcus looked away. 'What blanks?' he said finally.

'Oh, come off it Marcus!' Gnaeus said, trying to not let his irritation show, 'the blanks you used to fake the attack on the Slave camp. The ones that clearly Quintus did not know about, and I assume neither did Tiberius, or he is doing a pretty good job of pretending that Quintus' wandering off and being taken by the Reivers wasn't down to Titus' lie.'

Marcus did not reply, his face trying to remain blank.

'I imagine you did not tell Antonius—he could not keep a secret,' Gnaeus continued, 'I do not know why you did not tell me, we can come back to that later if you like, but I trusted you enough to bury the few blanks you carelessly forgot to clear away. So the real question I guess then is this, my friend. Why go to all that trouble? Would it not have been simpler just to kill the Slaves, rather than end up in this elaborate game that has probably already taken the life of one of us?'

'He did not mean for Quintus to get hurt,' Marcus protested.

'That I believe,' Gnaeus said.

'Would you not sacrifice a friend if the stakes were high enough?' Marcus asked.

'Perhaps,' Gnaeus replied, 'perhaps for my family, or for the life of the woman I loved. Not for some Slaves.' He shook his head and then realised the look of pain his last few words had caused in Marcus' face.

'What is it, my friend?' he said, concerned.

'There is a lot I should tell you,' Marcus said, sighing deeply.

Gnaeus and Marcus sat together under the great oak by the temple of Jupiter for half an hour, during which time only Marcus spoke. Once he had finished talking they sat in silence for some time before Gnaeus finally opened his mouth. 'I always knew something was wrong with the way we treated Slaves.'

'I think we all did, it's just...'

'It's just what everyone has always done,' Gnaeus said.

Marcus nodded in agreement; they could both think back to times in the past where they had treated Slaves badly.

'You were right though,' Gnaeus said, getting to his feet.

'Right about what?'

'Not telling us. I think Titus was right. You could have told me though.'

'I'm sorry,' Marcus said, clearly meaning it.

'If we find Quintus,' Gnaeus said, 'I will speak no word of this to him. If he found out the truth...'

Marcus stood up to leave but Gnaeus stopped him, 'tell me the rest of the story.'

Marcus laughed, 'but I've done that, we've sat here for nearly an hour.'

'No, that's also a lie Marcus, you still haven't explained why you are here? Why did you leave Londinium? Surely Titus needs you there to petition for Quintus' rescue?'

'I never went to Londinium,' Marcus said, and then to Gnaeus astonishment his old friend began to cry.

'Well sir, can I just say what a pleasure it was to meet you at last, and that it will be with great sadness that we close your account.' The man in the suit shook his head as he closed the ledger open on the desk before him.

Titus nodded. 'It was a difficult decision. But sometimes the best business decisions are.' He was frustrated; he had tried his best to tease information out of the man who sat before him, yet he had been so terse in his replies that Titus still had next to no idea what Strabo's accounts here were regarding. All he knew was that they had paid Strabo an insane amount of money for something, and yet they were sad to lose his custom. Whatever he was meant to have been providing them must have been precious beyond measure.

'How do you plan to continue without my assistance?' he said, as offhandedly as he could, 'if you don't mind me asking.'

'I must confess sir, it will be difficult. Supplies are hard to come by, increasingly so. The laws are as strict as ever,' he sighed with exasperation. 'We need more forward thinking people such as yourself. A Slave is useful during life yes,' he gestured to Cyric who sat behind him, the only other person in the office, 'but in death he can be so much more useful.'

Titus felt sick as he began to realise what happened here in this building. But he needed proof for himself before he could act.

He blew his nose noisily into the fold of his toga, much like he thought Strabo would have done. 'My Slave,' an idea suddenly appeared half formed in his mind, 'is reaching the end of his usefulness.'

'You wish to sell him to us?'

'It would save the hassle of returning him to Luguvalium.'

'You realise we cannot take him...' the man paused, 'like this.'

Titus hoped Cyric could maintain an obedient expression.

'Can nothing be arranged? Surely, in special circumstances, we could, how shall I put it? Bypass these little legal issues.'

The suit sat back down, staring at Cyric whose face was mostly obscured by the cowl. Eventually he nodded, 'the first day of Saturnalia, an ironic day to be selling a Slave, but we will see what we can do. Tell me Strabo, how is your Slave?'

'He is a fine worker, very strong.'

The suit laughed, 'no, of course I mean his health! No problems with his heart, lungs, kidneys?'

'None that I know,' said Titus, his fears being confirmed.

'Excellent.' The suit clapped his hands summoning a beautiful girl in an instant. 'Go and tell Plubius that there may be hope after all; we may have found him a match.'

The girl bobbed her head, 'oh, and make sure he has been taking the anti-rejection medications.'

'He has sir,' the girl replied, 'he will be most grateful.' She glanced at Cyric and smiled.

The suit hissed with pleasure as he relaxed back in his chair. He folded his arms behind his head. 'Seems we have a deal my old friend.' He reached out his hand for Titus'.

Titus calmly reached under his toga and brought out his concealed sonifex. He had won. He was so close to being able to ruin Strabo. 'I want all your paperwork. Now. In the name of Rome.'

XXXII

Ceinwyn sat at the entrance to her cave in the evening air. The day had cleared up nicely she thought, as she watched the sun begin to set, casting shadows over the tarn far below. A thin dusting of snow lay upon the now frozen ground. The earth was cold without its blanket of cloud. She shivered against the chill, drawing the blankets she and Marcus had brought with them tightly over her legs. She should have thought to buy some warmer clothes, yet the chance for another shopping trip would likely not come again for some time, if ever. She shivered again as she thought about Strabo and his podgy hands closing on her skin. Where was Marcus?

The sound of footsteps crunching through fresh snow startled her, and she drew back into the deepest recess of the cave—it was not far from the entrance, it was not a large cave. There were clearly two men coming; Marcus bringing Titus perhaps? Her heart leapt at the idea, but she knew it to be unlikely, Titus had been gone less than a week. It was more likely to be Strabo's men, or even worse, Reivers. Would Strabo really send men out to search the fells for an escaped Slave? Of course not. It would be Reivers, and they would rape her until she was dead, and then probably rape her some more just for good measure. She picked up the frying pan from where it lay on the cave floor. It had served her well in the past she remembered as she tried out a few practice swings.

The footsteps were getting closer now. Ceinwyn breathed deeply, remembering how she had felt before entering the facility beneath Strabo's compound. She had felt brave then; she had felt that she was in control of her destiny. She could control this too. The Reivers would suffer if they entered the cave. Still, she hoped the footsteps would continue past the cave entrance and down the long indistinct path to the tarn below. Few knew about the cave, and it was not easy to find. She should be safe.

Ceinwyn caught her breath as the footsteps stopped. She heard voices outside, two men, but their voices were muffled by the moist dusk air and the cave walls. Something about them sounded familiar. Her grip on the pan faltered. The men were coming towards her. She tasted blood in her mouth suddenly aware that she had bit her lip. She brought the pan back behind her head. The men were in the cave now. A voice spoke quietly but she could not make out the words. It was a voice she had never heard before, cultured. She liked it.

'Ceinwyn?'

Her name echoed in the confined space; the familiar voice of Marcus.

Safe now she stepped out from the recess, discarding the pan. Two men stood together, crouching in the low space. Marcus she recognised, though he looked haggard from his nights on the mountain. He tried to meet her gaze but seemingly could not. His companion was half a foot taller than he was, thin, not wiry even, just thin. But she could tell from the way he carried himself that he was stronger than he appeared. His hair was dark, nearly black, he wore it longer than Titus. And he looked young, although she knew from Titus that all his companions were the same age, for they had all joined the army together.

'I am Gnaeus,' the man spoke again; Ceinwyn enjoyed hearing his voice. It was educated, like Strabos' but tinged with warmth and humour, rather than malice. The thought suddenly entered her head that she should be afraid, Titus had explained why he had not told his men about her: they would not understand.

'Marcus told me about you, about your people.' He paused. 'It makes sense at last.'

'What does?' Ceinwyn asked, finding herself whispering.

'My life.' At Ceinwyn's gesture to do so he crossed the cave and took a seat, the others joined him around the small fire.

'My whole life has somehow failed to make sense; war, killing, slavery. Don't get me wrong,' he said, accepting a drink from Ceinwyn, 'I'm pretty good at those things. But they never made me happy.'

'Material things rarely do, I have never really owned anything. Those who had plenty never seemed as happy as they should,' Ceinwyn replied.

'An old truth,' Gnaeus replied, 'you would have thought more would have learnt it by now.'

'Where would they hear it from? You have a god of money do you not?' Ceinwyn asked, laughing at the idea.

'Marcus does, he has several in fact, the '*Dia Lucrii*'.'

'And you do not.'

'No.' Gnaeus replied.

'But I thought...'

'You thought we had to worship them by law.' Gnaeus said, 'many think that, but it has never been the case. I must worship them publicly in their darkened shrines or accept ridicule. Personally, I prefer the idea of ridicule.'

Marcus snorted, 'wouldn't it be easier just to go along with it rather than suffer needlessly.'

'My God suffered for me. It's the least I can do.'

'I have never met a Christian who was not a Slave,' she said surprised.

Gnaeus looked utterly surprised, 'you know the name of my faith?' he exclaimed.

'Of course!' She laughed, 'for it is mine also.'

Gnaeus blushed, the first time in that evening he had not seemed completely composed, despite the strange circumstances. 'Forgive me,' he said, 'I didn't think. Of course your people must have faiths as well.'

The three sat awkwardly before Ceinwyn broke the silence, 'thank you for coming back Marcus,' she walked over to him and reached her arms out to embrace him; perhaps he could forgive her?

He looked at her, and for a moment she thought that everything might go back to how it had been a week ago, and that he would smile back and reach out his arms in return. But then his eyes suddenly flashed with anger, and in one swift motion he got to his feet and stormed out into the night, his cloak billowing in the chill air.

Ceinwyn looked across at Gnaeus and opened her mouth to try to explain, but before she could articulate what she meant to say Gnaeus nodded at her.

'It is difficult,' he said, sipping from the warm drink Ceinwyn had given him. It was some sort of tea and very good—he made a mental note to ask her what it was later. 'When you love someone,' he continued, 'you cannot change how you feel, even if to not do so would destroy the ones closest to you. Marcus loves you in that dark, consuming way.'

'What can I do?'

'To make things better?' He shrugged his shoulders. 'There is nothing that can be done. But know this, Marcus understands, if he did not he would have stayed and argued with you, tried to make you love him in return. It is the unassailable truth that his cause is hopeless that makes him so angry. If he thought that you choosing Titus was the wrong choice he would try to make you see it rather than just run away.'

'But he will be so angry with Titus,' Ceinwyn said, her voice tinged with guilt.

Gnaeus nodded. 'That is true, but you should not see that as your doing alone, Marcus has a far greater reason to hate Titus than, forgive me saying this, just you. It's just that he has not let himself realise it yet.' He sipped from his tea again.

'But they are old friends,' Ceinwyn said, confused.

'The oldest of friends, but Titus did something long ago that Marcus has never been able to forgive.'

'What did he do to him?' Ceinwyn asked, hanging on Gnaeus' every word.

'He saved his life.'

The pair sat in silence around the fire before Ceinwyn finally spoke, 'Marcus is a proud man.'

Gnaeus nodded, 'you understand. We will see what happens. I know that it often seems as if Titus needs no-one's help, but he does, he needs us all. He needs Marcus. Marcus will have to make a choice. But to hurt Titus would be to hurt you—he is not stupid.'

'Sometimes he seems it.'

'Intelligence and common sense rarely go hand in hand. Marcus is probably the most naturally intelligent man I have ever met, but also probably the most foolish and infuriating.'

Gnaeus reached into the folds of his cloak and brought out a small leather book. Ceinwyn had never seen a book so battered, even the oldest books that Strabo had owned were in better condition. 'You are brave, Ceinwyn, you have endured so much.'

'My life is what it is, was, I mean. Until I was saved from it.' A dreamy look crossed her face as she thought of Titus again.

'Do you want him to kill Strabo?' Gnaus asked, jolting her back to reality.

Ceinwyn laughed, 'he could not, Strabo is the most powerful man in Luguvalium. The best we can hope for is escape.'

'Escape and a safe life?' Gnaeus asked.

'That is better than just vengeance, I would rather live un-avenged, than die for vengeance.'

Gnaeus nodded, the girl was sensible. 'What would Titus do in your situation do you think?'

'He would take revenge.' Ceinwyn replied without a moment's hesitation, remembering her teasing request of him on the first night they had met.

'Even if it led to his death?'

'Even if.'

Gnaeus gazed into the fire. 'Strabo is a dangerous man.'

'You think I should persuade Titus to leave, and not take revenge.' It was not a question, it was a statement.

'I want you to do what you feel is right,' Gnaeus replied, ' no one would want him dead more than you. But yes, I think that would be for the best. When he returns from Londinium and when he has found Quintus, alive or dead, then we should leave, all of us together and find somewhere safe from this man.'

'I will try, if it will keep him safe.'

Gnaeus nodded. 'It will keep us all safe,' he said sighing inwardly with relief.

'Were you allowed books?' he asked her changing the subject again.

'Living with my father, yes, in secret. He made me read even before I wanted to. Otherwise, only the ones I could steal.'

'Then take this one.' Gnaeus handed her the battered volume. 'I have had it since I was 16. It has travelled all over the Transmaritanus, to Rome, to Dacia, and then finally to here. And now it is yours if you want.'

'What is it?' Ceinwyn asked, reaching out for the damaged volume.

'It is not one book, but instead a library of smaller books, trust me, you will have heard of it.'

Ceinwyn took the volume and opened it, the first thing that struck her was the smell, then she noticed the handwritten annotations that covered most pages. She laughed, 'you obviously don't respect books.'

'My thoughts, over many years. It is hard when you have no-one to discuss your faith with. Read it, you will see that once upon a time Christ's followers were safe to meet together and discuss his teaching.'

Ceinwyn drew her attention away from the scrawled notations that ran in crazy lines around and throughout the page and began to scrutinize the text itself. It was small. 'I don't understand,' she said, closing the book and offering it back to Gnaeus.

'You have opened it in the middle,' Gnaeus explained patiently, 'the library is in two parts. You can start at the beginning, but I think you will be more familiar with the second section.' He reached over to her and flipped the pages forward to a well thumbed page. 'See here, do you recognise this?' he asked pointing to a line.

Ceinwyn leant forwards eagerly, peering at where Gnaeus' finger lay on the mud stained page. Then with joy, she finally understood what lay before her, because the line presented in front of her read:

'For God so loved the world that he gave his only son, so that all who believe in him shall have eternal life.'

'I know these words, my father told me them,' Ceinwyn replied excitedly but still confused. Then her eyes lit up as she suddenly realised what she was holding, 'is this...'

Gnaeus laughed at her amazement, 'yes it is, there are not many of them, I have no idea when one was last printed. You would not want to possess one in Rome these days.'

Ceinwyn passed the book back to Gnaeus again, who shook his head and closed her hand over it. 'Thank you, but as I said it is yours now. Keep it. Take it as an apology from me for every time I have insulted one of your people.'

Ceinwyn smiled and reached out to put her hand on his shoulder, 'I have already forgiven you for that. Before I even met you I forgave you.'

Gnaeus smiled sadly, 'but how can I forgive myself?' he muttered, and stared into the dying fire before him.

XXXIII

'What do you want?' The voice was desperate; the once confident businessman now humbled before the menacing barrel of the sonifex. Titus noticed the way that the man could not keep his eyes from staring into the dark emptiness of the bore. It was the usual reaction of a man who had never faced a weapon before.

'Proof.'

The man's mouth just flapped open and shut like a fish drowning in air.

'Proof of the nature of your business and of your clients,' Titus added to clarify.

'But sir, you have all of that yourself surely.'

Titus laughed. 'You still hope I am Strabo?' He picked at the edges of his threadbare toga and laughed. 'You are lucky to have never met the man.' He thrust the barrel of his sonifex a little closer to the man, but not close enough to risk being disarmed. 'Trust me,' he said earnestly, 'Strabo is not a man who you would want to die to protect.'

The businessman nodded slowly, 'the files are kept downstairs, you will be able to find yours... *Strabo's*,' he corrected himself, 'in the vaults.'

'And how many of your guards will I need to circumnavigate on the way to those? I imagine your clients are not generally encouraged to visit the records room?'

The man nodded, dislodging a bead of sweat that had formed on the end of his noise under the intense scrutiny of the sonifex barrel. 'If you would prefer, the information you require can be found on our internal omniajunctus, you can access it from any scire in the building.'

'I prefer.'

The businessman swung his omniajunctus terminal around with his shaking hands, leaving sweat marks around the edge of the screen which now faced Titus. 'You will need the password then all you need do is search for Strabo's name. All you want is there.'

Titus nodded, 'if this is true then you have nothing else to fear from me.'

A hiss from behind alerted Titus to Cyric's displeasure. He clearly did not like the idea of him letting anyone involved in this project escape with their lives. In many ways Titus agreed with him; it was a disgusting business. But his need to find something to use against Strabo was far greater than his desire to destroy this building and all those within it.

He turned back to face the businessman, 'the password?' he asked, and as he did so, something at the back of his mind raised a warning. He looked down at the businessman's hand beneath the desk clamped hard to the wood above, and realised he was pressing an alarm button. How long had he been doing it for? Titus remembered the armed guards at the entrance and a cold sweat broke out over his forehead as he looked down at the small sonifex he held in his right hand; it was all he had.

'Tell me it now,' he roared as he got to his feet.

At that moment the door behind swung open revealing a second suited businessman, except this one had an earpiece and a small silenced sonifex.

'Thank the gods,' the businessman shouted as he got to his feet and began to run towards the open door.

The man raised his evil looking black sonifex.

'I didn't tell him anything!'

The guard remained expressionless as he shot the businessman in the head at near point blank range, splitting his skull and splashing blood and brain matter over every inch of wall, ceiling and floor in the small room. The terminal in front of Titus spluttered and died as the blood boiled onto the circuitry within.

Still seemingly emotionless, the killer suit turned the weapon towards Titus who was already half way through a dive towards the comparative safety of the back of a filing cabinet. As he leapt through the air he fired two shots in the direction of his assailant, cursing silently as they struck the door and the lintel respectively. He knew that if it had been ten years ago the man would have been dead. He was out of practice.

The splintering of the wood as the bullets struck it drove the guard away from the doorway, and allowed Titus the space he needed to make his move. 'Now,' he shouted to Cyric, who crouched low at the far end of the office as he leapt from behind the cabinet and tore across the room, firing a burst from his sonifex blindly around the corner as he swung out into the corridor. The guard lay dead on the thin carpet of the hall-way; one of his shots had been lucky. Titus breathed a quick sigh of relief, but he knew reinforcements would be on the way. 'This way,' he gestured down the corridor to Cyric with his sonifex.

They retraced their steps, and to Titus' surprise met no resistance. The sonifex fire had clearly rung out through the whole building and a mass panic was ensuing, with businessmen, scientists, and patients alike milling around in every corridor. A Slave and a Roman, even one wearing a sheet for a toga, blended in reasonably well in the commotion.

Much sooner than Titus expected they came out into the great marble atrium. The three guards they had spotted on the way in now marched around the polished floor trying to instil a sense of order into the milling crowd.

'Come on,' Cyric hissed to Titus, 'we can slip past them easily.'

Titus shook his head and began to drag Cyric down a second corridor leading to the stairs, 'we cannot leave with nothing.'

'Are you insane Roman?' Cyric said as he jogged along at Titus' heels. 'We are going the wrong way!' Titus did not reply and began to descend the stairs.

'Where are we going?' Cyric asked.

'The vaults.'

'There's no time! They will find the office then they'll hunt us down.'

Titus grunted to silence Cyric for he knew that if they left now they had no proof whatsoever of what Strabo was up to. He paused at the sounds of boots on the staircase below him. Peering over the glass banister he saw that three guards were charging up from the basement. Presumably they were heading to help clear the atrium of panicking Roman elite. They clearly expected to meet no resistance, and they had certainly not heard the pair descending.

Titus picked his moment and as the first guard rounded the corner he leapt at him. The guard shouted in surprise. Before he even had a chance to bring his sonifex to bear, Titus was on him, striking him with his shoulder and his full weight in the centre of the chest. The guard was lifted off his feet with the blow and was thrown headlong back down the stairs careering into his companions, knocking one unconscious. Titus rolled to his feet ready to meet the one remaining guard, who was desperately trying to disentangle his sonifex from beneath the body of the first guard Titus had attacked. Titus did not give him the chance. He crossed the five steps down to him in a single bound and, as the guard raised his free arm to protect himself, struck him a powerful blow to the side of the head. The guard reeled drunkenly and Titus struck again, this time to the body. The blow forced the guard against the glass banister which fractured under his weight allowing the screaming man to pirouette backwards down the centre of the staircase. Titus and Cyric did not hear the impact of his body on the cold concrete below for several seconds. They clearly still had a long way to descend.

Titus began to jog down the stairs, hopping over the bodies of the other two guards. Cyric followed him, gingerly stepping around them trying not to look into the open eyes of the dead one. Their footsteps echoed on the marble stairs as they descended deeper into the bowels of the facility and the commotion upstairs faded away to be replaced with a faint but oppressive humming sound. The omniajunctus hub must lie close.

There was no reception party for them at the bottom of the stairs, instead a white corridor lay ahead with doorways leading off regularly along its length. The humming sound was much louder down here. Titus took a deep breath, and began to walk down the corridor towards the sound's source. Cyric followed, closer to Titus than he had ever considered acceptable before. As they approached the first doorway, a figure stepped out suddenly. Cyric jumped and let out a cry of alarm. Titus already had his sonifex drawn, but as his finger tightened on the trigger his brain managed to stop the reflex in time. The figure frozen before them was simply a cleaner. The man stared at the pair, eyes wide with fear before bolting in the direction of the stairs.

Titus let him go. The cleaner might tell the guards where they were, but equally he might not. He had spilt so much blood already today. Besides, he knew they would only be down here for a few minutes before they made their escape. He did not want to dwell on how they would manage that, for he knew that Cyric had been right: in the commotion they could have easily slipped away. Now, he had no idea if they would ever see daylight again. But to have left with nothing was beyond contemplation.

There was no cleaner in the next room, but no source for the sound either. Instead simply a gleaming operating table. Cyric shook with rage as he saw it. 'Is there no limit to your race's cruelty?'

There was nothing else for Cyric to say. He had known the truth ever since the businessman upstairs had as much as said what took place here, but to see evidence of it was too much.

'Where do they kill us?' He asked Titus, his voice quavering.

'Until today I did not know they did,' Titus replied, not sure if Cyric believed him or not. But Cyric did not seem to be in a state capable of making the decision himself. 'I know one place where they do now.'

'At my master's, I mean Strabo's, compound?' Cyric asked, already knowing the answer.

'Without doubt,' Titus replied, 'I have seen the rooms myself, in the West wing of the facility. But I did not understand their significance until today.'

'What will you do about it?' Cyric asked, desperate. But Titus had no time to reply. He strode off towards the buzzing sound, as Cyric slumped down onto the ground by the operating theatre door, and silently began to weep.

XXXIV

]

Quintus woke with a start. Staring around with bleary eyes it took him a few seconds to remember where he was. Then it became clear. The currus had lurched to a halt and within the dingy interior he could make out the filthy bodies of ten angry Reivers. Their dogs lay at their feet slumbering, their snoring reminding Quintus of their growling as they had pursued him last night.

He had no idea how long he had been asleep, but it could not have been for long as the currus had only retraced his own journey. He had run fast but it could only have been a few miles at the most. He laid his head back against the reverberating metal of the rusting currus. If only he knew where he was. The forest was thick, and although he knew he could not be more than a few days journey on foot from Luguvalium, he still did not have any idea in which direction it lay. His escape last night had been desperately foolish. Reflecting on it he realised that he had been in as much danger of dying at the hands of the forest itself as the Reivers.

The Captain had seemed to respect him, had seemed happy to keep him prisoner, but now Quintus was not so sure. He remembered what the Captain had told him—that he kept him alive to draw out his fate. He thought he had been joking. But as he remembered the empty eye sockets of the man they had cut down from the tree only a few months ago, he was not so sure. He imagined the birds flying at his eyes, the little ones he would be able to shoo away by waving his head to and fro desperately, but the bigger ones, the ravens, the crows; He would tire quickly. He felt sick at the thought of his arms struggling to free themselves as the birds drove their claws into his cheeks and their hungry beaks into his face.

Voices in the old Britannic language interrupted his unpleasant thoughts. The back of the currus was hinged down and at last Quintus could breathe fresh air again. He was forced to his feet and kicked down the ramp at the back of the currus. He rolled awkwardly and hit the ground heavily on his face.

He looked around spitting out a mouthful of mud. It was early morning and the first light of the sun was streaming in over the tops of the trees around the glade that formed the centre of the Reiver camp. All around, men were waking and getting ready for their day's pillage as wood smoke rose from the makeshift huts, twisting in the chill morning breeze. Quintus wondered why anyone would want to live like this. Not everyone in Britannia had Roman citizenship, but that only prevented a career in politics or religion, these men could theoretically do anything else they wanted to, even if their job prospects were admittedly worse. Why were they here?

He caught sight of the young Reiver Captain striding purposefully towards him, his breath condensing in the cold morning air. He looked pale and uncomfortable with the sonifex he held in his hand. The other Reivers cheered him on as he marched towards Quintus, who now knew that he was going to die here. All thought of the birds pecking at his helpless face disappeared; they would just shoot him right here on the ground. Quintus felt his resolve beginning to harden, and some of his strength returned to his exhausted muscles. He got to his feet. He was not going to die on the ground. The Reivers had not bound him, obviously feeling he was too weak from his ordeal in the mud to attempt escape.

He would strike first. He would still die but he would die at the hands of a man he fought rather than begging for mercy on his knees. He deserved death anyhow for the way he had failed Titus, but he would die in a manner which would bring him honour. Titus would find out what he done in the next world. Perhaps , Quintus thought, one day they might walk side by side again in Elysium. One day perhaps Tiberius would join him there, maybe finally when they were both dead, he would then be able to tell him how he felt.

His soul prepared, he took a step towards the Captain. The ground behind him began to shake. The captain looked over his shoulder and Quintus watched as the colour drained from his face and his mouth dropped open. Quintus swung around and saw a fully armoured military currus burst out of the forest, chips of wood flying high into the air behind it. As the currus cleared the forest edge its twin rotating saws slowed and the vehicle's speed increased a notch. Two hatches on each side opened revealing heavy calibre sonifi.

The Reiver Captain forgot Quintus in an instant and began to shout to his men trying to form them into a defensive cordon. But it was too late. The currus was upon them. The sonifi mounted to its sides began to whirr into life. They fired much more slowly than Quintus' assault sonifex would have done but each round threw up a cloud of dust and flame where it landed. The Reivers by now had managed to gather what weapons they could and fired back at the currus which ignored them and instead began to circle the camp firing into the makeshift buildings. Shards of wood, branches and piles of leaves flew into the air as the buildings were destroyed. Fire began to spread as gas canisters exploded, bringing warmth to the otherwise chill morning. The noise was deafening. The Reiver captain was roaring orders again, trying to organise his men. Quintus could see it was useless. He laughed to himself, knowing that the Reivers possessed nothing that could damage this machine. He had used similar vehicles years ago in the army. If the Reivers could only see some of the other machines the Roman army had, they would count themselves incredibly lucky to just be facing this.

Quintus saw a woman dragging a screaming child behind her, escaping from one of the burning huts, and sprinting for the perceived safety of the huddle of armed men. Quintus had not realised that anyone was still in the huts, but looking around he saw a few women and children. They must have been in the buildings when the attack had started. The currus was ignoring the men and massacring their families. The driver must have spotted the fleeing woman for the sonifi stopped, the currus swung round, and the saw blades began to turn once more. As it headed straight for the woman and child, its engine roared as it built up electrical charge from the glowing conduits on its rear. Suddenly the charge was released in a great burst of speed. The currus tore across the glade throwing turf up in the wake of its rear tracks.

He looked across to Armstrong and saw that he was held tightly by two of his Lieutenants; his face contorted with a mixture of rage and desperation as he fought against the men. This woman was his wife, and the boy his son. The currus crossed the distance between itself and the pair in a moment.

The Captain bellowed and his wife, seeing his terror turned and froze at the sight of the blades bearing down on her. It was over in a moment. The pair were there one moment and the next they were simply gone, their bodies dissolved in a haze of gore which coursed up and over the front of the currus. Bone fragments and pieces of flesh splattered the glade for fifty yards in every direction as the chipper behind the blades made short work of the Captain's family, blasting the remains out in a crimson stream through a duct behind the machine.

Armstrong sank to his knees, his mouth open to cry out, but no sound came. Quintus looked around; most of the Reivers were sobbing, or staring in anger at the currus. Nearly everyone had lost someone in the raid. But who had done it? Why? And most importantly why had they not attacked the armed men?

The currus pulled up before the men and a loudspeaker mounted outside began to hiss. 'This is the price you pay for not giving your master what he is due,' the voice blared out over the glade, but Quintus barely heard it from the cabin of the abandoned rusty currus as he slowly rolled away from his captors.

XXXV

Titus stood at last in front of the source of the faint buzzing that filled his head. Row upon row of scire databanks stretched before him in the dimly lit vault. Stored in this system along with presumably thousands of medical records, linking client with disease, disease with organ, organ with Slave donor, lay the details of Strabo's dealings with the *VivIter*, details which Titus knew could bring him down.

It wasn't the illegality of the company, so much as the taint that dealings with a trade in Slave organs, would have on the man in the eyes of the Senate. Strabo would do anything to avoid that. You just had to look into the eyes of any of the rich Roman clients desperately waiting upstairs for their organs to be matched with those from a hapless Slave. They were terrified of being seen there. That was the worst part of it: a Slave would die to save their life, and not only would they not be grateful, they would actually be ashamed of it. He was more desperate than ever to kill Strabo. He knew it was a daydream. Strabo was too powerful for that. Before him lay the key to blackmailing his former employer. The key to rescuing his friend, and then letting them simply walk away.

But how to access that key? Not for the first time since he had been in Londinium, Titus wished he had brought Marcus with him. His veiled excuse that he needed to look after Ceinwyn had never fooled Titus, but he had let his friend stay with the girl if it made him happy. He shook his head at his foolishness as he examined the touch screen on the far side of the room. From here he could access the data, send it anywhere in the world probably. He didn't want to send it very far really, just to Luguvalium, to Marcus' reader. But he might as well have had to send it all the way to Asia Minor. The system was beyond him. He turned to Cyric, 'do you know how to work this thing?'

Cyric simply nodded, his expression blank. Titus knew he was angry. He understood why. He had asked him to save his friends from Strabo, and punish the man for what he had done. He had not even replied; he did not yet know how to answer. He wanted to hurt Strabo so much.

As Cyric reached to touch the screen, it shattered before him as a sonifex round struck it; its vibrant colours suddenly dead in a shower of broken glass. Titus leapt sideways, throwing Cyric to the ground, and to safety, as three armed men rushed down the aisles towards them threading their way between the databanks. Titus, sitting in temporary safety with his back to the nearest cabinet, pulled out his sonifex and reloaded it. It was his last magazine. Each shot would have to count. Cyric was on his feet, crouched down, peering between the aisles. Titus reached under his toga to where his belt lay against his vest and drew his sword. He slid the drawn gladius across the floor to Cyric who picked it up gratefully and tried a quick practice swing. It was obvious he had never used a sword.

These guards were trained, moving quickly but quietly with their weapons drawn. But they were not as good as Titus. He heard the patter of the first guard gingerly approaching the broken screen. He waited. Every part of him wanted to flip his weapon around the corner, and shoot the man, he could not miss from here, even without looking. But he needed to conserve the rounds for he knew that upstairs lay many more guards. He picked his moment well, swinging his arm out as the guard rounded the corner.

Titus' braced outstretched arm caught him at the top of the chest and threw him onto his back. Titus cursed as he realised he had misjudged the man's height from his glimpse of the three entering the room. A little bit higher and the blow would have taken the man at the neck. Stunned the guard tried to roll away, but was stopped by Titus stamping on his chest. He brought his other foot down hard on the pinned man's contorted face and was rewarded by the crunch of bone against his boot.

Titus stalked after the other two men. He kept low, his sonifex ready and his breath catching in his throat with to his surprise, excitement. He had missed being a soldier for too long. He was pleased with the way he crept up on the second guard; the man was pacing around, peering round every corner looking for him as all the while Titus followed silently, ready to pounce. When he did so, he drove his elbow into the back of the man's neck, throwing him to the ground. But as he bent down to check that the guard was unconscious a blow struck the side of his own head, dazing him and throwing him to the floor. Through the sparkling lights that flooded his vision he saw the third guard swing his boot back ready to kick again. He had been so engrossed in stalking his prey amongst the row's of scires that he had not realised he too was being hunted.

He tried to parry the blow, but in his prostrate position on the slippery floor was only able to take the blow on his left shoulder rather in his face. The pain shot through his arm and into his chest like a bullet. He tried to lift his arm to stop the next blow, but he could not. Something was wrong with it. He tried to use his other arm but the man stamped down on his wrist hard, holding him in place. Grinning, the guard pointed the dark barrel of his sonifex towards Titus, ready to send him to the Underworld.

Suddenly a bloodstained metal point burst from the guard's chest, showering Titus in gore which continued to spurt as the point was withdrawn through his back. The guard's grin changed to a grimace, before relaxing into a blank expression as he fell forwards onto Titus. The spurting arterial blood soaked the bed sheet Titus was wearing and covered his face and hands as he tried to push the heavy man off. Cyric placed Titus' bloodstained gladius down carefully, and together they hefted the man away.

Titus looked up at Cyric through the haze of pain from his shoulder and enjoyed the look of pride on his face. It was his first kill. Titus smiled back at him. 'Well done lad.'

224

He reached behind him with his good right arm and pushed himself to his feet, trying his left arm in the process and being rewarded with another shot of agony. He could barely move it. There was no time to examine it now. He grabbed Cyric, who was still staring at the man he had slain, by the arm and began to drag him back towards the operating theatre corridor.

'No', Cyric protested, 'this way,' and pointed to the wall next to the screen where a lift stood open. 'More guards will come down the stairs surely?'

Titus nodded, the boy was right. The pair ran for the lift.

As if to prove Cyric correct, at that moment three more guards entered the room. As the bullets thwacked into the wall around them, Titus threw Cyric into the lift, leaping after him. The doors shut maddeningly slowly as the pair tried to press themselves as far into the side wall as they could, the side of the door barely shielding them from the oncoming attackers. At last the doors closed and with a sigh of relief Titus realised that they were moving up at last. Leaving the guards far behind.

'What's wrong with your arm?'

Titus tried to move his left arm again but the pain stopped him, 'not sure,' he gasped, 'here, help me with this.' He proffered the arm of his blood sodden toga towards the Slave.

Cyric helped him ease it off the wounded arm. 'The blood is not yours,' he said hoping he was right.

'Quite right. I'm not sure what injury the guard did to my arm though.' Titus' hands moved down over his arm. The forearm worked fine, some little electrical shock like pains when he moved it but otherwise no problems. It was his upper arm that stayed immobile against his side. He felt further up trying to find a fracture; but there was none, it didn't even hurt to press the bone. He began to palpate his shoulder joint, and almost immediately fainted from the pain. 'It's dislocated,' he groaned at Cyric. The lift had begun to slow, approaching its final destination. Titus suddenly remembered the lifts to his left as they had first entered the building. They were going to come up into the main atrium, which when they had last seen it, had been teeming with guards.

'Quick,' Titus motioned to Cyric to come over, 'I need you to hit me.'

'What?'

'Hit me,' Titus repeated, 'hard on the shoulder.'

The boy pulled back his arm, and looked into Titus' eyes. He was terrified.

'Go on, do it,' Titus insisted.

The boy struck.

Agony shot up Titus' arm and his vision clouded. Fighting off the urge to faint he realised that, despite the pain, the blow had not been enough. 'Again,' he shouted, and gritted his teeth as the elevator came to an abrupt halt.

The Slave boy thought of the operating tables downstairs, drew back his arm, and struck much harder the second time. An explosion of agony shot through Titus' shoulder into his neck, forcing him to his knees as a loud click signalled the relocation of the shoulder joint. Blinking the tears of pain from his eyes and wiping from his brow the cold sweat which had developed, he turned back to Cyric.

'Well done.'

The doors of the elevator swung open. With his good arm Titus gathered Cyric by the shoulder and propelled himself through the doorway at a full sprint, dragging the young man behind him. There was no point in stealth for there was no cover of any description in the huge open foyer. The pain in his shoulder focused him and he took in the scene in a fraction of a second. There were two guards at the far end of the atrium, too far away to be any threat in the period of time Titus planned on staying in the huge open space. A third guard stood with one arm on the reception desk and appeared to be in deep conversation with the receptionist, and indeed extremely receptive to her obvious charm. The fourth and final guard stood directly in front of the revolving glass doors which separated death and freedom.

He still had four shots. That was plenty. The guard at the reception desk turned around open-mouthed as the bloodstained pair tore across the marble floor. Titus couldn't risk leaving him alive. He swung up the sonifex, and fired across his body as he maintained his sprint. The guard dropped as Titus continued his run at the fourth guard. The man swung round as if in slow motion to Titus' heightened senses, shooting wildly

226

from the hip. Titus fired two shots. He would have liked to have aimed for the head, but even he could not be sure of success at a range of fifteen metres whilst at full sprint. Both shots struck the guard in the centre of the body propelling him backwards into the mechanism of the revolving door, which jammed immediately.

Titus flipped around, the final two guards were running towards them but they were still fifty metres away on the other side of the atrium. He had one shot left. He pointed the sonifex at the nearest of the two, using his left hand cupped around his right to steady the aim. He could not guarantee to hit, and besides there would still be one guard alive even then. He cursed, turned to face the jammed doors, and pulled the trigger.

The glass exploded. Titus grabbed Cyric again and threw him through the opening in the doors before jumping after him. Leaping down the steps together, dazzled by the sun, they headed for the road. Their currus remained where they had left it wrecked by the rubbish skip. Would it work? There was only one way to find out. Titus flicked his head around; the guards would be out on the street in seconds. They dashed across the road.

A currus, roaring at breakneck speed around the corner, saw the fleeing pair at the last minute and slammed on its brakes skidding to a halt. It was heavily modified, large exhausts, customised non military body parts, even the sonifex mounts had been entirely removed. Someone had spent a lot of time and sestertii on this vehicle and Cyric, who understood such things, broke out into a wide grin at the sight of it.

'What the fuck are you doing in the road, you blind fuck?' shouted the driver, his eyes wide with rage.

The man was only a few years older than Cyric, Titus thought, but with much more irritating hair. From the driver's expression it was clear that his rant had been composed before he had realised that it would be delivered to a man wearing a blood stained sheet, carrying a still smoking sonifex.

'Get out.' Titus said calmly to the young Roman, who nodded meekly, and quickly and silently obliged. The pair leapt in as bullets struck the road and sides of the currus. Titus hit the accelerator hard and the vehicle screamed away leaving a trail of black rubber, its owner staring forlornly as it tore around a corner and disappeared.

As *VivIter* receded into the distance, and Londinium began to fall away behind them, at last Titus let himself breath a sigh of relief. He turned to Cyric, who sat there with the same glum expression as always etched on his face.

'Why did you help me in there, Cyric?' Titus asked.

'I only did it to save myself.'

'What do you mean?'

'Without you I would have died, I can admit that, you can fight better than me. That's why I saved you.' He didn't seem entirely convinced by his own reasoning.

The pair drove in silence for a moment before Cyric asked what he had wanted to ask since they had first found the grisly secrets of *VivIter*. 'Why will you not try to stop this from happening?'

'How?' Titus asked.

'Well, you could try telling people for a start, I mean you are a noble, they will listen to you.'

'Dishonoured nobility,' Titus cut in. They had had this conversation before.

'Or, even on a small scale, you could save my fellow Slaves from Strabo, even kill the man for what he has done.' His voice rose in anger, 'for God's sake Titus, you know what goes on in there, how can you let it continue?'

'I want to kill Strabo.' Titus replied earnestly. 'I want to kill him for you, but even more I want to kill him for Ceinwyn. I even promised her I would do it. But he is so powerful, and he has the Praetorian guard. I can't risk the retribution, I can't risk what might happen to Ceinwyn.' He waved his hand back in the direction of *VivIter*. 'That databank was my last chance for a peaceful solution to finding my friend, and bringing Strabo down, and it has gone.'

He thought for a moment. 'Therefore there is one last option: to leave without Quintus, as I now have no hope in blackmailing Strabo to help me rescue him. That way I can still leave with Ceinwyn and my other friends. I hate myself for even suggesting it but it must be the correct thing to do; Quintus is probably dead. But to me it still seems like nothing but pure cowardice.'

228

'You would run?' asked Cyric, incredulously.

'Yes, because I love Ceinwyn, and I cannot think of any other way she will be safe.'

'Then it is not cowardice,' replied Cyric, earnestly.

'You think not?' asked Titus, not sure why it suddenly seemed to matter to him so much that he received this boy's approval, but nonetheless suddenly it did, more than anything in the world.

'You actually love her, don't you?' Cyric said.

'Yes, with all my heart,' Titus replied, his heart soaring at the thought of her.

'You deserve her,' Cyric replied, looking away from Titus so that he could not see his tears. 'And you are right, you cannot risk her or her love for you on attacking Strabo.'

'Thank you Cyric.'

Cyric drew a deep breath, and made a decision, 'I have never trusted a Roman in my life, but I think I can trust you. Perhaps we can save your friend's life too.'

Titus looked at the boy, confused, 'how will you manage to do what I with my men and weapons, cannot?'

'You say that you could blackmail Strabo to help you?'

'Probably, with the data from *VivIter*, but now I have no proof. I have nothing that I could threaten to send to the Praetorian Guard in Londinium.'

'Yes, but he will have files that will implicate him in his own compound.'

'I'm sure he does, but most of the files are encoded.' He remembered his initial raid on the compound over a month ago.

Cyric brought out a piece of paper from a pocket in his cowl and finding a pen on the floor of the currus began to scribble. When he had finished he handed the paper to Titus.

It had a single word on it:

Ignis Avis

'What does this mean?' Titus asked.

'It's the name of a fifty year old racing currus, very well modified; one of Strabo's favourites, and mine for that matter.'

'How does that help us?' Titus asked

'Because it is also his password.' The boy sat back in his seat with his arms folded looking smug.

Titus could have reached over and hugged him. He didn't even care that the boy had withheld this information from him for over a month. He understood the turmoil that had raged in him, and which he had only just overcome. 'What do you want in return?' he asked, knowing that he possessed nothing that was worth the information he had been given by the boy.

'Look after her for me,' Cyric said quietly.

'I will.'

There was nothing else to say, Titus understood the courage it must have taken the boy to admit that Ceinwyn did not, and never would love him.

'I will.' He put his hand on Cyric's shoulder and waited, looking away out of the windscreen onto the road whilst the boy struggled to suppress the hot tears that wouldn't stop.

But Titus' heart felt joy for the first time in over a week. He looked down at the speedometer—he was doing just over a hundred miles an hour, the fastest this currus could go, which was considerably faster than most. He smiled as the miles inexorably ticked away, each one closing up a small fraction of the distance between him and Ceinwyn.

XXXVI

The currus was closing fast. Quintus cursed again; he should have checked whether the Reivers had any other curri. He had had plenty of time to do so. At first, in his arrogance, he had thought that he was not even followed, but then the sleeker and, obviously much more powerful currus, had appeared in the mirrors. He had not managed to shake it yet. So far all that had saved him was the narrowness of the track. Despite his memory of there being a proper road not far from the camp he had been unable to find it. Now after driving over ten miles he was still wallowing in deeply rutted mud tracks. It was no surprise to him; no-one lived here, so why bother metalling the roads? Only farmers would use this track, farmers and mercenaries.

The currus tried to get alongside him again; it had tried this trick earlier and failed. The track was far too narrow. Quintus looked ahead and noted the approaching passing place, the Reiver had seen it too and realised he had an opportunity to get alongside. His passenger was none other than Graham Armstrong, the Reiver Captain. Quintus went pale as he saw the brutal looking assault sonifex held tightly in the hands of a man who had just seen his family literally destroyed. Quintus knew he was dead if they managed to get alongside. As if to punctuate his thoughts, the Captain fired a volley at the ancient currus. The bullets ricocheted harmlessly off the rear of the vehicle. That was one thing to be said about military hand-me-downs, even when they were as ancient as this one they stayed bullet proof. But the side windows and windscreen were far from impenetrable however. Quintus had to protect them at all costs.

He punched the accelerator pedal hard and twisted a dial on the dashboard, waiting for the power to build. The currus lurched forwards, its cogs straining under the amount of load he was putting on them. The induction coil beneath the vehicle glowed a deep red as it absorbed the power he was demanding. He looked back. The other vehicle was still closing, despite his best efforts, but he realised he had done just enough. As the passing space approached, the Reiver realised that he had no time to get alongside, and hammered on the brakes to prevent himself driving headlong into the trees thickly lining the track.

Quintus shook his fist in victory. But he was not safe yet. He still had no idea where he was in the thick wood, and he was not sure what the range of his vehicle's induction coil was. Modern coils could induct charge from hundreds of miles away. Quintus wondered exactly how far he could move from a node. The nearest one would probably be in Luguvalium. There was no range indicator on the dashboard, nor did it have any GPS. He cursed the currus once again.

Then the road began to open up in front of him and, glancing in the mirror, Quintus saw the Reiver Captain's face glow with savage victory. He was about to reach the metalled road. He could no longer block the more powerful currus. It would be a straight race; one which he knew he had no hope of winning. The Reivers would pull alongside and would simply shoot him through the window. He turned the corner with the realisation it could be his last, and suddenly saw where he was.

For there was no metalled road. Instead there was an open plaza, from which a single track led up to an embankment. And on the top of the embankment, bristling with various artillery, stood the Great Wall. 'Caledonia,' he whooped, almost leaping to his feet with excitement and banging his head on the metal canopy above him. He was safe. Looking back he saw the Reivers still close on his tail, but the look of victory on the Captain's face had been replaced by a scowl.

Quintus wrenched the wheel round to the left as he reached the far end of the plaza. The rear tyres squealed at the punishment and he was nearly jerked from his seat as the nearside one burst under the pressure, leaving a trail of flailing rubber; it did not matter. He was safe now. The Reiver vehicle had come to a halt out of range of the wall. Quintus could already see weaponry being aimed in its direction lest it should dare come into the Wall's area of control. The gunnery captain stared implacably through the death mask of his protective suit as he manipulated the controls on the nearest cannon. Gouts of oily smoke poured from the nozzle—a warning of what could come.

To Quintus' surprise the fire thrower came to rest pointing directly at his vehicle. 'What the hell are they playing at!' he muttered, before realising that he was in a battered old currus decorated with macabre Reiver trophies.

He abandoned the vehicle hastily, and stood alone in the plaza his arms folded across his chest. The thought occurred to him that maybe he should hold them out in a gesture of submission. He shook his head. He was a soldier of Rome. He would not submit to his own men. Small flecks of powder snow decorated his filthy tunic as he stepped purposefully towards the imposing gate. He wished that he still had his jacket, at least then he wouldn't look like a vagrant. He threw a cursory glance behind him and was surprised to see the Reiver Captain had left his vehicle too, and was slowly following him. Quintus looked up at the battery. Whilst some of the wicked looking weaponry was pointed at the Reiver, an equal amount was tracking his every move. His jubilation at his good fortune began to slowly fade. He fished into his pockets with increasing desperation. He found nothing that could prove who he was. He would have to talk his way through.

As he reached the gate he nodded in greeting to the border guard. Although all the world was Roman some parts were more directly controlled than others. No-one cared about Caledonia. Once upon a time the great General Hadrian had built a wall to keep out the crazy warriors who painted their faces with woad and the blood of their vanquished enemies. The woad was gone; the wall was not. The war was over; the bloodshed not entirely. There was no need for the full might of Rome to keep control, but a visible strong hand ready to come crashing down kept the peace.

It also made valuable taxes for Rome. At the same moment Quintus had arrived at the border gate, a currus rumbled up from the other side laden with bales of wool. There were plenty of sheep in Caledonia. The Guard held out his hand to Quintus. It was not a greeting; the palm was outstretched in a clear signal to halt and the sonifex slung over the soldier's back emphasised the point. The soldier waited whilst a comrade opened the gate and beckoned the currus through. The driver hastily handed a bundle of sestertii over to the solider, who placed it into a pouch in his webbing which hung down beneath his khaki body armour. Quintus had once owned a suit like it; he would have given anything for it now. Turning anxiously he saw the Reiver Captain only a hundred yards away, walking slowly but purposefully towards him, the look on his face still murderous.

'I am a soldier of Rome,' it was a gamble. But if he waited his turn it could be too late.

'And I've fucked the vestal virgins.'

The joke wasn't actually that bad, for the soldier was extraordinarily ugly and his sneer only made his face look worse. Quintus felt like telling him this, but managed to bite his tongue. 'Let me past,' he demanded angrily. He had presence, and he knew it. Even coated head to toe in mud he made the guard think twice.

'Perhaps, when this is through,' the soldier replied gesturing to the vehicle which was ambling through the gate irritatingly slowly.

'There is no time,' Quintus said raising his voice.

'Why the hurry?' Asked the guard purposefully gesturing at the driver to stop.

Quintus pointed over his shoulder as if it was obvious. 'That man means to kill me.'

The soldier laughed and shrugged his shoulders, 'does he now?'

'Do you know who I am?' Quintus shouted indignantly, and immediately wished he hadn't.

The soldier's gazed hardened and Quintus realised that, despite the rude exterior the man had only really been joking with him until now.

Knowing that he had to follow this approach through now he had started it, Quintus continued, 'I am a soldier of Rome, I was once a Military Tribune in the Transmaritanus, my commander was a man called Titus Aquilinus.'

'Papers.' Replied the guard, disinterestedly.

Quintus heard purposeful footsteps crunching on the gravel behind him. 'What?'

'Your papers,' the soldier looked at Quintus as if he was stupid.

The footsteps stopped. The Reiver was right behind him. Quintus wanted to reach forward and shake the guard into action. He turned round expecting to feel a sonifex pushed into his back. But instead the Captain stood a couple of yards behind him patiently waiting his turn. 'I have been a prisoner of the Reivers, do you think they let me keep my papers?' Quintus replied sarcastically.

The soldier's eyebrows furrowed in deep thought for a moment, 'and I suppose this is your captor here?' he said gesturing over Quintus' shoulder.

'Yes. Why don't you seize him, he is a criminal!' Quintus shouted.

The gunner wandered over to the edge of the parapet to watch the altercation. 'You look more like a Reiver than he does,' he called down at Quintus, laughing.

The gate guard nodded at his friend's comment. Quintus looked behind him at the Captain dressed in his thick jacket, and then at what remained of his own bedraggled clothing.

Then the Captain's voice boomed out over all of theirs, 'he is no Reiver.' The soldiers turned to look at him. His accent was thick, but he was able to command respect nonetheless. 'He is my Slave,' he continued.

Quintus turned to the soldier to protest. But saw that the disgusting smirk had returned. His heart sank.

'He does not look like a Slave,' the soldier said, 'he bears no signum.'

'No, but looks can be deceptive,' replied the Reiver Captain, smiling confidently at the guard.

The soldier stepped forwards and took Quintus by the shoulders. 'Slaves should always obey their masters,' he sneered, and brought his knee up into Quintus' groin doubling him over as the Reiver Captain signalled to his driver, who quickly brought the vehicle over.

With tears forming in his eyes at the pain and humiliation, Quintus stared at the solider with eyes as cold and calculating as he could muster, 'one day you are going to seriously regret that.' He did not believe the words; he was going to die well before he could take revenge. But the words in perfect Latin seemed to shake the man a little. He could not seriously believe he was a Slave. Had the Reiver somehow bribed them?

But the Reiver Captain did not seem to hand anything over to the soldier. Quintus was forced into the front of the cockpit and sandwiched between the two Reivers. The vehicle started with an ominous rumble, and drove Quintus away back into the forest.

There was silence in the cab for some time. Quintus spent it trying to think of some choice last words. He was finding it trickier than he had expected, eventually he decided that this was probably because he did not have any idea how he would want to be remembered.

'I lost my family today.' It was the Captain who broke the silence.

Quintus nodded, not sure what he should say to someone who had lost so much.

'I do not expect you to mourn them,' he continued, as if to answer Quintus' thoughts. 'I thought your presence in the camp would protect us, that you had importance and that our master would never risk killing you. I was wrong.' He stared into the distance for a moment and then changed the subject, 'that soldier was right—you do not look like a Slave.'

'Your money changed his mind,' replied Quintus, angrily.

'I paid him nothing.'

'Then how...' Quintus replied, exasperated.

'Blood is thicker than water.'

Quintus just stared at him blankly so the Captain continued, 'or for that matter, allegiance to a country or government.'

'But that man cannot be of your blood?'

'Why not?' the Captain asked, 'do your armies not come from all over the world, including Britannia.'

'But he has sworn allegiance to the Roman Legion; that makes him a citizen.

'Yes, but he is also an Armstrong. But that would be to state the situation in its inverse; for he is very much an Armstrong first, and a Roman second.'

Quintus was stunned into silence.

'You wonder who we Reivers are don't you?' asked the Captain.

Quintus nodded dumbly.

'I was born here,' the Captain explained, taking out a pre-rolled cigarette from beneath his cap, 'my family were not Roman citizens so I had little in the way of job prospects and so I became a soldier at the age of sixteen, and escaped my dull life in Luguvalium. Your people care little for their provinces don't they?' He shook his lighter before striking it, the light filling the dingy cabin. 'The war in the Transmaritanus gave me a purpose and a cause. But I lost everything when the war ended.' He drew on the cigarette hungrily, blowing curls of smoke that eddied around the edges of his thick beard. 'Eventually I stopped moping about how I had been promised citizenship in return for my service, and instead I found the woods; I used my skills to form a new life. Much like you have I think?' he said staring at Quintus who stared back intently, interested now. 'I found in the woods many others who felt the same, some like me—disillusioned soldiers turned mercenaries; others who had lost their lives at the hands of others lower down the pecking order in Rome. But the Reivers captured my imagination most: wild men who had never quite accepted a wall, of all things, dividing them from their relations in Caledonia. Men who had no interest in Rome, or citizenship for that matter. But they preyed on each other continuously causing trouble for none but themselves.' He paused and reclined in his chair with pride, 'until I found them that is. Now they cause much trouble, do you not think?'

'When the war ended many fell on hard times, but we soldiers swore an oath to Rome,' replied Quintus angrily, 'how dare you defile it?'

'Spoken like a true Roman. Those who were born within the Pomerium of the great city may indeed never be able to turn their back on it, which I understand. But in turn you have to understand that for me, and a great many others you in the past called comrades, Roman citizenship through soldiering was nothing more than a stepping stone; one that was torn out from under my feet in midstream by that bastard Marcus Albus. He provided nothing for the veterans.'

Quintus had no answer to this. He told himself this was because of the shock of his capture, but the truth was that the Reiver was right. Marcus Albus had treated the armies poorly when he became Consul in Rome; yet people had continued to vote for him in the Senatorial elections and his majority grew stronger each year. Standing up to that would have been to face a vast tide, and no-one had.

'How are there so many of you?' Quintus asked, surprised that so many felt this way in Britannia; there could surely not be this many destitute soldiers from Luguvalium?

'You think that we are all soldiers?' The Captain laughed bleakly. He pointed to the driver, his voice melancholy, 'Plubius once ran a successful fish wholesale business. He had his own ship, until Strabo took everything he had.'

Quintus looked at the driver, realising suddenly, and with horror, that he recognised the man. Quintus himself had stood and watched as Titus took his money on Strabo's orders only a few months ago. The man looked different now, leaner and purposeful. Confronted with the results of his own actions for the first time he tried to speak, but his mouth opened and shut noiselessly.

Plubius grinned and spoke in the salty accent that Quintus remembered. 'Your master. He did it. Not you.' He took a grubby, calloused hand from the wheel and offered it to Quintus.

Quintus took it, looking at the Reiver Captain. There was no grin—the events earlier in the day had taken that from him, but he had no malice in his eyes. Suddenly, with joy, Quintus realised that he was not going to die.

'When I first asked you why I was still alive you said you wanted to draw out my death.'

The Captain laughed. 'My reputation. The truth be told, I simply had had enough of killing for no reason. My men,' he turned to Plubius, 'current company excepted, expect me to lead by vicious example. Mercy wasn't an option.'

'So why did you not ransom me?'

The Captain looked at Quintus like he was mad, 'did you want to end up hanging from a tree?'

Quintus did not understand.

'You know your master, he wouldn't reward the incompetence of being captured. It would have been as good as killing you myself.'

'But I work for the Governor, Strabo,' Quintus said, correcting the Captain.

'And he thinks that we work for him too.'

Quintus was stunned. 'Sorry, the Governor, employs you?'

'No, just takes a cut of what we make, and allows us to go about our business. A very good business arrangement until recently.' His eyes narrowed as he thought about Strabo. 'His demands got out of hand, I refused them. I wish that I had just paid him.' He stared ahead at the road for some time.

Quintus thought about the implications of what the Reiver had said. 'So that man we found hanging from the tree, with the document case, Strabo ordered that.'

'He did, and he ordered us to leave everything exactly as we found it, take nothing except his money,' the Captain replied.

'Why?'

'I'm not sure, we searched him anyway and found nothing of any interest.'

'We were asked to return the body to Strabo. It was our first mission for him.'

The Reiver Captain nodded with interest. 'If he wanted the body he needed someone more reputable than brigands to deliver it to him; we couldn't exactly just turn up and leave it outside his compound!'

Quintus agreed, 'funny thing is though, he wasn't interested in the body, it was the briefcase he wanted.'

The Captain laughed again, 'That makes no sense either—I searched that too. Boring. I can't see why he would have wanted anything that was in it.'

'What was in there?' Quintus asked intrigued.

'You mean you never even looked! You are trusting of those you work for. I think the man was some sort of architect, the briefcase was full of schematics for pumps, water tanks, piping. None of us could work out how they could help him make money, and that is *all* Strabo is interested in.'

It made no sense to Quintus either, so he settled down in the seat and thought. All thoughts of escape had now left him. He had no idea what he would be escaping to anymore.

XXXVII

Titus' legs ached with each torturous step, yet he gathered pace with each and Cyric trotted behind him eagerly. It was early morning; they had driven through the night with no break for sleep. Titus had not needed it, fuelled only by the desire to see Ceinwyn again. The sun was no more than an idea on the horizon, but for the first time since Quintus had been lost he could see his path clearly. He would see his Ceinwyn, and take her to safety. Then he would blackmail Strabo, and rescue Quintus. That part of the plan was unfinished, however with Marcus at his side he knew he could not fail. The good old days were back once more.

The pair travelled in silence apart from the sounds of their hearts beating heavily in their chests with the exertion of the climb. To the right a small stream cascaded over rocks, plunging down the valley far below. Titus had never travelled the path before, but he had seen the place where he was travelling to on a map. The cave, however, existed only in his dreams, and since Ceinwyn had been hidden there he had had many of them.

He had spent much of his life wondering what it was to truly love. Girls had always liked him, and he had taken much advantage of this, but since the army he had kept a distance from any woman who took too much of an interest in him. But this was love. Here he was climbing a mountain in near darkness to see a woman who he had only been parted from for a matter of a week.

The path twisted beneath their feet around the steepest escarpments; it was the time of night just before dawn where it was at its darkest, for there was no trace of the moon nor the sun. Looking up he scanned the terrain for any sign of the cliffs he was meant to be passing between. He waited, cursing his eyes for taking so long to accustom to the gloom.

'There,' the boy's voice whispered quietly behind him, 'it is beautiful.'

'And your eyes are stronger than mine,' Titus grumbled, but as he stared ahead the cliffs did indeed began to appear, faint outlines of black on black to start with, but, as he took his time, gradually they took on shape and texture. The sun was rising, but the cliffs before him kept it from him. He pressed on, his breath catching in his chest. The gangly boy kept pace easily behind him, in another world perhaps the army could have made a decent soldier of him Titus acknowledged, grudgingly. A Slave soldier; Titus' upbringing made it immediately hilarious to him, but why was it so stupid? Titus shook his head at Cyric's earlier suggestion that he should tell people about Slaves not being just animals, if he could only just manage to believe it himself how could he expect anyone else to? He sighed—the habits of a life time were hard to break.

He wondered what Ceinwyn would say if she could only read his thoughts? He could see her laughing and shaking her head at his stubbornness; his fear of the ridicule of others was nothing in comparison to the life she had been forced to live, yet she had accepted that life, and let it mould her in the way she wished to be moulded. He could hardly believe she had been oppressed her whole life; she seemed freer than he did.

Maybe he should start telling people? He could start with Gnaeus; he'd probably understand. But the thought of announcing to the vast majority, the closed minded men that he had lived and fought beside most of his life, filled him with fear. He would rather walk into Strabo's compound single

242

handed, and punish the man for every minute of mistreatment Ceinwyn and her friends had suffered at his hands. Smiling at the thought of humbling the fat Governor, he could not stop himself from thinking of how much happiness that would bring to Ceinwyn, and how grateful she would be. And altogether how easy in comparison it seemed to telling the world the truth about Slaves.

The sky above the cliffs was navy blue now, the sun clearly up but still hidden by the bulk of the fell side before them. Titus took the last steps of the path at a bound and suddenly came to a standstill as he reached the top, his breath taken away. Before him, stretching quarter of a mile, surrounded by crags on three sides lay a beautiful mountain lake. Ceinwyn had a different word for it in her old language: a tarn. To the side of it, five hundred paces away she herself stood, the object of Titus' wonder, a slender girl filling a jerry can with water. Her hair glowing rich copper in the morning light. She stood up, heaving the can out of the tarn with difficulty. Standing in the dawn light with the jerry can resting against her, she looked around, clearly enjoying the beautiful morning. She turned slowly until she faced the pair standing on the lip of the escarpment. Her mouth opened to give a cry of alarm, which either never came or never carried across the distance. Then she recognised Titus.

The jerry can fell onto the path beside her.

The water glugged back into the tarn noisily.

She ran towards them.

XXXVIII

And then there was yet more ascent but his legs ached no longer. The tarn glittered far below in the morning sun which now streamed over the cliff tops. His arm tightly gripped the waist of the girl he loved; it was the middle of winter but he was warm. As they walked together Titus told her everything he had discovered in Londinium, whilst Cyric trailed behind following sullenly.

They gained height quickly and by the time they reached the cave Titus realised he had spoken for almost the entire journey. But then he had had much to say, and Ceinwyn had been amazed and disgusted in equal measure by the revelations about her old master. Pausing a short distance from the cave he stopped, and apologising, asked her how her time in the cave had been. She smiled at him, and his obvious embarrassment in not asking her sooner, but in truth there was not much for her to say, apart from that she had missed him. She had thought hard during the last days in the cave as to how she would tell Titus about Marcus, but even now she could not find the words.

And so finally they came to the lip of the cave where she had spent the last week, with him still oblivious. Titus strode forwards ahead of her and called into the cave, 'Marcus, you old bastard, come on out!' There was no reply, 'we've got a job at last, a proper one, we're going to go back to Strabo's mansion, and then...' He stopped in mid sentence as he caught sight of Gnaeus sitting on the cave floor.

'I must congratulate you on finding this wonderful cave,' he spoke, getting to his feet and running his hands along the moss covered walls. 'A good hideout. A bit far from civilisation though, anyone would think you had been trying to hide something.' Titus didn't know what to say. 'What you have been hiding is priceless beyond measure however,' Gnaeus exclaimed as Ceinwyn scrambled into view. 'Why you didn't ask me to protect her is beyond my understanding.'

'I asked Marcus.'

'And where is Marcus?'

Titus shrugged so Gnaeus told him: 'back in his house moping about how his friend's lover wouldn't leave his friend for him. You should have asked me,' he reiterated.

'I'm sorry Gnaeus.' Titus said, thinking how best to explain why he had not told Gnaeus anything at all, but he realised that he couldn't explain it. It had made sense to him at the time. He cursed himself; he should have trusted his friends.

'Cup of tea?' Gnaeus asked, changing the subject and gesturing to the battered pot teetering on the crackling fire in the far corner of the cave.

Ceinwyn and Titus both nodded, and Gnaeus collected a couple of cups from the shelf on the wall and began to pour the green liquid. He laughed hollowly as he handed the tea to Titus, something was troubling him.

'It's good to see you again,' he said.

The three of them drank together, happy to be reunited at last, although Titus worried about Marcus. Marcus was, if nothing else, proud and easily hurt. He needed to talk to him. Even then he wondered if he would be able to get his help.

He took a deep breath and spoke, 'I don't know what to do.' Immediately he felt as if a huge weight had been lifted from his chest. He had never admitted that to anyone before.

Gnaeus laughed. 'Do any of us?'

'At least I have you back,' Ceinwyn replied, hugging him. The pair kissed, and when they had finished realised that Gnaeus had left them alone.

'I missed you.' Titus whispered to Ceinwyn, the words still echoing in the cave.

'I love you.' Ceinwyn replied.

'I love you too.' They kissed again.

'I will always look after you, and I promise never to leave you behind again.'

'And I will never let you leave me behind again.'

The pair stared into each other's eyes in the gloom of the cave, Titus' dark brown, hard and black in the darkness; Ceinwyn's almost glowing with a deep green luminescence. 'Marry me.' Titus said.

'Marry me.' Ceinwyn replied, coyly.

Titus became acutely aware of the fact he had not brought a ring, but then he had not planned any of this.

His thoughts were interrupted by Ceinwyn. 'There is one condition,' she was looking down at the ground.

'Go on.'

'Let me withdraw my request to you, the night you saved me. Leave here with me. I would rather we be safe than my master dead. Take me to Rome.'

'Rome,' Titus was taken aback—Ceinwyn would not be allowed in Rome, not with Marcus Albus' new rules. But they could cross that bridge when they came to it, and for now he would grant any wish for his wife to be. 'Of course,' he replied.

'We should go now.'

'It will only take me a day or two to get a plan together to break into Strabo's compound.'

'No,' Ceinwyn was insistent now, 'you must not,' she was almost in tears.

'Ceinwyn, I can do it! Cyric has a password that will get me information I need to bring Strabo down.' He had to press on with the plan; he had to rescue his friend; and he wanted to punish Strabo for

Ceinwyn. She might pretend she did not want revenge anymore, but he knew she would never be truly happy until he was gone.

'Quintus is dead Titus.' She looked down at her feet, finding it difficult to meet his gaze, 'Gnaeus told me, there was a report from the wall. He was seen there. They think he had escaped—he looked awful. But the Reivers caught him just as he reached the wall, and executed him in front of the soldiers before they could act. I'm so sorry.'

Titus could not speak. He had suspected that Quintus might have been killed, but still the confirmation of it felt like a blow to the stomach. 'Strabo must pay, for my friend, and for what he did to you,' he growled.

Ceinwyn shook her head. 'I no longer want my master ruined,' she said. 'I take what I said back. I cannot risk your life. You must not go back there. He will kill you.'

'I will kill him then,' Titus replied proudly.

Ceinwyn shook her head at him, 'on your own?'

'Marcus and I.' Titus said, and then realised the flaw in his plan.

'I don't think he will help you,' she came to him and put her arms around his shoulders. 'I am sorry, for it is my fault.'

'It is his alone.' Titus replied coldly.

'Promise me then.'

She stared at him with her eyes wide and penetrating and her jaw set defiantly; she looked more beautiful than ever before, he could not refuse her.

'I promise.' The words sounded hollow even to him.

She nodded. It was agreed. They would be married, and they would live together for ever far away in Rome, if they could somehow smuggle her in there. And neither they, nor Cyric, nor the memory of Quintus would ever be truly satisfied, and Titus knew it, and the truth hurt him more deeply than Strabo ever could. They could not be happy like this.

They arrived to a Luguvalium in uproar. Hordes of hungry people roamed the streets in packs, and Marcus was nowhere to be found. As they sat in Titus' front room keeping a watchful eye on the street outside, yet another small explosion gently rocked the house. 'We should leave this place now,' Ceinwyn said.

'Not until I have seen what is going on.'

Gnaeus grimaced at the idea, 'come on Gnaeus, you are coming with me. There is something going on in the square, we need to see it.'

'I have to admit that it does sound rather more terrifying than interesting,' replied Gnaeus, who, despite his reservations, grabbed his coat and followed Titus onto the street outside. The air stank and became increasingly rancid as they neared the square.

All along the main road there lay the ruins of shops, previously boarded up, now looted as the depression over the town had deepened. 'I was only gone a week,' Titus said to Gnaeus, who just shrugged his shoulders.

'What the hell has happened here?' Titus asked as they entered the square.

'War,' Gnaeus replied. 'With the Reivers. All the shops are shut and no food has been distributed for days.'

The square was strewn with the bullet torn bodies and possessions of several dead men. A huddle of men, women and children stood at their side of the square. At the other end, with the bodies separating the two parties, stood a group of Praetorian Guard protecting a supply of food which it appeared they had, up until recently, been rationing out.

'A proper war?' Titus replied incredulously.

Gnaeus shook his head, 'I don't think Rome knows,' he said, as the smoke rose all around them burning their noses with its acrid sting.

'But surely Strabo would tell Rome; it would be embarrassing to have an uprising of course, but if he needed help...'

Gnaeus shrugged, 'or if he had something to hide.'

'Which we know he does.'

A group of Slaves huddled clustered for warmth in the foyer of the main hotel on the square. They looked thin, haggard and ill. As Titus watched, an elderly male Slave vomited on himself and lay back down, seemingly without even the energy to clean himself.

'So soon, to have people starving on the streets in just one week.'

Gnaeus shook his head, 'I don't think they're starving. Most of the Slaves in the city are like this now. The chief medical officer says it is some type of Slave disease, but they haven't told us its name.' He pointed up at a half torn poster on the side of the clock tower.

'Vos ipsos ex mortem liberate!'

The other half of the poster was mainly torn away, but showed a diseased looking Slave.

'Save yourselves from death!'

'Strong words,' Titus said, worried.

'Effective words. People won't help the Slaves, they just run away,' Gnaeus said.

The pair walked over towards the group of diseased Slaves who shuffled away in fear as they approached.

'Do not be afraid, we are not going to hurt you,' Titus addressed them. 'What has happened.'

The old slave they had seen vomiting earlier looked up at them from the ground. He was stick thin and his yellowing eyes were sunken with dehydration, but his abdomen bulged grotesquely as if full to burst with some sort of corrupt fluid. The stench of the Slaves made Titus retch. None of the Slaves would speak, perhaps partly from fear, but many of them seemed so close to death that speech was now beyond them.

'There is nothing we can do for them,' Gnaeus said quietly. 'But there may still be time to save other Slaves. One's who have not been exposed yet to whatever disease this is.' He clearly meant Ceinwyn.

Titus nodded, and they began to hurry back towards their houses. But Titus couldn't stop thinking about the dying Slaves. Maybe there was nothing medical that could be done now, but only Slaves seemed affected so there seemed no reason that other people couldn't nurse them safely. The scaremongering poster had clearly put paid to any hope of that though. Angry at the way Strabo was running the situation, Titus stopped.

'What about these people then?' Titus said to Gnaeus gesturing around at the beggars in the square, and the pitiful supply of food guarded by the Praetorians.

'We cannot help them either.'

'Yes we can,' shouted Titus, grabbing him by his collar and shaking him. 'This can end here, now. If you help me.' He paused, 'please Gnaeus, help me destroy him.'

Everyone was staring at them now. The Praetorians began to move towards them, then looked at the hungry crowd and returned to guard the stockpile of food.

'Why are you even here Titus?' Gnaeus shouted back angrily. 'Of all the God forsaken places on this Earth, why this one? Dacia: that was a load of fun wasn't it? We were proper mercenaries. But it wasn't enough for you was it, playing soldiers. You had to be one again; be in command once again. So we come here, the only place in the whole world which is still 'at war'. Except it isn't really 'at war', because the Picts are completely subdued by that giant wall. You were so disappointed by that weren't you? But now we do indeed eventually have a war. Strabo against the Reivers, and in actual fact it seems to be Luguvalium which suffers, which does not surprise me.'

Titus nodded agreement at this; they had both seen enough war to realise that it was common people minding their own business who came off worst when powerful men clashed over them.

'You wanted another war, Titus,' Gnaeus continued, 'and now you have it. But there are only five of us, and neither side would welcome us within their ranks. That leaves us only one sane option.'

'Kill Strabo,' Titus hissed.

'So the Reivers win?' Gnaeus asked, exasperated. 'Remember the man with no eyes? Think Titus! They can't be allowed to win. You would have Rome lose this province?'

'Rome must win.' Titus replied.

'Then you cannot kill Strabo. So if you want to join in the war your only option is to offer your help to him! We must leave—it's our only choice.'

'But Strabo does not stand for Rome.'

'Then Rome has already lost Luguvalium,' Gnaeus replied bitterly.

'*We* are Rome,' Titus replied slowly, '*we* must win.'

Gnaeus laughed and shook his head with exasperation, 'you are the bravest man I have ever met. She deserves you.' His eyes closed briefly, almost in regret, for a moment before he continued. 'Once, like you, I would have charged in too. We did that together many times remember. But the time has come for us to start using our heads rather than trusting to our sonifi. Would you truly risk your life to destroy one man?'

'Gladly.'

'Even if that meant Ceinwyn going through her life alone, with no one to protect her?'

Titus thought hard, realising he had not entirely thought his plan through. 'If,' he paused, 'if *that* did happen, you would care for her.'

Gnaeus laughed again, 'of course I would. But she doesn't love me Titus. She loves you. There would be no lack of people willing to look after her. Marcus would also gladly look after her, but do you think for a minute that that is what she wants? She loves you so much that despite her desperation to wreak vengeance on Strabo, she has instead implored you to take her away. She is trying to protect you.'

'And you think I need protecting?' replied Titus, his pride hurt.

'You cannot go in there and come out alive and victorious without an army, and you have no army. There is no shame in admitting that.'

The pair stared at each other in the devastated square. Eventually Titus nodded. 'You are right my old friend.'

'Thank you.'

'It's a shame that I can't go and get Strabo's head for Ceinwyn; it would have made a nice wedding present.'

Gnaeus wrinkled his nose with disdain, 'a little macabre don't you think.'

'Perhaps.' Titus replied laughing, 'but did you actually listen to what I just said?'

Gnaeus nodded. 'So I guess congratulations are in order. I was merely trying to think of an empty slot in my diary to take the service,' he flicked through the pages of his logbook, trying to look as serious as he could, 'how about three nights from this?'

'Saturnalia itself?' Titus replied, surprised.

'I prefer to call it Christmas.'

'Seeing as I am letting a Christian marry us...' Titus laughed. 'Ceinwyn would like it to be then I'm sure.'

'Then it is set, three nights from now,' Gnaeus replied and the pair began to walk back towards their houses leaving the crowd far behind. But Titus' thoughts were never far from the dejected people of Luguvalium, and the desire for vengeance still burned deeply inside him.

'Where?' Titus asked.

'In secret.' Titus nodded his assent.

'A small island on a lake surrounded by the mountains. There is an old cross there, it will do nicely.'

'I know the place,' Titus replied, 'the local people call it Lord's Island.'

Gnaeus nodded, 'you have three nights to prepare.'

'Would it not be safer for us to marry here in the town?' Titus asked, concerned.

Gnaeus nodded, 'possibly. But Ceinwyn will want to get married in a Christian ceremony.'

'That is fine, it means something to her. It doesn't matter to me where it is. Surely though,' he added, 'there must be somewhere in the town?'

'Do you see a shrine to our God?' Gnaeus asked.

'It would be illegal,' Titus said, understanding the problem.

'So you can imagine our sacred places are not in the middle of cities and towns.'

The pair continued in silence for some time; the streets were deserted now. It seemed they were the only ones foolish enough to brave the streets now that martial law had descended.

'Will you return to Rome with Ceinwyn?' Gnaeus asked.

Titus nodded, 'and you will come with us, if that is what you wish?'

'I have missed Rome,' Gnaeus replied, blushing at his obviousness.

'I can barely remember it.' Titus replied, thinking of the tumbledown townhouse and his father's meaningless scribblings; those would be worth less now than the land his mother was buried in.

'You will love it once again when you return, and so will Ceinwyn.' Gnaeus continued, oblivious to Titus' thought furrowed brow, 'I hear that many of Ceinwyn's kind remain in the city despite the laws. They can make themselves look almost like usual Slaves until you get close up.'

252

Titus nodded, not really listening. 'I guess so,' he replied as he continued home, deep in his own silent thoughts. He had a plan.

XXXIX

The data banks whirred and clicked menacingly. Titus wished once again that his old friend Marcus was alongside. Maybe he could have helped him here, and maybe he would have talked him out of freeing Tristan. Freeing the broken young man was a needless risk, but Titus had felt a pang of regret as he saw him lying in the cage, no different to two months before. He did not know why he had done it, for he could not take the boy with him, and indeed Tristan had not moved when he opened the cage door. Did he even realise he was free? Titus had worried at first that he would leap at him, but he just knelt there with his mad eyes fixed on Titus'. Unblinking black pools staring into his soul. Mercifully he had stayed silent, but still Titus could not shake his fear that somewhere higher up in the compound Tristan would be stalking around, stirring up the guards. With difficulty he forced himself to turn his mind back to the task at hand.

'Ignis Avis'. He whispered under his breath as his fingers worked the small keyboard awkwardly. The databank alongside him beeped in acknowledgment, causing Titus to jump sharply. The screen before him glowed faintly before suddenly lighting up. Titus couldn't resist a small chuckle as he took in the information before him. It was everything he needed. The list of names, amounts and descriptions of services rendered

254

was the fine detail of all of Strabo's actions for years. Tomorrow it would be on the desk of the serious fraud office in the Praetorian Headquarters in London. He would have revenge eventually.

He thought of his wife to be, sitting beside the fire in their house this very moment, and dreaming of their wedding, now just two nights away. Gnaeus had helped her pick out the dress from a pile of many which a shopkeeper had been desperately trying to flog before fleeing the area. He should not be here either, he thought about what Ceinwyn would say if she knew that he was. But what better wedding present than the destruction of her old master? What better revenge for Quintus.

His eyes drifted towards the total balance at the bottom of the spreadsheet. It ran into millions of sestertii. A faint idea drifted into his mind, and he began to smile. Rummaging in the equipment bag he had stolen from Marcus, he fished out a small grey metal scire. He connected it into the entirely illegal box that he had stolen from Marcus' house earlier, and with difficulty located the correct interface at the back of the databank. Sweating now, he tapped the screen again, clenching his fists in triumph as Strabo's accounts were downloaded onto the machine. His fingers traced thick outlines on the screen as he worked through the menus one by one. Then he found the link he was looking for.

It only took a single click and then the money was his, every single sestertii. Except it wasn't quite his. It was Marcus', for it was Marcus' account terminal, and Titus did not have an online account. Having seen the ease with which he had stolen money from one though he felt that this was probably no bad thing. Everything that Strabo owned was now theirs. Revenge was his. Strabo would be ruined, disgraced and bankrupt.

He sat down on the cold concrete floor as he took in what he had just managed to do. Ceinwyn would be so proud of him, once she had forgiven him of course. She still thought he was preparing for their wedding. He smiled proudly as he scrolled through Strabo's accounts, now downloaded to Marcus' online account. A sudden worry crossed his mind that Marcus might log on and wonder why he was suddenly the richest man in the whole of Britannia. He would have to tell him soon enough. He would not be impressed with the idea of the wedding, still seething with resentment as he was, but telling him would be nothing compared to

255

telling the others. He had to do it though, and before the wedding. He laughed to himself as he realised that the idea of telling his friends that he was in love, was more terrifying to him than breaking single handed into Strabo's facility had been. He smiled broadly in the dark room: he had won.

A piercing shriek ran out. Titus leapt in the air in surprise. The pitch rose and fell, deafening him. Titus ran. The white corridor shot past in an instant, and almost immediately he was at the massive door that lead to the cloisters outside. He entered the keycode frantically as he heard the sound of running boots clanking close by on the sheet metal that floored the corridor. The door began to open, the first light of the day beginning to stream in through the opening to the outside world. He could not fit through it yet. He almost screamed with exasperation as the door continued to open inexorably slowly.

Suddenly a shout of alarm rang out in the corridor, and a salvo of sonifex fire ricocheted off the door just beside his head. A fragment of hot metal struck Titus on the cheek. He angrily flicked it away, ignoring the blood on his hand. The small concealed sonifex was all he had, but it sprung to his hand in an instant as Titus threw himself down onto the ground firing in mid flight. The anti personnel rounds tore into the guard leaving trails of blood and viscera plastered up and down the hitherto pristine white corridor. Another guard took his place and fired. The recoil caused him to slip in the remains of his companion, and the rounds struck the ceiling above Titus' head, showering him with plaster.

In one move Titus threw himself back onto his feet, and backwards out of the door into the fresh morning air. Bullets struck the wall around him as he drew himself out into the early light of dawn and into the deserted cloister. His hand slammed down on the emergency override button by the door and it began to close, again far too slowly for his liking, but he had no time to wait and see if a guard could make it through the opening.

He turned and ran through the dimly lit quadrangle. Casting rapid glances from side to side he thought he saw a guard in every bush. But he ran on doggedly, and the shots he dreaded never came. Then he caught a glimpse of a shadow in the cloister alongside, an animal form which shifted in the half light and disappeared into the foliage alongside him. Spooked, he began to sprint, his breath beginning to tear in his throat.

Out of control he fled in the direction of the gate. As he crossed the final edge of the quad he bent low and charged headlong into the portion of the gate he had purposefully weakened on the way in. The impact nearly knocked him unconscious. Dazed, he stared at the door. The hinges were still in place. He had filed them earlier—why had they not burst open? Then he saw the shadows of the reinforced bars at the other side of the gate, now slid into place. He had been locked in. He rolled to his feet, desperately thinking of another way out. But he knew there was none. Had this been a trap all along?

A laugh sounded out behind him. He turned slowly, knowing who he would see.

XXXX

'Titus Labienus Aquilinus,' the voice was as whiny as always, but filled with menace. 'By the gods I have been looking forward to this day.' He had grown fatter, if that was possible, and he was flanked by a score of his Praetorian Guard alongside his usual house guard. 'Did you really think you could just walk in here? That you could blackmail me! Who did you think would listen? The Praetorian Guard? I own the Praetorian Guard,' he shouted. He cast a sideways glance at the Guards around him, but there was no reaction. 'Not just the Guard here, but the one in Londinium as well. I own you. I own your family. I own that half-breed you helped escape.'

Titus tried to keep his expression neutral, but he knew it was hopeless.

Strabo laughed again, a foul raucous sound, out of control, 'just as I thought. You have taken her as a lover! The very thought disgusts me.'

Titus smiled at him, knowing that Strabo's thoughts on that subject had been very different a month ago.

Strabo stopped laughing abruptly. He took out his handkerchief and wiped at the drool that had begun to collect at the corner of his mouth, hissing as he inhaled, sucking the remainder of the spit back in. When he spoke to Titus again his voice was as calm as it had ever been, 'now my dear friend. So you come to the end. You have struggled so hard, but it is time to die. Where will you go? Elysium? Or Tartarus perhaps? Which would you like?'

Titus stared back, defiantly.

'Then, if you permit, allow me to choose for you,' he stroked his chin as if in deep thought, 'Tartarus I think. Will the gods look with pleasure on all those terrible things you did in the Transmaritanus?' Seeing the look in Titus' eyes he continued, 'oh yes, I know all about you my old friend. I know you better than you know yourself.'

'You know nothing about me,' Titus snorted back.

'Tartarus then,' the Governor nodded sagely, 'it is decided. Come forwards Titus, it is time to meet your eternal torment.'

Titus looked over his shoulder, but there was nowhere to run. His mind worked frantically. There must be a way out of here. His mind cast back to a time long ago when as a young man he was in a similar situation. Surrounded by his enemies, but then his friends had appeared on the walls around him. His friends didn't even know he was here; he hadn't trusted them enough to tell them.

Strabo took a silver plated sonifex out from beneath his toga, and carefully polished the barrel. 'Time to die Titus,' he said pointing the barrel at Titus face, only three feet away. 'Any final words?'

'*Virtutis Fortuna Comes,*' came to his lips. To say his family motto as he died in battle would be appropriate. But he was not in battle, nor did he wish to die. Then his mouth opened and he began to speak, the words forming all by themselves almost without conscious thought: 'Saturnalia is in two days, and I promise you a Saturnalia to remember, one in the ancient vein where Slaves' and masters' roles are reversed.' He had no idea how he could make his promise come true. The possibility of the Slaves turning on their former master, and tearing him apart had never seemed further from reality, but it would indeed be fitting.

He took a deep breath and stared into the deep dark depths of the sonifex barrel, chuckling to himself at the irony that if he had been shown this barrel six months ago, he would likely have embraced it, and its dark oblivion. Ceinwyn had given him something to live for, something to lose. He was not ready to die anymore. Strabo's finger closed around the trigger. Titus closed his eyes.

Suddenly a pale animal figure leapt from the bushes to his right and landed with considerable force on Strabo's back. The sonifex went off, a sharp crack in the partly enclosed quadrangle, which startled the birds roosting in the shrubs all around. They streamed off into the dawn air with a receding cacophony of sound. Strabo rolled onto his back screaming with fear as he battled his assailant, who roared an inhuman cry of rage with each mad blow. The assailant pinned Strabo to the ground with his wiry body and looked up, his eyes meeting Titus' and transfixing him. It took a second for him to recognise the torn face under the matted hair: it was Tristan.

'Run.' His voice was guttural, inhuman. Titus nodded in mute thanks, and leapt sideways, rolling and charging into the cloisters. A scream rang out from behind, clearly belonging to Strabo, maybe Tristan had bitten him? Titus hoped it was the case. As he reached the edge of the quadrangle he leapt at a full sprint to clear the dwarf wall. He landed awkwardly on the smooth marble of the cloister and went down hard on his left ankle, sliding on the floor and hitting his chin. Pain shot up his leg and he tasted blood in his mouth. He forced himself to get back to his feet, to run, to make Tristan's sacrifice worth something. His leg collapsed under him. He threw himself forward and tried again. The leg buckled. He heard a crash as another heavy body threw itself into the cloister behind him. He gyrated his body forwards, trying to keep moving, but his foot would not obey him. A pair of arms grasped him hard around the chest choking the breath from his lungs. Then suddenly he was flying over the dwarf wall again and into a ragged panting heap on the grassy quadrangle. The guard who had thrown him approached again and took a well aimed kick which caught Titus under the chin, throwing him onto his back. His vision dimmed, but he did not black out.

Across the quadrangle two guards held Tristan who was still screaming his cries of rage at Strabo. Unable to help him, Titus watched as the silver sonifex silenced him; the shots ringing out again and again over the compound. The shots paused for a moment as Strabo reloaded before one final shot rang out. Strabo rubbed his hands together, proud of a job well done, and marched purposefully towards Titus.

'Sorry for that interruption in the proceedings my dear friend.' He lifted the sonifex again.

Titus tried to calm his breathing; he wished to live, but if there was no choice he would die quietly and bravely. Strabo's finger tightened on the trigger. Titus forced himself to keep his eyes open this time.

'Sir, sir!' The voice came from the command centre at the other side of the quadrangle.

'What is it!' shouted Strabo, apoplectic with rage at this second interruption.

'Sir, my apologies,' the guard was shaking with fear, Strabo's sonifex was pointed straight at him, 'but I must report... Sir, I am sorry but...'

'Tell me what you have to say now, and leave.' Strabo's voice was calm and measured now; he was in control of himself once again.

'The accounts, they have been interfered with.'

'What do you mean, interfered with?'

'Sir, I am sorry but, your money. It's been taken.'

'What?' Titus watched what little colour there had been drain away from Strabo's fat jowls.

'Someone hacked in, they took it all. Every last sestertii.'

The sonifex rang out over the quad. The guard seemed to hang in midair for a second before plunging hard into the earth beside Titus. Strabo took a long time in cleaning the barrel, deep in thought, before he turned back to Titus.

'Well then, it seems you have earned yourself a reprieve, for now. But trust me, you will regret not dying here; the Tartarus that I can provide will make the real Tartarus seem a mercy. I promise you that by the end of today you would happily take your own life, and by the end of the week you will beg for death. By the end of the month? Well, you would happily kill your own family if only then I would let you die.' He gestured to the powerful guard beside him. Titus groaned as he was lifted bodily into the air and the guard strode purposefully back towards the basement door.

XXXXI

A trail of blood ran down the white corridor behind him. Every
step drew fresh blood from his crudely bandaged feet. 'You are
hallucinating again! Come on!' The voice before him hissed
imploringly, 'we are nearly there.'

Titus groaned through broken lips, his body on fire, his voice an
unintelligible moan. He tripped, and the world faded to darkness around
him.

'Come on.'

It was the voice again. Titus knew he must obey it, after all it was
trying to save his life. But he needed to sleep. He slumped to the ground;
his vision dimming as he felt the white coated figure tugging at him,
slapping him, rousing him, as it had done earlier in the day.

*'Good, good. He is conscious again. Time for some more fun.' Strabo's voice dripped
with barely concealed rage, and a disturbing undertone that Titus could only place as one
thing, arousal. The footsteps approached from behind again. He was strapped down to
a cold metal chair, tilted backwards at forty five degrees, his hands and feet manacled
tightly to the sides of the chair. He was exposed, like a piece of meat on a butcher's
block. The footsteps stopped, inches from him, he twisted his head against the restraints*

262

trying to keep his eye on the torture doctor, but they were too tight. A searing pain rose from the base of his spine, tearing its way up through the tissues of his back and into his neck. He had long given up trying to stay silent.

'Where is my fucking money!' Strabo's face appeared only inches from his, swollen contorted and almost purple with rage.

Titus spat in his face. 'Fuck you.'

A nod from Strabo, and the chair began to vibrate again. Titus began to scream in anticipation; then the agony came. His body twisted violently and he felt like his muscles would tear from their sockets as they contracted against his will.

Then there was calm, his vision dimmed, the pain diminished. Had he lost consciousness again? He wasn't sure. The white coated, young but balding torture doctor leaned over him again. A sharp prick in his arm, and then the world slowly came back to life. The doctor's figure began to blur as the drug he had just injected took effect.

'My colleague here has many infusions at his disposal.' Strabo pointed at the drip needle now in Titus' arm, a great grey cap, his open vein beneath it. The sight of it made Titus retch. 'Right now he had just given you a benzodiazepine, a simple truth serum. He can do much worse.' Strabo smiled as he looked over Titus to the many other infusions lined up on the wall. 'Now, let me ask you again. Where is my money?'

Titus' eyes rolled back in his head. A crashing punch in the face from Strabo focused his attention. 'Lean closer and I'll tell you,' he spoke through the haze of sedative and blood.

Strabo eagerly leaned in. 'Go on, tell me and this all ends.'

Titus gathered as much blood in the back of his mouth as he could and spat it hard into Strabo's face. A broken stump of tooth followed and rolled down Strabo's chest leaving a thin trail of gore on his toga.

Strabo howled with rage and gestured to the doctor, who gathered a pale plastic bag from the wall and began to set up a drip stand. He lifted the end of the giving set and allowed it to flow carefully expelling every drop of air. A tiny drip reached the end and dropped onto the bare concrete floor of the torture chamber.

'Only 10ml of air is needed to stop your heart. Wouldn't want that would we?' Strabo hissed as the doctor connected the infusion. 'This is a concoction I devised myself, a nerve stimulant,' he continued, signalling at the doctor to start the drip running.

Titus desperately tried to pull his arm away from the giving set, but the doctor easily connected the bag despite his struggles. At first he felt nothing at all, but as Strabo watched on with a wide grin, he began to feel a tingling in his left arm. His eyes widened in fear and Strabo laughed at his discomfort. 'Modern medicine is a wonderful thing, don't you think Titus. We have the power to stop pain completely and to cause pain so severe it can kill you all by itself. There is no need to even leave a mark on your body.' Titus' arm was burning now and the tingling was moving into his neck. He twisted, trying to get away, but the pain was coming from inside; he could not escape. 'At the present rate within five minutes your whole body will feel like it is immersed in fire. But you can stop it. Whenever you want it to stop it stops.'

'Go to hell.'

'No, Titus, you go to hell.' He signalled to the doctor again, who shook his head. 'Increase the rate!' Strabo shouted angrily.

'But sir, it could kill him,' the doctor's tone was almost pleading.

'Increase the rate or you will find out what it feels like too,' Strabo said menacingly.

The doctor nodded and reluctantly turned the wheel. Titus felt nothing more at first. He watched the doctor as he twitched nervously in the corner, not able to meet Titus' accusing gaze. Then he understood why. The pain rose quickly, and now was uncontrollable. He howled as he contorted in the chair, fighting against his restraints. His breath came in short bursts, he could not breath deep enough, he could barely breath at all. He bit his tongue, and ground his teeth, tasting blood but feeling nothing but the pain in his arm and neck. The pain that was now spreading everywhere.

'Sir, his heart rate is two hundred and forty,' the doctor said, reaching across to reduce the infusion rate.

'Keep going.'

'Sir, he will die,' replied the doctor.

'If he dies, you die too.'

Titus had run out of breath even for screaming. His agony continued, but was only shown through the bulging of his muscles against the chair's cold metal restraints, and in the rolling of his eyes.

Then suddenly the pain stopped. Titus retched and looked up to see that the doctor had stopped the infusion and was injecting a second agent into the line, seemingly neutralising the first. Then a familiar object was thrust in front of his eyes by Strabo. It was his observation ball which he had left in the facility weeks ago. Strabo was sweating—he looked worried. Titus felt his resolve harden; he was winning.

'Do you remember this?' Strabo asked. 'It's a very interesting piece of kit, whoever looks through the little hand held receiver can see through the ball. Of course you know this though, it is yours after all.' He tossed it from hand to hand. 'A fascinating piece of kit, but wouldn't it be better if we could do it the other way? See who is watching the ball?' He flicked the large wall screen on behind him, which glowed faintly before bursting into life.

Titus stared at the screen, and to his surprise into his very own sitting room. 'As I said before, I know everything about you, I know your old friends in Rome, even Marcus Albus. And for the last months I have known everything you have been doing.' Strabo pointed into the room. Titus felt sick at the thought. How long had Strabo been able to spy into his house? What had Strabo seen and heard? Then with a sudden shock it dawned on him that the room was empty. Where was Ceinwyn? Was she safe? He craned his head as if by doing so he would be somehow able to look outside the confines of the little receiver screen's view. Then he saw a vision in white coming down the stairs. She trod slowly so as not to slip on the bare wood and faced away from the screen, but then she turned and Titus caught his breath involuntarily.

Her hair was pinned up into a beautiful pile of copper curls, a few of which still cascaded down to the nape of her neck and around onto her bare shoulders. The dress started at her shoulders, a simple white shift brought in at the waist with a blue tie and stopping just below her knees. He had never seen her look so wonderful. Then through the haze of his tortured fragmenting mind he realised why, for it was now Saturnalia eve, and she was about to set off for her wedding.

'She looks wonderful doesn't she? Shame really that she has to die.'

'If you even think of touching her...' Titus growled.

'You'll do what?' Strabo asked sarcastically. 'Seriously Titus, what will you do?'

'What I promised you two days ago, I will kill you. Remember it is Saturnalia tomorrow,' he replied hoarsely. He did not know where his bravado came from; with the drip needle in his arm he certainly did not feel brave. Strabo fumed with anger and advanced towards where Titus lay on the reclined metal chair. He fumbled around on the table and picked up an evil looking monkey wrench, matted with the blood and bone of a previous victim. He picked up the ball.

Titus watched Ceinwyn stare up at the screen; she was looking at one of the pictures on the mantelpiece beneath it.

She sighed wistfully, 'my love. I don't know where you have gone, but I know you will meet me tonight, for our special night. I love you Titus.'

265

The screen flickered and then went black as Strabo crushed the ball with the wrench.

'Don't worry Titus, she won't be going anywhere, I've got your houses watched and if she leaves tonight, she will be followed.'

Titus groaned.

'And if she stays put...' Strabo continued as the door burst open and three Praetorians filed in, coated from head to toe in body armour. Their eyes were barely visible through the slits in the black helmets. They were armed with fasces and the lead one held a new assault sonifex which glistened in the bright lights.

'Sir, we have come as you asked.'

'Good. You know your mission?'

The lead Praetorian nodded and spoke with a muffled voice through the faceguard of his helmet, 'to capture the half-breed.'

'Yes, and to bring her here,' Strabo added and nodded, dismissing them.

'We will assault the house at the stroke of midnight, sir,' the Praetorian saluted and turning on his heel marched out with his comrades. Strabo turned back to Titus.

'So you see Titus, one way or the other she will come to me here. And then, you will tell me everything.' Titus paled at the thought of Ceinwyn's flesh being touched by Strabo, at the tools hanging on the wall burrowing into her flesh, exploring her, violating her body. He cursed Strabo, and fought against the restraints once more.

'Calm down Titus,' Strabo cooed, 'she isn't here yet! We have plenty of time left to enjoy ourselves. Now let's have a look at those toes of yours.'

Titus felt his socks being pulled down over the ends of his feet and the cold metal of the monkey wrench against the first toe on the left. He tightened his grip against the chair's sides in anticipation. The cold metal touched, tickling at first. Then it began to squeeze, gently at first, but with increasing insistence. Then Strabo twisted the wrench.. The pain shot up his body, he arched his back, opened his mouth and screamed. Over his own involuntary screams he heard the cracking as the bones in his toe broke, followed by a splashing sound in the corner of the room. The doctor was vomiting loudly over the cold concrete floor.

The slapping woke Titus again, dragging him from the haze of pain and drugs. It was the doctor once more. They were still in the white corridor. Why would he not just let him sleep?

'Listen Aquilinus, we are nearly there, you have to keep moving.'

Titus heaved himself to his feet with the help of the doctor.

'We can get out, look the doors are just ahead.' The humming of the white corridor filled his ears; it reminded him of the chair earlier. He collapsed to his knees and vomited on the white floor. The vomit was yellow and tasted foul; he had not been fed for his two days of capture.

The doctor grabbed him by his shoulders and pulled him forwards. 'Come on Aquilinus, you can be free. We can get you out in time, there is still time to save her.'

The thought of Ceinwyn spurred Titus on. The pain in his feet was incredible but he forced himself to go on, each step squelching fresh blood from his ruined feet.

'I can fix those for you, give you pain injections, splint the toes, I just need to get you outside.'

Titus nodded. The doctor had caused him much suffering earlier, but Titus could see how little the man had enjoyed it—he had had no choice.

The doctor slapped his hand down hard onto the button that operated the swinging door and, as it began to slowly creak open, turned his attention back to Titus. 'Do you know the code Aquilinus?' Titus looked back blankly. 'The code to the account where you put the money? Do you know it?' Titus shook his head, panting hard against the pain. 'If you give me it I can use it to get you out of here, book curri off the island for you and your friends?' Titus did not reply. 'All I ask is that you take me too,' the doctor continued. It was clear from his expression that he was terrified that he was risking his life to save Titus'.

Titus tried to reply, but he had no energy left. He slumped to the floor again. The doctor walked over to him and, his question seemingly forgotten, gently helped him back to his feet.

Slowly, with the doctor's help, Titus managed to lurch across the threshold and out into the courtyard. His feet shot agony up his legs with every step but it was worth it, for he was almost free, and dusk had never been so beautiful. A chorus of sultry birdsong greeted the pair as Titus limped onto the cool grass, breathing in the cold winter air. The sun hung low and red in the sky. Snow was falling gently over Luguvalium, twisting in the eddying air above the compound and falling in his hair and around his bloody feet.

The doctor led him further on, beckoning insistently as he guided him back down the colonnades which edged the quadrangles. Titus took in deep breaths of the fresh air, allowing himself for the first time to realise what was happening. He was being rescued. He would be free. The gatehouse loomed ahead. Surely the guards would see him. The doctor reached the gatehouse and peered through the window nonchalantly, before ducking down and waving Titus on. The way must be clear, it was suppertime and the guards must be in the mess. Titus limped across the last quad, allowing himself a quick glance backwards and realising that his ruined feet were leaving a trail of blood behind him. He remembered the doctor's promise that he could fix his feet. He hoped with all his heart that the doctor was right, the thought of being crippled was worse than death itself.

'You are free Titus.' The doctor spoke again, raising Titus' spirits. 'Quick,' he continued, 'through the door, then run back to your friends, there may just still be time to save her.'

Titus nodded, not trusting his voice to reply. His hand rested for a moment on the cold metal of the latch, he twisted it. The door swung open. He was free.

A savage blow from the gloved fist of a Praetorian Guard caught him off balance as he darted through the door. The blow threw him off his feet and back through the door as he crashed awkwardly to the ground, the force of the impact driving the air from his lungs. He struggled to a sitting position on the quadrangle floor, panting with pain and confusion. Through the open gate of the compound walked Strabo, flanked by two Praetorians. Strabo walked past Titus and clapped the doctor on the back. He smiled sycophantically, and darted off in the direction of the mess without even glancing in Titus' direction. Strabo slowly meandered over to Titus who tried to curse, but could only cough.

'So, Titus. Do you understand at last?' He leant forwards till he was at Titus' level, inches from his face. 'No one will help you. You will rot here and die when I deem there is nothing else of use left in you. You will be an empty husk, whimpering in the dark, no better than Tristan was. And then, and only then, will you be allowed to die.'

268

Titus couldn't help but cast his mind to the memory of the crazed young man in the cage; he could not end up like him.

'But first you will live to see your woman and friends suffer.' Strabo punctuated these last words by slapping Titus across the face with the back of his hand; a blow of surprising strength for such a man.

Titus flopped back on the hard concrete of the quad. He had been so close to safety, but it had all been a sham. The thought of further tortures when he had been so close to freedom was too much. He felt closer than ever to breaking, all he had to do was give the code to Marcus' account. He did not know if he could cope with more torture, but he could not let Strabo break him. He would hold out as long as he could.

'Take him back to Tartarus,' Strabo barked to the Guards, who marched a pace forwards grabbing him under the shoulders, and dragging him, helpless, back to the west wing, his ruined feet leaving a trail of gore across the freshly falling snow.

At the same time as the last rays of the sun fell below the horizon, only half a kilometre away, three Praetorian Guard stealthily moved from their hiding place and began to slowly tail the cloaked figure who had just left the house. 'Just follow,' the leader muttered to the others gruffly as the figure pulled the door of the house closed gently. The Praetorian Captain and his men were powerfully built, dressed in tatty cloaks and armed with wooden cudgels; they would be Reivers to any passer by, who would then undoubtedly flee without taking a proper look, which suited their purposes perfectly. 'Be ready to strike on my command,' he hissed as the group moved out, 'but remember we want her alive.' The men nodded, smirking, and carefully lumbered after the figure ahead of them, who ploughed on, head down, into the driving wind.

XXXXII

Ceinwyn pulled the door closed gently. She did not want to wake Cyric. She had thought of inviting him to the wedding, but he seemed to have pre-empted this by retreating to his bed in the cellar. Clearly he had no wish to see her marry his enemy, but Ceinwyn wondered whether there was more to it than simply that. He had barely been out of his room in the last two days, and she had heard him retching down there. She had heard about the plague that was sweeping the city; it was said only to affect the Slaves. She shuddered at the thought of Cyric taken with it, or catching it herself. There seemed to be no cure, or perhaps there was but no Roman could be bothered to look for or administer it. She stepped out onto the street, the weather had calmed now, but it was still freezing. In the distance she could hear explosions and gunfire as the Reivers and Praetorians fought just outside the city.

Ceinwyn did not care much for the fighting, for she wanted neither side to win. All she cared for was Titus, and their rendezvous tonight on the island. Gnaeus had shown her the way on a map yesterday. Although she had never seen the lake and its islands before, she had heard of their beauty and could picture it in her mind perfectly. It would be an amazing place to marry. She had not seen Titus now for nearly three days. She had been upset, but understood his need to prepare for the wedding alone, besides she knew that wherever he had been, right now he was heading for the island too. Gnaeus should already be there at the old cross, everything would be prepared. She could imagine the cloth he would use to bind their hands, the brittle bread that they would eat together and the perfumed wine that they would drink to cement their new lives together, by the body and blood of her God.

The last rays of the winter sun still hung in the sky, but the cold was all encompassing none-the-less. She pulled Titus' great cloak around her shoulders tighter; Titus was tall enough for it to cover her wedding dress entirely. She looked like any normal person, except that she was a Slave, and Slaves would not usually roam the streets alone. This night very few people should be roaming the streets at all—the Praetorian's would be on patrol enforcing martial law. She would have to move stealthily.

She stole along her street quietly, passing the house that Tiberius, Antonius and Marcus lived in. There was a light on upstairs. She moved past quickly, looking up furtively to check that she was not spotted, but there was no flicker of the curtain. She scuttled across to the edge of the road and turned left onto the main road. It, too, was deserted.

She walked along the road, bolder now in the near total darkness. A crash to her left made her jump as two local men rolled out of a pub and onto the street. At first she thought they were fighting, but then she realised that they were only supporting each other as they tried to haul their drunken bodies down the street. She looked down as she passed them.

'Cheer up lass!' they shouted raucously as they stumbled past. She breathed a sigh of relief as they continued down the road behind her, their voices receding into the distance.

She reached the edge of the town without further incident. Luguvalium had no wall, but there were guard posts on the roads leading into and out of it. Normally it would be no trouble to pass them, but she was an escaped Slave. She doubted even that Titus could pass one safely now having antagonised Strabo. She knew as well as anyone that Strabo was not a man who had the capacity for forgiveness. He would never let

Titus leave without a fight. Once they were married they would have to leave together stealthily, just as she would have to do now.

The gate house was manned. Ceinwyn's heart sank. Two Praetorians sat at a rickety table in the hut, puffing furiously upon a hookah of low quality tobacco. She had discussed yesterday with Gnaeus the best way of getting to the lake, for she had never been shown how to drive a currus. Gnaeus had chosen to walk on ahead earlier in the evening, claiming it as some kind of pilgrimage. He had never been to the holy place on the island before and wanted to be in the right frame of mind to perform the ceremony. She would walk on behind and arrive once everything was prepared. She looked at her watch—it was only six in the evening. She had six hours yet before they were to be married.

She crept up to the side of the guard hut, she was so close now that she could hear the Guards talking. They were playing cards. Above her head was the first of a bank of cameras ready to catch her face. Another pace forwards would put her into the observation area. She pulled the cloak around her face and crept forwards.

'Full house.'

The voice made her jump—the Praetorian was only inches from her head as she crouched beneath the window.

'Pocket aces! Add the flop, turn, and river, gives me trip aces and a pair of queens.'

Ceinwyn heard a sharp intake of breath from the other Guard. The first Guard laughed, 'wishing you hadn't put these in, eh?'

She heard the swishing of keys being swung around and more laughter. She looked across to the other side of the road to the military currus parked there, the ownership of which was clearly about to change hands. 'Well in which case you shouldn't have put these in, should you?' the second Praetorian mocked, grabbing at some papers on the table.

'Give the deeds back!' the first Praetorian shouted in mock outrage, 'you've got no chance!' He added hastily.

'Your land is mine and so is my car!' replied the second Praetorian, mocking and grabbing back his keys with a loud jangle.

'What, so you think you can beat my full house! You've got shit!'

A moment of silence ensued as the Praetorian revealed his cards, 'a pair of queens' he said triumphantly.' Ceinwyn could imagine his smirk.

'You lucky cunt. Four of a kind? You piece of shit!' Ceinwyn heard the first Praetorian lunge for the other and the sound of the table creaking with his weight. Suddenly there was a thud as the table collapsed and the keys flew through the window, landing on the tarmac in front of Ceinwyn as the guards struggled. She reached forwards and, gathering the keys, crawled past the hut. The alarm did not sound. She was past. She breathed again—suddenly aware she had been holding her breath. She tossed the keys deep into a gorse bush and then she ran. She had done it. She was out of the town.

She glanced over her shoulder again; she had thought for a moment earlier that she had seen a light gliding over the fields behind her, following her, keeping its distance. It had gone now, however. She crouched down and waited, but she heard and saw nothing more. The lake lay just ahead, glistening in the pale moonlight. Snow fell gently around her as she wrapped her cloak tight and skipped down the narrow steps that led to the lake shore.

A rustling in the bushes behind spooked her, and she whirled around staring wide eyed into the tree-line—was someone watching her? The bushes rustled again in the gentle evening breeze as if a man was running through them frantically. She dropped to the dry earth and lay still. The sounds receded into the distance. It must have just been the wind, she thought; but she couldn't shake the feeling that she was being watched. She crossed the shingle to the lake shore watching the tiny waves form far out under the moon, and followed their short life as they travelled inexorably towards their fate, to break upon the shore line. The gentle sound soothed her as she scrunched her way along the shore.

The islands were faint silhouettes over the water, the fells towered behind them, surrounding the lake. It was beautiful, she could think of no better place to marry Titus. Suddenly the hairs stood up on the back of her neck and she had that uncanny feeling of being watched again. She shot a look over her shoulder but there was no one there. She turned her attention back to the lake. Gnaeus had explained that there was a boat she could use to get to the island, which was used by the few pilgrims who wished to visit the old cross. She doubted she would meet any pilgrims tonight. Gnaeus and her father were the only other Christians she knew. But if illegal religions were to thrive anywhere, they would exist in the far flung provinces of the empire such as.

She found the rope more easily than she had expected; it was fixed to a small wooden pole which seemed to be dug deeply into the earth beneath the shingle. Attached to it by a smaller thread of rope was a boat, if you could call three planks of wood lashed together with string a boat. Ceinwyn was pleased she hadn't chosen a full length dress; she didn't want it getting ruined before the ceremony. She quickly checked her watch again, two minutes to midnight. She had made good time. She placed one foot on the raft which swung wildly even under her slight weight.

She heard the unmistakable sound of a footstep crunching on the gravel behind her. The hairs on the back of her neck shot up and she felt the sickness in her stomach as the adrenaline coursed out into her blood. Her worst fears were realised: she had indeed been followed.

Her heart sank—she had got so close. But now she would die, so close to her love, but separated by a deep gulf of water. She stood up slowly, and stared at the island out on the lake, it seemed impossibly far away now. She wished that she could see Titus just one last time, but it was a hopeless wish. The wind suddenly gusted cold, whipping her skirts up around her. Terrified, she turned around to confront her pursuers. She had no hope of defeating them, but at least she would die looking them in the face.

XXXXIII

The Praetorians stepped out onto the path directly behind Gnaeus. 'Stop right there girl!'

Gnaeus swung around sharply and took in the scene, 'evening gentlemen.' He spoke casually, more at ease than he felt, for he carried no weapon. The three men ahead of him carried thick wooden cudgels which hung loosely at their sides for now. The tallest of the men, clearly the leader, opened his mouth to speak and then shut it again. His brow furrowed and then finally he spoke, 'I thought you were a woman!' The tone of his voice was jeering and the men either side of him laughed, but Gnaeus could see the confusion and disappointment on their faces.

Gnaeus looked down at his ceremonial robes, laughing in irony at himself, hoping to placate them. He needed time to think. The fact that he was dressed like this would only harm him. These local people would probably either worship their own gods, or possibly the Roman ones. They were hardly likely to share his minority belief, they probably didn't understand what the robes meant. Then a sudden realisation dawned on him. These men had been following him for some time, possibly all the way from Luguvalium, and they had been following him because they thought he was a woman. He looked again at their sneering expressions and he suddenly realised with fear that they did understand what religion he was representing and they found it amusing. They were not Britons. They were Romans. He nodded in understanding; he knew who they thought he had been.

At that moment the leader grinned menacingly and advanced with the club. Gnaeus dropped his shoulders and allowed the bulk of the robes to slide off his back. As they slid to the floor he used the moment to weigh up his opponents. Confidently he stood still, waiting for them to come to him.

The leader approached, his club held lightly at his side. Gnaeus crouched down slightly, lowering his centre of gravity. The man charged and swung the club at Gnaeus' head. He waited till the man was upon him, then he rose up and caught the blow in his ribs rather than his head. It hurt but it did not wind him. Gnaeus caught the leader's club with both his hands and drove his head into the man's chin. The Roman grunted and reeled backwards, dazed. Gnaeus pulled hard at the club, but the man had a deathly strong hold and would not relinquish it. His companions cheered him on with shouts of encouragement. Gnaeus wondered how long it would be before they joined in. He could easily kill all three of them. They were making this too easy.

As his assailant wouldn't let go of the club Gnaeus used it as a lever to swing him towards him. The man crashed against Gnaeus' outstretched leg as he was swung across, and tumbled headlong into the nettle bushes by the side of the path. He emerged roaring with pain and anger, clearly no longer dazed by Gnaeus' blow to his chin. 'Come on you bastards,' he shouted to his companions, the pretence no longer important, it seemed, as he bellowed in perfect Latin, 'kill this priest quickly—we have a job to do.'

Gnaeus turned around to see the other two men running at him across the path, their clubs held high ready to strike. He leapt at the nearest and dived under his blow, taking his legs out from under him. Gnaeus swung himself round and back onto his feet in an instant, and kicked the wooden cudgel out of second man's hands. He turned once more and threw himself onto the prostrate first man, punching him over and over again in the face. He heard the crunch of footsteps behind him, and swung to one side just as a cudgel came down. Roaring with anger the Roman struck, but the strike instead hit his other assailant hard in the stomach.

Gnaeus took advantage of the confusion to attack the leader again. The man was wary of him this time, dancing from side to side, carrying his club lightly. He would not be so easy to trick this time, Gnaeus thought. The man struck a short jab of a blow which caught Gnaeus on the arm, shooting pain up into his shoulder, which he tried to ignore. He punched with his uninjured right arm and caught his assailant on the side of the head. Using his momentum to close the gap he hooked a leg behind the struggling man, tripping him. They fell together onto the gravel of the path. Gnaeus reached to grab hold of the cudgel, but found that his opponent seemed to have dropped it. The man's hands went for his neck. Gnaeus smiled as the Roman's hands tightened; his deception had worked. He felt the inexorable tightening in his chest as his breathing was forcibly stopped. He waited for a few more seconds, his vision starting to dim. The Roman glared up at him triumphantly. Gnaeus winked at him, and drove his thumbs into the man's eyes.

The Roman roared in pain and the grip around Gnaeus' neck loosened immediately. He kept pushing, feeling the wetness of the man's tears against his thumbs. The Roman's hands had released his neck completely now and were, instead, struggling with Gnaeus' fingers. He pushed furiously, ignoring the pain in his left arm. He managed to work his thumbs beneath the eyelids and felt his reward as the soft white of the eye gave beneath his pressure. The Roman screamed a high pitched wail as blood spurted onto Gnaeus' hands from the blind sockets. He placed his hands on either side of the man's thrashing head and twisted sharply until his neck snapped. The screaming stopped abruptly.

Rolling the dead man aside, Gnaeus turned his head and saw that the other two Romans stood ten paces away. They were staring in horror at what they had just seen, their quarrel forgotten. Gnaeus rose, showed them his bloodied thumbs, and laughed. The men paled, grasped each other, turned, and fled into the trees. Somewhere in the woods they would have a currus. He let them go. Strabo was onto them. He had to get to Ceinwyn.

'How dare you follow me!' Ceinwyn shouted at the tall slender figure of Cyric in front of her on the shore.

He held out his arms towards her, palms upwards in a gesture of submission, 'I was worried about you, I didn't want you to get hurt.' His legs were covered in grazes.

'You wanted to interrupt the wedding!' She shouted, wagging her finger at him, reminding him that their friendship was being tested.

'No!' Cyric exclaimed, shocked by the accusation. 'I just wanted to see you get married, you're my best friend.' He started to cry, and turned away so that Ceinwyn could not see. He looked pale and thin.

'It's just that this is meant to be a special time, just for Titus and I,' she said.

His expression drooped further.

'Are you OK?' she asked.

He glared at her. 'What a stupid question.'

'No, I mean. Are you ill?'

He could not meet her gaze. His skin had a yellow tinge; it could have just been the moonlight but Ceinwyn knew it was more, 'they say there is hope.'

Cyric started to cry again.

Ceinwyn reached to hug him.

'No!' Cyric cried out and backed away, his yellowing eyes wide open. Blood trickled from his bleeding gums as he shouted. 'Stay away.'

'Please, let me help you,' she begged, wishing that she had paid more attention to her friend over the last few days. She should have been there for him. But he had locked himself away, hidden from her.

'Don't touch me,' he whispered, 'you must not catch it.'

Ceinwyn began to cry. 'Cyric, I...' her voice faltered. 'I wish that I could have made you happy.'

Cyric tried to laugh. 'Ceinwyn, you don't love me. I understand now. I didn't come here to try to change that. I just thought that someone from your old life should be there at the beginning of the new.'

Ceinwyn nodded. 'I would like that very much.' She stepped towards him and took his hand and kissed it.

Cyric looked aghast.

'It only affects Slaves remember,' she said. 'And I am only half a slave.'
'I hope you are right,' Cyric whispered.

Ceinwyn turned her attention back to the boat leading to the island. It was more of a small raft really. She managed to get onto it and helped Cyric on. Despite his illness he still seemed to have most of his strength. For now. She crouched low to keep the planks stable on the lake. She thought about how lucky she was that the wind was low, proper waves would have made the crossing impossible. She reached down into the water and grabbed the rope that lay across the boat attaching it to the shore. As she tugged on it she pulled the boat a little bit nearer to the island.

The rope stretched out in front of her all the way to the island, the vast majority of it submerged. As she pulled again they began to move faster, the small length of twine that attached the raft to the main rope tightened as the light wind tried to take the raft off course. She gave a little whoop, quickly suppressed, as she gathered speed under the power of her tugs. Now she understood why the raft had to be small, one person would never have the strength to pull a proper boat in this way. Water sprayed off the rope as she continued to pull on it, drenching her wedding dress. She laughed, it didn't matter now really, she was going to see Titus soon. The island was close now. She would arrive just on time, ready to make her big entrance.

She dropped the coat off her shoulders as she arrived at the island's shore. It too was covered in small round pebbles. On a hot summer's day they would have been perfect for skimming, but she had no time for that now. Dressed only in her white dress she wandered into the interior of the island. To her surprise a thin track showed her the way; there must have been more pilgrims than she had expected over the years. Cyric followed a few paces behind—he did not want to spoil her grand entrance. The moon shone strange patterns onto the path ahead of her through the foliage. She smiled as she imagined how she would look to Titus as she stepped out, bathed in white light. Then she saw it. The cross lay ahead, it was as Gnaeus had described it, all alone in the middle of a tiny clearing in the trees. It looked ancient, weather-beaten over hundreds of years. She closed her eyes and stepped out into the clearing. She waited, imagining how she looked to Titus and Gnaeus. She opened her eyes and looked around. She was completely alone.

The journey back across the water was much slower.

Ceinwyn sobbed as the cold water soaked into her dress. Cyric helped as best he could, but his co-ordination was poor at the best of times, and with each pull on the rope he tilted the raft dangerously to the side. It was left to Ceinwyn's blistered, frozen hands to do the bulk of the work. When they reached the shore they stood for a moment not sure of what to do.

'Strabo must have him.' Ceinwyn spoke at last.

'Cold feet?' Cyric asked, immediately regretting his words as Ceinwyn's glare silenced him.

'He has been gone two days. I thought it odd at the time, but this confirms it. We have to get back and tell his friends. We have to save him.' Cyric nodded. Despite his childish daydreams, he knew in his heart that Titus loved Ceinwyn and would never jilt her.

After fifteen minutes of running they realised that they were lost. The track was thinning out and no longer looked like the track they had used when first heading down to the lake. Ceinwyn asked Cyric's advice, but he seemed exhausted from the run. The plague was weakening him quickly. 'Come on,' she said, and wrapped her arm around his sweaty waist dragging him further on into the forest. There was no time to go back, perhaps this track would join the one they wished for. Moments later Ceinwyn heard voices up ahead. She dropped down low, pulling Cyric down into the cold damp grass with her. She crawled forwards. There was the sound of a currus as well, and the voice was not just one man's but that of several. She kept crawling forwards, her heart beating quickly with fear and anticipation. A currus could get them back to Luguvalium far faster than on foot. But the men guarding them could be difficult to deal with. She thought of Titus at the hands of her former master, she thought of Tristan, and what had been done to him. She would find a way to save Titus.

The sound of the currus was close now and the voices seemed to come from right in front of her. She crawled slower now, turning her head over her shoulder to check on Cyric, who was right behind. She could see his face clearly now for there was a light not far ahead of them. His eyes were almost bright yellow. He looked terrible. She crawled to the lip of the small crest she was crawling up and peered down.

Beneath her was a huge hole in the ground. A trench, about twelve feet deep and over a hundred metres wide and long stretched into the distance. A currus with a huge digging attachment was moving earth from the end nearest them. The trench was nearly complete. Almost beneath her, two Romans stood in full Praetorian uniform sharing a few beers. Cyric crawled up alongside her.

'What is it?' she mouthed at him.

'I don't know,' Cyric replied in a whisper, and pointed to the far side of the trench where a basic currus stood. Ceinwyn nodded in agreement and the pair crawled around the side of the small slope they were on. As they descended it and drew level with the side of the trench, the foliage grew deeper and they were able to crawl more quickly whilst still remaining hidden from the guards.

'We are miles from anywhere,' Ceinwyn exclaimed to Cyric as they crawled. 'Why build here?'

'No idea,' Cyric replied breathlessly. 'Lets just get out of here, I don't know how much longer I can crawl for.'

They crossed a huge track leading away from the trench, pointing out from the hills, in the direction of Luguvalium. 'They are building a road as well,' Cyric stated. 'A big one.'

Ceinwyn shook her head, it made no sense, they were building a huge road to service a purposeless trench in the middle of nowhere. They rounded the corner and the currus was directly in front of them. They circled behind it so that they would be out of sight of the Praetorians until the last minute. 'Cyric, do you know how to start this.'

Cyric nodded and reached under the vehicle and started pulling at wires. The door nearest her clicked open and she was about to climb in when she noticed what the vehicle had concealed from their vantage point earlier. She tapped Cyric on the shoulder. 'Cyric, what are those.' She pointed at a collection of metal barrels that lay a score of yards away, partly buried in the undergrowth. Cyric shook his head, and hurriedly wrenched the door of the currus open. They looked in and found to their surprise another of the barrels on the passenger seat. This must have been the currus that had brought the barrels up here. Cyric reached in to pull it off the seat, but stopped when he saw the chemical symbol written on the side.

'CaO'

Cyric turned even paler. 'This is quicklime.'

Ceinwyn looked confused, 'what is it for?'

'For making the dead decay quickly in the grave,' he replied, his voice shaking.

Ceinwyn felt her stomach lurch. She looked out of the driver's window at the trench and imagined it full of the bodies of her friends. The plague was man made. This was planned genocide. 'We have to get out of here,' she hissed at Cyric, who was already on the floor of the currus pulling at the mass of wires that he had freed from the under the wheel.

'Give me a second.'

Ceinwyn felt a sharp tug at her ankle. She turned and looked into the masked face of one of the Praetorians, who shouted to his companion and pulled at her savagely. Ceinwyn screamed and kicked out hard at the guard who was knocked backwards. 'Come on!' she shouted at Cyric, who was working as fast as he could. The Praetorian was back on his feet. He lunged at her again, his masked face evil in the bright artificial light. She twisted away, still in the passenger seat of the currus and punched him in the chest—his face was not a target with the full mask. He brushed away her punch and gripped her left arm tightly, trying to drag her from the currus. 'Cyric!' she shouted. She raked her fingernails at the back of the Praetorian's hands, it was the only unprotected part. He roared with anger and drew back to strike her with his huge fist. The engine roared into life.

Cyric hit the accelerator pedal to the floor and the currus sprang away, throwing up clouds of earth and vegetation behind it. The Praetorian was thrown clear, and Ceinwyn pulled the door tightly shut panting with fear. They had been so close to death. She thought of the huge trench, the mass grave hungry for their bodies. Death was still close. They had to stop this plague somehow before it was too late.

XXXXIV

Titus tried to calm his breathing. He tried to forget how near he thought he had been to escape, and to focus on what was about to happen. A second bout of torture. Strabo paced in front of him.

Just like before, the Praetorians had come in first and given him a going over with boots and fists. Just to warm things up. Then, like before, Strabo had entered and the questions had started again.

'Pain doesn't seem to bother you,' Strabo said calmly. 'No problem. There are many other natural fears that we as animals cannot bear. Pain is but one. Separation is another. Drowning, being unable to breath, your lungs crying out for air, but yet unable to draw breath. That is yet another. We can try them all, one will work, one always does.' He clicked his finger at the torture doctor, who circled around with a syringe containing a small amount of colourless fluid. Strabo nodded and the doctor reached down to Titus' struggling arm and undid the cap of the cannula. The liquid was injected quickly and Titus gritted his teeth waiting for the pain. But none came. Strabo reached forwards and undid the straps binding him. Titus looked at him incredulous and stood up to strike him. He managed to lift his hand a couple of inches before it fell back. The muscles in his arms and legs began to ripple as they fasciculated. He groaned with the pain. Then the pain began to subside, but he could no longer move his limbs.

Strabo laughed. 'Suxamethonium!'

Titus' eyes widened with fear as his breathing slowed.

'A muscle inhibitor—its used in operations when the patient is asleep so that they can have a breathing tube shoved down their throat.'

Titus could barely move his fingers now, they were rigid, all his muscles working against each other. He tried to scream, but no sound came.

'It blocks the neuromuscular junction by blocking acetylcholine and depolarising the synapse junctions,' Strabo said, proud of his knowledge.

Titus' breaths were so shallow now that they were insufficient. He felt like someone was crushing his chest, preventing him taking breath, but he was simply sitting in a chair, completely unrestrained, completely helpless against what they had done to his body.

'It lasts about three minutes. You will feel like you have died, but trust me, you won't actually be granted that mercy. Whilst you are suffocating yourself into unconsciousness have a little think about that code I want. Unless of course you want to find out how many vials of this we have?' He knelt down so that his face was opposite Titus'. Titus tried to scowl at him, but he couldn't move the muscles in his face. 'Trust me Titus,' Strabo said, patting him on the cheek. 'We can keep suffocating you to the point of death all day if need be. Happy dreams.' He turned around and walked out.

Titus felt his vision dim. As he began to panic, the inability to show any outward sign of his terror amplified it. Every fibre of his body told him to breath, but he could not. He wanted to scream with fear, but no sound came. His vision faded and his mind began to wander as his consciousness faded.

13 Years Ago: AUC 2751

The Transmaritanus

'Marcus!' Titus' desperate shout rang out down the dark, concrete tunnel. The floor shook again, nearly throwing him to his knees. The artillery was firing again. He wondered if the shallow earth above the drainage tunnel would be enough protection from it. 'Marcus,' he shouted again. There was no reply. He pulled himself to his feet and charged along the shifting floor. A figure leapt out of the gloom from a vent above and to the right. Titus flicked his sonifex into position by reflex and firing from the hip continued to run; the figure turned over in midair and sprawled on the hard concrete. The natives were everywhere.

'Marcus,' his voice was desperate now. Where was his friend? Why had he run? They had been safe, and besides Marcus' duty was to their General not to himself. Titus' breath began to rasp in his throat as he realised he had been sprinting for a full five minutes. He paused to catch his breath; he was young and at the peak of his fitness, but even he couldn't continue for ever. He stared around, the concrete corridor continued into the distance. There was no other way that Marcus could have run. As he stood there he imagined the conversation in the command bunker that must be taking place right now—they would be deciding what to do with him. The General could have him executed. Another dead Centurion would mean little, they wouldn't even have to do it by the book if they didn't want to, but Titus knew they would do it by the book: the Legate was one of the old guard and a stickler for regulations.

He shuddered at the thought of his friends being forced to beat him to death. Gnaeus wouldn't join in, he knew that for sure, and then they would beat him to death too, for insubordination. It didn't bear thinking about. He wished, and not for the first time, that his legion was under the command of another Legate, Marcus Albus was the Legate of the 8th Legion, a thousand miles away. He had heard much about the command style of that man, he was only five years older than Titus, and he did things his own way, regardless of the rules in the book, much like his father, one of the two Consuls of Rome.

He shook his head. Marcus Albus was not his Commander, no matter how much he might wish it; even if he saved his friend he would face a court martial for certain.

But whilst he cursed himself for his stupidity in abandoning the defensive cordon, in his heart he knew he had made the right choice; he could not abandon Marcus even whilst his friend was in the darkest depths of his cowardice. He drew himself back up straight, ready to move again. He needed to reach Marcus before the rebels did—maybe they already had.

A cry of triumph rose up behind him; the sound was high pitched and the tone foreign, and it set Titus' pulse racing. Two hundred yards down the concrete tunnel behind him stood five rebel warriors, their reddish skin glistening in the dim glow of the electric lamps which illuminated the sewer. They must have clambered in through one of the many maintenance shafts that ran from the surface far above. Above them lay a no man's land that had once been a beautiful valley which the inhabitants called Rowena. Now it was just churned mud, blood and poisoned earth. He hoped that Marcus had not taken one of those inviting tunnels to the surface in his panic, far better to stay in the comparative safety of the maze of sewers. He began to run, listening over the pounding of his heart to the distant sound of the rebels feet splashing through the shallow storm water.

The sewer began to narrow ahead and straightened. A volley of sonifex fire cascaded into the water around him from the pursuing rebels. They were too far away to allow an accurate shot, but he could not risk them getting lucky. Titus turned and fired his assault sonifex high into the roof above, the armour piercing rounds cutting into the concrete bringing it down behind him in great chunks which shook the ground as they fell into place. The sewer was partially blocked. It would hold them off for a while. He shouldered his weapon and continued to run.

As the sewer continued to narrow it also began to twist as if the Romans who had built it when they had first conquered this land hundreds of years ago, had been unable to pass it straight through the rock and instead had had to avoid the toughest outcrops. Titus ran through the twisted passages. He had been at a near sprint for fifteen minutes now, and was beginning to tire. But he was young and he knew he could push on for as long as was needed, he prided himself on that. Somewhere ahead Marcus needed him.

He was running so fast that he nearly ran into the end of the sewer. He came up against it sharply and stood with his hands pressed against the cold stone as a torrent of grey water poured down the metre wide hole, cascading down the sides and over his body. Through the centre of the waterfall he stared up, eyes blinking hard against the rainwater, to the bright sky above. They had been trapped down here for a month. It had been worth the run just to see the sun again, if nothing else.

286

He turned around and began to walk back down the sewer and nearly tripped over a long metal canister that lay half way across the corridor. He tapped it with his foot and the echo rang out down the sewer. He bent down and brushed some of the dust away. Beneath was a label. The skull and crossbones stared at him out of the metal. The symbols beneath told him more: $\underline{C_5H_{11}Cl_2N}$. The blistering gas. Titus had only seen it used once, for it was an old weapon largely superseded by other more potent methods of mass destruction. But his skin still crawled as he remembered the effects on the rebels they had fired it at. It had taken a few hours to take effect after the shells had been fired, and they had not seen the deaths. But Titus had heard the screams, and he had seen the corpses the next day when they took the town. It was clear that the gas did not bring an easy death.

He shivered as he rose to his feet and continued back down the sewer. As he walked he sighed with disappointment—Marcus must have climbed out through one of the maintenance ducts after all. He cursed his friend's stupidity and cowardice. At least he would have seen the sun as he died though, cut down by the automatic sonifi which covered the no man's land above. He brought his sonifex down so that it rode at his hip with his quick stride. He would have to fight his way back to the Legate's compound.

A whimper of fear off to the right made him jump, his sonifex flying up to his shoulder in an instant. 'Titus,' Marcus' voice was choked with tears. His face illuminated by the laser sight through which Titus was staring at him. The light shone on the water below; an eerie glow in the otherwise dark sewer. Marcus fell forwards.

Titus caught him, holding him tightly and shaking him. 'Come on!'

Marcus groaned.

Titus slapped him hard on the face and shouted again. 'We have to get out of here!'

'I can't go back,' Marcus moaned.

'If you stay here you die for certain.' Titus pushed Marcus back onto his own feet, 'can you run?'

At that moment the shouts of rebels came from further back down the corridor; they had managed to get around the rock fall he had created. The sound seemed to galvanise Marcus. 'In here!' He shouted, dragging Titus into the small recess where he had been hiding.

The footsteps were closer now, nearly upon them. They found themselves crouched in an ancient store room which was no more than 10 feet across in either direction. The wall behind them had crumbled with age, and Titus immediately began to make the most of it gathering rubble and stray bricks which he piled up in the entrance. He grabbed Marcus, who sat dejected in the corner, forcing him to his feet. 'Get your sonifex!' he shouted, gesturing to the completed makeshift barricade.

Marcus shrugged his shoulders; perhaps he had not brought it, or perhaps he had lost it. It was too late to rectify that now. Titus pulled out the concealed sonifex he kept in the inside pocket of his jacket and tossed it over to Marcus. It was loaded with twelve anti personnel rounds, but he had no spare magazine. He doubted that Marcus would be much use in this state though.

As the footsteps hurried closer he heard commands shouted excitedly in the rebels' foreign language. They must have heard the two of them as they had shouted in the corridor—there would be no hope of remaining hidden. He pulled the magazine out of his sonifex and quickly replaced it with his second one loaded with anti personnel rounds; the rebels he had seen earlier had been wearing no body armour.

A figure flitted past the entrance to the storeroom. Titus listened warily as the figure stopped running a few yards beyond. He must have found the end of the sewer, and would come back. Then the search would begin. The man walked back into plain view and passed them again, this time at a slow walk before speaking with a further unseen rebel back down the sewer. Titus heard him turn and slowly begin to walk back towards them. Titus' breath came raggedly after his long run, impossibly loud in the confined space. They could not avoid detection. Suddenly the rebel's face appeared directly in front of them, the only part of him visible from behind their barricade. His eyes widened in shock as he came face to face with Titus.

Titus fired a controlled burst of three shots. The first armour piercing round still in the breach left a neat half inch round red hole in the man's neck, a fatal speck of red. The second round which followed was from the antipersonnel magazine, and collapsed as its soft tip met the rebel's flesh. Spinning awkwardly upon its axis as its drilled grooves caught in the tissue of the rebel's neck, the round bored through his body and drove its way out through his back leaving an exit hole the size of a dinner plate. The force of the impact catapulted the rebel's head high into the air, as his neck exploded in a torrent of blood, which coated Titus' face and dripped down onto his tunic beneath the flak jacket.

For the briefest of moments there was silence. Then the warcrys came, and the air was filled with smoke, dust and blood. Titus fired short controlled bursts at every shape he saw in the corridor outside. He had no idea how many rebels there were. Suddenly he was pushed backwards, as the top end of the barricade collapsed under a weight of a rebel Chief, clothed in his ancient traditional battle dress. Titus fired a burst into his bare chest, tearing his painted body apart and showering Marcus with gore, as he

288

covered in the corner. Titus pulled himself from under the rubble, firing instinctively as another rebel framed the archway. The unmistakable clang of a grenade on the concrete floor registered in Titus' brain. It had landed close by. He made a quick swoop for it and tossed it back through the opening out into the sewer, where it exploded with a force that almost threw him to the ground and covered him in dust loosed from the ceiling. His ears hissing from the shockwave he fired at another intruder. The man's ruined body was tossed aside by the brutal rounds. Titus tossed the empty magazine away and loaded the armour piercing magazine, cursing as he realised it was his last.

A piercing war cry rang out as another rebel tried desperately to clamber over the dilapidated remains of their barricade. Titus fired; the rebel's body jerked as the jacketed rounds tore through his body with ease, ripping great chunks out of the sewer wall behind him. Another metallic click, this time on the far side of the room from him. He dived for the grenade, but fell far short. There was no time. He twisted on the ground desperately and launched himself in the opposite direction. As far away from the grenade as he could.

The world seemed to implode around him as he felt himself launched through the air, and tumbling out of control, crash against the far wall next to Marcus. Time seemed to slow down as he reached for his discarded battered sonifex. The sights had gone, but he did not need them in here. His right arm didn't seem to work anymore. The dull roar in his ears rose to a high pitched wail. Marcus was mouthing at him but he couldn't hear him. He looked down at his right arm which hung loosely at his side, clearly broken; he could even see the bone sticking out, but the wound was entirely painless.

Another painted face appeared in the archway, pointing his sonifex into the gloom. Titus switched his sonifex to his left arm and fired. The face disappeared as the rebel was thrown back. He smiled grimly as he heard the thud of the body striking the bare concrete of the sewer. He had not been permanently deafened after all.

A new hissing began to penetrate over the sounds of the rebels outside. At first he thought it was just his ears recovering from the confined explosion, but the rebels had heard it too. They were screaming, panicking in their foreign tongue. Titus did not understand the word they were shouting, but he knew what it must mean and the realisation terrified him. The grenade that he had thrown back must have punctured the blistering gas cylinder, and now they were all going to die.

He grabbed Marcus with his good hand, his sonifex hanging loosely at his elbow and launched himself towards the opening of the sewer. He clawed his way past what remained of the barricade and dragged Marcus into the corridor. The rebels had gone;

their shouts echoing from further down the sewer back in the direction of the command bunker.

'I can't smell it!' Marcus exclaimed.

'Its odourless, and dense, keep your head high,' Titus replied as he sprinted along the corridor, trying to breath as little as possible. He could not help but remember the screams of those dying from the blistering gas, he shook the thoughts from his head and kept running. Marcus kept pace easily next to him now; the fear of the gas giving him the impetus he needed.

As they came out into the wider part of the sewer they caught sight of the fleeing rebels again, trying to climb over the rubble that Titus had dislodged earlier. One rebel turned around, having clambered onto a flat topped piece of broken concrete, and caught sight of the pair. Shouting a warning to his colleagues, he fired a couple of shots from his sonifex before continuing to climb. His companions stared for a moment as Titus and Marcus bore down on them, their hands reaching for their sonifi, but then they turned back to the barricade and began to climb desperately, their fear of the gas triumphing over their desire to kill the Romans.

Titus and Marcus crossed the gap in a few seconds. Titus launched himself at the rock with his left arm, his sonifex slung over his back, and dragged himself up onto a concrete lump; the rebels were only five metres above them now, oblivious to anything but the gas insidiously flowing nearer. Titus reached up for his next hold and hauled himself between two concrete blocks, finding an easier route up the mountain of rubble. He reached up with his good arm and grabbed the boot of the nearest rebel. The man turned as he felt the pull, his eyes opening wide with fear as Titus pulled him off the block. His body flailed as it tumbled down over the concrete to fall awkwardly into the sewer water below. Titus took his place on the concrete plinth. Two other rebels remained, one, limping heavily, being helped by his stronger comrade. The stronger of the two reached for his sonifex but was cut down by Marcus who had taken up a position alongside Titus on the top of rubble mountain. The final remaining rebel started to run as fast as he could, his sonifex forgotten in the flood water. Marcus raised his sonifex to bring him down.

'Leave him,' Titus said, 'he can't do us any harm.'

Marcus nodded, holstering his sonifex, as the pair descended the rubble and retreated towards the command bunker. Marcus' face was red with embarrassment and he could not meet Titus' eye. No words were spoken.

Then up ahead they heard the rebel begging for his life. He was crying in his strange barbaric language, his words interspersed with sobs. They could not understand what he said, but it was clear he was facing imminent death. They rounded the corner. The command bunker was right ahead—he had run right up to it in his panic to escape. Now he knelt in the damp silt, his arms held out, imploring the man who stood before him not to shoot. But the rebel had no chance, for the man who stood holding the sonifex casually to the side of his head was none other than Antonius, and he had never spared a life.

Titus opened his mouth to intervene, but something stopped him. He was not sure why he stayed silent. Perhaps he knew that his words would have no effect on Antonius anyway, yet it seemed wrong to him that this rebel, who had endured so much in escaping the gas, should die now on his knees on the muddy concrete.

The man begged again and Titus watched as Antonius' fingers closed tightly around the trigger. Antonius looked deeply into the eyes of the rebel, sneering at him. Then something strange happened.

The rebel fell silent and closed his eyes, accepting his fate, and at that moment Antonius released his finger from the trigger. The sonifex fell back to his side. His right hand worked the action so that the weapon unloaded, pinging the jacketed round out onto the concrete floor, where it rolled in slowly diminishing elliptical circles before finally coming to a halt against Titus' boot.

The rebel opened his eyes slowly and looked up at Antonius, who stared down at him, his expression unreadable. The rebel gingerly got to his feet. Still Antonius did not move. Then suddenly his other arm came up and the rebel cowered once more. Antonius laughed and waved his arm at the rebel, gesturing for him to run. He obliged, his legs scrabbling for purchase on the muddy ground. He bolted past Titus, and began to climb out of one of the ventilation shafts to the surface above.

Titus looked quizzically at Antonius, who said nothing. He reached down and collected the unspent round and handed it back to Antonius. The big man took it before turning around, still deep in thought, and walking back into the bunker. The door swung shut automatically after him and Titus and Marcus were alone once more.

Titus leaned against the metal bulkhead of the bunker. Neither of them wanted to turn the wheel which would unlock the door and lead them towards the wrath of the Legate.

'You saved my life,' Marcus spoke thoughtfully.

'Whatever happens in there, remember that I would do it again.'

'I didn't deserve it.' Marcus replied.

'No, you didn't. But I would do it for any of my friends. We have been through too much together for me to just let you die.'

'I cannot repay you.'

'You do not need to.'

Marcus shook his head, 'I must, and I will start with a promise,' he was nearly in tears, 'I promise that I will never disobey you again.'

'Don't promise that, I don't want that.'

'Trust me, I will repay you,' Marcus said earnestly.

Titus shook his head and turned the wheel on the door which swung open gently. Inside they could smell freshly cooked beef stew. Titus immediately became ravenously hungry, and that was when he realised how much his arm hurt; he had never felt pain like it.

XXXXV

As Titus' vision slowly returned he was aware of two things: first of all, the drug was wearing off but his breathing was still very fast and shallow. Secondly, Strabo was *still* gone. He wanted to scream, beg for help. But he suppressed that desire. No one was going to help him. He had to save himself. That meant being brave and trying to control his tortured breathing. The doctor walked in front of him. Titus tried to keep his eyes still and stopped blinking. The doctor looked concerned. Titus held his breath. His oxygen starved body sent waves of pain rushing through his arms and legs, and he felt as if his head would explode from the effort. The doctor reached forwards to check his pulse. 'Hurry up!' Titus thought. The urge to breath was unbearable now. The doctor placed his index finger on Titus' carotid artery; his hand was shaking. Titus remembered Strabo's words earlier, 'if he dies. You die.'.

The doctor's fingers dug into Titus' neck, desperate to find him alive. This was his one chance. He jerked forwards, grabbed the struggling doctor's head and snapped his neck like a twig.

The drug had worn off.

He ripped the grey capped cannula from his arm. Pressing firmly as blood poured out of the hole and down his arm, he limped out of the chamber.

Dressed only in a white vest and shorts coated with his own blood and vomit, he hobbled down the white corridor meeting no-one, but then it was the middle of the night and all the workers would be safely in bed. Apart from Strabo and a few guards he was alone. The corridor stretched ahead of him; another torture chamber like the one he had been in was off to the left but it did not appear to have been used for some time. The room next to it caught his eye. He peered in and saw a bare metal operating table.

Now he recognised where he was. The West Wing of the compound. He could find his way out from here. He hurried as quickly as the pain from his broken feet would allow, trying to find the vent in the wall that he and Marcus had used. Voices in the corridor ahead stopped him. The were heading his way. He turned and tried to ignore the pain in his feet as he scuttled back into the operating room and hid beside a machine at the far wall. The voices grew closer. One was clearly Strabo's, the other, presumably, a guard.

'What do you mean, he's gone!'

'The doctor is dead. The prisoner is missing,' the guard's voice shook with fear.

'You had better hope that he is easily found.' Strabo replied menacingly, as the pair marched past the entrance to the operating theatre. Titus backed away further, trying to draw himself as close to the wall as he could. His lower back came up against a metal mesh. He turned around. There was a large vent, much like the one Marcus and he had climbed into all those nights ago when they had first broken into Strabo's compound. Perhaps it led to the surface as the other one had all those nights ago? He crouched down and hooked his fingers beneath it, gently hinging it up. The vent creaked, seeming deafeningly loud to Titus as he climbed in. He turned around, and as gently as he could, let it slide closed.

The vent was narrow, dark and echoey. He crawled slowly, but was sure that sound from his passage would ring out in every room the vent passed through. After five minutes he saw some light up ahead, and

294

eventually dragged himself out into a large windowless maintenance room. It was almost exactly the same as the one that he and Marcus had climbed out of when they had first infiltrated this compound. Above him lay a hatch with a wheel, above it would be clear night air, and hopefully no guards. They would most likely all be down in the facility looking for him.

Climbing the ladder was horrifically painful. He tried to just use his arms, but his muscles ached from the suxamethonium he had been given earlier. With great difficulty he reached the hatch and turned the wheel. It was rusty and he needed to use his last reserves of strength to open it. He braced his ruined feet against the rungs of the ladder and pushed up on the hatch screaming with the pain. The hatch opened two inches and came up short against a thick chain. It was padlocked shut. Titus could reach the padlock but he had nothing with which to pick it. He stared out of the two inch hole, breathing in fresh, winter air. It was completely dark—he must be just outside Luguvalium. Safety lay just a few inches away. He cried out in frustration and pushed harder against the hatch, but it would not budge. This way was blocked to him.

He looked back down at the vent he had crawled through. There was no point in going back, the place would be crawling with guards. Should he just stay in the maintenance room until he died? That would be relatively painless compared to more torture. But he needed to get out and rescue Ceinwyn before the Praetorians brought her to Strabo. There had to be another way. His eyes fixed on the hatch in the floor; he remembered from last time what would lie below it. Water, Luguvalium's water supply.

He climbed down slowly and knelt down by the hatch. The wheel turned easily—it had clearly been used recently unlike the one to the surface. He opened it and peered down into the darkness. Far below, a small platform stood, illuminated above a torrent of water. The ladder was better maintained than the last one, but each step was still an agony, as he could not take all of his weight on his arms.

He let himself fall backwards off the ladder onto the platform to avoid landing on his ruined feet, the sound echoed over and over again in the dark cavern. He peered over the edge at the torrent below. If this was indeed the water supply for Luguvalium he should be able to follow it. He

295

noticed a thin gantry that connected this platform to another a few hundred yards away. He decided to travel in the direction of the water and started to hobble along. The first two gantries passed without incident but the third was much bigger and contained a machine that was dribbling liquid into the stream below. Perhaps it was waste from Strabos' compound he thought, but this was Luguvalium's drinking water. He tottered closer, blood pouring from his feet through the gantry into the water below. He put his hand out into the stream of water. It smelt of nothing. He tasted it and nearly retched. It was so bitter. He spat over and over again trying to rid himself of the taste. He wandered behind the machine to inspect further. A pipe connected it to the wall behind it which led further into Strabo's compound. There was a door next to it. With foreboding Titus turned the handle and pushed the door open. He walked into a small scire room. The pipe was connected to a large circular tank which glowed blue in the light from the scires. A layer of yellow scum floated on the top.

'It's bacteria.' A voice boomed out in the room. Titus cowered, the voice belonged to Strabo.

'I can still see you,' the voice continued.

Titus looked around and caught sight of the camera in the corner.

'I have been watching you all the way from the first gantry. Don't worry you won't be alone for long, some Praetorians are coming for you.'

'Why are you pumping bacteria into the water?' Titus asked.

'Idiot. It's not the bacteria I am pumping in but what the bacteria make—what I have engineered them to make to be precise.'

Titus thought about the diseased Slaves. 'A poison to kill the inhabitants of Luguvalium? Why?'

'Again, you are greatly mistaken. I have no desire to kill my subjects. The poison only harms Slaves. You could drink as much of it as you liked, and it would have no effect. Your liver can process it. It won't fail like the liver of a Slave's will under continuous exposure.'

Titus remembered what Cyric had said about Slaves not being able to process alcohol well. Perhaps there were other chemicals that they could not process as well. The stomping of heavy boots in the corridor focused him. He had seconds only before capture. He hoped what Strabo had just said about the poison being safe for non slaves was true. He dived at the glass tank hitting it with the full weight of his body behind his shoulder. The glass shattered and Titus landed in a pile of broken shards, bacterial biofilm and poison. The pump outside faltered as its supply of liquid ran out and it choked and spluttered before coming to an eventual halt. The door burst open and five Praetorians ran in. They grabbed Titus, who had no energy left to resist, and forced him into a metal box. Slamming the lid shut they began to drag him back up the corridor. 'Solitude Titus, solitude!' It was Strabo's voice again from the loudspeaker in the room. 'But don't worry. Not for long. Next time I see you we can have a nice chat with Ceinwyn too.'

Titus screamed abuse at the Governor from inside the box as the Praetorians dragged him clumsily down the corridor, but there was no answer. He was completely alone.

XXXXVI

'Now,' whispered the lead Praetorian. He had been waiting in position for four hours now and had become thoroughly bored. But his master's orders needed to be followed to the letter. They would be asleep, far more chance of seizing the girl without a struggle then. He hoped she would be there, the master had warned him that another detachment were watching the house in case anyone should leave. Perhaps they had already captured the girl? He fingered the controls of his fasces in anticipation. He hoped the girl was still in, that way the glory would be his. If there was any doubt he would tear the house apart to be sure before he left. He had no desire to risk his master's wrath.

He nodded to his two companions who clicked their magazines into place. The three of them were lurking down an alley not far from the target house. Their assault sonifi glistened in the pale moonlight as they ran silently across the street, keeping low, the snow twinkling where it had settled on their body armour. They crouched down on either side of the door. There was no sound from within—they had not been spotted.

There was no light from the windows; the girl must be asleep. The leader nodded to his companions, stood up, and kicked down the door.

Tiberius was roused from sleep by the sound of crashing. He rolled over and tried to sleep again. He had been having a good dream for once; his dreams had been dark of late, ever since Quintus went missing. He closed his eyes. The banging came again, it was from coming from further down the street and sounded like someone was trying to move house with scant concern for the contents. He shrugged his shoulders—there was a battle raging in and around Luguvalium. Best to stay out of it. He wondered if Marcus would wake up and go and investigate, but then he remembered that Marcus had been gone for weeks, along with Titus. He did not know where they were but they were clearly planning something, hopefully another mission. Tiberius missed action, which was why he and Antonius had started hiring themselves out independently for the last two weeks. It kept his mind off Quintus, even though all they had ended up doing was being a 'presence' at criminal underworld meetings. It was Antonius they really wanted for that. He smiled to himself as he tried to go back to sleep despite the sounds from outside—soon they would have real work again.

Then a shot rang out. Tiberius jumped from his bed, reaching for his assault sonifex as a reflex, it leant up against the bed side. He had it in his hands and had flicked off the safety catch before he had even woken properly. Something inside his head told him that the shot had definitely come from outside. He could not be sure, he had heard it only in his sleep, but Antonius had heard it too, he could hear the huge man leaping down the stairs two at a time. Tiberius followed and the two met in the sitting room at the front of the house.

'What's going on?' Antonius asked, blinking the sleep from his eyes.

'How the hell should I know,' Tiberius replied grumpily. 'A house is being torn apart down the road. It must be the Reivers.'

'We could go and kill them.'

It was always so simple to Antonius, Tiberius thought, smiling to himself. 'The Praetorians will be on their way soon, they must have heard the shot.' He gestured for Antonius to stay still, but in his heart he did not believe his words. He knew that the Praetorians would be more likely to be off fighting the Reivers in the forest. Another shot rang out from down the street. Antonius' hand rested against the door knob impatiently.

Tiberius shrugged his shoulders.

Antonius swung the door open and peered out into the street before stepping out into the thickening snow.

'What's going on out there?' Tiberius asked anxiously.

Antonius peered into the darkness.

'I can't see anything.' Tiberius said, exasperated. Then another crash rang out and the pair stared down the road where they could hear the sound of wood splintering.

'It's coming from Titus' house!' Tiberius exclaimed and marched down the street, Antonius tailing along behind.

The house was only a few yards away, the front door hanging off its hinges. 'Reivers!' Tiberius whispered, 'so much for marshal law! The looting seems to have started already.'

Antonius nodded in agreement.

'She's not here.' A voice rang out from inside. To Tiberius' surprise it was in perfect Latin, no trace of a local dialect. He stepped through the doorway to investigate. Moving quickly and silently into the sitting room he was confronted with a bizarre scene. Two men dressed in body armour and wearing black helmets were tearing through Titus' house. The room was almost unrecognisable. The furniture was lying in disarray in the centre of a dishevelled rug and holes had been blown in the walls with the sonifi the men carried, which were more advanced than any Tiberius had used before. He reached for his own instinctively, cursing as he realised that he had left it by his bedside. The men were busy ripping a sofa away from the rear wall of the room and had not yet noticed him. Tiberius stepped into the centre of the room and drew himself up as tall as possible. He cleared his throat.

The pair whipped around and stared at Tiberius and Antonius. The sofa fell from their grip, crashing down hard on the carpet. The shorter of the two men looked to the larger man, who was clearly the leader. He nodded, answering a silent question. The men charged Tiberius. The shorter man reached him first and leapt into the air with a loud shriek, Tiberius was off balance and tried to twist aside but was caught by the knee of the man and was flung onto his back. Behind him he heard the sounds of Antonius wrestling with the other intruder. Tiberius lunged for the sonifex which hung forgotten at the side of his opponent, but all he succeeded in doing was drawing the man's attention to the fact he was carrying it. He tried to wrestle it from his hands but the man was stronger and threatened to tear it from his grip. When that happened Tiberius' knew both he and Antonius would be dead.

A crash from behind him told him that Antonius was still dealing with the other interloper. His opponent, sensing victory grinned viciously at Tiberius. He had no choice but to take a gamble. Releasing one hand from the weapon he flicked his arm up in a swift cut. The angle was difficult and, half crouched on the carpet, the blow lacked any real force, but it still caught the man in the throat. His opponent gave out a strangled cry and reeled backwards.

Tiberius launched himself at the man and threw a punch at his face. The blow connected well, into the small unprotected face area of the helmet sending his assailant backwards and splaying him out over the sofa.

Tiberius shook his hand to ease the pain; he had caught the top of the helmet's faceguard with the blow and cut it open. He reached down for the sonifex and felt the man's hand tighten over his wrist as his other gloved fist flew into Tiberius face. The glove was lined with armour and the punch threw Tiberius onto his back and dazed him. His vision dimmed as he tried to get to his feet, and he collapsed back to his knees.

He felt burning on his left arm and looking down realised that he was leaning on a glowing ember. Antonius had thrown his opponent into the open fireplace and the fire was now spreading throughout the room. He turned back to the man who stood above him, smiling down at him as he lifted the sonifex. As he flicked off the safety catch a red laser dot lit up from the end of the muzzle. It was a beautiful weapon and Tiberius wondered how these criminals could have got hold of it. He closed his eyes against its glare.

The sound of wood connecting savagely with human flesh brought him back to his senses. His opponent slumped to the ground, his helmet and skull smashed by a four foot long chunk of broken table. Antonius laughed as he hefted the piece of wood back under the crook of his arm and reached out his other hand to Tiberius who took it gratefully.

'We need to get out of here,' said Antonius as soon as he had hauled Tiberius to his feet. The fire was spreading.

Tiberius nodded and turned for the door. Suddenly the cellar door burst open and a third armoured man charged out. Antonius turned in a moment and, with a movement surprisingly swift for such a large man, swung his makeshift club straight at the chest of the man. The blow catapulted him several feet through the air, sending him crashing to the ground on his back. Antonius stepped forwards and raising the wood high above his head brought it crashing down with a dull thud. A thin trail of blood oozed out from the side of the man's helmet as the pair turned and abandoned the stricken building.

'Who the hell were they?' Tiberius asked Antonius, rhetorically, as he rubbed his face where the punch had connected. It ached but no serious harm seemed to have been done. 'They almost looked like...' his voice tailed off as he saw an elegant figure walking towards him. He stared: it was a girl, wearing a white knee length dress traced with mud at the base. But it was her face that drew his attention. She was beautiful, and unusual.

Her pale white face, framed with deep red hair piled in loose curls, seemed somehow at odds with the rest of her body, but he couldn't quite place why. She marched up to him, placed her hands on her hips, and defiantly returned his stare.

'Who the hell are you?' asked the handsome man gruffly. His sidekick, a huge beast of a man tossed a thick beam of wood between his hands testily. The wood was matted with hair, flesh and what appeared to be bone fragments which twinkled in the light from the fire that was engulfing her house. She did not wish to know what had taken place here.

'My name is Ceinwyn. I think you must be Tiberius.'

The handsome man froze and fixed his piercing eyes on Ceinwyn. 'Now how on Earth do you know that?' he asked calmly.

'Because I am in love with your General,' she answered proudly.

Tiberius peered closer, inspecting her in the light cast from the embers of what remained of her and Titus' house. 'But you are a Half-Breed!'

Tiberius laughed as he realised. 'Do you really think Titus would bother with you?'

Ceinwyn shrugged her shoulders, 'if that is all that I am, then perhaps he would not.' Tiberius face contorted as he thought deeply.

Antonius tapped him on the shoulder, interrupting.

'Yes, Antonius,' he replied curtly.

'She does look like a Half-Breed.'

'Yes Antonius, but she is right. She can't be.' He looked at her again, scrutinising her, still unsure.

Ceinwyn just smiled back.

'She is telling the truth you know.'

A polished voice boomed out from behind the burnt out building, and all three of them turned to stare. A figure stepped out into the street, trailing ash from his thick cloak which scattered and eddied in the gentle night breeze.

'Gnaeus, you are safe!' Ceinwyn exclaimed and ran towards her friend who embraced her. She felt a thud which shook the earth and turning around she saw that Antonius had dropped his makeshift club in astonishment.

'I am sorry,' Gnaeus whispered to her as he came alongside, 'I was intercepted by some Romans. I think they were Strabo's men.' Ceinwyn recoiled at the sound of the name of her old master, 'I came back to look for you and make sure you were safe, but I couldn't find you.' He smiled at her and hugged her before turning back to his friends. 'This girl is indeed half Slave and half Roman; it makes her rather striking do you not think.'

'But she is intelligent,' stated Tiberius, confused.

'Yes,' replied Gnaeus, 'yes, she is. And so are they all. We got it wrong Tiberius. We have oppressed a people for so long that we have forgotten that they are people too, and in turn they have ignored us, and given us no reason to see intelligence in them.'

'You expect me to believe that?' asked Tiberius with a sneer. 'Sounds like something you made up from that damned contraband book of yours.'

'Yet Titus believes it too.' Gnaeus replied, 'and he fell in love with her, despite what you think of her. Tonight he was due to marry her, in secret, because he knew this would be your response, and that of the rest of the

303

world for that matter. But he did not arrive, and I was accosted by Praetorians on route to our rendezvous.' He rubbed his arm at the memory of the attack. It was still acutely painful. The cosh had bruised the bone but mercifully it seemed to be unbroken. He looked around at the scene of destruction, 'what has happened here is the key to his whereabouts no doubt.'

Antonius reached into the building and hauled out a brained body. He jerked the helmet clear of its black body armour, effortlessly exposing the head and neck of the dead man. Yanking hard on the dog tags he snapped the chain easily and threw them over to Gnaeus who nodded gratefully and knelt on the ground to inspect them. It was as he had thought. 'Praetorians,' he said softly, 'so these are Strabo's men too.'

'And Strabo holds Titus?' asked Tiberius. 'Why?'

'Because of this girl who was once his, and because Titus opposes all the evil that Strabo does. He is ruining Luguvalium, and Titus is trying to save it.'

Tiberius shook his head, 'I need some evidence Gnaeus, you know he told us nothing of this.'

Gnaeus shook his head with frustration at Tiberius, 'he needs your help, you have to trust me.'

'Why should I trust you?' Tiberius asked angrily.

'And more importantly, why should we help Titus at all?' a voice boomed out, echoing in the dark street. Everyone turned to look down the street as a portly figure marched angrily towards them, 'why help him when he has betrayed us all?'

Gnaeus groaned inwardly, Marcus had not forgiven. As Marcus approached he opened his mouth to speak again, condemning Titus to remain a prisoner of Strabo's till he died. It was deeply unfair, but Gnaeus understood why he did it, for he had also met Ceinwyn and spent time with her. And he had seen the look of resentment on Marcus' face after Titus had saved him beneath Rowena Valley all those years ago. It struck him that jealousy was possibly the greatest motivation a man could have. Marcus' every word dripped with it. He began to speak again, gesturing angrily at Gnaeus. Then his mobile phone beeped. He cursed, and reached into his pocket angrily to examine it.

'Message?' Gnaeus asked, still exhausted from his ordeal on the road earlier.

'Yeah,' Marcus said and started putting the phone away.

'Aren't you going to read it?' Antonius asked slowly.

'Yeah, you should, it could be from Titus, telling you that you are a lying, betraying bastard,' Gnaeus snarled at Marcus, stepping towards him.

To Gnaeus surprise tears came to Marcus' eyes. He had expected him to shout back, to make a proper fight of this. Instead all the fight seemed to leave him and he deflated visibly in front of them. He stared at Ceinwyn as tears began to roll down his face. 'Don't *you* understand?' he said to her, his voice breaking as he crossed the last few steps between them. 'I love you,' he croaked through his anguish, 'Titus took you from me, I never had a chance to show you how much I love you.'

Ceinwyn walked a pace towards him, and replied, her voice cracking as well as tears welled up. 'I am so sorry Marcus. I knew you loved me, and I used you. But you have to understand, I always loved Titus, and never you.' Marcus looked as if he had been struck around the face, the colour drained from his cheeks and he lost balance and nearly fell to the snowy ground.

'I want to prove it to you,' he said.

'You don't need to,' she pointed to his tears, 'I know you love me, but I am sorry. I don't love you,' she said, firmly now. Tears began to pour down her beautiful face, soaking into her mud stained wedding dress. Her voice broke, 'I love Titus.'

'He doesn't have the best way of showing it then does he! Getting himself locked up by Strabo when he should be off marrying you,' Marcus said vehemently.

'You don't understand!' Ceinwyn rounded on him angrily, 'he did it because he loves me. You have no idea what that animal, Strabo, did to me; what he is still doing to my people. At least Titus wanted to do something about it.'

Gnaeus shifted awkwardly from foot to foot, he knew that if he had helped Titus then perhaps none of this would now be happening. But then he had thought he had talked him out of his insane plan altogether.

'He lied to us all,' Marcus said looking around at Tiberius and Antonius. 'Titus could have told us about Ceinwyn and the Slaves and about Strabo's plotting. But he didn't, he kept it to himself. He doesn't trust us. Why should we help him?'

'He is our friend,' Antonius replied. The gruffness of his voice incongruous with his words, 'and our boss. We must help him.'

Sensing victory slipping from his grasp Marcus turned to Tiberius, 'Quintus would be here now if it wasn't for Titus. Titus lied to him—that's why he ran away.'

Tiberius nodded. Gnaeus cursed Marcus under his breath for arriving at exactly the wrong moment. He thought frantically, desperately needing something to swing the argument his way. Then Ceinwyn spoke.

'Please,' she said to Marcus falling down onto her knees in the snow, her voice choked with tears. 'Save my husband for me.'

She looked up at Marcus with her big green eyes glittering in the reflected light from the snow, 'you are right: he does not deserve it. But I love him, I cannot abandon him.'

Marcus opened his mouth in defiance, ready to condemn Titus to imprisonment, and death. But he did not speak. Instead he stared at the girl he loved kneeling before him in the snow, weeping. Walking forwards he reached out his hands towards her, taking hers gently and helping her rise to her feet. Tears poured down his face into the snow. He could not speak at first, and simply held her in his arms. Eventually he managed to control his emotions and spoke at last, 'I love you, Ceinwyn.'

She opened her mouth to speak, to brush away his words.

'No listen,' he cut her off with a whisper. 'I will always love you, no matter what you do, and no matter how you feel about me. I can't change that, even if I wanted to.' He drew breath and fixed her with his piercing eyes. 'Watching you with Titus hurts so much, I can barely stand it. I have tried my whole life to be as good as him, but I could never manage it. Do you think that I didn't know myself from the start that I could not really make you happy? I was desperate to prove that I could, but no matter how hard I tried I could see you getting closer and closer to Titus. It didn't surprise me, I have never made any woman happy,' he laughed, a hollow sound. 'He makes you so happy doesn't he?' He stared into Ceinwyn's tear filled eyes which could not help glowing with love at the thought of Titus. Marcus smiled back at her, acknowledging her feelings. 'You love him, not me, but I love you and so I cannot refuse you.' His words were kindly now.

'So yes,' he continued, putting his arm on her shoulder and kissing her cheeks, tasting the hot salt of her tears. 'Yes, for you I will save him.'

Gnaeus resisted the urge to clap. 'How?' he asked bringing them back to the stark reality of their predicament, 'how will we do it?'

Marcus pondered this, and whilst doing so, absent-mindedly reached into his pocket for his phone to read the message he had received earlier. He stared at the screen, his face becoming more and more confused, before bursting into a wide grin.

'What does it say?' Gnaeus asked.

'It's from my bank in Rome!' Marcus exclaimed, his mouth widening with shock. 'I appear to have become rather wealthy.'

XXXXVII

Titus awoke slowly. It was pitch dark, but he thought it was morning. He could not be sure; his body clock was completely out of sync.

He could not tell where he was. The box was about four foot across and four foot high. You could sit up, but not stretch out your legs, or alternatively stretch your legs but have to stand crouched. His legs and back were in agony, it was a wonder he had slept at all. From the way the box swayed to and fro, he imagined that he was suspended somehow from the ceiling.

There was another prisoner as well. Titus had not seen him, but he had heard sobbing coming from somewhere above him in the night. At first Titus had thought the sounds had been coming from him and he had panicked; the idea of losing his sanity scared him more than anything else that Strabo could do to him. He had hammered on the side of his dark box in greeting, but either the other prisoner could not hear or would not reply.

The box wobbled and the creak of metal told him that the pulley was starting up again. Pain shot up his legs as the box shuddered on its

308

descent. Titus tried to control his breathing. He would be free for a few seconds in a moment, too heavily guarded to escape. He knew in his heart now that he could cope with any torture that Strabo could throw against him—it was about vengeance now. He could tell Strabo the code at any moment, he cared nothing for the money; but he knew that there was more to this for Strabo as well, the torture would not end no matter what he told him. Far better to take the secret to the grave and leave Strabo penniless.

But Strabo's final threat last night left him shaking with fear and rage. He cursed himself for his stupidity. Ceinwyn would have been safe in the cave. Why did he take her from there? He could not watch her suffer. He had made up his mind last night, if Strabo captured her, he would tell him everything. He did not trust Strabo to let her go, but there was a slight chance that she would be left unharmed. He shook his head, knowing that Strabo would probably torture them both anyway once he had the code. Some wedding present, being tortured to death.

The box stopped suddenly and the door swung open with a squeal. Light streamed in blinding Titus. Rough hands hauled him out onto the concrete floor. The lights on the white ceiling stared down at him as he was hauled to his feet to begin the long hobble to the torture chamber.

Strabo was waiting. Titus fixed his eyes on him, not wanting to see Ceinwyn bound to the chair. He kept focused, looking for that hint of triumph he was expecting to see glimmering on the Governor's face. But he looked drawn. He had slept worse than he had, Titus realised, and a slight hope surfaced in his mind. He looked around the room. It was empty apart from him and the chair. He smiled and his heart soared; somehow Ceinwyn had evaded the Praetorians. Strabo looked away, unable to meet his gaze. The guards flung him into the chair and retreated as the door swung to gently, closing with a metallic click. Strabo and he were alone again.

Strabo walked over to the far corner slowly. He looked exhausted as he picked up the bare metal stool and, placing it in front of Titus, took a seat. Titus was surprised to find himself unbound.

'Don't even think of trying anything.' Strabo said as soon as he had sat down. 'This room is monitored and there is a whole score of the

Praetorian Guard in the compound. You'd be dead before you even touched me.'

Titus nodded, confused. Why did Strabo not simply tie him up like last time?

'I have decided to level with you. We need to talk properly, man to man.'

'You mean your plan to torture the code from me failed, so you are going to bore me to death instead?'

Strabo tried to conceal the anger that briefly furrowed his brow. 'You and I are very much alike.'

Titus didn't even try not to laugh. 'Really? When was the last time you saw me capture Slaves so I could sell them for their organs? Or subject the town I am meant to be protecting to the predations of bandits so that I could take a cut of their profits? Or try to commit genocide for that matter?'

'I am a Roman, just like you.'

'Rome abandoned me!' Titus spat, surprised by his vehemence. He had never realised how much anger he had bottled up. Strabo smiled.

'It abandoned me too! I could have been Consul by now, I had a good family, a good career in the Senate! But instead I ended up Governor of this shit hole in the middle of nowhere. Even if I manage to kill these Slaves for them I don't think I'll ever be allowed back into politics.'

'Kill Slaves for them?' Titus echoed his words back, confused.

'You think I would slaughter all the slaves in my province for personal gain? I slaughter them for their organs Titus, it makes me a fortune. Why would I want to kill them all and bury the bodies?'

'So why then, why commit genocide?' Titus asked.

'It's hardly genocide!' Strabo laughed, 'to kill a bunch of animals. The Senate told me to. Not that they provided any means, I had to do all the work myself,' he said angrily.

'The Senate would never condone that!'

'Don't believe me then—I have no reason to lie to you.'

'And what would you get in return?'

'A place in the Senate.' Strabo turned red.

A place in the elected Senate. Titus could not believe what Strabo had just said to him. 'How would they manage that?'

'Easily. They would simply manipulate the vote using the omniajunctus as they have done for years.'

'Rome is not that corrupt.'

'Your father doesn't agree with you. Did you even read a *single* thing he wrote?' Titus couldn't meet Strabo's gaze. 'What a great son to him you have been,' Strabo mocked.

'I still don't believe you.'

'If you are so loyal to Rome then why not join me? Give me my money back, and together we will fight the Reivers—they are a common enemy.'

Titus looked at Strabo, bright red with anger, and suddenly understood. For the first time in the three days of his imprisonment he felt something approaching happiness. 'The Reivers are winning aren't they?'

'Of course not!' Strabo said, rising from the chair and leaning over Titus.

'But they are, aren't they! You protected them from Rome so that they could grow strong and make you a fortune. But now they are killing your Praetorians. They have outgrown you Strabo. I hope they destroy you!'

Strabo raised his fist to strike Titus, but thought better of it and sat back down. He took a moment to compose himself before he went on. 'With that money, I could fight them off. I need to pay the Praetorians. I need to pay bribes to the Reivers. I could buy them off!' He was almost pleading now, his voice becoming increasingly desperate.

'Tartarus beckons, Strabo,' Titus snarled.

Strabo rose from the chair and stood above Titus impassively, 'in which case Titus we have nothing left to say to each other.' He made a signal to the cameras studying them and at that moment the restraints whipped tightly across Titus' limbs. 'You will be tortured until you talk, or die,' Strabo continued, 'if your friends or woman are found, the same will happen to them. You have missed your last chance to save them and yourself.'

Titus felt calm envelope him. He had no more choices to make. The fates were set.

Strabo sneered at him and grabbed a chainsaw from the table. The blade snarled into life and Titus' eyes opened wide with fear. The blade screamed as Strabo revved it harder and pushed it closer towards Titus' face. 'Your last chance Titus. The code?' Titus shook his head. 'Then it is time to die.'

The door burst open and a shot rang out. The blade flew across the room scattering fat yellow sparks as it gyrated across the concrete floor. The chain snapped and the motor whirred madly. He was aware of a group of people bursting into the room behind him. Titus twisted in the chair trying to see them properly. He could hear the intruders fighting with the guards behind him. Strabo reached into his toga and drew out a small sonifex. Titus watched grimly as he pulled back on the barrel and levelled the weapon at his head. Suddenly a slender figure leapt from behind his chair and struck Strabo hard in the face. He yelped and staggered backwards dropping the sonifex. The figure struck him again, and Strabo staggered and fell, crawling away on the concrete. The figure turned and looked at Titus.

It smiled at him.

It was Ceinwyn.

She was wearing the most beautiful dress.

XXXXVIII

The restraints came loose immediately as someone twisted the dial on the back of the chair. Titus rose to his feet to take Ceinwyn in his arms; his first instinct being to protect her. He teetered on his ruined feet and slumped forwards towards the ground with a startled cry. Ceinwyn caught him under the arms and hugged him tightly to her. He felt her mouth on his forehead as he half lay across her and the chair. Then stronger arms hauled him up to his feet again. He turned around to see his rescuers properly.

'Marcus?' he said, confused upon seeing the face of the man who was supporting him. 'What are you doing here?'

Marcus smiled, 'you owe me.' He didn't need to say anything more.

Titus nodded—the debt was finally paid.

Marcus' attitude suddenly changed, 'we need to get out of here,' he spoke quickly and with, to Titus' surprise, great authority. Marcus and Gnaeus helped him across the room, whilst Tiberius and Antonius moved ahead to the door, sonifi drawn.

'Wait,' Titus said, stopping them all in their tracks, 'we must finish off Strabo.' He tried to look over his shoulder, but to his irritation could not turn properly in the grip of his friends.

Marcus looked back instead, 'he has gone!' he said, bemused.

'He can't have gone!' Titus said, 'there is only one door and we are blocking it,' he gestured to Antonius who with his great bulk was indeed blocking the only exit.

Marcus shrugged, 'there must be a secret way out of the room, all the more reason to get out now. If the alarm hasn't already been put out it will be any moment!' He pulled hard on Titus, thrusting him through the door as Titus nodded in agreement, but in truth he needn't have done—Marcus was in charge here.

For once he enjoyed the feeling of being led, rather than the burden of having to make tough decisions which had been his life for the last fifteen years. His broken feet barely touched the white floor as the group pounded up the white corridor. Apart from Ceinwyn in her wedding dress, they all wore full battle gear and were smeared with oily camouflage paint.

'Why are you carrying a gladius, Marcus?' Titus asked, staring down at Marcus' webbing, it was much plainer than Titus' own sword, in fact it was much more like the ones they had been first issued with at the age of sixteen.

Marcus blushed, 'it never hurt you to carry a sword into battle when you led us.' Titus tried to smile despite the pain from his feet.

Then suddenly they were free. They burst out of the facility and into the bright light of a new winter's day. A foot of snow lay in the courtyard and was kicked up to sparkle in the fresh sunlight as the group tore towards the main gate. Dozens of dead guards littered the courtyard; there had been a massacre on the way in it seemed. Suddenly two guards vaulted the side of the quadrangle to their right. Continuing his sprint Marcus fired from the hip cutting them down, their bodies spinning down into the snow, churning it red with their pulsating arterial blood. Marcus pulled harder on Titus' shirt. It was covered in his own blood and vomit and stank with sweat. Titus wished that Ceinwyn didn't have to see him like this, but she did not seem to care. She was running along with a small sonifex in her hands, scanning the courtyards for any further guards. Titus wondered if she knew how to use the weapon. The look in her eyes told him she did.

Four more guards closed in behind them as they reached the gate. Tiberius, calling for the others to continue, spun round and flung himself down low as he fired a burst which cut the first two men down. Laughing, he fired again drawing the line of fire from the next man's groin up to his head, splitting him in two. The last man, seeing the fate of his companions, skidded to a halt on the snow and desperately tried to turn and run. Tiberius took his time to aim and put a single measured shot through the man's skull leaving a trail of crimson blood splattered through the snow for twenty yards behind the guard.

The others were through the gate by the time Tiberius' rejoined them. Titus looked around in disbelief for they were outside the compound. He turned to hug Ceinwyn.

'No time,' Marcus barked, clearly enjoying being in command. 'We need to get out of the town.' He thrust Titus in the direction of a Praetorian currus which was parked haphazardly outside the compound.

'Have you got the key for this?' Titus asked confused.

'Cyric hotwired it,' said Ceinwyn proudly.

Titus raised his eyebrows at Ceinwyn, not understanding.

'She used it to escape from the lake, to bring us the alarm that you had gone missing,' Gnaeus explained. 'The Praetorians it belonged to are probably still lost, wandering aimlessly in the woods!'

Titus smiled in admiration at his wife to be as she hopped up into the currus. Marcus kept nervously glancing back into the compound, expecting at any moment to see more Guards heading towards them. Titus tried to leap up but his foot caught awkwardly on the side of the sill of the door and he slipped, grunting with pain, onto the floor of the currus where he lay in an undignified heap. Looking up he caught sight of the driver.

'Hello Roman,' Cyric's voice was as sarcastic as usual. His eyes were sunken and yellow, however he still had his strength. Titus remembered that he had been able to drink some alcohol. Perhaps he was lucky enough to possess some of the enzymes that other Slave livers lacked?

He tried to pull himself into a seat without grimacing whilst Cyric laughed mercilessly at his attempts. 'Now you understand what Strabo really is?'

Titus nodded in reply as Ceinwyn helped him into a seat. The rear of the currus was open, so Titus felt the breeze in his hair as he rested back in the chair. He closed his eyes. He was safe and sitting next to his nearly wife. 'Cyric,' he said, 'you're going to be OK. Just don't drink any more tap water for the next few hours. The plague was man made.'

'I know,' Cyric replied, and he told them about the mass grave which they had seen being prepared.

A salvo of gunfire ricocheted off the currus's side as a group of armoured Praetorians burst out of their headquarters across the street. Marcus, half way onto the back of the vehicle, watched incredulously as their leader led them, firing from the hip, to a huge military currus. It was Strabo himself.

Marcus shouted to Cyric to drive and the currus screeched away onto the tarmac road. As they turned onto the main road out of Luguvalium Titus looked back over his shoulder. The Praetorians were almost half a mile behind. The sonifex point on the front of the Praetorian currus fired at their fleeing vehicle, but the shots were wild and none came close. Titus watched apprehensively over his shoulder as the man released the heavy weapon and took a seat in the cab. 'How fast is this vehicle?' he called through to Cyric who sat next to Tiberius in the cab.

'Fast enough Roman,' he snapped back.

He looked back at the Praetorian vehicle. Was it gaining on them? He couldn't be entirely sure. He put an arm around Ceinwyn as if somehow that could protect her from a heavy calibre round tearing into her flesh. He shuddered at the idea.

The sonifex point remained unmanned until they started to climb into the mountains. Then it began to dawn on Titus with a mounting dread, that the Praetorian currus, whilst not faster on a straight road, was far more powerful. Titus could see some of the features of the driver now, they would certainly be in range of the great sonifex that stood proud on the top of the cab. He instinctively reached for his own sonifex, but of course he had no weapon, just his filthy clothes stained with the blood and vomit that Strabo had forced from him.

'Where are we going Marcus?' he asked with exasperation. They had been driving for thirty minutes now.

'Just a little bit further,' said Marcus obliquely, 'I have a fantastic surprise for you, and for them, possibly, if we are lucky.' He gestured with his hand at the Praetorians following.

'Give me a weapon, just in case we need to fight before we reach this surprise of yours.' Marcus nodded and reached into a compartment next to him. He drew out a sonifex, handing it to Titus, who studied it carefully. 'This is mine!' he said.

'Indeed,' Marcus replied, handing over some webbing with an old ceremonial gladius. Titus drew the gladius and cast his eye over the inscription in bone running around the pommel, 'Virtutis Fortuna Comes,' he whispered to himself before cutting his hand gently and sheaving the weapon.

Marcus shook his head and laughed. 'You have some very strange traditions in your family, Titus.'

'It has never been drawn without drawing blood, not for three hundred years,' Titus replied proudly, staring back at the currus as it rose over the lip of the pass.

It was only a few hundred yards behind now, and as it appeared again the heavy calibre sonifex fire recommenced. They all ducked low behind the headrests of their seats, which were armoured, but not to withstand this sort of round.

'How far Marcus?' Titus shouted as a bullet tore through the side of the currus, ripping a seat behind them off its mounting.

'A mile, maybe a bit more,' Marcus said turning white as another bullet struck the back of the currus, causing it to skew around as they charged down the mountain road.

Titus shook his head. 'We won't make it.'

'I know,' Cyric shouted back angrily.

'It doesn't matter where we fight then,' Titus said.

Marcus shook his head, 'put your foot down Cyric. We have to get away.'

The vehicle surged forwards with a whine as Cyric threw caution to the wind. The currus approached the next hairpin bend at full speed. Titus closed his eyes as Cyric hit the brakes and wrenched the wheel around. For a moment he was sure he was going to be dashed to pieces on the rock wall. But then Cyric lifted the handbrake lever and the back end spun around with a sharp screech in the thin layer of snow, leaving black sticky rubber on the road behind them. At the last moment Cyric plunged the handbrake back down, releasing its grip on the wheels. The engine whined again as Cyric accelerated down the next stretch of road.

Titus' eyes remained fixed on the corner they had just passed, his hands gripped the chair tightly as he watched the much larger heavily armoured currus hurtle towards it. He watched the balance in the vehicle change as the driver hit the brakes and the way it shuddered as it struck the rock wall sideways on. He shook his head with disappointment as the driver managed to pull the vehicle round, and was about to turn to push Ceinwyn down below the seat for safety, when he saw that their back right wheel was spinning uselessly. The Praetorians had a broken rear axle. He couldn't resist shouting for joy as he tried to imagine the look on Strabo's face.

Titus and Marcus whooped with jubilation again as Cyric brought their currus down into the vale beneath the pass. Behind them the Praetorians still followed, but far out of range for any further attacks. Their little stolen currus whirred gently as the electric motor propelled it along the thin country roads towards Marcus' destination, still a mystery to Titus. The vehicle had been badly damaged by the sonifex fire earlier and Titus was not sure if it could have survived another hit. They had been lucky, if it had not been for Cyric's driving and for the ungainliness of their pursuing vehicle they would still be up there on that ridge, most likely being executed.

'Are you going to tell me where we are going?' Titus asked Marcus again.

'We are very near to where you and Ceinwyn were going to marry,' said Marcus, answering the question obliquely.

'Yes, but I'm hardly going to marry her right now am I.' Titus replied, gesturing at the pursuing vehicle about to finish its lumbering descent from

318

the pass. He looked around though trying to catch a glimpse of the lake. There was a hill to their left and he guessed the lake must lay somewhere beyond that. He hugged Ceinwyn tightly and kissed her.

Then Titus felt the vehicle shudder. Then it began to slow. It was doing half the speed it had been when coming down the pass. He looked back, the Praetorian currus was still far back with its damage, but, worryingly, it was starting to close on them again. 'Come on Cyric,' he called into the cab, 'we aren't safe yet.'

'It's not my fault!' the boy called up irritably, 'the currus isn't working properly.'

They were travelling at barely a crawl now, and Titus could imagine the victorious face of Strabo as he climbed down from his currus alongside. It would happen soon if they didn't get moving. He clambered forwards into the cab trying to ignore the stabbing pains in his feet. The vehicle coasted down to a gentle standstill. Titus watched as Cyric pounded the accelerator over and over again. There was nothing, not even a gentle whir.

'What's happened?' Titus shouted to Cyric who raised his arms in confusion and irritation. The vehicle was dead. Titus glanced over his shoulder, the Praetorians would be with them in minutes.

XXXXIX

'It is the induction coil,' Marcus said as he leant over the side of the cab. He struck the chair with his fist in frustration and hissed at the pain. The coil was still glowing, but only ever so faintly. 'We are out of range,' Marcus said quietly as the realisation of their predicament registered fully.

Titus gestured back up the road to the Praetorians, 'they seem to have power.'

'We did back there!' Marcus shouted angrily at Titus for failing to comprehend, 'there is a range that the power is sent over. We cannot collect enough power here to drive the vehicle.'

'But they can?'

'Probably not. It's our position between the mountains that is weakening the signal. When they reach this spot they may also end up becalmed.'

'And there is no way we can get more power?' Titus asked, trying to stay calm. His feet began to throb again.

'No!' Marcus shouted, 'of course not! The power is sent remotely. If we can't receive it, we have no power.'

Titus nodded, 'so we must fight.'

'We can't beat them,' replied Marcus, 'we have nothing like that sonifex.'

'Then we must abandon the vehicle and flee. We must make them come to us on foot.' He clapped Marcus on the back, trying to enthuse him, but his old friend looked completely deflated.

Running was completely impossible for Titus, so it fell to Antonius to carry him. He roared with pain every time his feet brushed the ground and each time this happened Antonius stopped, until a grunted command from Titus through clenched teeth forced him to continue, despite Titus' obvious agony.

They were running through bracken up the hill he had seen earlier. A thin layer of snow lay on the ground here, with the threat of more in the low dark clouds around them. The Praetorians were not far behind. Strabo was there with them, Titus could sense it, and he longed to plunge his gladius into the man's foul, blubbery flesh. Ahead he could hear Marcus and Tiberius arguing. He tried to tune the other thoughts out of his head to concentrate. He could not catch everything they said but what he heard was enough, they had barely any ammunition left. Most of what they had brought must have been used in the quadrangles, and Marcus had obviously not expected to fight two battles today. Titus tried to think of a plan, he didn't need to look backwards; he knew how close the Praetorians were. He shouted encouragement to Antonius who bounded forwards like a bear and cleared the top of the rise. Titus looked up expecting to see the view from the top of the hill. But they were not at the summit, instead a plateau stretched out before them and the summit lay some several hundred yards away.

Ahead of them lay a circle of stones fifty yards across. Most of the stones were just over four feet high, but some were as tall as a man. Titus smiled grimly, this was a natural killing field. Marcus clearly realised this too and gestured to Antonius to bring Titus in to the stone circle. Hurriedly they took up positions at the far side, crouching down behind the cold damp stones. Antonius lowered Titus gently into place next to Ceinwyn on the snow covered ground and ran off to take his own position, from which he leaned out, his sonifex held menacingly, in the direction of the slope they had just ran up.

Titus reached for his sonifex and examined the magazine. It was empty. They had given him no ammunition. Marcus dropped to the ground beside him. 'We only have ten rounds left between us,' he whispered, 'all anti-personnel.'

Titus shook his head, 'we need armour piercing against Praetorians.'

'I know,' his face was thunderous. 'We're fucked.'

Silence fell over the circle as Marcus counted three rounds into Titus' cupped hands. He had left himself with only two. Ceinwyn held her little sonifex angrily by her side, Marcus had given her one round only. It was clear she understood why, but Titus doubted that she would really use it on herself. If it came to that she would use it to kill Strabo, even if that meant a fate worse than death at the hands of the Praetorians.

That left Antonius, Tiberius and Gnaeus with four rounds between them. Titus thought of the vehicle that had carried the Praetorians. How many could have fitted in it? Surely at least ten, possibly more. He tried to ignore the pain in his feet and thought back to that time facing the Chief all those years ago when he had hoped to die well. The hope remained. He could not die here. Not like this, clothes sodden with mud and snow, and his feet broken. He would fight. He would protect Ceinwyn and his friends. He would die for Rome, even if out here Rome no longer seemed to count for anything any more. He thought of Strabo's words. He would die for Rome, even if Rome was not all he thought it was.

The first Praetorian appeared over the lip. All five men looked at each other, not wanting to waste a shot by firing together. Titus gestured for them to wait, holding up five fingers. The message seemed to get through. His men held their fire. Another Praetorian appeared, and then another. The first was getting close to the circle now, keeping low, glancing left and right as he jogged towards them. The man suspected a trap, which was not that surprising. Their trap was extremely obvious, but the best they could manage in desperate circumstances.

A fifth Praetorian mounted the top of the rise. Titus raised his sonifex to his shoulder again and brought it to bear on the nearest Praetorian. The others took his lead, aiming at the others. Titus stared at the man down the sights, watching his eyes roving to and fro as he searched for the unseen danger he knew lurked somewhere ahead. Suddenly the Praetorian caught sight of Titus leaning out from behind the megalith and stopped in his tracks, his eyes widening with fear. The slit for the eyes in a Praetorian helmet was not wide, but it was one of the few parts that was not armoured. Titus held his aim on it and squeezed the trigger.

Blood burst out of the eye slits and the bottom of the assault helmet as the grooved round tore the Praetorian's head apart in the confined space. His body jerked spasmodically as it crashed to the ground. At that exact moment four other shots rang out sending three of the other Praetorians to the ground. The fifth was thrown onto his back, dazed as the round crashed off his armoured helmet. A second round from Titus through the groin finished him off. That left him with only one bullet left. He could feel his heart pounding in his chest with the excitement of battle. The agony in his feet was at last forgotten.

The next group of Praetorians mounted the slope at a run and were at the edge of the circle before a shot was even fired. They took up their own positions behind stones on the other side. Titus tried to control his breathing and listen. He peered out from the side of the stone to try to take a shot, whipping his head back instinctively as a bullet cracked into the side of the stone next to him. Chips of stone flew into the air and cut into his face.

Then he heard a sound that cut through that of his own breathing and the pounding of his heart. It was the sound he had been waiting for. It was the sound of a fat man struggling up a hill. He took a risk and leant out from the other side of the stone. Strabo was running, trying to get to the stones, but he was too slow. Titus looked across at his companions and saw they were all ready to fire.

'No!' he shouted, his blood boiling with anger, 'he is mine.' He had no idea if the others would obey him or not, it was pure selfishness on his part and he knew it, but he was the only one of them who had had to suffer so extremely at the hands of Gaius Strabo. It was his right to punish him for it. He focused in on the scarlet face of the man, watching his rubbery lips flap as they sucked great volumes of air into his starving lungs. He pulled the trigger with delicious ecstasy, already visualising the grotesque face bursting as the antipersonnel round twisted within it.

He heard a sharp click, the firing pin on the cartridge. His sonifex had misfired. He heard shots around him as his companions fired, but it was too late. The shots kicked dust up all around Strabo as he dived for cover, and then it was over: Strabo was behind a stone and safe from them. Titus sank down to his knees in the slush behind his own stone taking the weight off his tortured feet. The situation was now truly hopeless. They had perhaps one or two bullets left between them, if that.

Then the cloud rolled in.

It had only been brushing the top of the hill behind them when they had arrived, but now it descended fast, covering the hill in thick white tendrils. All Titus could see was Ceinwyn huddled up next to him, safe for now behind their narrow stone. Marcus was a thin outline to his left, only a few yards away.

The mist had the odd property of muffling sound. He heard the crack of sonifex fire, and felt the distortion in the air as shots came in over their heads but he could not tell its direction properly. A Praetorian suddenly loomed out of the mist to his left, before disappearing again as Marcus struck him down with the butt of his empty sonifex.

Titus looked down at Ceinwyn, her face even paler than usual. Her copper coloured hair seemed almost to glow, the only colour in the whiteout. 'Thank you,' he said, his voice nearly breaking.

'What for?' she replied. He had forgotten how much he loved her accent.

'For saving my life.'

'Then thank you,' she replied.

He looked puzzled.

'For making me want to live mine,' she added.

They kissed one last time.

'I only wish I could have died as your wife.'

Titus nodded, not able to tear his eyes from hers.

The sonifex fire roared out again, so close. The Praetorians were all around. He had no time. He drew his gladius.

'No,' she said softly shaking her head, 'there must be another way.'

'I must,' Titus said his voice breaking.

He held the blade towards her as tears sprang into his eyes. 'Strabo will...' his voice faltered again, 'you know what he will do.'

She nodded, and held her wrists out making it easy for him.

He held her chilled hands in his staring at her veins, deep blue under her pale skin.

He touched his blade to them.

She closed her eyes.

He lifted the blade away.

'Marcus, give me your sword,' the words were a growl. Ceinwyn opened her eyes. She stared in awe at the figure before her, standing tall, proud despite his broken feet, all trace of fear somehow gone.

Marcus unsheaved his sword and with shaking fingers placed it into Titus' outstretched hand. He stood there between them a sword at each of his sides, the pain in his feet seemingly forgotten. He tilted his head back and opened his mouth wide.

'Virtutis Fortuna Comes.' He bellowed the words out into the fog and sprinted off into the centre of the stone circle.

His senses were heightened, partly by the pain and partly by desperation. He could not bring himself to kill the woman he loved so he had no choice but to attempt the impossible. At least ten Praetorians remained, all armed with state of the art sonifi. He had two swords, one blunt. A dark shape loomed out of the mist to his right. He charged towards it, his feet obeying despite the damage he wrought upon them with each step. The Praetorian tried to turn as he heard Titus' approach, but it was too late.

Titus slammed his gladius into the man's neck and then bent low, following it up with an uppercut to the groin led by the point of Marcus' blade. He pulled back hard on the blades; the Praetorian's body jerking rhythmically as it fell spurting gore onto the frozen ground. Titus spun around as two Praetorians charged in firing their sonifi. He leapt at them, striking down at their necks from above with his gladii. The first man collapsed under the strike, but the second screamed as the blade lodged in the space between his collarbone and second rib. Titus ripped his sword out of the first man and swung it with all his force into his opponent's mouth, who gurgled as blood and teeth ran out from around the sharpened decorative blade. Titus' felt the Praetorian's weight fully as he at last died, and let him run off the blades onto the ground. Three more Praetorians ran in from behind. He spun around and leapt at them. He drove the points of his gladii into the chest of the nearest, then using the man's dying body as a springboard, he twisted and lashed out at the other two Praetorians. His blades found the hinges in their neck armour and they fell back, clutching at their severed throats. He stooped down, suddenly exhausted, as pain shot up from his feet. Looking down he saw the snow around them was soaked with blood, clearly his own. He would probably never walk again.

He heard footsteps behind him. He tried to swing around to take the fight to the remaining Praetorians, but his feet at last failed him and he teetered and fell into the red slush. The Praetorian advanced triumphantly, his sonifex swinging in time with his footsteps. Titus watched as the black shiny boots got nearer. He readied his sword to strike if the Praetorian gave him the chance. All he wanted to do was to get to Strabo.

Then he heard pounding footsteps from his other side. Groaning he twisted his head to look and saw a terrifying sight looming out of the mist. A man with a huge beard and armed with a battered ancient sonifex was bearing down on him. The armour he wore was old and had clearly survived a great deal of sonifex fire. Titus could smell him from the twenty paces away that he was, but he was closing fast. Then he recognised him; it was the Reiver Captain he had met in the woods months ago. He roared and drew back his sword ready to strike. The Reiver snarled and ducked down low, rushing at Titus who struck wildly with his gladius. The Reiver contemptuously brushed the weak blow aside with the edge of his sonifex and leant over Titus' shoulder, firing upwards into the Praetorian who collapsed to the ground, just feet away from Titus.

The Reiver stood up, towering over Titus who lay on his back in the snow staring up in bewilderment. Suddenly the Reiver's severe face broke into a wide smile and, laughing, he reached a filthy hand down to Titus who took it gladly. He stood up, leaning for support on the Captain and stared around. All through the mist the dark figures of Reivers ran, carrying sonifi and in some cases brutal looking axes which swirled in the

326

mist as they cut into the fleeing Praetorians. Titus watched as two of the Guard desperately fought back to back before one was cut down by a bare-chested Reiver, who split his upper torso in two with a heavy double handed blow. The survivor was quickly cut down by sonifex fire as he fled.

Then as quickly as the mist had come it began to evaporate. The cloud base rose until it was once again just brushing the top of the hill above them and the stone circle was once again exposed to view. Titus stared down in awe at the devastation around them.

A dozen Reivers were sifting through the dead. There had been close to twenty Praetorians in all. Titus looked up at the Reiver Captain, wondering what had led him to save his life. He followed the Reiver's gaze; it fell upon Marcus who waved. The Reiver saluted him back.

'We come to receive the ransom money,' the Captain barked across the battlefield.

A cry rose a few yards away from a still live Praetorian, cut off by a volley of fire from a sonifex.

'As agreed,' Marcus said.

'You paid a high price for your man,' the Reiver said.

'The money was not ours.'

The Reiver smiled at this, and gestured to some of his men who had held back just below the hill. They jogged off behind the lip at his signal.

'You did not arrive for our rendezvous,' said the Captain.

Marcus held his arms out at the destruction wrought around them in explanation. 'We were delayed.'

The Captain nodded. 'Saving your lives was not part of our deal, it will cost you extra,' he said, smiling at Marcus' obvious discomfort.

Titus thought he detected a hint of playfulness in the smile; all was perhaps not quite as it seemed.

A figure was led out from around the hill. He was chained, but loosely and he walked easily with a spring in his step. His clothes were filthier than those of the Reiver Captain yet it was unmistakably Quintus. Tiberius whooped with joy and ran over to greet his old friend. The pair embraced at the edge of the circle, whilst a Reiver undid the leg irons, allowing

Quintus free. The pair bounded back to the circle towards Titus and the Captain.

'It will be a shame to be deprived of your company,' the Captain said. 'You would perhaps, given time, have made a great Reiver.' Quintus nodded awkwardly and turned to Titus who smiled at him.

'I do not know what to say,' Titus spoke, breaking the silence between them.

'Perhaps you should start with sorry.'

'I have not treated you well.'

'You could have trusted me—why didn't you tell me Strabo was so evil?' Quintus replied, exasperated. Titus did not reply; he could not tell Quintus the truth, that he could *not* trust him. Should he trust him now? He had no choice. He had to make a new start. No more secrets.

'Let me show you someone,' he said, gesturing to Ceinwyn who sat with her back to one of the great stones. Quintus watched with interest as she walked over towards them through the shallow snow, head high and proud in the late morning air. Red hair strewn beautifully across her face by the wind.

'Quintus, I want you to meet Ceinwyn.'

She offered her hand to him. 'It is an honour to meet you Quintus. Titus tells me you are a doctor?' She smiled kindly at him trying to put him at his ease.

Quintus refused her hand and stepped back, staring accusingly at Titus.

'You are with this?' he shouted. 'A Half-Breed!' Everyone was silent now, watching the three of them together in the centre of the circle.

Titus' expression was thunderous as he turned on Quintus. 'I love her Quintus, and you will respect my decision and her.'

Quintus took a couple of steps forwards so that he was only inches from Titus' face. 'I understand now,' he said finally, 'you betrayed me, for this. You tricked me so that I thought I had failed, and that I had ruined the mission for you and for my friends.'

He was as composed as anything, but Titus would have rather had him screaming with rage.

'I ran off in disgrace, I endured capture and humiliation because of this.' He pointed at Ceinwyn, 'she has poisoned you against yourself, your true nature as a Roman. Can't you see it?'

'What I did to you was wrong,' Titus said, 'but it is not her fault that I lied. That fault is mine alone.' He held out his own hand to Quintus now, but he turned on his heel and, walking over to Tiberius, joined him squatting on the frozen ground. An uncomfortable silence fell once again over the stone circle.

Suddenly a squawk echoed over the stones and everyone turned to see a figure being forced to his feet and frogmarched into the centre by a burly Reiver.

'He was trying to hide in the guts of one of his own men!' The Reiver shouted as he hurled the figure to the ground between Titus and the Captain.

The man's face was obscured by congealed blood and faeces, but from its bloated size and foul appearance it was clearly none other than Gaius Strabo. He moaned pitifully on the floor, trying to get into a kneeling position from which he could better petition his captors. His mouth flapped open like a drowning fish as he stared up in astonishment at Titus. He opened his mouth to speak, to beg for his life.

Then his eyes fell on Titus' broken feet, and on Ceinwyn standing alongside him. Her piercing green eyes bore into his with their accusing stare and he turned away, unable to meet her righteous anger.

'Well!' said the Reiver Captain, louder than he need have done, turning to Marcus, 'it is time to discuss the matter of payment.'

Marcus shook his head, 'we have already paid! We have nothing else to give you!' he said holding out his open hands wide.

'I think you do,' said the Reiver Captain stroking his bearded chin and looking down at Strabo.

Marcus' gaze followed his, and Strabo cried out in fear as he realised what was going to happen. 'You want him?' Marcus asked surprised.

'He killed my wife,' said the Captain, staring bleakly at the hapless Governor, 'and my child.'

Strabo tried to screech in protest but didn't seem to be able to suck enough air in to make a sound. His voice was a thin warble, 'I am a

Roman citizen like you,' he hissed at Titus imploringly. 'You have a duty to protect me.'

Titus whistled through his teeth as he inhaled thoughtfully, 'but today is Saturnalia Strabo, don't you remember? Slaves get to rule their masters today. So it is up to Ceinwyn really.' He smiled at the Governor, 'and she isn't Roman,' he continued, as if Strabo needed reminding.

He turned to his wife to be who stared at Strabo for a long time before nodding slowly, condemning her old master. Strabo scrabbled in the snow and tried desperately to get to his feet and run, but he was kicked back down by the Captain, who gestured to a pair of his men to run and get the necessary materials.

The Reiver Captain sat down in the snow next to his old Governor, the man who had destroyed his life. He sat and spoke to him. He whispered so quietly that even Titus who stood next to him could not make out the words, but suddenly Strabo went white. And screamed. A piercing shriek which shook Titus, for even in his darkest moments at Strabo's hands he had not felt despair great enough to cause a wail such as that which he had just heard. He paled at the thought of what must be to come, and for a moment almost regretted handing Strabo over to the Reivers. Justice should be done in Rome. But then he thought about Tristan, his mad brains blown out over the floor of the compound, of his father and Strabo's threats, of Ceinwyn and her terrified life at his hands. The governor of Northern Britannia deserved whatever he got.

The net was made of chicken wire.

As the currus skidded away from the now empty stone circle overlooked by the one bleak, solitary tree, Titus looked back and saw the birds beginning to gather. At first there was only one, its black head tilted slightly to one side staring downwards; Titus could imagine its dark, empty eyes.

As he looked back, a second landed and joined its companion. It sat stock still upon the bare branch, watching and waiting with infinite patience. Then a third and a fourth landed at once, shaking the branch and squawking loudly to entice more. Titus shuddered in the cold breeze blowing into the back of the currus; the snow was falling heavier now. He looked back one last time as the circle fell out of sight entirely; the tree was now outlined with dozens of birds, all staring down to where their victim hung from the lowest branch, he was still too strong to attack, but the birds would wait for days if necessary. They would just keep on staring down at him with their cold, unblinking eyes.

Titus looked up at the sky and closed his eyes. He remembered the old Slave, smiling as he was murdered by him, all those months ago. He whispered thanks to him for the account numbers; which had led him to bring his old master down, and realised that he had unwittingly fulfilled the old man's dying wish. He turned to the beautiful girl beside him who was almost his wife. Her green eyes shone with the light reflected from the snow, and they shone even brighter when she smiled at him. He slipped an arm around her waist, laid his head back on the bullet torn headrest, and closed his eyes. At last, for the first time in ten years, Titus Labienus Aquilinus was content.

XXXXX

Ceinwyn took a deep breath and closed her eyes. The summer air rippled the edges of her dress, warming her as she stepped barefoot on the soft turf. She knew the way. She had trod this path before.

The dappled sunlight streaming through the trees played as flashes of red through her closed eyelids. She was nearly there. Her life had already changed beyond measure in the last months; how much more wonderful could things be after this?

She walked forwards another ten paces; she had counted them hundreds of times in her mind. Then she stopped. As she reached forwards, her hand explored the cold stone she found, enjoying its texture, its age. She thought about her dress, chosen with Marcus' help. This time there was no mud staining it, or water making it cling to her. This time she would not be alone.

She opened her eyes.

Titus was standing there. She had barely ever seen him wearing anything that wasn't military, let alone something smart. His toga was new, but as the acting governor of Northern Britannia he could afford it. He could afford anything. All around stood their friends, Titus' old comrades from the Transmaritanus at one side, and opposite, her friends from Strabo's compound. Titus had freed all of the Slaves but most had chosen to continue to live at the compound, it was the only home they knew. Cyric stood in the centre of her group of friends, all trace of the yellow hue gone from his face. Once the biological poison had been washed from the water supply most of the Slaves had recovered very quickly.

Gnaeus smiled at her as she approached the altar and reached out for her hand. Taking it, he looked into her eyes for a moment before placing her hand in Titus'. He looked at her, watching her face beaming with joy as Gnaeus began the service, it was only a matter of minutes until they would be husband and wife.

A snore from a tree behind her startled Ceinwyn, but then she realised it was just Decimus. The old head of the Praetorian Guard had been doddery for years apparently and had slept even more of late since his ordeal at the hands of Strabo. They had found him locked in a small box. From his weakness it seemed he had been a virtual prisoner in it for months. Titus had to run the Praetorian Guard as well whilst Rome found a replacement. It was hard work, but she helped him and together they seemed to be able to deal with any problem that occurred in or around Luguvalium. She hoped that they would be able to stay there for ever, but she knew in her heart that eventually another Governor would be appointed by Marcus Albus in Rome. She would just have to enjoy it whilst she could. She chided herself for worrying about the future and turned her attention back to Gnaeus and her husband to be beside her.

And then almost as soon as the service had begun it was over. She said her vows, a ring was pushed onto her finger and in turn she tried to force one over Titus' huge digit. Then they kissed. She was married.

The applause came from all around and filled the tiny island, drifting across to the deserted shore. The mountains towered around them—the only other spectators to their happiness.

Marcus walked forwards and hugged each of them in turn. He seemed so happy for them; Titus and he had talked almost every day since they had abandoned Strabo to die in the hills. It seemed that they had sorted through most of the differences, but Ceinwyn couldn't help but remember what Gnaeus had said in the cave months ago, that Marcus could never forgive Titus for saving his life. Did Marcus still resent Titus? From the way they were talking now it seemed impossible, but from what she knew of Marcus he would be perfectly capable of hiding something like that from anyone, even from himself.

On the far side of the island Quintus stood in deep conversation with Tiberius. As she watched he paused in conversation and for a moment looked down at the ground. He was preparing himself to say something to Tiberius, but he looked petrified. Tiberius sipped from his drink, seemingly oblivious. Ceinwyn watched on as Quintus eventually seemed to make up his mind. He looked up, placed a hand on Tiberius' shoulder and opened his mouth to speak. Tiberius looked at him confused. Quintus didn't seem to say anything, but then Quintus turned away embarrassed. Looking up, his eyes met hers and his face flashed with anger as he stormed away. Tiberius looked across at Ceinwyn and shrugged his shoulders. She returned the gesture.

An old hand drifted over her lace covered shoulder, and she looked around to see Decimus Petronius behind her. He smiled at her; she wasn't sure how sane he was after what had been done to him but he was kind to her and she trusted him.

'Congratulations,' he croaked at her. He used his voice little; it seemed he had grown accustomed to silence during his incarceration.

'Thank you, I am pleased you could be here today.'

Decimus laughed, 'as am I. I thought I would die in that place.' Tears came to his eyes but he quickly brushed them away. 'I am pleased your husband thwarted Strabo's plans. He would be living it up in Rome by now if it hadn't been for him. Senator Strabo,' Decimus laughed again. 'I would have rather died than live to see that.'

Titus came into view in front of her and smiled. She walked towards her husband and took his hands in hers.

'I love you,' he said.

'I love you too,' she whispered and kissed him.

They walked together slowly to the edge of the island and sat down on a rock next to the old boat they had used to get across. Holding hands they stared around at the view, listening together to the tiny waves slapping against the base of the boat. The mountains towered over them as they kissed again.

They were interrupted by the sound of splashing from further out on the lake. Looking up they saw a figure pulling angrily at the rope lying across it. He was sitting on the tiny raft she had used to get to the island all those months ago, and was tugging it away to the far shore as fast as it could go. It was Quintus.

'You should go after him,' Ceinwyn said, concerned. Quintus still refused to speak to her, and had barely spoken to Titus for months.

Titus shook his head, 'I cannot reason with him—he has to learn for himself,' he replied sadly.

Ceinwyn frowned.

'I don't understand,' Titus sighed staring out over the lake.

'For now we see through a glass, darkly,' Ceinwyn replied.

Titus turned to her, 'and that puzzles me even more,' he said laughing.

'It means that one day we will understand, that one day we will see the world clearly in its true colours,' she explained.

Titus looked even more confused.

It's from a book. A contraband book,' she added.

Titus laughed louder, 'that makes sense. I can't imagine you ever obeying the law!'

Ceinwyn hugged him closer to her as she followed the line of the rope back to their own island, and realised that another figure was watching Quintus disappear into the distance. It was Tiberius. Sitting cross legged on the shore, he had the same forlorn look on his face that Titus had had at Quintus' departing. Except Titus was not sobbing.

A chill blew in over the lake, and Ceinwyn shivered in her thin dress despite the sun still beating down hard on the rocks. Titus squeezed her arm gently and wrapped the long edge of his toga around her. She leaned her head on his warm shoulder and closed her eyes.

She thought of Rome, the great space elevator towering into infinity receding into the distance as she was dragged away from her father all those years ago. She thought of her life at the mercy of the cruel Strabo, and the suffering of her friends at his hands. She had been rescued from all of that. She looked up into the face of the man she loved.

At last she was safe.

Epilogue

2754 AUC

The Slaves were dead; piles of corpses, torn and bloody in the bright midday sun, blood soaking into the sand. Marcus Albus clapped Titus heartily on the shoulder and laughed. 'Well done my friend, well done.' Turning sharply, his cloak flashing purple in the wind, he strode back to the command tent leaving Titus alone on the beach. The volacurrus that had been waiting for the Slaves hissed angrily as it rose from the sand and headed back to Rome; its presence no longer required.

Titus wandered silently amongst the dead. Many were still holding hands even in death, their hollow expressions cut into his soul. 'Animals, slaughtered animals,' he kept repeating it to himself, but he still couldn't make himself believe it. He had to believe it, he had to stay sane.

Then something, but he was not sure what, caused him to linger by the contorted body of a woman. Titus knelt down upon the warm sand, conscious of the sea lapping calmly close by, the only sound on the now eerily quiet beach. It was just him and the dead. A small part of him suddenly envied them. He pushed the thought aside angrily; he had so much to live for. The new command he had just earned for a start. Beneath the woman's body a small leg stuck out, the leg was attached to a head, and the head was covered in golden curls. He gasped involuntarily for beneath the curls was a dusty face, streaked with tears. His hand flew to his mouth in sudden realisation of what he had just done.

He was twenty one, a general of Rome, and he had just murdered a young girl. His sonifex fell from his shoulder thumping onto the sand with a muffled crash as a sob burst forth from his tightly clamped lips.

The girl opened her eyes.

Author's Note

Roman rule, as we know it, effectively ended in 476 AD when the Western Roman Empire fell to the very nations it had previously subjugated, the Goths. Although in name the Eastern Roman Empire survived (becoming known eventually as the Byzantine Empire), before itself falling in 1453 with the sacking of Constantinople by the Ottomans. These facts remind us that no civilisation, no matter how great and overwhelmingly powerful, has ever survived for four thousand years, as mine dares to do here. Yet we still dream of what the world would be like if the great civilisations that have preceded ours were still present, ruling over us.

If you could go back in time to the Roman withdrawal from Britain in the fifth century AD, you would be able to experience a world that contained buildings and infrastructure that would not even be imitated again until the twelfth century. Glass, sewers, and aqueducts, are just a few of the wonders that the Romans had mastered. Their departure from Britain marked the beginning of the period of history known as the Dark Ages.

And so it is no surprise that we wonder what would have been if they had not left. What if their power had grown, and their Empire had expanded around the globe. What sort of marvellous technologies would exist now? For to look at a modern day Rome would surely be like staring into a window looking upon a world six hundred years further ahead than us; a world that had had no Dark Age. That would be the case if it were not for, I believe, fundamental differences in the way our world and theirs operated.

For the Roman world was one of matching splendour and brutality. On the one hand they had a sophisticated and relatively fair system of government, yet they executed people with a barbarity that has been rarely equalled through history and mercilessly subjugated almost every people they came into contact with.

In writing this book I asked myself the question, 'what would the world look like now if the Roman Empire had never fallen?' This, of course, is an impossible question to answer and so I had to examine the idea further in order to answer it as well as I could; make my best guess if you like. The question quickly broke itself up into three, which together help piece together two thousand years of made up history.

1. 'What would a modern Roman people value?'

Although the values of a race do change over time it often seems to be regime change that precipitates this and so I allowed myself to imagine that the Roman people of my present day Rome would not be far different from their earlier counterparts, in terms of such fundamentals as their outlook on life, their society, and their treatment of others. So accepting this as the case, what then might our world be like today if the Romans were still here?

It would be ruled fully by Rome for a start. Conquering other races was how the Romans expanded; they were also masters at assimilating lands under their control. So they would need a strong military. Research over two thousand years would surely have allowed their army to be far in advance of ours today, both in terms of manpower and technology. But we shouldn't presume that the Roman world would have any more resources than ours, so if they spent so much effort on the military then surely this would be at the expense of other things. This is why the world that most of this novel is set in is relatively bleak, poor and if anything more basic than ours, full of military hand me downs. Of course it is important to bear in mind that this book is set in a far flung Roman province, a sort of Roman 'Third World' if you like. Rome on the other hand would perhaps have become a place of immense splendour in direct contrast to its far away and uncared for provinces; a theme that will be explored in the next book.

2. 'How would a modern Roman government react to modern day events?'

In writing the book I wanted the characters to live in a world that has the same problems that ours does now: the threat of terrorism and global warming are two good examples of this which are referred to within the book. The Roman method of dealing with them would, I think, be far different to our own though. Set in their ways, valuing tradition above all else, I find it hard to believe that the inhabitants of a Roman world would accept global warming as a problem, or change their ways to act against it. I also imagine that their reaction to terrorists would be different to ours; they would hardly want to admit that a province was revolting unless they had to, and if they were eventually forced to act they would most likely act decisively, with overwhelming force.

3. 'Why did Rome not fall in my world?'

I think this is the most important question of all, and shapes very much what the world would look like. It is also, in itself, completely impossible to fully answer currently. Historians are still very much divided on the subject of why Rome fell. Ever since Gibbon wrote his 'The Decline and Fall of the Roman Empire' in 1776 the question has been pondered, and there have been over two hundred separate theories put forwards over this time. The two of these which most captured my imagination are a general decline towards decadence eventually weakening the iron willed Roman people, who had once cared little for luxury; and another - the Roman empowering of their once conquered neighbouring races (i.e. the Goths) by everyday contact with Roman weaponry and society, which eventually gave them the strength to overthrow their rulers.

For a more detailed account of theories regarding the fall of Rome it is well worth reading 'The Fall of the Roman Empire' by Peter Heather, an excellent book which covers these theories, and more in great detail.

So armed with these theories I needed to decide how best to reverse them. When was the turning point in history? Could anything have stopped Rome falling?

If Rome ever had a Golden Age it could be said to be during its Republic, the system of government which it adopted for just over five hundred years and which lost its power after the civil war won by Julius Caesar. If Rome had remained a republic would it have been stronger? Perhaps.

It could be argued that the greatest excesses of the Emperors resulted in the ruling classes emulating them to some extent. Luxury, an idea abhorred by Roman people during the republic years, was suddenly flooding in from the provinces and being enjoyed. So perhaps a Roman Republic might have avoided some of the decadence partly responsible for the fall of the Empire.

This left me with an idea which eventually spawned my main character. Caesar brought about the end of Rome's Golden Age, The Republic, when he crossed the Rubicon with his army and marched on Rome, starting a civil war he would eventually win and in doing so set himself up as Consul in perpetuity; a King in all but name. To bring about my Eternal Republic I needed Caesar to lose. But would losing be enough? If Pompey, Caesar's opposing General during the civil war, won then perhaps he would have been set up as Consul in perpetuity instead to safeguard Rome, and maybe, eventually, his descendants would have become Emperors. So I didn't just need Caesar to lose; I needed the civil war to never happen.

In our real world a man called Titus Labienus, one of Caesar's generals could not bring himself to attack his beloved Republic and instead defected to Pompey, fighting against his old master during the Civil War.

So in the end it only took a small change in history to create my world instead of ours; to have this man take matters into his own hands and assassinate his master. The Republic lives on, Rome becomes stronger rather than weakening, and his descendant eventually finds himself dishonoured, living the life of a mercenary amongst the fells of Northern England.

I appreciate that in even mentioning the fall of Rome I will have antagonised a great deal of proper historians who will probably severely disagree with some or all of what I have written here. The truth is that every one of you reading this book probably has their own slightly different idea about how things might have turned out if the Roman World hadn't fallen, but the fact that a civilisation that ceased to have any real power fifteen hundred years ago can still make us day dream, shows you why I had to set my story within it.

I hope you will be interested in finding out more about my Rome, and about Titus and his friends in my next book. In the meantime for the benefit of those who have no Latin. . .

The direct translation of Titus' family motto,

'Virtutis Fortuna Comes,'

is 'Valour is Fortune's Companion', I would however myself favour a modern paraphrase of this,

'Fortune Favours the Brave.'

If you want to find out more about Rome, especially its golden era you really need to read a book by an actual historian, rather than the rambling notes of an author, albeit even one obsessed with the classical world. There is no place better in my opinion than amongst the pages of 'Rubicon: The Triumph and Tragedy of the Roman Republic' by Tom Holland.

Thank you
Dr Daniel Berkeley BMBS Hons BMedSci Hons

Please feel free to contact me at daniel.berkeley@hotmail.com or on facebook (Daniel Berkeley) or twitter (@sirdanthethird). I am always interested to hear your thoughts on my book and any advice you might have. If I can help you in any way too, please let me know. Please check out my amazon author page.

About the Author

Dan Berkeley lives with his wife and two children in Cumbria, near to the edge of the Lake District. He is a doctor at the hospital in Carlisle (Luguvalium). He started writing five years ago, but had the idea for this book five years before that, whilst awaking from a barely remembered dream. He has been interested in ancient history since he was a child, but was fairly useless at Latin whilst at school. Unfortunately he thought that to do medicine you needed A levels all in sciences, and so didn't do classical civilisation as a subject past GCSE. He therefore spent most of his time at medical school, reading books about ancient Rome and Greece, and drinking ale. Whilst at school he did try writing some short stories, but with no exceptions—these were awful. Even his English teacher told him they were awful. Having read ancient history, and enjoying the works of Bernard Cornwell, Conn Iggulden, Wilbur Smith, and Robert Harris, he felt it was time to try to combine three ideas: write an alternative history in the style of 'Fatherland', with the type of action, and characterisation, of an Iggulden or Cornwell novel, and the sickening descriptive brutality of a Smith book. At least he was writing what he wanted to read.

When he is not utterly failing to get his book published by an actual publishing house he also enjoys, strategic board gaming, medicine, brewing ale, drumming (badly), walking on the fells, and trying to eat as many different types of animal as possible. This is his first book, and will hopefully be followed up by some sequels, and a couple of other ideas he had recently, which may or may not actually turn out to be good books.